THE MAN'S BOOK

THE MAN'S BOOK

A Complete Manual of Style

Edited by James Wagenvoord

AVON
PUBLISHERS OF BARD, CAMELOT AND DISCUS BOOKS

THE MAN'S BOOK is an original publication of Avon Books.
This work has never before appeared in book form.

AVON BOOKS
A division of
The Hearst Corporation
959 Eighth Avenue
New York, New York 10019

Copyright © 1978 by Product Development International Holding, n.v.
Produced by Plenary Publications International, Inc.
10 East 49 Street
New York, New York 10017
Library of Congress Catalog Card Number: 77-92349
ISBN: 0-380-01899-3

First Avon Printing, April, 1978

AVON TRADEMARK REG. U.S. PAT. OFF. AND IN
OTHER COUNTRIES, MARCA REGISTRADA, HECHO EN
U.S.A.

Printed in the U.S.A.

Created By:

EDITOR

James Wagenvoord

DESIGNER

Sandra Forrest

WRITERS

Peyton Bailey   Douglas Colligan
H. Y. Coop   Joel Homer   Judd Howard   Dan Ross

ILLUSTRATORS

Sandra Forrest   Keith Right

ASSOCIATE EDITORS

Ellen Foley   Gail Newton   Susan Smith

PROOFREADERS

Maureen Hatch   Michael Hayes

INDEX

Maro Riofrancos

EDITORIAL ASSISTANTS

Janet Goldstein   Dewey McDonald Thompson   Tim Adams

MENSWEAR CONSULTANT

K. M. Fleck

FOREWORD

This is a book about the realities of being a social male in the final quarter of the twentieth century. It is a book of information, sources and guidelines—not boundaries. The material has been developed and shaped by a group of professional writers, editors and artists who were backed up by leading professionals from the social and cultural worlds that directly affect day-to-day lives. Throughout the months, the editorial focus has been on finding direct answers to questions often hinted at, others occasionally asked, and more left unphrased, but important nevertheless. The result, in the pages that follow, is a book about the social world.

CONTENTS

THE INNER MAN

THE OUTER MAN

THE SOCIAL MAN

Body image
Love your body? You probably don't. You try not to think about it. Men, you say, don't love *or* hate their bodies. They just accept them. A man's body isn't beautiful, and isn't supposed to be.

What rot. You're just as conscious of your body as a woman is, just as insecure about it. And you want and need to feel beautiful, just as a woman does. You worry that your chest isn't brawny enough, that your arms are too skinny, your stomach too pudgy, your penis too small. Do other men share your feelings? There's no way for you to know. Since no one talks about it, it's easy to assume you're the only one who's less than confident about the way you're built or the shape you're in.

You were raised with the notion that you've got to be BIG. It's better to be tall than short. To have big shoulders, a big penis. "Be a big boy now." "He's a big man on campus." "He's a big jock." If you were hurt when you were a boy, lost out on something, you were told to "be big about it." And even if you were physically big, you didn't feel tough. Not feeling tough felt terrible. Feeling terrible felt small. So you hid the way you felt. You figured you'd show 'em one day. You'd "make it big" in the world. Big money. Big power.

Come to terms with your body
It's OK now to confront the ridiculousness of all that. And you can improve your sense of well-being by coming to terms with how that conditioning caused you to develop negative feelings about your body. Recently men have begun to admit the truth: they feel

vulnerable. Their body image is poor. They need close, feeling relationships with other human beings—men and women.

Hearing other men be honest helps—a little. Being honest with yourself would help more. When you're insecure about your body, it shows in everything you do—the way you walk, talk, earn a living, make love.

Accept yourself

A good body image is essential to feeling great. How to get your body in tune with your whole self? First, confront the way you really feel about it. Is your body alien to you? Does it embarass you at times? Most of us judge our bodies according to an external, unreal standard. We can't accept that we can be below the standard and still be beautiful, that in fact we can be homely and still be beautiful to those who know us and love us. You can be admired for being strong. If you want to be *loved*, have some weaknesses too. Can you accept that you can be loved for you? When you roll back your fear of not living up to some standard of perfection and reveal who you really are, warts and all, you'll see your beauty reflected in the reactions you get from others. Sound contradictory? It's not. Need help? Self-exploration programs (see "Choosing the Right Self-Exploration Program," page 44) are a great way to learn to love and accept your whole self—body included.

Posture

The way you carry yourself says a lot about your state of mind, your self-image, your approach to the world. Think of a man you admire, one who's at ease with himself and in good physical condition. Chances are that his posture is neither a stomach-in-chest-out, I'm-all-man-and-I'll-chew-bullets-to-prove-it stance, nor a hunched-over, leave-me-alone one. He probably carries himself easily, naturally, and gives a sense of being at home in his body.

Good posture comes naturally to some. You may have to learn it. But a full-length mirror and steel reserve won't do it. You can't force yourself to have a better posture by following a set of rules. You have to work with your body until healthy movements and carriage become second nature. If you've picked up a lot of bad habits over the years—you have a lot to unlearn.

Do you have bad posture?

Most people have bad posture. You may think your posture's fine while other people see you as a walking question mark. How to know? Ask. Have a friend (or your doctor) analyze the way you stand, sit, and walk. And take a look at yourself. When you walk down the street, notice your silhouette reflected in a store window. Are you hunched over? Slump-shouldered? Rigid and stiff? Do you constantly gaze down at the pavement or up at the sky instead of keeping your eyes level? And how do you *feel*? Are you tired a lot, even when you wake up in the morning? Do you often have a backache, a stiff neck? Bad posture leads to daily fatigue that sleep doesn't relieve. It can put strain on your back, neck, and shoulder muscles. If you have bad posture you're supporting the wrong parts of your body with the wrong muscles, and you're creating strain throughout your whole body. It affects other physical processes, from the way you walk to the "posture" of your inner organs.

How to correct bad posture

What can you do about your poor posture? Developing the right mental attitude about your body is an important beginning, for if you come to like your body you'll want to tend it well, and if you work to get your body into good condition, your posture will improve. A good exercise plan will develop body coordination, balance, flexibility. A good exercise plan will also rid you of a double chin, a paunchy stomach, and sagging shoulders. All of this will help your posture.

If you need discipline, admit it and get yourself into an instructor-led exercise program. Some that are especially good for posture: The **Alexander** method, which concentrates strictly on posture correction, changes the way you move, rest, carry your body. **Yoga** is loaded with mental and physical benefits, and posture correction is an important one. **Massage** will help your posture too. Rolfing, for example, is a rough, ten-session massage technique that will rid you of muscular rigidity and physically force your body back into natural alignment. And if you don't want anything that tough, soothing Swedish massage, done regularly, can help to correct your posture flaws.

Of course, getting your posture fixed isn't going to transform you as a man. You must attend to your whole being—mental and emotional as well as physical. Getting your posture in shape is just one part of feeling great—don't forget the importance of a good self-image, increased self-awareness, a good diet.

Massage

If you've never had a true massage, the word may have a sleazy sound, reminding you of disreputable massage parlors, scented body rubs, paid-for sex. The proliferation of tawdry massage parlors in cities across the United States has given true massage a bad name. In fact, true massage performed by a practiced masseur can provide your body (and mind) with many benefits you badly need. Most masseurs are skilled specialists, serious about a profession that provides clients with muscle relaxation, reduction of tension, relief from stress. Massage, when done regularly, can give you better muscle and skin tone, improved circulation, a more balanced metabolism, and a feeling of relaxation and renewed vigor.

When you go for a massage in a health club or a masseur's private studio, you'll probably receive a Swedish massage. This technique (also called French or German massage) involves a set of different hand manipulations: **friction,** rubbing with the fingers; **pétrissage,** kneading of muscles to get the kinks out; **effluerage,** stroking in long, upward movements along the body to increase circulation; **tapotement,** firm tapping with the sides of the hands; and **vibration,** gentle pressing of fingertips while vibrating the hand.

Swedish massage

The first time you go for a massage, you may feel somewhat awkward. Knowing what to expect can help you relax. You'll be shown into a dressing room where you'll take off your clothes and wrap yourself in a towel. This towel will serve as a drape when you're on the table. Climb on the table, lie on your back, and tell the masseur about any aches or pains that need special attention. A tense neck? A sore calf muscle? Now settle back and let the masseur take over. What to do with your hands? While you're on your back, rest them across your stomach. When you turn over onto your stomach, put them under your head or let them dangle from the table—whatever's comfortable *for you.* Stay limp, completely relaxed. The masseur will move your arm, leg, foot, or head when he needs to; you don't have to help him.

What to expect

If you don't belong to a health club and can't get the name of a good masseur from a friend, check the phone book. And when you call for an appointment, ask questions. Will he take credit cards? How long will the massage last? Does he use any technique besides Swedish massage? Don't be timid. Be clear ahead of time about all details.

A masseur in a health club expects a tip. A private masseur has set a price with which he's comfortable. In either case, tipping is up to you. A good tip is 20 to 25 percent of the cost of the massage.

Massage tips

To get the full benefit of massage, you should go at least once a month. Go when you have no pressing appointments to worry about, when you're neither very full after a meal nor very hungry. A massage too early in the day may overrelax you, and if you schedule a massage after strenuous exercise, take a lukewarm shower before you get on the massage table.

By the time you have your second massage, you'll be much more relaxed. And after a few times you'll feel a rapport building between you and your masseur. If he does something you don't like, tell him. He wants to give you what's most beneficial for you.

Other forms of massage

Esalen massage, devised at the Esalen Institute in Big Sur, California, aims at increasing sensory awareness through touch. The massage may go on for up to two hours, and the masseur may linger on a single part of the body to induce total relaxation.

Rolfing, named after its founder, biochemist Ida Rolf, is based on the theory that your body has been thrown out of alignment and damaged by your physical responses to past emotional experiences. Through deep compression and (painful) massage, supporting tissue is "unlocked" and damaging emotional memories are released. The result is that the body is forced back into its natural shape. Many people who have been "Rolfed" say they feel looser, less tense, more positive about life.

Reflexology, or **Zone Therapy,** involves foot massage. Its practitioners hold the view that the soles of the feet have key pressure points that are linked to other areas of the body. Massaging specific spots on the feet produces a tonic effect on certain body organs. This massage can be self-administered.

Shiatzu is a massage technique that attempts to release blocked energies that cause discomfort. By exerting deep finger pressure on key points of the body utilized in acupuncture, the Shiatzu masseur releases tensions, induces relaxation, allows blocked energies to flow freely.

Health clubs

In the last few years health clubs have sprung up in cities and suburbs everywhere. Some are larger and more posh than others. Some have swimming pools; others don't. Some have elaborate exercise equipment; others offer more Spartan facilities. If you're serious about sticking with a regular exercise routine, a good workout in a health club can be invaluable. But if you're just kidding yourself about your desire for exercise and are likely to lose interest after using the club a few times, you might as well save your money.

Evaluate the situation. Make a tour through several clubs, and weigh your objectives against what each club has to offer. Basically, most will provide a locker room, steam room, sauna, pool, whirlpool, sun room, and gym with machines (jogging machine, weights and pulleys, slantboards, stationary bicycles). They'll also offer fitness classes (calisthenics, Yoga, Karate, for example) with instructors.

Variations in health clubs

Most health clubs have "package deals" to tempt you—a basic rate for the first 14 months, for example, with a reduced fee for the year that follows. A package deal can be a bargain if you'll keep coming for an extended period of time, but a waste of money if you won't.

Check out several different programs before you sign up in any club. And don't get drawn in by a sales person and sign a contract until you've decided what you need and thoroughly checked out how well this particular club fills your needs.

When you're ready to join a health club, you'll be asked to sign a contract. Read it thoroughly! Be sure any promises they've made are there in writing. Pay attention to what the contract says about when you have to pay fees. A contract usually states that:

· If you default on an installment payment, the balance is due immediately.
· Fees are not refundable.
· You use the facilities of the club at your own risk (are you insured?).
· The club is released from liability even if you have an injury due to negligence on their part.

Be sure you're willing to go along with everything the contract says. And keep a copy.

You don't have to join a private health club to have a place to exercise. There are also tennis clubs, squash clubs, dance or Yoga classes—the list is practically endless, and some things are relatively inexpensive. Tennis, on the other hand, can be expensive if you join a private club. Many town- or city-maintained courts are inexpensive and some are free, but court-time is often difficult to schedule.

Other places to exercise?

The best bargain for a regular exercise regimen is usually the

YMCA. A yearly membership is inexpensive, and in general the Y will offer the same space and equipment that's available in private health clubs (this includes classes in Yoga, Karate, dance, and calisthenics).

Spas

You may think a health spa is a place for wealthy and out-of-shape women to go to lose weight and get pampered and toned up. But as more and more men are finding out, spas can do wonderful things for a *man's* health and well-being. Businessmen as well as movie and television stars make regular once or twice-a-year visits to spas to relax and get recharged.

What goes on at a spa?

There are thousands of spas (at least 2,000 in the United States, several times that many worldwide) at which you can soak in a hot spring or a thermal bath; sweat in a steam room or sauna; get massages; join dance, Yoga, exercise, or body-awareness classes; play tennis or golf; swim; hike in the woods or up a mountain; ride horseback. And your spa might offer delicious, calorie-minded food; serve you an organic vegetarian diet; or help you embark on a fast.

Variations in spas

Some spas are very plush, tucked away on the grounds of lively resort communities where you need a strong will to stay away from the rich food, alcohol, and high living being enjoyed right under your nose. Other spas are smaller, more Spartan, and more secluded. At these you may follow a disciplined program (up at the crack of dawn for a pre-breakfast hike) and a strict diet (not a potato chip or an ounce of whiskey in sight). At either kind of spa, you can literally turn your body over for a week or two to a staff of expert dieticians, physical education instructors, masseurs, and cosmetologists who'll orchestrate a total overhaul for you—all under a doctor's supervision.

Spas vary in the facilities they offer as well as in atmosphere. You'll find any combination of gyms, pools, whirlpools, saunas, steam rooms, and outdoor sports. But whether you choose silky elegance or rustic tranquility, any spa offers the promise that if you stick to its regimen you'll look and feel better at the end of your stay than you did on the day you came in. The benefits of a week or two in a spa can be mental too. For one thing, seeing such a drastic improvement in your body in such a short time may be all the inspiration you need to adopt healthy eating and exercise habits for life. Spas have also been touted by men as terrific cures for nervous tension, depression, irritability, and inertia. Not all spas take men. Some take men only on certain weeks of the year, or during "couples' weeks."

Some men are chronic hypochondriacs who go to bed after the first sneeze and hide behind bottles of "magic" doctor-prescribed pills. A greater number are notorious tough guys who think doctors are for old people and can't believe that anything serious could ever happen to *them*. Both kinds of men have a distorted point of view of a doctor's utility.

Doctors

You do need a doctor. And you should call on him or her whenever you need advice. If you don't have a doctor, find one now—don't wait for an emergency. If you've just moved, ask your old doctor to refer you to an associate in your new area. Starting fresh? Ask neighbors or co-workers for names of doctors. Gather a list of at least five. Then check them out. The American Medical Association directory, available in most public and hospital libraries, will explain a doctor's specialty, office location, age, medical training (consider a "name" medical school a plus)—even the year he received his license. Do you prefer the up-to-dateness of a young doctor, or the experience of an older one? Sex shouldn't make a difference, but if you prefer a woman instead of a man or vice versa, take that into account—you should feel comfortable with your choice. Consider the office location (the more accessible the doctor's office to your home, the better).

How to find a doctor

When you make a choice, call for an appointment. Ask the fee for a regular office visit, a checkup, a complete physical exam, and find out whether you'll be charged for broken appointments. Ask if the doctor is connected with a teaching hospital (if he is, he'll probably be aware of the latest medical discoveries). Ask whether he gives phone consultations, if there's a fixed time of day when he receives calls, and who covers for him when he's out of town. When you meet the doctor, evaluate him as a person. Do you *like* him? That's as important as anything else.

On your first appointment your doctor should learn:

Visiting a new doctor

· Your complete medical history (past illnesses, operations, vaccinations, injuries), and whether you smoke, drink, take drugs; what you do for a living; how you exercise and relax; if your family life and/or sex life is happy.
· The current state of your health and any abnormalities (unusual bowel movements, shortness of breath, etc.).
· Your family's medical history (illnesses, etc.).

He should give you a complete physical examination, including:

· Blood count (for anemia, leukemia).
· Blood pressure check.

- Urinalysis (for diabetes, kidney disease).
- Examination of your eyes, ears, nose, throat, neck, chest, and abdomen.

The doctor may perform the following tests if your medical history suggests that they will be enlightening. Do not be concerned if he feels they are not necessary.

- Electrocardiogram.
- Chest X ray.
- Examination of other organs.

About checkups If you are under 40 and your doctor has given you a complete physical at some point in your adult life, you'll need only brief checkups every year or two—blood count, blood pressure, urinalysis. After 40, add periodic chest X rays and electrocardiograms, but you won't need those annually until you're over 50. Have an eye examination at least once every two years—such an examination will detect glaucoma, which can be arrested if it's caught early but can lead to blindness if left untreated.

After your checkup, appraise your doctor. Did he rush you through the exam? Did he give you any special tests without an explanation? Was he clear about any problems you have and the treatment he prescribed? Did he answer your questions? Don't let a doctor intimidate you. If he's too busy to answer questions or give you the confidence you need, tell him so. If he skips any part of your checkup, ask why. If you don't understand something, say so. Medical knowledge can be stated in simple terms—it's *not* over your head. You have the right to expect your doctor to be competent, compassionate, open to questions—including those about himself that are relevant to your treatment—and receptive to your seeking a second opinion on his diagnosis.

When you're sick When you're sick, you have the right to know the usual course of the illness and what impact it can have on your day-to-day activities. You should also be told why a specific form of therapy was chosen for you and given information concerning the possible side effects of any prescribed medicines. In most instances instructions will be written out by the doctor. If he doesn't write things down, make sure that you repeat his instructions and write them down yourself for future reference.

Once you choose a doctor, *use* him. Have periodic checkups. In the event of an emergency, have him notified. Consult him between checkups about any fears you may have concerning your physical well-being. If you exercise and watch your weight, you don't need a doctor to tell you that you're healthy. But if you have a sudden, drastic weight loss, change in bowel habits, shortness of breath, or peculiar lumps, call on your doctor—if only to ease your mind.

Acupuncture

Acupuncture has been practiced in China for centuries but has become popular in the United States only recently. It's a therapy that treats disorders through stimulation by very fine, sharp, pliable needles inserted into the body at specific points. The idea is that the body can only be healthy when its vital energy (*C'hi*) flows unimpeded. Disease or pain is considered a sign that the flow has been blocked. The acupuncture process is used to regulate the flow, to cure disease, and diminish pain.

Private medical opinion regarding this process is varied. Some doctors doubt its effectiveness. Others recommend it when conventional treatment has failed, and some are using it in conjunction with regular medical practice.

Acupuncture has been used to treat migraine headaches, deafness, backache, arthritis, asthma, diabetes, ulcers, insomnia, overweight, and disorders of a variety of the body's organs. Medical authorities are cautious about endorsing the use of acupuncture, fearing that it could become a tool for quacks (who might, for example, claim that they could cure cancer with it). If you are interested in trying acupuncture, it would be best to do so under the supervision of a medical doctor.

Chiropractic

Chiropractic healing is based on the theory that disorders are caused by the abnormal functioning of the nervous system. Through manipulation of the body, and particularly the spinal column, a chiropractor aims to give you relief from what ails you. A chiropractor has earned his degree from a school of chiropractic, not a medical school. Four years of training include basic anatomy, physiology, biochemistry, microbiology, pathology, and the interpretation of X-ray films.

For years, the American Medical Association has denounced chiropractic as quackery. And for years, chiropractors have tossed back the claim that the medical profession is afraid of the competition. The dispute has yet to be settled. Chiropractors and many of their satisfied patients profess that the practice has produced amazing relief from headaches, backaches, asthma, neuralgia, bursitis, arthritis, digestion trouble, and circulation disorders. Will it work for *your* aching back? The only way to find out is to try it. Check with your doctor first to rule out the possibility that your complaint is caused by an underlying disease, and then be sure to go to a chiropractor who's been recommended by a friend, or one whose credentials and references you've checked.

The right exercise for you

Face it. You're not happy with the shape you're in. You're getting fatter, thinner, lazier, flabbier, or more tense than you'd like to be. Your exercise routine is sporadic at best. You try and you fail over and over again, and you feel guilty. Yet with the right mental attitude and the smallest amount of effort and discipline, you can look as good as nature intended you to look—right into old age.

Some people are catching on to this. At times it appears that this country has gone mad for exercise. Sixty-year-old men running the 26-mile New York Marathon. More than 5,000 people mob together to run the 7.8 miles in the Bay-to-Breakers race in San Francisco every year. The number of entrants in the Boston Marathon is now limited because the crowds had grown unmanageable. Health clubs and spas, squash clubs and tennis ranches are everywhere. Packs of joggers trot through the park and around the block at six o'clock in the morning. People turn spare rooms into at-home gyms.

There is a lot of controversy about what kind of exercise is good for you and how often you should do it. How can you tell what to believe? How do you know if you're out of shape? And what if you hate exercise and find the whole thing boring?

Many doctors don't know how to prescribe exercise, and the only measure of how much and what kind of exercise you need seems to be the one you take yourself. How do you look and feel? If you're easily winded and less than firm and toned-looking, you're out of shape—and you know it. *Admitting* that you know it is the part that comes hard. But admit it you must, because you need exercise. Without it you become mentally slushy, physically flabby, and more susceptible to fatigue and illness.

Find a workout you'll love

Find an exercise routine that you can enjoy—look forward to, even. That way you're more likely to stick with it—for life.

First be clear about the kind of man you are. If you're unrealistic or overly ambitious about your exercise routine (planning to bike an hour before breakfast when you're a chronic oversleeper, for example), you'll just set yourself up for failure—and guilt. There's something for everybody out there. If the idea of huffing and puffing in calisthenics class jangles your nerves, consider solitary, contemplative Yoga or the rhythmic movement of aerobic dancing. If you love to jog but lack the discipline to do it, get into a group that will force you to stick with the routine. Find ways to incorporate exercise into the context of everyday life just by altering the body movements you already make. For example, never sit when you can stand. Never stand when you could be moving. Never ride when you can walk. Stretch when you reach for a book on a high shelf, or leap for it instead of getting a stool. Ride a bike or walk to work if you can. Instead of taking the elevator to your eighth-floor office, climb the stairs—*every day*. Find the kind of exercise that appeals to you, and *get going*.

Calisthenics or isotonic exercises consist of weight-lifting, toe-touching, push-ups, chin-ups, and the like. They build agility, coordination, muscular tone, and strength.

Different kinds of exercise

Isometric exercises involve pushing or pulling against an immovable object—pushing against a door frame or pulling up on the seat of a chair you're sitting in are both examples of isometric exercises. They build muscular strength through muscular contractions.

Aerobics are running, swimming, cycling, walking, tennis, skiing—exercises that get you moving and increase the action of your heart and respiratory system. These trim you down rather than build up muscle, and are considered the best overall conditioners.

Eastern exercises such as Yoga, Tai-Chi, Akido, Karate, and Judo aim at blending the physical, mental, and spiritual. They can give you flexibility, strength, body firmness, and a heightened sense of well-being.

Any exercise plan you take on should include doses of aerobic activity. (Yoga or weight-lifting alone will not be enough to keep you in the best possible physical condition.)

With the right exercise you can:
- Control your weight.
- Control mental and physical fatigue.
- Ward off disease.
- Improve your posture.
- Enjoy inner organs that function more efficiently.
- Experience less nervous tension.
- Improve your sex life.
- Retard aging.

It's better to exercise for half an hour a day than for three hours once a week. But if three hours of tennis on Sunday afternoon is all you're realistically going to do, it's better than nothing. The thing to avoid is overdoing. Murderous hours on a hot mountain trail when you've been hunched over a desk all week can be worse than no exercise at all. If you're beginning a new form of exercise, put yourself in the hands of a skilled instructor. He'll teach you the right way to breathe, how to pay attention to your body, how to have the right mental attitude about what you're doing.

If time and bad habits have taken their toll on your physical condition, reverse the process NOW, no matter what your age. You deserve a healthy, beautiful body. And you *can* have it.

Eight exercises to make you feel great

The best exercises build up your lung capacity, develop your heart muscles, and get your circulation going. For exercise to have a conditioning effect, it must push your heart rate to two-thirds of its capacity. (To determine your maximum-per-minute pulse rate, subtract your age from 220.) Ideally, you should work in an exercise session that lasts 20 to 30 minutes at least three times a week. WARNING: If you're out of shape, get a physical checkup before you begin any exercise plan, and aim for a gradual buildup of strength and endurance—it's dangerous to push yourself too far too soon.

Activity	Why it's good	What to watch for
Cycling	Good overall conditioner if done vigorously. Especially good for your respiratory system and legs.	Cycle long enough and far enough to get full benefits (include some hills in your route). Doesn't give your upper body much exercise.
Jogging	Excellent overall conditioner. Especially good for heart, lungs, and legs.	Build up to long distances gradually. Wear running shoes—jogging can be hard on joints and ligaments. Limber up before setting off.
Tennis	Fairly good overall conditioner. Good for developing reflexes and eye-hand coordination.	Benefits depend on how vigorously you play.

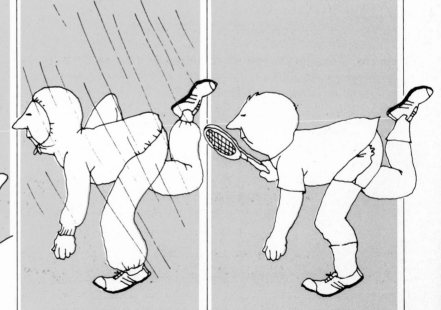

Skiing	Downhill skiing is good overall conditioner. Cross-country skiing ranks with swimming as one of the most complete workouts.	High altitudes and cold can strain the heart. You should be in good physical condition *before* you undertake skiing.
Swimming	Excellent overall conditioner. Exercises *all* your muscles, as well as the circulatory and respiratory systems.	Swim long and hard to get the maximum benefit. Mere water play is not as effective.
Walking	Excellent beginning exercise. Good for the heart, lungs, and muscle tone if done briskly.	Walk at a brisk pace (one mile in 10 to 12 minutes) to exercise the heart.
Modern dance	Excellent overall conditioner if it involves vigorous movement.	Attend regular classes, or be disciplined to get enough exercise to benefit you.
Yoga	Builds strength, flexibility, and balance but doesn't accelerate your pulse rate sufficiently. Benefits include mental serenity through quiet concentration.	Builds muscle tone slowly. Takes patience and concentration. You need to learn with an instructor. Must supplement with an aerobic exercise for sufficient heart conditioning.

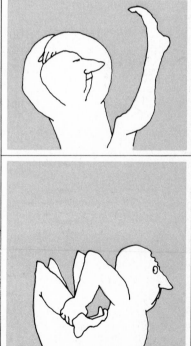
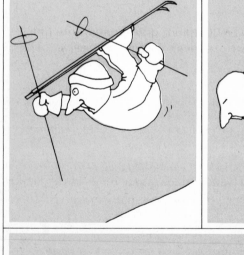

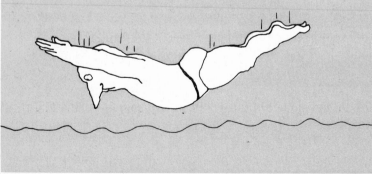

Five exercises for appearance' sake

These exercises will build and tone your muscles fairly quickly; however, they're not respiratory or cardiovascular conditioners. In other words, they may make you *look* better, but they're not enough by themselves to keep you healthy. To stay fit, you'll need to combine these exercises with some kind of aerobic activity (running, cycling, swimming, etc.). Use these exercises to stay toned, not to make yourself muscle-bound. Overdeveloped muscles can turn to fat. Well-toned muscles are leaner, more likely to keep you looking great right into old age.

The problem	The exercise that helps
Flabby stomach	Sit-ups. Hook your feet under something heavy, like a sofa. Lie back, knees bent. Put your hands behind your neck, elbows close together. Pull yourself up, bending at the waist, until your elbows touch your knees. Lie back down slowly. Do as many as you can. Work hard, but don't overtax yourself. Work up gradually to 25.

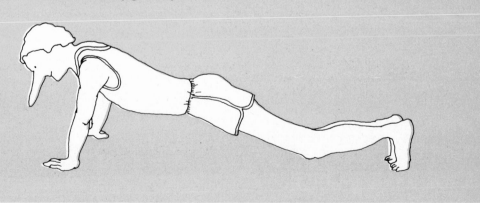

| Untoned arms, upper body; weak back | Push-ups. Stretch out, face down, on a mat (or the floor). Bend your knees. Place your hands palms down on the floor at shoulder level, out a bit past your shoulders. Push up, pivoting from your knees until your arms are straight, keeping your back straight. Lower yourself slowly until your nose touches the mat. When you master this, try the same exercise keeping your legs straight, so that you pivot on your toes instead of on your knees. Work up gradually to 25. |

Weak, untoned thighs

Squats. Stand with your feet 18–24 inches apart. Squat down slowly, pushing your knees forward as you go. Try to keep your back straight. Don't lower your hips below your knees. Exhale as you go down, pause, inhale as you go up. Work up gradually to 30.

Underdeveloped calves

Toe raisers. Stand with the balls of your feet on a two-by-four or the edge of a bottom stair tread—your heels will be unsupported. Pump yourself up and down. Work up to 20 or 30.

Underdeveloped biceps

Chin-ups. Place your hands on a chinning bar with your palms facing you, your hands eight inches apart. Hang straight down; make sure your feet don't touch the ground. Pull up slowly until your chin reaches the bar. Do this *once*. Work up until you can do four, rest, and do another set of four.

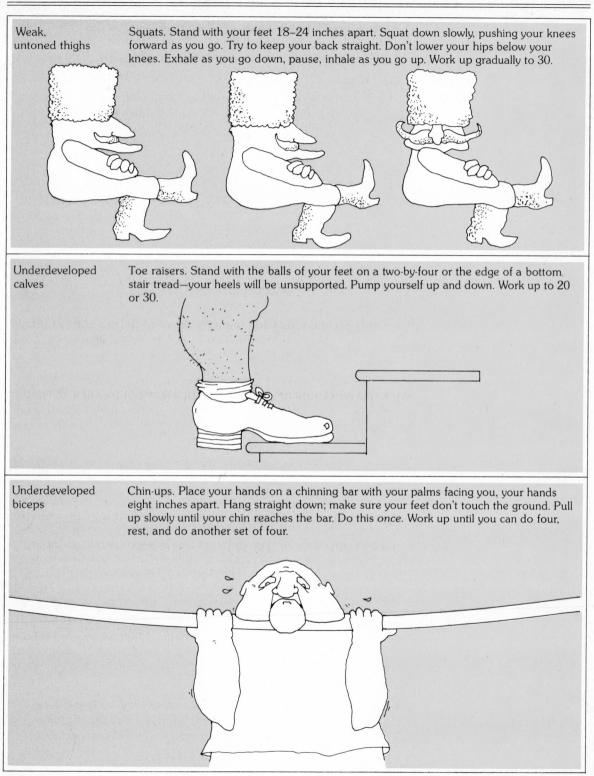

Six tension-relieving exercises

Exercise	How to do it	Benefits/Cautions

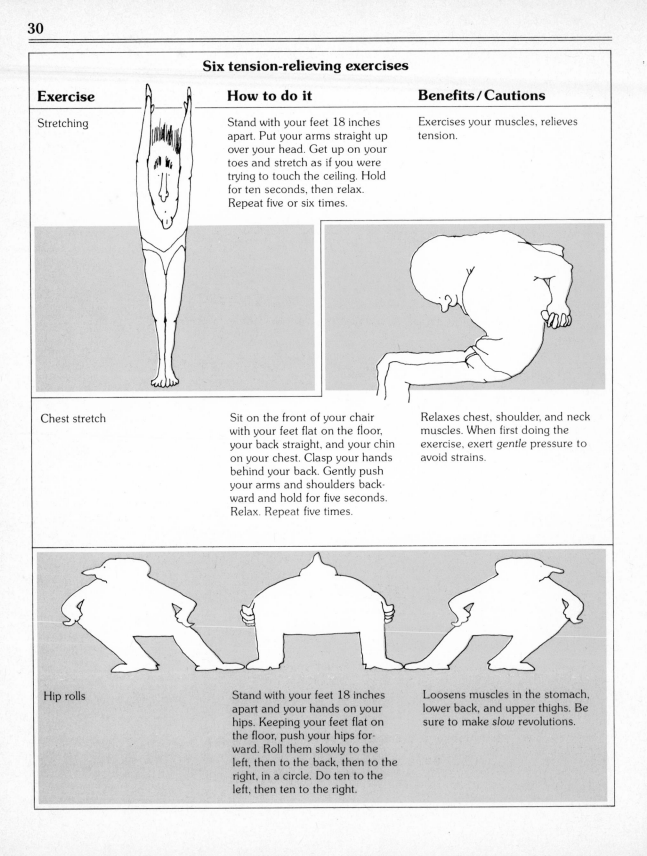

Stretching

Stand with your feet 18 inches apart. Put your arms straight up over your head. Get up on your toes and stretch as if you were trying to touch the ceiling. Hold for ten seconds, then relax. Repeat five or six times.

Exercises your muscles, relieves tension.

Chest stretch

Sit on the front of your chair with your feet flat on the floor, your back straight, and your chin on your chest. Clasp your hands behind your back. Gently push your arms and shoulders backward and hold for five seconds. Relax. Repeat five times.

Relaxes chest, shoulder, and neck muscles. When first doing the exercise, exert *gentle* pressure to avoid strains.

Hip rolls

Stand with your feet 18 inches apart and your hands on your hips. Keeping your feet flat on the floor, push your hips forward. Roll them slowly to the left, then to the back, then to the right, in a circle. Do ten to the left, then ten to the right.

Loosens muscles in the stomach, lower back, and upper thighs. Be sure to make *slow* revolutions.

Rapid breathing

Sit on the edge of your chair, feet on the floor, hands in your lap. Take a deep breath and let it out through your nose in short bursts, contracting your stomach muscles with each outward breath. Let the air back into your lungs slowly. Exhale again, sharp and fast. Continue this for 30 to 60 seconds. Finish by taking a deep breath, exhaling slowly, relaxing your whole body.

Clears your head, rids you of fatigue, strengthens your body. Smokers may feel dizzy (a sign that your lungs haven't been getting enough oxygen). If so, stay relaxed and breathe normally until the dizziness passes.

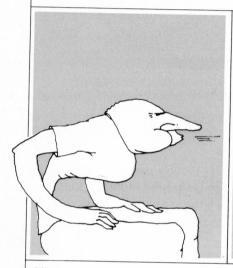
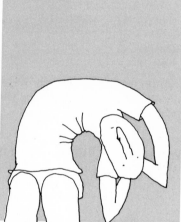

Elbow point

Sit down with your back straight and feet flat on the floor. Clasp your hands on top of your head. Bend to the left, raising your right elbow as far as you can. Sit up straight again. Now bend to the right, raising your left elbow. Repeat five times.

Stretches the back, underarm, and neck muscles. Again, start with *easy* pressure—let your body get used to the exercise.

Head rolling

Sit straight in your chair. Drop your head forward. Keep it down. Roll it slowly to the left, then to the back, then to the right, in a circle. Keep your shoulders down, your back straight. Finish by putting your chin on your chest and pushing your head down gently with your hands. Then move your head backward and pause for a few seconds.

Stretches and relaxes neck and shoulder muscles.

Twelve easy exercises to keep you going

1. Balance on one foot without support while putting on your shoes and socks. This tightens leg muscles, builds strength.

2. Climb stairs two at a time. This exercises leg muscles, and strengthens your heart.

3. Squeeze your washcloth out extra hard, holding the tension until the exertion feels heavy. This adds strength to your wrists and arms.

4. Yawn. Wide. This stretches your facial muscles and fills your lungs with air.

5. Have a good stretch before you get out of bed in the morning. Muscular contractions build muscular strength.

6. Lift something relatively heavy and hold it for five seconds. Taxing your muscles keeps them toned.

7. Polish something vigorously (your car, a pan, a mirror, a glass table). This is good for your cardio-vascular system and tones your arms and chest.

8. After a shower, give yourself a vigorous rub-down with a towel. Hard toweling of your body can stimulate your heart. You'll also slough off dead layers of skin and improve your skin tone.

9. Park your car a few blocks from your destina-tion. Walk fast. The more briskly you move, the more circulo-respiratory benefit you get.

10. Stand whenever you talk on the phone. Stand-ing for at least two hours a day is good for circula-tion and bone structure.

11. Go dancing. Dance until you're out of breath. This gets your heart working and helps build stamina.

12. Enjoy a vigorous sex life. Intercourse increases your heart rate, exercises your muscles, and increases your supply of testosterone.

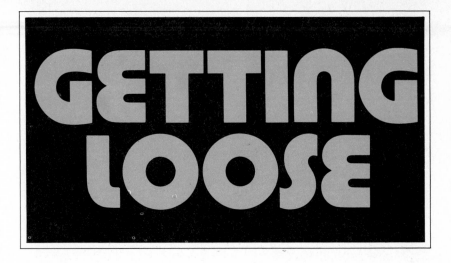

GETTING LOOSE

Living with stress

The high cost of high pressure

You face a certain amount of stress *every* day. You're under stress when you're late for work, when you get stuck in a traffic jam or in the slow line at the bank, just as you are when someone you love dies—or when you take off for a Tahiti vacation you've looked forward to for years. A stress situation can be pleasant or unpleasant. Joy, sorrow, heat, cold, pain, worry, trauma all induce the same physiological manifestations of stress in your body. You may sweat, your heart may race, you may frown, tense your muscles, perspire, cry. During stress, your body works to readjust itself so that it can go about its normal functioning. Stress is a fact of life. It's not bad—in fact, without the things that cause stress, life would be deadly dull. Everyone must face it. What makes you different from somebody else is not the amount of stress you face, but the way you deal with it. Losing your job may totally undo you; another person might be able to ride through it without too much difficulty.

Not handling stress well takes its toll on your physical and mental well-being. Medical research shows that a continual high-pressure reaction to stress can literally kill you. High-pressure people are more likely to suffer heart attacks, strokes, and mental breakdowns than people who can recover more easily from stress situations. High-pressure people set deadlines for themselves. They're impatient when things move slowly. They talk fast, walk fast, eat fast. They often have higher cholesterol levels than others. When they're under stress, they push even harder. They block any recognition of how tense they are. And though they may earn their life rewards, it's at a high cost to their bodies. People who can handle stress well have a quiet inner reserve that allows them to recover from the effects of stress rather quickly.

They are just as intelligent, just as highly motivated as high-pressure people, and though they can use stressful situations to excite them to high performance levels, they don't allow the negative effects of stress to tear them down. They know how, and when, to ease up. They don't over-pressure themselves. And they are actually able to reach higher levels of achievement than high-pressure people because the ability to relax (and replenish their energies) doesn't elude them.

If you're a high-pressure person who needs a drink or a tranquilizer in order to calm down, who can't take it easy or stop pushing even on weekends and vacations, you may be afraid to change. You may think that if you let up, you'll lose your ability to compete. And you may not understand what relaxation means. High levels of tension are *not* necessary for you to meet the goals you've set for yourself. Learning to relax doesn't mean you'll become a zombie or lose your drive. It simply means that you'll be able to handle stress better, be able to make it a positive force in your life instead of a negative one. You need to learn to build that quiet inner reserve. And you can. How?

Don't be afraid to relax

Start by taking a good look at yourself and the way you live. If your approach to life and to work is extremely fast-paced, look for ways to tone it down. Plan your schedule realistically, allowing time for unexpected phone calls and interruptions so that they don't knock you off balance when they occur. Be realistic about what you can and can't get done in a given amount of time, and don't panic if you sometimes fall behind. Force yourself to take time out. Instead of a drink, a tranquilizer, or a frantic game of tennis to "calm you" at the end of the day, find a quiet place where you can sit uninterrupted for ten minutes. Listen to some calming music and let yourself flow with it. Tighten your muscles one at a time, and let them go. Feel them relax. Better yet, do this whenever you feel tense and pressured (in the middle of the day if need be). Time out, even for a few minutes, renews your energy, equips you to tackle the jobs at hand in a more efficient way.

Another excellent way to build a protection against the effects of stress is through meditation. To the surprise of skeptics who just a few years ago thought meditation was a kooky cult, medical researchers have turned up evidence that meditation and relaxation techniques bring about distinct physiologic changes that slow down the nervous system. The practice of Transcendental Meditation, for example, decreases the body's metabolism, heart rate, breathing rate. Blood pressure remains unchanged while a person practices TM,® but blood pressure appears to be lower in general among people who meditate than among individuals who don't.

Why meditation helps

How to meditate   Want to meditate on your own? It's not difficult. And any kind of meditation technique will help you build a calm reserve that will, in turn, help you improve the way you deal with stress. You need a quiet place, a comfortable sitting position. Keep your back straight. Do whatever's comfortable with your hands and legs; just be sure you feel relaxed. Set a timer for 20 minutes. Close your eyes. Clear your mind of thoughts. Concentrate on your breathing—in-out, in-out. Don't slow it or hurry it. When a thought flits through your mind, allow it to pass. Don't dwell on it or let it distract you. Keep focusing on your breathing. If you have trouble concentrating, count your breaths, one to ten, and start over. Don't break your concentration. Twenty minutes can seem like a long time, and if you're very tense you may feel anxious about "just sitting" for so long. If the thought that you're wasting time occurs to you while you're meditating, note it and let it go. Realize that you're developing something valuable for yourself. If you meditate regularly (preferably twice a day, morning and evening) you'll get the best results. And your overall ability to relax will increase the longer you continue to practice meditation. You won't make much progress if you meditate only occasionally. Want to learn more about meditation? Bookstores are jammed with books about every kind of meditation technique. And see the "Self-Awareness Guide," page 46-49.

Facing depression   It's perfectly okay to feel depressed sometimes. Any sensitive man is bound to have days when he feels tender, insecure, lethargic, just plain blah. The feeling may last for days or even a couple of weeks before you return to normal. But if depression lingers or begins to interfere with your normal life pattern, there's something wrong. Telling yourself it'll go away, playing tennis or going to the movies to take your mind off your troubles won't help when problems run deep. You won't begin to get rid of what's bothering you until you're willing to take a good, hard look at what it is.

You're not Superman   This may not be easy. As a man, you've been conditioned not to look at your vulnerabilities—to tough it out instead. When you feel trapped by your responsibilities, in doubt about your career or your relationships with others or your own capabilities, it may seem safer to ignore the doubt and the fear than to look at it and acknowledge it. You're not likely to be comfortable with questions like, "Who am I?" "Where am I?", "Is this what I really want?" You feel that a man should know the answers. Doubts don't fit into the image you have of yourself. You want to be strong, assured, happy. And so you may pretend that you are, hoping that problems will just disappear.

This kind of ostrich, head-in-the-sand attitude is very dangerous. When you bottle things up you place a heavy burden on your emotions. Continue to do this for too long and your emotional machinery can break down altogether, resulting in a deep, incapacitating depression.

You can be in a depression and not even know it. It can build up around you gradually as you continue to push out the knowledge that things are *not* just fine. When you're in a depression, you feel fearful, angry, and irritable most of the time. You may feel lethargic and sleep inordinate amounts, or you may be incredibly tense and find your eyes popping open long before dawn each morning. The zest goes out of things; nothing seems like fun anymore, nothing seems to have the value and meaning it used to have. Worse, you feel hopeless, helpless, and can't believe you'll ever feel otherwise. A depression like that needs attention.

When depression needs help

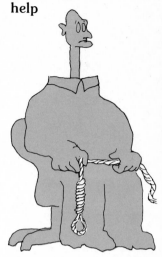

If you need help, get it

The idea of getting professional help frightens many people, even today, when being in therapy is fairly common. In your mind, a "shrink" may be okay for your friends, but not for you. You still may feel that to be a "real man" you've got to handle your problems alone. That, of course, is nonsense. Not getting help for problems you can't handle successfully on your own is as foolish as not asking for directions when you're lost in a strange town.

What can a therapist do for you? He or she can help break emotional blisters that have formed, provide you with a place where you can spill emotions, fears, and conflicts without fear of judgment. A therapist can give you support as you learn to examine your values, your needs, your view of society, your behavior, and the behavior of those around you. A therapist can help you to gain a perspective that works for *you*. Actually, the term "shrink" is a misnomer, since it implies that a therapist will bring your head down to size. A "stretcher" would be a better nickname for a therapist, for therapy can help you to expand your mind to a point where you're capable of handling and understanding much more than you ever did before. It may take weeks, months, even years for you to feel that your therapy is complete. But most people who go into therapy begin to feel better about their problems and about themselves right away.

How a therapist can help

How to find a therapist? Your regular doctor may be able to recommend someone. Ask friends for names of therapists; ask them about the kind of treatment they've received. You can get more therapists' names by calling a university medical center or a local hospital—these can refer you to private therapists or clinics—or by

Finding a therapist

looking in the telephone book under "Mental Health." When you've decided on a therapist you'd like to try, call for a consultation. When you make an appointment ask about the cost per hour and whether or not you'll be charged for canceled sessions. If you have questions about the kind of therapy that's practiced, ask that too. And when you go for your consultation, be open and honest, and trust your instincts. If you simply don't like the therapist, discuss it with him or her. And don't hesitate to consult with other therapists. You should feel as relaxed as possible and have a certain amount of rapport with the person to whom you'll reveal your deepest feelings. You may have to do some looking before you find the right person.

However painful it may be to confront your doubts and fears, doing so is the only way to grow and to increase your feelings of self-worth. Growing requires constant questioning, reevaluation, and willingness to make changes. As long as you're unwilling to deal with what's bothering you, you'll stagnate. Self-exploration, on the other hand, can give you the power to make your life flourish.

Alcohol and marijuana Man first encountered alcoholic beverages long before the advent of recorded history. And since then alcohol has been periodically damned and praised. Today alcohol is imbibed on a variety of occasions. Wine or beer is often drunk at meals to enhance the flavor of the food, and its sedative effect helps your body properly digest the meal. At social gatherings people drink to relax, lower inhibitions, and ease the aches and pains of the day. Several religious ceremonies include the drinking of wine. And alcohol is still occasionally used medically for its qualities as a sedative and muscle relaxant. Unfortunately, the widespread use of alcohol has not fostered a better understanding of its effects. Myth and hearsay confuse the issue. Here are some facts.

What is alcohol? Ethyl alcohol, or ethanol, is derived from the fermentation of fruits, honey, or grains. Alcohol has caloric value (that is, it can be burned by the body for energy), but no nutritional value. It constitutes 3 to 6 percent of beer and ale, 12 to 14 percent of table wines, 17 to 21 percent of dessert wines (port and sherry, for example), and 40 to 60 percent of hard liquor.

How does it affect you? Alcohol does not need to be digested; it is absorbed directly into the bloodstream through the walls of the stomach and small intestine. Ten percent of the alcohol is eliminated through the lungs and kidneys. The remainder stays in the blood until the liver can break it down for the body's use. Alcohol first affects the more developed brain centers (those dealing with judgment); then it affects the voluntary muscle control centers (those controlling coordinated movement) and, ultimately, if sufficient amounts are consumed, the involuntary muscle control centers (those controlling breathing, for example).

For the purpose of this section, one drink will constitute a 12-ounce can of beer, 5 ounces of table wine, 3 ounces of dessert wine, 1½ ounces of whiskey straight or mixed into one cocktail. Keep in mind in reading the following discussion that everything is relative; your level of intoxication will depend on how fast you drink and your drinking habits, body size, and personality as well as the amount of alcohol you consume.

A blood-alcohol level of 0.01 to 0.05 percent, brought on by drinking one or two drinks in about an hour, will make most people feel mildly intoxicated. At this level you will feel relaxed, talkative, and less inhibited, and minor aches and pains will fade.

Two more drinks in the next hour can raise the blood-alcohol level to between 0.06 and 0.1 percent. (The latter is the legal limit of intoxication in most states.) You will become erratic; coordinated movement will be impaired; thinking will become muddled; reactions will be slowed.

One more drink will probably raise your blood-alcohol level to between 0.1 and 0.4 percent. At this point, confusion sets in. Emotions are exaggerated, speech begins to slur, double vision may occur, and perceptions are disoriented.

Several more drinks in rapid succession will raise the blood-alcohol level to between 0.4 and 0.6 percent. At this point, standing or walking becomes impossible, consciousness begins to fade, and nausea may occur. Beyond this point one enters a coma. In very rare cases death may occur due to respiratory paralysis.

The body burns alcohol at a constant rate of about half an ounce per hour. If you linger over your drink for an hour and a half, no alcohol will accumulate in your blood. Otherwise, you will just have to wait for your body to burn the excess. Remedies such as black coffee, cold showers, fresh air, and exercise *don't* work to lower blood-alcohol levels, though they may make you feel better.

Abuse Alcoholism is a disease characterized by uncontrolled drinking. Trouble starts when drinking becomes a necessity or a means of dealing with problems rather than a pleasant addition to other activities. In the United States, there are about 95 million drinkers; roughly nine million are chronic abusers. If you suspect that you are drinking too much, or if your drinking interferes with your day-to-day activities, consult your physician.

Marijuana Marijuana, the leaves and buds of the cannabis plant, has a history as old and checkered as that of alcohol. Cannabis plants originated in central Asia. Explorers brought them to Europe for use in the manufacture of hemp for rope, twine, and cloth. The plant oil was used in paint, varnish, soap, and cattle feed. It was not until late in its history that its widespread use as an intoxicant occurred.

The effects of marijuana The active ingredient in marijuana is THC (tetrahydracanabinol). When THC is taken into the body by smoking or eating marijuana, the effects are varied. Among the more common are feelings of being relaxed, contemplative, and giddy. Fascination with the obscure may increase as time and space perceptions become distorted and heightened. The user may also feel confused, hungry, and mildly paranoid.

Studies of how marijuana use affects the body are numerous and conflicting. It has been said that there is more accumulated knowledge concerning marijuana than penicillin. Most of the research and reporting both pro and con pertaining to marijuana is affected by the bias of the writer or interpreter.

Advocates of marijuana law reform present a battery of arguments to support their views. They feel that legalization would make it easier to curtail the sale of the drug to minors; that quality would become consistent; that revenue could be generated through taxation. Their most potent argument, however, is that court time and expense could be saved. And there is the fact that many people's lives are destroyed by the police records and jail sentences imposed for using what *may* be one of the least harmful drugs. Those who oppose the modification of existing laws feel, simply, that the drug's (possible) detrimental effects far outweigh the (possible) benefits of legalization.

Abuse

Problems can arise from the recreational use of any consciousness-altering substance. Marijuana differs from alcohol in one important respect. Whereas a man may have a glass of wine because he enjoys the taste, the only reason for using marijuana is to get high. When obtaining a "high" starts to affect the rest of your life, you're in trouble. If you feel awkward about consulting your physician, call a drug-abuse hot line. They can usually give you the help you need.

To sleep or not to sleep

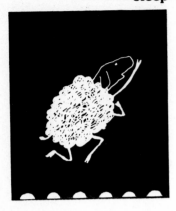

Some people need a regular eight to ten hours of sleep a night. You may get along just fine with five or six hours. Furthermore, the number of hours you need will vary at different times in your life. Obviously you need sleep to recharge your body; if you are deprived of necessary amounts of sleep, you can become cranky, mentally fuzzy, depressed, less efficient. If severe sleep deprivation goes on for a long period of time, you may hallucinate or even exhibit bizarre, psychotic behavior.

During a normal night, you'll float back and forth between REM (rapid eye movement) sleep and Delta sleep. In REM sleep you're just below the level of consciousness—and it's then that you dream. During Delta sleep you're in a state of deep unconsciousness, and your bodily functions slow down—breathing and heart rate, even body temperature fall off. You need *both* kinds of sleep to retain physical health and peace of mind.

What disturbs sleep?

What can disturb your sleep? Alcohol, drugs you take for other ailments, depression, or emotional problems can rob you of sleep. If you lose some sleep for a night or two, your system can adapt pretty easily. But if insomnia persists, you should do something about it. Sleeping pills may seem like an easy cure, but they're a bad idea. Sleeping pills (barbiturates, tranquilizers, sedatives, or anti-anxiety drugs such as Valium or Librium) are dangerous, habit-forming, self-defeating. For one thing, they can disrupt your REM sleep and deprive you of the necessary dreaming process. For another, you may develop a sleeping-pill tolerance: it takes one tablet to knock you out this week, two next week, three the week after that. And, since drugs leave your system only gradually, a residue will build up. Use sleeping pills too long and you'll store up a dangerous, even lethal dose of drugs in your body. Sleeping pills should never be taken for a period longer than four weeks. If you depend on pills to sleep and a stimulant to get you going in the morning, you're locked into a vicious, destructive, drug-logged cycle. If this happens you'll need to relearn to tune in with your own natural processes.

Healthy ways to induce sleep

Hypnotherapy: It's a kind of autohypnosis—you plant a suggestion in your mind that will help you to disassociate yourself from the anxiety or stress that's the cause of your tossing and turning. Hypnotherapy should be taught to you by a medical doctor or a psychologist. A qualified hypnotherapist can be found by consulting your doctor or the local medical society.

Relaxation exercises: Lie in bed, lights out, doors locked, any other necessary-for-sleep rituals performed. Now begin tensing and relaxing

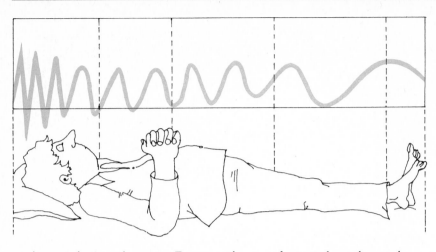

each muscle one by one. Begin with your feet and work up—legs, abdomen, back, shoulders, face. This not only relaxes your body, it slows your mental processes so whatever problems you're facing will be less likely to keep you awake.

Some other sleeping tips

- Cut down on your intake of coffee, tea, and cola drinks containing caffeine. Never drink them in the evening.
- Get plenty of exercise in the morning or afternoon. But don't exercise just before bedtime—it'll rev up your system. (Love-making, however, can relax you.)
- Take a warm, muscle-relaxing bath before bedtime.
- Drink a cup of warm milk laced with a spoonful of sherry or brandy. Toss in three or four calcium tablets. (Calcium is a natural tranquilizer.) If you wake up during the night, make yourself another warm cup of the same.
- Create a good sleeping environment for yourself—a dark, quiet, ventilated room is ideal. If unsettling light creeps over your windowsill, buy a blackout shade.
- Sleep on a good, hard mattress. If your mattress at home is soft and lumpy, get rid of it. If you can't afford a new one, slip a bed board under it while you save up. And when you shop for a mattress, test it out by lying down on it. You might choose a latex or urethane foam mattress (lightweight, and good if you have allergies) or one with innerspring construction—whatever the manufacturer calls his hardest mattress is probably what you want. It doesn't matter which, just as long as the mattress you choose gives your body good, firm support.

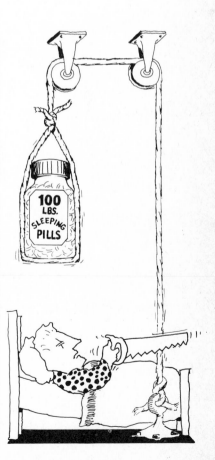

GETTING IN TOUCH WITH YOURSELF

Choosing the right self-exploration program

If you haven't joined the consciousness revolution, it may not be because you don't want to, but because there are so many cults, therapies, and awareness techniques that you can't possibly know which one to choose. Do you adopt a macrobiotic diet, begin doing Yoga, get "Rolfed," or head for a Zen retreat? Do you try TM® or go into Gestalt therapy? You may also wonder if you really need to do anything at all.

You probably don't. You can probably get along fine without getting your mind blown, having your consciousness expanded, or being zapped with enlightenment. And yet...

You notice a new serenity in your meditating friends. You watch someone making a long-overdue career change after a two-weekend encounter with est; you see a good friend quit blaming other people for his problems after becoming involved with Arica. You sense that some kind of awareness program might enrich your life.

There are literally thousands of ways to "wake up," to get in touch with your feelings, reevaluate your goals, broaden your perspectives, develop your human potential. Within the consciousness movement there are experimental psychologists, psychotherapists, mind researchers, gurus, lamas. There are cults, fads, and many, many different kinds of therapies that seem to focus more on helping normal people refine their sensitivities than on helping neurotic people function normally. Some popular therapies: Fritz Perls' Gestalt; B.F. Skinner's Behavior Modification; William Glasser's Reality Therapy; Arthur Janov's Primal Therapy; Eric Berne's Transactional Analysis. To find out more about any of these, look on the shelves in a good bookstore.

The Esalen Institute in Big Sur, California, has been a showplace for new techniques in the consciousness movement. Since Michael Murphy opened Esalen in 1962, it's become well known as a place to go to try out body-awareness techniques and encounter groups. People from many different disciplines have met and exchanged ideas at Esalen—major thinkers such as Abraham Maslow, Fritz Perls, Aldous Huxley, Paul Tillich, and Carl Rogers have been drawn to this serene Pacific cliffside setting with its relaxing, outdoor, hot-spring baths. Today's Esalen catalogue shows a wide selection of growth programs that blend Eastern and Western thought. You can go for a weekend or for a week, and your program might include Gestalt encounter, meditation, types of body awareness (such as Rolfing, massage, or martial arts). The catalogue alone is fascinating reading.

What should you expect?

Though self-exploration techniques can be fun and rewarding, they can be painful—mentally, emotionally, physically—at the same time. Beware of having unrealistic expectations about the amount of health, happiness, or enlightenment you'll get from self-awareness programs. Quality control is impossible to establish in a field like this, and you can be taken in by charlatans. There's a lot of disagreement about some consciousness-expanding techniques—one man's gateway to enlightenment can be another man's ripoff. Get into this and you're pretty much on your own. Remember that however tough you may think you are, your psyche may be tender; be sure you're willing to rake it over the coals. Check out any plan thoroughly before you sign up—if possible, talk to people who've been through the program to get a clear picture of what to expect. And if you're in therapy, be sure to let your therapist know if you make plans to sign up for any kind of self-exploration program.

> HOT SPRINGS

Self-awareness guide   Listed in the following pages, ten ways to work on your own enlightenment: body therapies to pound past traumas out of you or to teach your mind to counteract physical ills; encounters that offer emotional release and help in the healing of old psychic wounds; intellectual mind-benders that promise to stretch your awareness and enrich your life; meditation techniques to bring you serenity and peace of mind. WARNING: These things are for people who are fundamentally stable and are looking for ways to improve their lives and their relationships. They are not cures for psychological ailments.

Arica   In a 40-day program, a 16-hour weekend program, or a series of weekday evening sessions, you'll dance, do balancing techniques, exercise, chant mantras, meditate. One exercise, called "traspaso," has you sitting opposite another person for three to five minutes, staring into his left eye—a form of communication that's said to be exhausting and enlightening. Another Arican exercise is a system of movements called psychocalisthenics; they're designed to unify your body, mind, and emotions. Arica has been with us since 1971, when it was introduced by a Bolivian guru, Oscar Ichazo. Arica is a blend of Eastern and Western disciplines, and its ultimate aim is to help its students get beyond the ego in order to see the world properly, to find a permanent sense of inner harmony and peace with the rest of the universe.

Bioenergetics   While a therapist guides you, you'll toughen your muscles and let out your emotions with vigorous body exercise, deep breathing, traditional psychoanalysis, and various forms of Gestaltlike psychotherapy. Bioenergetics was developed 20 years ago by U.S. psychiatrist Alexander Lowen, a former student of Wilhelm Reich (who thought the source of all neurosis was blocked sexual energy). The idea here is that your natural energy is locked in, that you're emotionally and physically tied into a knot. To break that rigid state and to get your natural energy to flow freely, you must unlock your physical tensions and let out your pent-up emotions.

Biofeedback You'll be wired to a machine while you meditate and do other autogenic exercises that aim at controlling your body's involuntary systems. The machines tell you when you've achieved control as you modify your heartbeat, blood pressure, muscular and nervous tension. You can even control the rhythm of your brain waves. Several scientists, including Dr. Barbara Brown, Dr. Joseph Kamiya, and Doctors Elmer and Alyce Green, have worked with Biofeedback since the late 1950s. It's been found that the mind can control body processes to an extraordinary extent—and besides being used to train muscles and nerves to relax, Biofeedback has been employed to retrain damaged nerve-muscle systems, reduce epileptic seizures, and control insomnia. The mind can be trained to cure or prevent illnesses as well as to control thoughts and feelings. WARNING: The Biofeedback phenomenon has attracted faddists, cultists, and exploiters. Some manufacturers are marketing monitoring devices that could actually be harmful. Beware of products you haven't checked out with an expert. Look in your phone book under "Biofeedback" to find study centers near you.

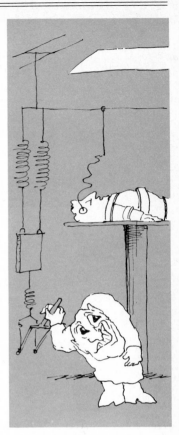

est In two consecutive weekends, you'll spend 60 hours in a hotel ballroom with 200 or more other people. You'll be yelled at, led through meditation-type exercises, put through processes that can be emotionally painful. You'll get in touch with your feelings, your past hurts, and the act you put on to protect yourself and to "survive" in the world. You'll hear other people "share" their feelings, and possibly you'll "share" some of your own. You won't be allowed to eat, smoke, go to the bathroom, or even leave the room except during specified breaks. The est "training" is boring, exhilarating, painful, and powerful. Started in 1971 by former businessman Werner Erhard, est is a blend of a whole basketful of philosophies, including Scientology, mind dynamics, Zen, Gestalt, Dale Carnegie. Its aim is to help you to shed your armor and find out who you really are; to help you end the constant rationalizing and blaming you do in order to avoid taking responsibility for your life; to help you stop wishing things were a way they aren't and to get on with the way they are. Results seem difficult to describe, and satisfied graduates say est must be experienced to be understood. There are est centers in 16 major U.S. cities coast to coast.

The Feldenkrais Method You do slow-moving, meditative exercises to relearn coordination. (For example, as you lie on your back you'll be asked to check out where various parts of your body touch the floor, to notice how they are doing so.) You'll do hundreds of easy movements that borrow ideas from the martial arts, yoga, the twirling dances of the Sufis. "Functional integration," which is what Moshe Feldenkrais (now in his late 70s) calls his method, is based on the idea that if you're attuned to your body, you can establish a rapport with your environment and reduce stress. It also holds that expansion of body awareness expands your consciousness, heightens your self-understanding. The method eliminates tight, stiff muscles, relieves the symptoms of diseases of the nervous system (such as multiple sclerosis), and inhibits the symptoms of aging.

Psychosynthesis Through group and individual therapy, you'll be led toward a greater inner freedom. You'll work on developing intuition and creativity. You'll get a taste of guided imagery, meditation, journal-keeping. Developed over the last half century by the late Italian psychoanalyst Roberto Assagioli, Psychosynthesis aims to restore balance to the self, to help you recognize the conflicting elements of your inner life. This multidimensional growth therapy holds that your true self is a center of awareness and that you have other subpersonalities that revolve around that center. When one of your subpersonalities becomes dominant (the child in you, say), your true self is thrown off balance. Psychosynthesis brings it all into focus.

Silva Mind Control® In a series of four 12-hour classes you'll learn to "count down" to inner consciousness levels and to reach an alpha state that is beyond time, space, and the physical senses. In the alpha state your attention is turned inward; alpha brain waves are associated with creativity, awareness, intuition. You'll also use visual exercises for problem-solving—with "mirror of the mind," for example, you'll visualize your problem in a full-length mirror, study the problem, and mentally remove it. You'll program yourself to solve problems in dreams, to wake yourself up at a predetermined time, to learn to control pain. Developed 30 years ago by a Texan named Jose Silva,

Silva Mind Control® aims to bolster your confidence, motivation, and leadership qualities; to develop your innate psychic ability; to improve your concentration, memory, creative imagination, and verbal artistic expression. There are Silva trainers operating in most major U.S. cities as well as in Mexico, Canada, England, and Israel. Check your phone book.

Transcendental Meditation In four two-hour sessions with a teacher of TM®, you'll be given a mantra (a simple word that you'll repeat during meditation) and taught how to use it. TM® involves an effortless form of meditation that induces a state of rest that's deeper than sleep—yet in this state your mind is still alert. Your mind will be taught to experience subtler and subtler levels of the thinking process until thinking is transcended and your mind comes in contact with the source of thought. TM® was introduced to the United States by Maharishi Mahesh Yogi in 1959. Scientific research, begun in 1970, has shown that the TM® technique lowers the body's metabolism, heart rate, and breathing rate and provides a lot of other benefits, including relief from insomnia and stress, increased creativity, and overall well-being. There are TM® centers in major cities all over the world.

Yoga You begin, with a teacher, with exercises that improve your health and physical fitness, and gradually work up through the mental to the spiritual. Yoga, a science of physical and mental self-development, has been around for centuries. Its aim is to develop the physical, mental, moral, and spiritual forces that are already within you. There are many different aspects of Yoga. A natural place to begin is with Hatha Yoga, which concentrates on regulation of breathing and other body disciplines. From there you can move on to take up meditation (Raja Yoga), concentration (Laya Yoga), and the quest for enlightenment (Kundalini Yoga). Check your phone book for names of Yoga teachers near you.

Zen is the meditation school of Chinese and Japanese Buddhism. One Zen meditation technique will have you follow your breathing without attempting to control it, and you'll work with koans (phrases that seem to make no sense) and perhaps puzzle over their meaning for years. Wrestling with a koan helps you to push through outer layers of consciousness, to tear away the veils between self and reality. Zen training, undertaken with the guidance of a teacher, is long and difficult. The reward to aim for: "Satori"—enlightenment, an awareness of an ultimate reality that's beyond the limits of your own consciousness.

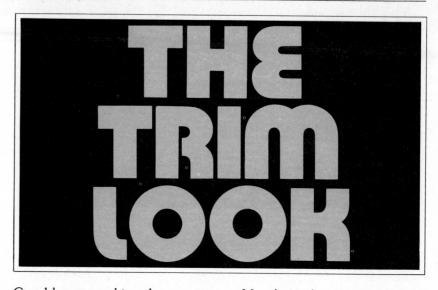

Cook for your health

Good home cooking does not mean Mom's apple pie or a glass of milk and a plateful of cookies at bedtime. By the time you reach your mid-20s you have outgrown the quick-energy needs of adolescence. Unfortunately, you may not outgrow your appetite for the wrong foods. Whether you're married, living with someone in a strictly "he or she cooks" arrangement, or doing the cooking yourself, you should know and care about what goes into your kitchen cabinet, your refrigerator, and your stomach. Good home cooking means taking good care of yourself.

You don't have to be a health food advocate or a food faddist to break out of the mental laziness that creates poor eating habits. Poor eating is bad for your health, vigor, sex life, looks. Eat right and you'll look better, feel better, and get more energy from less food.

But what does eating right mean? You can be overwhelmed by conflicting information about what makes a healthy diet. How bad are fat, sugar, salt, cholesterol, carbohydrates? You know that junk food is the enemy, but sometimes you'd rather toss a TV dinner in the oven than try to figure it out.

A healthy diet is easier than you think

It's really not as complicated as it sounds. You need milk products, meat or a meat substitute, vegetables, fruits, and breads and cereals to stay healthy. You need a certain amount of protein, fat, and carbohydrates (found in sugar and starches); these are elements of food that furnish heat and energy to the body. Even the popular villain, cholesterol is necessary for proper body functioning. However, as there is a correlation between high blood cholesterol levels and the incidence of heart disease, it is wise to limit the amount of high-cholesterol foods you eat.

Moderation is the key to proper eating habits. Here are some guidelines to help you maintain a healthy diet:

Some simple guidelines

· Vary your diet. Eating a variety of foods will help ensure that you obtain the necessary vitamins and nutrients.

· Don't overeat. Your digestive tract has to work overtime to make up for your overzealousness. Consequently, your body uses the food less efficiently.

· Although a few additives are sometimes necessary, avoid foods containing long lists of preservatives and other chemicals. Your body has to do a major sorting-out process to discriminate between the useful and the useless. Don't burden it with useless extras.

· Cut down on salt. A normal diet supplies you with six times as much salt as you need. Excess salt is related to high blood pressure and heart and kidney failure. The taste for salt is acquired; break the habit by substituting herbs such as dill and basil or by seasoning with pepper, onions, etc., instead. Also try to eat less bacon, ham, herring, fewer hot dogs, pretzels, salted nuts, and do your body a favor.

· Eat less sugar. Sugar in any form (raw, refined, honey, etc.) supplies the body with glucose. This can be obtained from other foods that supply other nutrients as well (most fruits and starches supply glucose), and is also derived from your protein intake. You might try sweetening your diet with such fresh or dried fruits as melon, berries, raisins, prunes, apricots.

· Be discriminating about the *kind* of fat you eat. Your body needs *some* fat in order to obtain fat-soluble vitamins and to aid in digestion. Saturated fats, however, allow fatty deposits to form on the walls of your arteries; these can cause an insufficient flow of blood to your heart and increase the possibility of heart attack. The troublemakers: milk, cream, eggs, butter, lard, hydrogenated fats (read the labels to find these), cheeses, and shellfish. Good kinds of fat: oils derived from corn, peanuts, safflowers, sunflowers, wheat germ, soy beans; and margarine made without hydrogenated fat.

· Eat more fresh fish, chicken, turkey, and veal and less red meat and shellfish. This is not to say that steak, for example, is bad for you; simply don't eat too much too often.

Cooking for yourself

· Don't peel vegetables with edible skins. Most of the vitamins and minerals are found right under the skin. Scrub them with a vegetable brush instead.

· Steam, don't boil vegetables. This can be done by putting an inch of water in a large pot, then placing a vegetable steamer (available inexpensively in housewares departments) in the pot and the vegetables in the steamer.

· Eat the outer, darker leaves of salad greens. The deeper in color *any* green or yellow vegetable, the higher the nutrient content.

· Don't overcook food. Cooking begins the process that your body is to complete: digestion. It also serves to eliminate harmful bacteria and to make food more palatable. Overcooking, however, lowers the vitamin and nutrient level of any food.

· Skim fat from soups and casseroles after refrigerating. Fat will congeal on top so that you can simply lift it off.

When you shop

Read the labels on all canned, packaged, or processed foods. The law requires that any food claiming nutritional value provide the following information:

Other shopping tips:
· Buy fresh fruit and vegetables when your budget allows.
· Pass up canned, packaged, or processed foods whenever possible.
· Have all visible fat trimmed from your meat purchases. This is not only healthy but economical as well.

· Net weight.

· A list of ingredients. These are listed by quantity present in the product—most first, least last.

· Nutrition information. This must appear directly to the right of the main panel. The label will give size of serving and number of servings per container. Number of calories and the amounts, in grams, of protein, carbohydrates, and fat are listed first. This is followed by percentages of the U.S. Recommended Daily Allowance (RDA) for protein, vitamins A, B_1 (thiamin), B_2 (riboflavin), C, niacin, calcium, and iron. Optional information may appear listing cholesterol, fatty acid, and sodium content as well as other vitamins and minerals.

Getting rid of the junk

While developing healthy eating habits it will be necessary to clean out the kitchen cabinets and delete items from the grocery list. Start by getting rid of the following: sugared breakfast cereals, white bread, candies, bleached flour, lard, hydrogenated margarines, saturated fats, potato and other snack chips, sodas (including the diet variety), TV dinners, sugar-filled jams and jellies, packaged frozen French fries, and canned puddings.

Health food shopping

You may have been into the neighborhood health food store with every intention of bringing something good and nutritious home. Then, inside the store, you became confused and discouraged. What is rose hip tea? Carob powder? What are you supposed to do with those sacks of dried fruit? Do you really need any of it? (It's

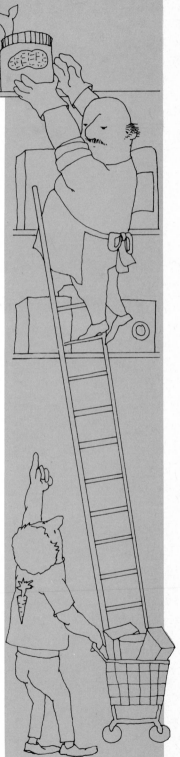

expensive.) And what would taste good? Herewith, a shopping list of health food store fare that's worth trying.

Raw honey—It's delicious and a large jar is worth the price. Try it in place of sugar.

Brewer's yeast—Get tablets to swallow or powder to mix with liquids in your blender. It's rich in vitamins and it's good for your hair, skin, and disposition.

Carob powder—It's a chocolate substitute that's rich in B vitamins and doesn't have the caffeinelike stimulants that are in chocolate.

Sea salt—If you feel the need to season with salt (everyone should limit salt intake), try sea salt. It provides iodine and other necessary minerals.

Desiccated-liver tablets—These provide all the healthy benefits that you get if you eat lots of liver—shining healthy hair, good skin tone, extra energy. These tablets are especially worthwhile if you don't like liver.

Wheat germ—The toasted kind is the tastiest. Try it as a breakfast cereal with milk, use it instead of bread crumbs when you cook. It's full of vitamins, minerals, and protein.

Wheat germ oil—Rich in vitamin E. Use it in salad dressings and for cooking.

Fresh peanut butter—It's better for you than the grocery store variety that usually has added oils to make it smoother.

Sprouts—Mung, soybean, alfalfa. Use them in salads and sandwiches. Buy them fresh as you would salad greens, or get the seeds and sprout your own.

Herbal teas—The benefits of herbal teas are based more on popular belief than fact. Most do not contain caffeine. Devotees claim that camomile calms nerves; wild strawberry acts as a laxative; rose hip provides vitamin C; papaya helps digestion. You may not like all of them, so sample a few before you buy a quantity of any one kind.

Vitamin-rich snacks—Try sunflower seeds, raw almonds or cashews, toasted soybean nuts, dried apricots.

Check out the store before you buy anything. Are there open sacks of dried fruit, beans, or flour? Are sacks stored on the floor? Is the food being stored in a manner that you would find unacceptable in your house? If so, try another store.

Vitamins and minerals   All of the vitamins and minerals you need are in food. The government has established recommended daily minimums for a variety of vitamins and minerals—these are amounts that adults should consume each day in order to stay healthy. The problem is that most of us fall into eating routines—having the same breakfast, the same lunch, day in and day out—and may not eat foods that give us all the vitamins and minerals we need. If you feel that you are not getting enough vitamins and minerals, you can buy a multivitamin supplement. Vitamin tablets, however, will not replace your need for food. There are many nutrients and trace elements that the body requires that are not present in supplements.

How many vitamins and minerals *you* need depends on your diet, your metabolism, and your overall health. Serious vitamin deficiencies are rare. And it would take over a year of a severely depleted diet for such a deficiency to be recognizable. Consult your doctor if you have a question about whether you have a vitamin deficiency. If necessary he can give you a blood test, a urinalysis, and check your dietary habits to determine whether a problem exists. You may balk at this, preferring to follow the latest vitamin theory, but since it can be harmful to take overdoses of certain vitamins and minerals and wasteful to take supplements you do not need, it's more practical (and a lot safer) to get the advice of an expert.

Taking vitamins   Some vitamin do's and don't's:

• Do take vitamins and food together. Vitamins are used more efficiently this way.

• Do take vitamin C if you smoke. Each cigarette destroys 25 milligrams of vitamin C.

• Don't take vitamin E and iron simultaneously. Most iron salts destroy vitamin E. If you take both, swallow one in the morning and one in the afternoon.

• Don't waste your money on separate vitamin B_{12}. Get all of the B vitamins together in a proper balance in a pill that supplies you with all of the B complex.

• Don't diagnose your own vitamin deficiency symptoms. Dry, itchy skin probably means you're allergic to the soap you're using, not that you need vitamin A.

What about megavitamins?   Massive doses of common vitamins are used in megavitamin therapy, a treatment for mental and physical disorders. Some biological imbalances (certain types of alcoholism, depression, and senility, for example) can be treated with massive doses of the proper vitamins. Megavitamin therapy (also called orthomolecular medicine) is a new, controversial type of medical approach, formulated by biochemist and Nobel Prize winner Linus Pauling. However, megavitamin therapy is not designed for home experimentation. The popular belief that you can make up for a poor diet with huge amounts of vitamins is a dangerous fallacy. Popping large quantities of vitamins can do you more harm than good—an overdose of vitamin D, for example, can cause liver and kidney damage and, in rare cases, can be fatal. If fat soluble vitamins (A, D, E) start to build up in your system, deposits of calcium can accumulate in your blood and cause high blood pressure, kidney disorders, and muscle weakness.

If you think you need massive doses of vitamins for therapeutic reasons, consult a doctor who specializes in preventive medicine—don't experiment on your own. You need to get your basic nutrition from food, not vitamins. Megadoses can't make up for the harm done by a poor diet. Vitamins don't supply energy or build muscle and bones, nor do they supply the digestive bulk of fiber foods, fat, and water. What *do* vitamins do? Read the vitamin and mineral chart on the next two pages.

Chart of basic nutrients

A

Promotes healthy skin, hair, nails, teeth, bones, eyes, and mouth, nose, and throat linings.

Found in deeply colored fruits (apricots and watermelons, for example); dark green, orange, and yellow vegetables (carrots and beans, for example); liver, eggs, and milk products.

B_1 (thiamin)

Helps release energy from carbohydrates; promotes healthy digestive and nervous systems; maintains the appetite.

Found in lean pork, fish, poultry, eggs, whole-grain and enriched breads and cereals, meat, various nuts, and dried beans and peas.

B_2 (riboflavin)

Releases energy from food; helps the cells use oxygen; promotes healthy skin, tongue, lips, eyes, and nervous system.

Found in milk, liver, mushrooms, dark green leafy vegetables, meat, fish, poultry, eggs, and whole-grain and enriched breads and cereals.

B_3 (niacin)

Promotes healthy skin, nerves, and intestines; aids in the release of energy from food.

Found in peanuts, liver, dry beans and peas, poultry, fish, whole-grain breads and cereals, potatoes, and milk.

B_6

Helps the body use carbohydrates, fats, and proteins, aids red blood cell regeneration; promotes healthy skin, lips, tongue, eyes, and nervous system.

Found in whole-grain breads and cereals, meat, potatoes, dark green leafy vegetables, tuna, salmon, liver.

B_{12}

Necessary for normal functioning of cells; promotes healthy digestive and nervous systems; prevents some forms of anemia.

Found in eggs, fish, meat (especially liver and kidneys), and poultry.

C (ascorbic acid)

Promotes healthy skin, gums, muscles, blood, and blood vessels; helps manufacture the "cement" that holds cells together; helps heal wounds and broken bones.

Found in citrus fruits, strawberries, cantaloupe, tomatoes, broccoli, green peppers, white and sweet potatoes, raw leafy greens, and cabbage.

Calcium

Works with phosphorus in building bones and teeth; helps blood to clot, and nerves, muscles, and heart to function; helps regulate the use of other minerals by the body.

Found in milk and milk products, dark green leafy vegetables, and enriched breads.

D

Helps calcium and phosphorus to form bones and teeth.

Found in vitamin-D fortified milk, fish-liver oils, salmon, tuna, egg yolks, liver, and sunshine.

E

Protects the cells from aging by oxidation. NOTE: Some nutritionists and natural-food enthusiasts feel that vitamin E aids in hair growth; cures acne, sterility, and impotence; eases arthritic pain; prevents ulcers; and more. The Food and Drug Administration and vitamin manufacturers are cautious as there is no conclusive proof of these benefits.

Found in liver, eggs, milk, green leafy vegetables, whole grains, and vegetable oils.

Iodine

Helps the thyroid gland control cell activities and controls the rate of energy use.

Found in seafood, products from the sea, and iodized salt.

Phosphorus

Works with calcium in building bones and teeth; helps regulate chemical activities in the body.

Found in milk and milk products, liver, fish, whole grains, and nuts. Almost all foods contain some phosphorus.

Fats

Provide a large amount of energy from a small amount of food; carry vitamins A, D, E, and others; provide necessary fatty acids (which help keep skin smooth and healthy); protect important organs.

Found in butter, margarine, cream, cheese, mayonnaise, vegetable oils, animal fats. NOTE: Polyunsaturated fat is fat that is liquid at room temperature (for example, vegetable oil). Saturated fats are those that congeal at room temperature (for example, most animal fats).

Iron

Works with protein to produce hemoglobin (the substance in the blood that carries oxygen to the cells).

Found in organ meats (liver and kidneys, for example), eggs, oysters, dried fruits, green leafy vegetables, enriched and whole-grain breads and cereals, and dried beans and peas.

Zinc

Used in many cell activities involving proteins, enzymes, and hormones—especially wound healing.

Found in lean meat, liver, eggs, seafood (particularly oysters), milk, and whole-grain breads and cereal grains.

Cholesterol

Essential to cell structure; necessary for synthesis of some vitamins, hormones, and bile salts.

Found in foods of animal origin; cholesterol is also synthesized by the body.

Magnesium

Helps the body's enzymes metabolize carbohydrates; promotes healthy nerve and muscle tissue.

Found in whole grains, nuts, green leafy vegetables, dried beans and peas, soybeans, milk, eggs, and meat.

Proteins

Promote the formation of antibodies that fight infection; build and repair all body tissues; supply energy.

Found in meat, fish, poultry, milk, cheese, nuts, bread and cereal grains, and dried beans and peas.

Carbohydrates (sugar, starch, and cellulose)

Supply energy and provide the bulk necessary for proper intestinal-tract waste removal.

Found in breads, cereals, pasta, rice, potatoes, corn, fruits, sugar, syrup, honey, and jellies and jams.

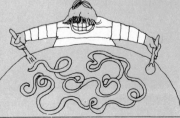

Vegetarianism

Why do people become vegetarians? For economic reasons—a meat-free diet is cheaper. For health reasons—vegetarians feel that when you eat meat you ingest germs left over from diseases the animals had and that the chemicals used to fatten the animals for market are harmful, if not poisonous. And it's known that consuming excessive amounts of animal protein can lead to arthritis, gout, cancer, diabetes, or arteriosclerosis. For moral or political reasons—it takes eight pounds of grain to produce one pound of beef. This fact bothers people who feel that we should be providing grain for the starving in this country and abroad. If we all ate less meat, they reason, there'd be more grain to go around. For humanitarian reasons—killing other creatures in order to live better seems cruel and unnatural to some people. (Some researchers say man is naturally a vegetarian since he doesn't possess certain physical characteristics of carnivorous animals, such as a short intestine.) For reasons of squeamishness—the idea of eating dead flesh simply turns some people off.

Confirmed vegetarians say that instead of *replacing* meat in their diet they are experiencing food in a broader, more imaginative way than people who eat meat. The rigid, four-course square meal that's centered around a main meat course is not the vegetarian style. Vegetarians approach food in a smorgasbord fashion, spreading out an array of foods (perhaps fruits, vegetables, grains, soup, cheese) with each dish given equal importance. They fulfill their protein requirements with eggs, milk, cheese, yogurt, or with protein-rich lentils, soybeans, and wheat germ.

A vegetarian may be a **lacto-ovo vegetarian** who eats animal products—milk, cheese, eggs—but no flesh. Or he may be a **vegan** who excludes all animal products from his diet. Or he might eat the flesh of fish but not of land animals. Or he could fall into some other category he's devised for himself.

Know what you're doing

To adopt a vegetarian diet sensibly requires a thorough knowledge of nutrition, and more care and thought about diet than most of us are willing to devote to this. You have to know how to mix legumes and nuts, when to add soy protein; you have to be sure to get enough iron and calcium. If you're a strict vegan you run the risk of becoming deficient in vitamin B_{12}, which is only found in animal products. (Vegans should definitely add vitamin B_{12} supplements to their diets as a deficiency could lead to anemia and, over a period of 10 to 12 years, could do damage to the spine.) Lacto-ovo vegetarians must be careful not to eat too many eggs. The amount of cholesterol in egg yolks is particularly bad for the adult male. (The American Heart Association advises that you eat no more than three eggs a week.)

The awkwardness and inconvenience of being a vegetarian are also drawbacks. What do you do when the restaurant menu offers nothing more than salad and baked potato with its meat entrees? What do you say to the proud hostess who presents you with a shishkabob that's been marinating for three days in her special sauce?

Many contented vegetarians find that it's all worth it. They are less likely to be overweight than meat eaters. They get a lot of good bulky fiber in their diet, and fiber is purported to help prevent cancer of the colon (the second highest malignant killer in the United States). And they report that they feel more vigorous, less aggressive, mellower, and healthier than they did before they turned their backs on meat.

Fasting

Fasting—going for a period of time without food—is a way to lose weight quickly. (On a true fast, you consume only water.) And according to fasting enthusiasts, it purifies the body—at the end of a fast, they say, they feel younger, fresher, healthier, and happier than before.

What happens to your body when you don't eat? When you stop eating, your body uses up its store of glucose (a sugar solution that is stored in the liver as glycogen) and begins to burn protein (muscle tissue) as fuel. Before damage is done to the muscles, the body shifts to burning fat. At this point, substantial water weight loss occurs, blood pressure drops, and ketosis takes place.

Ketosis is an overproduction of ketones, chemicals derived when the body burns fat for fuel. As fasting continues ketones are used, in the absence of glucose, by the brain and central nervous system. They are expelled through the urinary tract and through respiration and are the cause of the foul breath usually associated with fasting. Leading doctors and nutritionists feel that self-induced, unsupervised ketosis can be dangerous.

The effects of fasting

Many people report feeling revitalized and purged after fasting for one to three days, and they do it routinely every month or so. If you plan to fast longer than that, a doctor's guidance is essential. When you fast you may feel nauseated, fatigued, headachey, dizzy, nervous. During a fast, your body does *not* get the rest that enthusiasts claim. Because you are no longer consuming the necessary nutrients, less efficient chemical processes become responsible for maintaining normal body functions. This means that your body must work harder just to keep going.

If a fast lasts longer than five days, you'll need a lot of rest. And you'll have to slow your working pace down considerably. This fact makes prolonged fasting impractical for most people.

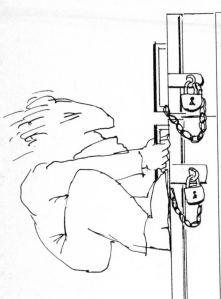

Some fasting guidelines.

• Never fast if you suffer from any chronic ailment—ulcers, liver problems, infections, or any form of diabetes.
• Learn about fasting before you begin. Read at least one good book on the subject.
• Plan your fast at a time when you expect an easy schedule (a weekend?). You need to get plenty of rest when you fast and to avoid strenuous exercise.
• Prepare for any fast by cutting your food intake down to just raw vegetables for a day or two ahead of time. Heavy eaters find fasting most difficult, and they may need even longer to prepare.
• Don't extend your first fast beyond three days.
• Do drink plenty of water—and juices, if you've decided to include them—it's important to avoid dehydration.
• Don't drink coffee or regular tea (herb teas are fine, though) when you fast. You want to cleanse your system, not add caffeine to it.
• Reintroduce food slowly at the end of your fast. Start with an orange or grapefruit. The next day add a portion of steamed vegetables to the fruit. Build up gradually from there.
• Don't return to poor eating habits. Now that your body is getting a fresh start, keep it healthy by eating right and never stuffing yourself.

Diet summaries There are so many diet books on the stands that it's overwhelming. Some popular diets (ice cream diets and lollipop diets, for example) make losing weight sound like fun. Others (high-fat or gorge-your-way-to-thinness diets) make dieting sound impossibly easy. Which of these diets work?

Almost *any* diet will work if you follow it strictly. But unless you change the eating habits that made you fat in the first place, you'll probably regain the weight soon after you go off the diet. Are some diets unsafe? The medical profession thinks so. A diet that deprives you of any of the necessary foods (milk products, meat or meat substitutes, vegetables, fruits, breads and cereals) should not be followed for long periods of time. And if you undertake any strict diet regimen without first getting a physical checkup and a doctor's OK, you're asking for trouble.

Basically, diet plans can be classified in the following ways: low-calorie, low-carbohydrate, high-protein, high-fat, and fasting.

Low-calorie diets are based simply on the fact that to lose weight you must consume fewer calories than your body burns. Your build, weight, and activity level determine the number of calories you burn each day. To go on a low-calorie diet, you figure out how many calories you must cut out of your daily diet to reach your ideal weight and cut your intake by that amount until you accomplish your goal.

• How fast do you lose? Two to three pounds a week at most.
• What's good? This plan gives you a well-rounded diet since you eat *all* foods in moderation. This is one of the more sensible diets, for it can be maintained indefinitely and really does change your eating habits. You learn to use a calorie guide and in the process learn to avoid fattening foods. Calorie counting, despite rumors to the contrary, is the one diet technique that endures.
• What's bad? The temptation is always there (just one slice of bread, just one more piece of cheese). This plan requires self-discipline and the patience to wait for results.

Low-carbohydrate diets require that you limit your intake of carbohydrates (found in sugars, starches, breads). As long as your carbohydrate consumption doesn't exceed 60 grams a day (a difficult level to maintain for most Americans), you can eat anything you want. The idea is that when your carbohydrate intake is below normal, your body reacts by burning its own fat reserves.

• How fast do you lose? About two pounds a week.
• What's good? You can still eat sweets, as long as you stay within your carbohydrate limit.
• What's bad? If your carbohydrate consumption falls below 50 grams a day, you'll suffer fatigue. It is easy to slip up and take too big a piece of watermelon or cake. You must be conscientious if you expect this kind of diet to work. You'll need a carbohydrate gram counter and you'll have to be willing to play a fairly tricky numbers game with it.

High-protein diets are just what the name implies—a diet of lean meat, a few dairy products, and lots of liquids. A high-protein, low-carbohydrate diet causes your body to break down its fatty tissue in order to provide energy.

• How fast do you lose? About five pounds a week. Initially, this will be water weight loss.
• What's good? You lose fat fairly rapidly. And when today's food is the same as yesterday's and tomorrow's, the lack of variety may cause you to eat even less. It's a simple plan to follow—no decisions to make.
• What's bad? This diet can be dangerous if you have a history of liver or kidney disease. You must drink a lot of liquids to flush out the fatty acid residues that can irritate your kidneys. You'll need to take a vitamin and mineral supplement. It does not promote good eating habits, it causes bad breath, and it can be *boring*.

High-fat diets hold the highly controversial theory that by eating lots of fats you stimulate your body to burn fat at a faster rate—thus, you burn not only the fat you eat but the fat you've accumulated over the years.

• How fast do you lose? About seven to eight pounds the first week; less after the first week, but loss continues at a steady rate.
• What's good? You get thin while literally stuffing yourself with food.
• What's bad? This kind of diet, known as a ketogenic diet, has been heavily criticized by organized medicine and by nutritionists.

It is considered a health hazard to the heart, and it also causes weakness, apathy, dehydration, calcium depletion, nausea, and fainting. Studies have shown that, because of the unpalatable menu, many people lose weight because they choose not to eat instead of following the diet. In any case, the diet should not be undertaken without a doctor's OK.

Protein-sparing fasts, the latest hope for the obese, involve total abstinence from food for a month, or two, or three, or more. This diet is designed to take off fat as fast as possible while preserving muscle tissues and other vital body protein. Each day you take seven to eight ounces of a predigested protein formula that is supposed to give you all the necessary amino acids. You also take vitamin supplements and drink one-and-a-half to two quarts of liquid (water, black coffee, diet soda) every day.

• How fast do you lose? Seven to 15 pounds the first week, 25 pounds the first month. Loss drops a bit after that, but continues at an impressive rate.
• What's good? Besides the drastic weight loss, it's said that after a fast has begun it's actually easier to eat nothing than to eat a little bit.
• What's bad? Buying predigested protein over the counter and taking an unsupervised (protein-sparing) fast is *very* dangerous. Besides fatigue, dizzy spells, hair loss, dry skin, bad breath, and constipation, the unchecked diet could cause serious or even critical health problems—especially for people with undiagnosed kidney, liver, cardiac, vascular, or metabolic problems. Not recommended for people with less than twenty pounds to lose. If this diet is undertaken, do so with strict supervision by your physician.

Staying slim   Getting yourself slimmed down on a diet may have been hard. Staying that way is even harder. To stay trim you must use your head about nutrition (see "Cook for your health," page 50), and you have to be sure that calories won't sneak up on you when you're not looking.

You know the excuses you make for yourself: "It's a business lunch—what choice do I have?" (Or it's a party, or it's a special evening out.) The only way to stay trim is to pay attention constantly to what goes into your mouth.

Here, some fairly obvious (but often ignored) advice about what to eat—and what not to eat—when you're in a restaurant or having dinner in someone else's home.

At cocktail time

If liquor is served, try a glass of quinine or mineral water with a twist instead. Remember that alcohol has no nutritional value—only empty calories. One and a half ounces of whisky contains 105 calories, a scotch old-fashioned 179, a martini 140, an eight-ounce glass of beer 114, 3½ ounces of wine 80. Two glasses of white wine are better than one cocktail.

Pass up the peanuts, the olives, the potato chips, and the other high-calorie hors d'oeuvres (remind yourself that they just spoil your dinner). Instead reach for the carrots, pickles, and celery on the relish tray.

When you sit down at the table

At the table, skip the bread and butter routine everyone gets into while waiting for the food to arrive. Sip your water and watch how unconsciously other people keep eating out of nervous habit.

If you are in a restaurant, remember when you look over the menu that poultry and seafood (except shellfish) are kinder to your waistline than pork chops or steak, that broiled food is better than deep fried, that a baked potato is better than French fries.

Eating to maximize enjoyment

• Eat slowly. Digestion begins in the mouth, where food is broken up and mixed with saliva. If this step is minimized by gulping your food, your body does not obtain the full complement of nutrients present in the meal. Also, the feeling of being full is caused by the expanding stomach pressing against the surrounding organs. This expansion does not happen immediately upon the food's reaching the stomach. It is therefore possible, if you are eating too fast, to consume more than would normally be required to make you feel full. So slow down and enjoy the meal.

• Ask for a lemon to squeeze over your vegetables. Don't smother them in butter.

• Trim the fat off meat, and the skin off chicken, skip the gravy, leave the rich sauces in the serving dish.

• Have fruit and cheese for desert if you can. One ounce of Camembert cheese is 85 calories; an apple, 80. If your hostess presents you with a slice of apple pie—377 calories—or a slice of layer cake—274 calories—eat half of it, tell her it's delicious, and stop eating.

Basic care   Basically, your skin is composed of two layers. The top layer, which is the layer we see, is called the *epidermis*. You continually shed the surface of the epidermis as new cells form to replace old ones. (Every fifteen days or so you have a completely "new skin.") The nourishing underlayer of the skin is called the *dermis*. It's an intricate network that includes blood vessels, oil glands, hair follicles, nerve tissue, and sweat glands.

What makes healthy, handsome skin? Protecting it from the elements (sun, wind, pollution) and keeping it clean are part of it. More important, though, is that you nourish it from within. If you're not eating a balanced diet, your skin will suffer. Acne can be a sign that you're consuming too much of the wrong kinds of oil. Easy bruising may mean that you need more oranges and other vitamin-C foods. Splotchy redness on your face may result from an overload of spicy foods (chili or curry, for example), which, like too much alcohol, can cause vasodilation (expansion of the blood vessels). Dry skin may indicate that you need more vitamin-A foods, such as carrots and fish.

What can threaten healthy skin? Undue amounts of stress, emotional upsets, hormonal imbalances, some medications (such as cortisone, taken for allergies or arthritis), and too much exposure to the sun all can have ill effects on your skin.

If you have a serious skin problem, you should talk to a doctor or a dermatologist. You need advice on how to handle excessive acne, dermatitis, allergic reactions, an outbreak of boils, or strange blotches or growths that you suspect could be skin cancer.

A certain amount of sun is *good* for your skin. Besides helping your body to produce vitamin D, the sun speeds peeling of the epidermis; this unblocks pores and is good for acne and skin diseases like psoriasis.

Tanning sensibly

When you tan, the ultraviolet rays of the sun cause melanin (the color-producing protein in the outer layer of the skin) to disperse. The amount of pigment in your skin determines the degree to which you'll tan or burn. Mild tanning is fine. Overexposure to the sun season after season, year after year, can do your skin a lot of harm. Besides giving your skin a tough, leathery look, years of overexposure to the sun can harm the collagen and elastin contained in the dermis. (Collagen and elastin give your skin healthy tone and elasticity.) Too much sun can create premature wrinkles, liver spots, brown pigmented patches, and scaling. It also increases your risk of skin cancer.

Something else to look for: Certain drugs, such as the thiazide you may take for high blood pressure, oral diabetic drugs, or tranquilizers can make you photosensitive—that is, you'll burn more easily. Deodorant soaps that contain halogenated salicylanilides, essences of lemon or lime (found in some after-shave lotions, colognes, and bath soaps), can make your skin sun-sensitive too.

Sun protectors

You can see why it makes sense to approach the sun with a certain degree of caution, and to avoid the temptation to turn yourself into a bronze god (which is not only unhealthy, but is also the too-much-of-a-good-thing that can be really unattractive).

Protect yourself. Find a good tanning lotion, and calculate carefully how much sun your skin can take without burning or becoming leathery. Basically, sun protectors are classified in one of three ways: as **sun blocks,** which will screen the sun out completely; as **sunscreens,** which will screen out burning rays and allow a minimum amount of tanning; and as **suntan lotions,** which allow tanning while providing a minimum amount of sunburn protection. The most effective chemical to look for in a suntan preparation is para-amino-benzoic acid (Paba for short). Whatever suntan preparation you use reapply it frequently during your time in the sun, especially after swimming or after exercise that's made you perspire.

How long should you stay in the sun? The American Medical Association guidelines are cautious: For light-skinned people—15 minutes the first day, and an additional five minutes each following day. For dark-skinned people—20 minutes the first day and an additional five minutes each following day. You may want to alter this according to your own propensity for burning and according to your locale (a midwestern poolside is less burn-inducing than a sandy tropical beach). Altitude, season of the year, hour of the day, and whether the sun is bouncing off sand or snow or filtering through the trees all play a part in how much your skin is exposed to ultraviolet radiation. Don't *ever* fry yourself to a burn, and don't *ever* allow yourself to get too dark and leathery, and you'll minimize the sun's harmful effects.

Getting clean   Should you bathe *every* day? Once you realize that the epidermis is constantly shedding dead cells and that your sweat, decomposed by the bacteria on your skin, begins to smell, a daily scrubbing seems like a good idea. A shower does the job well—and fast. A shower is bracing. It wakes you up in the morning. It sends all those dead cells down the drain.

A lot of showering can dry your skin, however. Solution? At least once a week, soak yourself in oil-treated tub water. A bath? For a man? If you visualize yourself with your knees drawn up under your chin in two inches of tepid water, it's time you discovered what women have always known: that there are times when there's nothing like a leisurely bath to soothe your tired muscles, calm your frazzled nerves, bolster your morale, improve the condition of your skin.

How to take a bath   Before you begin to run your bath, you'll need to get bath granules or oil to add to the water. (Scented oils are fine if you like them—their fragrance can be more subtle than after-shave or cologne.) A few drops of baby oil in the water or smoothed over your skin before you bathe will work well too. If you want your bath to have a reviving effect, toss in some Epsom salts. While the water runs, set a tubside table with a pumice stone (to slough off rough, dead skin on heels and elbows); a loofah (a fibrous scrubber to remove dead cells from your shoulders); a long-handled, natural bristle brush (to get all those bumpy imperfections off your back); a big bar of hard-milled soap (stands up to bath water best); an orange stick (to push back softened cuticles); and a newspaper or book (to read while you soak). Give your skin ten minutes to soften up before you give it a going-over with your bath tools. Suds up with the bar of good soap; rinse yourself in warm water (run the shower for a minute at the end if you want to). Rub yourself dry with a nubby, oversized towel. Splash on an astringent—or rubbing alcohol. Slather on a moisturizer. Stretch out on your bed for a few minutes to relax.

If all this sounds terribly feminine to you, and you haven't the least idea where to *find* all that equipment, wander up to the men's cosmetic counter in a department store. You'll be amazed at the number of bath products there are to choose from. Some may seem unnecessary to you. But remember, your skin needs moisturizing just the way a woman's does. Astringents can help tighten up your pores after a bath. And working yourself over with brushes, manicure tools, and the like may seem like pampering, but it does good and necessary things for your skin.

Perspiration and odors

Perspiration is the way your body maintains its normal temperature. Two kinds of glands create sweat: the *eccrine glands* that are located all over your body (they respond to heat and emotions and are constantly secreting small amounts of clear, odorless liquid) and the *apocine glands* that are concentrated in the underarm and pubic area. These glands, which begin to function at puberty, respond only to emotional stimulation. When the apocine glands get going they secrete a milky liquid that's odorless until it is decomposed by the bacteria on the skin.

American men have an aversion to body odor and to the idea of sweat-soaked clothes; European men seem to feel that it's natural, and it doesn't bother them. If excessive wetness and body odor are a problem for you, you're probably frustrated to find that at times of stress no deodorant or antiperspirant seems to do the job.

Minimizing body odor

Daily scrubbing will get off odoriferous bacteria. Antibacterial soap, a good antiperspirant, and a moisture-absorbing antibacterial powder offer you the best protection until your next shower comes around. If, up to now, this regimen hasn't been working for you, it may be because you haven't given it a chance. Antiperspirants work by altering the perspiration process. The aluminum compounds in them (aluminum chloride and aluminum chlorohydrate) cause the cell membranes to reabsorb the perspiration before it reaches the skin. However, if you are perspiring when you put your antiperspirant on, it will wash away before it can produce the desired effect on your skin cells. How to remedy this? You might try putting on an antiperspirant after a nightly shower, before you go to bed. At that time, when you're in your most relaxed state, perspiration is minimal, and the antiperspirant will have a chance to condition your skin before you sleep. You may have to do this for a few nights before the system reaches full effectiveness.

What causes foot odors?

Feet give off odors when rubbed-off skin cells become decomposed in the moist, closed environment of your shoes. How to prevent this? Scrub your feet when you bathe or shower; soap up between the toes and across the soles. Towel dry, being sure to get in between each toe. Try out foot deodorants, antiperspirants, and antibacterial powders. Spray them on your feet, shake them into your shoes. Wear fresh socks *every day*. Give your shoes a chance to air out between wearings—never wear the same pair two days in a row.

What is jock itch?   Jock itch. A rash in the groin. Embarrassing. Uncomfortable. What causes it? It could be *intertrigo*, a rash that's created when your sweating thighs rub together (as when you play tennis, jog, etc.). Men with heavy thighs seem to suffer most from this kind of rash. It's a help to wear boxer shorts instead of tight-fitting Jockey shorts, and to dust your legs and shorts with antibacterial powder. If it's a fungus infection (characterized by water-filled bumps), you'll need an antifungal cream, liquid, or powder. It's best to put the cream or liquid directly on the rash, but put the powder in your shorts.

Saunas   Opinions vary about the beneficial and harmful effects of taking frequent sauna baths. The Finns take the extreme view that the sauna is a cure-all. Sauna-bath critics (including the U.S. government's Federal Trade Commission) claim that since dry or moist heat raises blood pressure, body temperature, and pulse rate, elderly persons and people suffering from diabetes, high blood pressure, or heart trouble may suffer ill effects from taking sauna or steam baths. If you are one of those people, it's probably sensible to follow that directive. However, if you are healthy and approach the sauna bath sensibly (see sauna rules, below), harmful effects of the sauna can be avoided.

The modern versions of saunas (there may be one in your health club, or in a friend's ski house) are modeled after the traditional Finnish wood cabin on the edge of a pond. Inside, unpainted benches of porous, slow-heating wood provide a place for you to sit or stretch out and relax while a stove (cast iron or brick) heats the cabin to temperatures up to and beyond 200 degrees Fahrenheit. On the stove sits a pile of stones. Occasionally, ladles of water will be poured over the stones to raise the room's humidity. You stay in the sauna (naked, or with a towel drape) until sweat seeps out of every pore and your heartbeat and circulation speed up. When you reach your limit of comfort (usually in about 10 to 20 minutes), you leave the hot room to jump into some cold water or snow. This closes your pores, slows your circulation, and contracts your blood vessels all at once—a pleasant shock. You may repeat the cycle two or three or more times before you finish with a slow cool-down in the open air.

Some people find the sauna extremely relaxing after strenuous exercise. Some find that it relieves the miseries of a cold or reduces mental strain. The sauna is especially praised for its cleansing power. The heat opens your pores and you sweat out deep-lying dirt. The cold plunge closes your pores before more dirt has a chance to settle in. Because the sauna does dry out your skin, it's vital that you slather yourself with moisturizer after you've cooled down and your pores have closed naturally.

Some sensible sauna rules

• Don't wear glasses with plastic frames, or contact lenses, in the sauna. Plastic frames may soften and bend; contact lenses will dry out and irritate your eyes.

• Don't wear clothes in a sauna. Clothes will impede your perspiration and can cause a rash to break out on your skin. If you want to be modest, drape yourself with a towel.

• Don't wear jewelry or watches in the sauna. They'll get too hot and can burn you or become damaged.

• Don't take a sauna right after eating. A full stomach puts your cardiovascular system on overload at high temperatures.

• Don't take a sauna when you are ill.

• Never take drugs, tranquilizers, antibiotics, or narcotics before you sauna.

• Take your first sauna at a lower temperature (160 degrees Fahrenheit should be fine). As your body becomes acclimatized to the sauna, increase the temperature to 190 to 200°F. Anything higher than that is too uncomfortable.

• Get out of the sauna immediately if you find it hard to breathe; if you feel dizzy, headachey, or nauseous; if your heartbeat becomes highly exaggerated; if you have any abnormal pain; if you are so hot that you're *really* uncomfortable.

• Don't remain in the cold environment too long after you leave the hot room. Cool off, but don't get chilled.

• Always put on lots of moisturizer after you've cooled down. If you don't you'll dry out your skin.

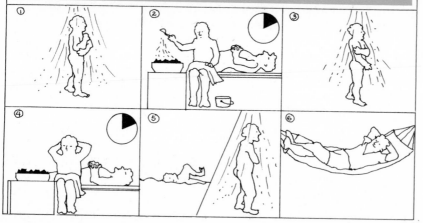

More than any other part of your body, your face is *you*. When other people visualize you, they think of your face. And your face is the "you" you confront every time you look in the mirror. It naturally follows that skin problems on your face will be more disturbing to you than skin problems anywhere else on your body. Your face is a barometer of your inner weather. When you're overtired, anxious, nervous, unhappy, or undernourished, your complexion is likely to look dull and lifeless. When you're well fed, well rested, and well loved, your state of being is likely to show in a complexion that glows with healthy color.

Basic care   Does the way you care for your complexion affect its healthy state too? To a degree, yes. If you don't keep your face clean or attend to the problems created by too-oily or too-dry skin, your complexion will suffer. Women, it seems, have always known this. Men have tended to ignore the fact that to look their best, they must pay attention to caring for their complexions properly. If, up to now, your routine has been to suds your face with a deodorant soap while you shower, then give it a once-over with a razor and a splash of after-shave, you have a lot to learn. If your skin tends to flake, get red patches, or wrinkle prematurely, you can do something about it. (By the way, where age lines add character to your face, wrinkling due to arid skin conditions simply looks unhealthy.) If you're getting more than your share of pimples or blackheads, you can clean up the oily excess that causes them. Of course, the kind of care you give your skin will vary according to time of year—exposure to cold and to indoor heating can cause winter dehydration; the climate you live in—Arizona is more skin-drying than New York, for example; and your skin type.

Your skin belongs, basically, in one of three categories: oily, dry, or normal. How do you know which type of skin you have? Just looking in the mirror will tell you a lot. If you are acne-prone, it may be that there's excess oil in your skin that's clogging your pores. (A test for oily skin: Rub a strip from a brown paper bag over your forehead—do it first thing in the morning, before you wash your face. If the paper becomes translucent from the oil it picked up from your skin, you have oily skin.) You have dry skin if dry, flaky patches often crop up or if your face often feels itchy. Your skin is normal if it rarely gives you problems other than an occasional oily or dry spot and a stray pimple every now and then.

How to tell your skin type

Your skin type will dictate a specific kind of cleaning regimen that involves soap and possibly moisturizers or astringents. The amount of shampooing you do and the kind of shampoo you use can have an effect on your complexion too.

Composed of fatty acids and alkalis, soap is *the* basic dirt-cutting agent. The texture and quality of a soap depend on the quality of the vegetable and animal fats it contains. Different types of soap vary due to the way the soap curd has been manufactured into a final product. **Milled soaps** are the most common, inexpensive type. They are fine for normal skins but may be too harsh for problem or sensitive skins. **Superfatted soaps** contain an additional portion of fatty materials like lanolin. They don't clean as thoroughly as ordinary soaps, but they are milder. **Transparent** or **glycerin soaps** are less drying and less likely to irritate the skin than the more alkaline milled soaps. **Floating soaps** contain a lot of moisture and air bubbles. They are good-quality soaps, but a bar of this kind of soap melts more quickly in water than a bar of hard-milled soap. **Special soaps** include deodorant soaps, cold cream soaps, antibacterial soaps, soaps with abrasive granules. Some of them may be drying or allergy-provoking. Some deodorant soaps contain ingredients that can promote a bad sunburn. And soaps with abrasive granules may be fine for gritty hands, but are too strong for your face.

What different kinds of soap do for you

Other skin aids **Astringents,** usually in clear liquid form, contain either alcohol or acetone. They are extremely good for ridding skin of the grime and excess oils that clog pores and cause pimples. You can buy them in bottles (rubbing alcohol makes a good astringent) and in presoaked pads. Astringents leave your skin with a tingly, tight feeling. Since they are drying, they are not good for dry skin.

Moisturizers don't actually put moisture into your skin—what they do is help retain the moisture that's already there. It's a good idea to smooth on a moisturizer when your skin's still damp after washing and let the moisturizer act as a protective film over your face throughout the day. There are two types of moisturizers: water-based and oil-based. Water-based moisturizers are lighter textured than the oil-based kind, and they disappear right after application; they're fine for normal, dry, or slightly oily skins. Oil-based moisturizers are good for dry skin but are not recommended for people with oily skin because they are likely to clog the pores.

Oily skin **Washing:** The more you wash your face, the better. The minimum: three times a day. The idea is to scrub away excess oil that creates acne. If your skin is mildly oily regular milled soaps can work well, but if your skin is very oily, try one of the acne soaps designed especially for oily skin. Take it slowly, though—acne soaps contain strong drying agents (such as sulfur and resorcinol) that may be *too* drying for your skin until you become accustomed to them. If you're black or very dark-skinned, avoid soaps with resorcinol—it can cause your skin to blotch.

Astringents: After every washing, swab your face with an astringent-soaked cotton ball. (You can buy astringent in towelette form to make it easy to do when you're away from home.)

Moisturizers: They can clog the pores of oily skin—a problem you don't need. If you *ever do* use a moisturizer, make sure it's water-based, not oil-based.

Shampooing: Shampoo every day if you can, and in any case at least four times a week. Strong detergent shampoos cut oil best but, as with acne soaps, it may take you a while to get used to them. Some shampoos are for acne-prone people. Some contain tar, others zinc pyrithione, and it's good to alternate brands, for you can become immune to the active ingredients. Whatever shampoo you buy, be sure it states that it's for oily hair.

Washing: It's best if you wash your face just once a day. If your skin is really dry, avoid soaps altogether in favor of "imitation" soaps which will be less drying. Avoid acne soaps with sulfur and tar, and deodorant soaps that can irritate dry skin.

Astringents: Use none at all.

Dry skin

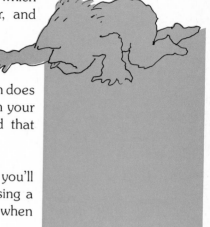

Moisturizers: These will help you retain what moisture your skin does have, and it's a good idea to dab on a bit whenever you wash your face. Look for moisturizers that contain urea, a compound that attracts moisture and prevents its loss.

Shampooing: The less frequently you wash your hair, the less you'll dry out your complexion. Shampoo every five or six days, using a nonalkaline, low-detergent shampoo. Using a hair conditioner when you shampoo is a good idea too.

Washing: You can use just about any soap that appeals to you, as long as it doesn't dry out your skin or make it oily after you've used it a few times. You may want to try some of the fancy kinds of soap you see in the drugstore, such as cucumber, almond, and buttermilk. They don't have any special cleaning power—they just smell good.

Normal skin

Astringents: They're not really necessary. But if you like the fresh, clean feeling they give, use them. Don't use an astringent more than once a day, though—it can dry out your skin.

Moisturizers: You won't need a lot of moisturizers, and maybe you'll want to use them only at times when your skin feels particularly dry. The best moisturizers for normal skin are the water-based ones.

Shampooing: You can shampoo whenever your hair needs it—and almost any shampoo labeled "for normal hair" will be all right for you. Just be sure the one you use leaves your hair soft and manageable, the way you like it.

A professional facial is a deep-cleaning treatment for your face. Many women's salons and some of the posh barber shops do facials for men. A facial usually involves an hour-long treatment, though in some salons you can get a half-hour version. Or you might want to go for "the works"—shampoo, haircut, manicure, and hour-long facial.

Facials

Facials are not just for women any more than good clean skin is just for women. And though facials involve the kind of pampering that used to be considered feminine, men are now coming to realize that it's OK to be pampered every now and then. In a facialist's chair, you'll not only get rid of blackheads and learn how to take better care of your own complexion, you'll find yourself in a calming atmosphere that can give your mind a rest and your spirits a lift. Men who are facial enthusiasts go regularly—usually once a month.

Some doctors and dermatologists claim that facials do nothing more than clean your skin and that soap and water do it just as well. Cosmetologists feel that facials give you preventative skin care too. They contend that the deep-down cleaning a facial gives makes skin eruptions less likely to happen. Facials, however, can't cure skin problems—in fact, they shouldn't be given to unhealthy skin. If you have serious skin problems, such as advanced acne, you should be treated by a dermatologist and get the problem cleared up before you have a facial. A facial does plump up your skin, make your pores look smaller, and give you a rosy, healthy glow that lasts for a few hours after you leave the salon. And it feels good.

What to expect from a facial in a salon

Each salon has its own facial "routine," but the kinds of things you can expect from a facial will include all or some of the following.

Your skin will be analyzed. The technician will check over your face under a magnifier to determine what kind of skin you have, where any flareups are, and what your skin problems might be. Then you'll be led to a private room, be given a robe to wear, and be seated in a deep, comfortable chair. A misting machine will moisten your skin and open your pores before you get a facial massage. Done with creams, this massage will relax your face and neck while cleaning your epidermis, toning the underlying tissue, and stimulating your circulation. After the creams are removed with cotton, a soft, automated brush may be used to whisk off surface dirt. A vacuum-cleaner-like machine may draw out other impurities before the technician goes over your face to remove blackheads and plugs from your pores.

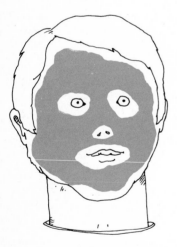

Now your face will be clean and you'll be ready for a facial mask. The kind of mask you get will depend upon your skin type. As it's applied, you may feel a cooling sensation at first, then a warmth and a tightening of the skin. The purpose of the mask is to remove dead skin cells from your face and to refresh your complexion. Once the mask is removed you may be sprayed or misted again and any residue of creams, gels, or masks that were used will be stroked away.

At-home facial masks

There are facial masks you can give yourself at home, too. Prepackaged masks come in four types: A **clay mask** has a mineral clay base that hardens on your skin and absorbs oil and dirt—good for oily skin.

A **massaging mask** has a plastic base and is applied to your face in lotion or cream form. After it's dried, you remove it in small pieces by rubbing. It removes dirt and dead cells—good for oily and normal skins. A **peel-off mask** may have a rubber or wax base. It's put on in lotion or cream form, peeled off in one sheet after it dries; it's good for slightly oily and normal skins. A **moisturizing mask** has a jellylike base that often contains protein. It cleans, adds moisture—good for dry and normal skins.

A good homemade mask: Brush the white of an egg evenly over your cheeks, forehead, and chin with a pastry brush. Avoid the area around your eyes. Let the egg dry and then wash it off with tepid water. If your skin feels dry afterward, rub on a little cold cream or other moisturizer.

No mask should be used more often than once a week. If you use masks too often you can irritate your skin. If after using any mask you find that your skin is unusually dry, flaky, irritated, or acting peculiar in any way, stop using the mask.

Although masks do give your skin a good cleaning, feel good, and are kind of fun to use, they are not necessary for routine skin care. If you don't want to be bothered, don't worry. You can have healthy skin without them.

Shaving

You probably remember your first shave with the same kind of nostalgia that you remember your first love—it was a big step across the threshold into manhood. And it's likely that today you're still using the shaving method with which you started. That may be fine or not fine, depending on the kind of skin and beard you have.

If you have a heavy beard and you're using an electric shaver, you are probably bothered by more five o'clock shadow than you would be if you used a safety razor. If you're plagued by razor burn or razor nicks, it's probably because you aren't using the right method to soften your beard before you shave.

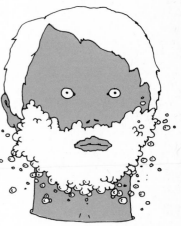

The best razor for you? It depends on what you want. Electric razors are quick and convenient. You can carry one in your pocket if you like and, in a pinch, shave in your car. Though it doesn't give you as close a shave as a safety razor, a *good* electric razor won't pinch, burn, or cut your skin. It will get into nooks and crannies and not leave any stray whiskers. The way to find a good electric razor is to try several out in the store. Shave a spot on your face with razor A. Then go over the same spot with razor B. If razor B picks up whiskers that A left behind, it's a better razor for you.

When you shave with an electric razor, you may be tempted to dispense with the preshave treatment for the sake of speed and convenience. Except in emergencies, don't. A beard that's not preconditioned is tougher to remove. Shaving unprepared skin is rough on your face. A preshave treatment will remove the skin oils that can bog your razor down, provide a lubricant that helps the razor slide easily over your skin, and stiffen the whiskers so they stand out and let you shave closer.

Safety razors take more time. They confine you to a sink and hot water. And yet the refinements that have been made in safety razors over the last few years have been excellent, and a good safety razor (the twin-bladed kind are superior) will give you a close, long-lasting shave.

When you shave with a safety razor, be sure to give your beard plenty of time to soften beforehand (shaving is easiest after a long hot shower). Spread lots of rich, foamy shaving cream on your face (be sure to use a shaving cream that doesn't irritate your skin) and let it stand for a few minutes. Wet your razor with HOT water, and rinse it often during shaving—if your blades fill with residue, they'll slide over your face without catching the whiskers.

Whether you shave with a safety razor or an electric, finish with a good rinsing. (Safety-razor users may need to rinse many times to get off all the shaving cream.) Make the last rinse cold, in order to close up your pores. *If your skin is oily,* smooth on an astringent or an after-shave that will cut any soap residue. *If your skin is dry,* skip the astringent/after-shave routine and instead cream your skin with a moisturizing lotion.

Whichever shaving method you choose—stick with it. It takes your skin a while to get accustomed to a shaving style, and if you switch back and forth from electric to safety razors, you'll be continually breaking out in a rash.

Men's fragrances   After shaves, which usually contain some perfume, alcohol, and emollients (moisturizers), are intended to soothe your skin and make you smell good. Recently they've lost out to other, new men's skin-care products.

The number of different types of men's cosmetics now turning up on the shelves is staggering. These products seem to pay more attention to helping your skin than to making you smell good—which is a good thing and about time, too. Instead of being called after-shave lotions, skin-care products are variously tagged "after-shave balms," "all-weather skin conditioners," "face conditioners," "moisturizing after-shaves," "sport lotions." The best way to find out which one does what is to step up to the men's cosmetics counter in a department or drug store and *ask*. Read labels, too. If your skin is dry, look for products with oil-rich ingredients like lanolin; if your skin's oily, alcohol-based products will be better for you. This caution, however: If you are planning to wear a fragrance, pick a lotion that has no scent. If you use a fragrance as well as a highly scented skin conditioner, you can create a mixture that smells *awful*.

The biggest problem you're likely to have with a man's fragrance is with using too much of it. Many men (and women too) figure that if a little bit of this stuff will make me smell good, a lot of it will make me smell *great*. And the result is an overpowering onslaught on other people's olfactory systems. The trick with cologne is subtlety—you want to give just a vague, tantalizing hint that there's something delicious going on with your skin.

Be sure a cologne smells good on *you*

The second biggest problem is in choosing a fragrance that smells good on you. Fragrance in the form of cologne (or super-cologne—a euphemism for perfume, which is more concentrated than cologne) can smell very elegant or very cheap. What smells good on another man may smell just awful on you. In fragrances, you get what you pay for—most of the time. But if a cologne doesn't mix harmoniously with your body chemistry, it won't matter if it's the most expensive cologne in the world—it's worthless to you. The only way to know which cologne will be compatible with your body chemistry is to try some out. In the store first, and then out in the world. Wear one you like and ask your friends what they think. If three people tell you it's terrible, believe them, and get rid of it.

As there are more than 200 fragrances to choose from, you may have to do some hunting until you find a cologne that's "you." The kind of scents you'll encounter: citrus (sweet); spicy (rich, floral, herbal); woodsy (earthy); oriental (heavy, full-bodied); leather (smells like tanned leather).

Scents to choose from

It's impossible to tell from a description what you'll like. A cologne that's described as floral may sound too sweet and feminine to your ear but smell quite heady and masculine to your nose. Since response to smells is totally irrational and emotional, there's just no way for you to know what will appeal to you until you go up to a cosmetics counter and literally put your nose right into things.

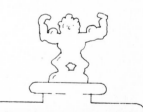

Some better known scents

Old Spice—crisp and spicy
Aqua Velva—woodsy
Braggi—dry, oriental
Aramis—dry, oriental, with woodsy notes
Bill Blass—dry, oriental, woodsy, *and* spicy
English Leather—leathery, with sandalwood notes
Eau Savage—citrus, herbal

Some fragrance rules:

• Sample before you buy. Rub a cologne you like on your arm, walk around the store for ten minutes—it takes that long for the cologne to blend with your body chemistry. Then if you still like the way it smells, buy it.

· Test different fragrances on different spots. If the scents get mixed together they'll smell terrible.

· Realize that woodsy scents linger on your skin longer than citrus ones, that oily and normal skins retain scents longer than dry skin.

· Apply cologne *sparingly.* Put it on your neck and shoulders. If you wonder whether you've used too much or too little, ask a friend.

· Use less fragrance when the weather's hot. Scents intensify on a hot, humid day.

· Wash off cologne before you go out in the sun. Colognes contain elements that can cause a bad sunburn or permit the sun to permanently streak your skin.

· Store fragrances away from windows and radiators. A bottle of cologne may look attractive on your windowsill, but heat and light will make it deteriorate.

· Throw out cologne that's been around longer than a year—it won't smell the same after 12 months.

Skin problems

Everyone has an occasional pimple or two. A blackhead here and there, clogged pores that need squeezing out—these are facts of life. But many adults are surprised to find that the acne they thought was a teenage nuisance has followed them into adulthood. Some people, it seems, are genetically susceptible to acne all their lives.

Your sebaceous glands protect your skin by sending sebum, a collection of fats and waxes, up to the surface. When the sebaceous glands produce too much of this oily substance, the pores can become blocked. The waxy plug that blocks a pore (called a comedo) obstructs the normal passage of sebum to your skin's surface. If the pressure of the comedo causes a follicle wall to break, sebum and fatty acids will filter into the surrounding tissue. The result is an inflammation—a pimple. A profusion of pimples gives you the condition called acne.

What makes you acne-prone

Chocolate does not cause pimples. Nor do fried foods. In fact, some experts argue that since the sebaceous glands operate quite independently, diet may have no effect on acne at all. Others argue that some foods, particularly those with high iodide, bromide, or androgen content, do create an acne-prone condition in some people. The food on this forbidden list is surprising: saltwater fish, spinach, artichokes, and cabbage have high iodide contents; some multivitamins are high in iodides or bromides; wheat germ, shellfish, and organ meats such as liver, kidney and sweetbreads are androgenic.

Some other reasons you may be acne-prone: **Heredity**—If your parents had acne, you're likely to. **Medicines**—Many over-the-counter medicines are likely to cause acne. Bromides are found in hundreds of drug products. Cortisone in poison-ivy treatments may be a culprit. Iodides in cough and cold medicines are suspect. **Cosmetics**—Hair-grooming aids often cause pimples. The vitamin E oil found in some soaps can cause problems. Any oil-based moisturizing cream may clog your pores. **Stress**—When you're under pressure, your sebaceous glands produce more oil. If you've got a big business deal or social event coming up to make you tense, watch out for pimples.

If you find yourself with an outbreak of acne, consider the possible causes. If you're under stress, can you take steps to cope with it better? Have you begun taking any kind of medicine that may be causing the pimples? Have you started using any new soap, hair or skin cream, or after-shave lotion that might be making you break out? Have you been out in the sun for the first time in a long time? (Exposure to sun is usually good for acne, but at first it can cause temporary skin eruptions. A few washings with a good acne soap often clear this up.) Is there anything in your diet that could be to blame?

What can you do about acne? Of the countless creams, cleansers, lotions, soaps, gels, sticks, scrubs, masks, and medicated swabs that are sold without a prescription, there are only a small number that will actually help your acne problem. The over-the-counter remedies that are considered most effective are those that contain one of these four ingredients—benzoyl peroxide (the strongest); sulfur, resorcinol (not recommended for black or very dark skin because it may cause blotching), or salicylic acid. Products with these ingredients all work by causing your skin to peel. This opens up the comedones (plugs) so that the sebum can move to the surface. Some of these medications are quite strong, however. If your skin becomes *too* dry or scaly, stop using the medication for a while.

The best acne medications

Another sensible way to help your skin is to cut its excess oil as much as possible by using an acne soap, acne shampoo, and applying an astringent after you wash your face.

If none of this seems to help, you're a candidate for the dermatologist. What will a dermatologist do about your acne? There are several kinds of treatments, and the one chosen for you will be geared to your particular kind of problem. You might receive an oral antibiotic such as tetracycline. This is aimed at diminishing the amount of fatty acids contained in your sebum. And you may need to take the medication for six to eight months before your acne is completely cleared up. Your acne might be treated topically—with a soap or cleanser that

How a dermatologist may treat your acne

contains abrasives or sulfur. These will scrub the skin's surface, loosen comedones, remove oil and bacteria. You might receive doses of ultraviolet rays from a quartz lamp. You might undergo cryotherapy (use of extremely cold temperature). With this treatment, your pimples are daubed with cotton that's been soaked in liquid nitrogen. This freezes the pimples for three to five seconds. Your skin reddens, and blisters form; these may last for a few days while the treatment takes effect. You might get a vitamin A acid treatment. In towelette, cream, or liquid form, this hardens the skin's surface and halts the formation of comedones. Vitamin A acid treatments are applied daily, and during treatment your skin will become extremely sensitive to other substances like aftershaves and will also become highly photosensitive. Acne begins to clear up in four to five weeks.

If the inflammation of acne has spread to the dermis, the skin's deeper layer, scars may form. If these scars are profuse you may want to have them removed.

The best way to stop acne before it starts is to pay careful attention to keeping your skin as clean and oil-free as possible. Wash your face often, using an acne soap when you need to, and using an astringent regularly. When a pimple does crop up, treat it gently by extracting the comedo without rupturing the follicle and causing infection to spread. A help: A "comedo extractor" that carefully loosens the oil plug and cleans out the pore. These are inexpensive and available in most pharmacies.

Plastic surgery Maybe your ears stick out. Maybe you have deep, disfiguring acne scars. The tattoo that was cool at 20 embarrasses you now that you're 40. You've always hated your enormous nose. Lately you've noticed that your skin has become paunchy, or you despair at the jowls that have formed around your jaw. The bags under your eyes don't go away, no matter how much sleep you get.

Would it be vain to have plastic surgery if any of those problems belonged to you? Not necessarily. Of course, part of loving and accepting yourself involves being open to the changes in your appearance that inevitably come with age. The laugh lines around your mouth or at the corners of your eyes have been etched by years of merriment—a delightful thing to see. And the mellowed richness of an older man's face is powerfully sexual to many women. But a specific facial flaw that makes you miserable is something else. If you wake up every morning and feel a stab of pain when you look at your sagging jowls in the mirror, you have a problem. If being miserable about your appearance is costing you your self-esteem, if looking ten years older than you are is making you feel and *act* ten years older than you are, then the price you're paying is high. And then you might want to have cosmetic (plastic) surgery. Vidal Sassoon, in his health and beauty book, describes the operation he had to remove the bags under his eyes: "Plastic surgery did not change my lifestyle, my habits, my friends.... To expect this kind of miracle is asking too much of plastic surgery. You are the only one who can effect these changes in your life. The surgeon can merely remove certain physical impediments to the fullest expression of your pride in yourself and joy in life."

If you think cosmetic surgery will make you happier, why not look into it? Different types of cosmetic surgery include:

Rhytidectomy (face lift)—An incision is made from the temple down in front of the ear to the nape of the neck. The skin is pulled taut to remove deep folds of skin around mouth and jaws. Excess skin is trimmed off and the skin is stitched back in place.

Blepharoplasty (eyelid correction)—Removes excess skin and fatty tissue from upper and/or lower eyelids with a technique similar to that employed in face lifts.

Rhinoplasty (nose correction)—Changes the bridge line; can shorten the nose or lengthen it; can straighten or alter the shape of the tip.

Chin surgery—Implants bone, cartilage, or silicone into the chin to build it up or removes fat to minimize it.

Ear surgery—Can correct ears that stick out by removing an ellipse of skin from the back of the ear and trimming the cartilage beneath.

Salabrasion—Removes unwanted tattoos by a method that involves brisk rubbing with a salt-impregnated sponge.

Dermabrasion and chemabrasion—Remove acne and other scars and fine wrinkles that are the result of aging. What these methods do, literally, is give you a new epidermis—dermabrasion by sanding the face with a rotating wire brush or a steel burr; chemabrasion by applying highly irritating chemicals that burn off the top layer of skin. Both methods require a recuperation period of about two weeks. You apply lubricating oils religiously as your skin forms a new epidermis.

A serious decision

All forms of plastic surgery require a recuperation period while scars heal and bruises disappear. And the decision to undergo this kind of treatment is a serious one.

To find the right cosmetic surgeon, you may have to do some shopping around. Since this isn't an emergency operation, you can take your time to look, to talk to friends, to consult with various doctors. As you look them over they'll look you over too. Cosmetic surgeons take care to ensure that their patients are emotionally stable and are seeking surgery for sound, healthy reasons.

What does plastic surgery cost? The cost of this kind of surgery varies greatly according to the area you live in (you'll pay more in a city like New York) and the kind of surgery you require. You might pay anywhere from $1000 for a simple eyelid correction to $5000 for a total face lift.

Teeth Unless your teeth give you a lot of trouble, you probably don't think about them very much. You brush twice a day, make haphazard visits to the dentist every few years, and consider that you've done your duty to your mouth. And, since you begin having fewer cavities when you reach your 20s, you feel pretty secure that your good healthy teeth are here to stay.

This is the attitude that allows many people to be caught off guard by an insidious disease called periodontis. Periodontis causes millions of adults to lose teeth, year after year. (Millions of people in the U.S. are completely toothless and periodontis is the major cause.)

Why special tooth care is vital to you It all starts with a sticky, colorless layer of bacteria called **plaque.** Plaque is constantly forming on your teeth. Some of the foods you eat contribute to it, particularly soft, sticky, sugary foods. When it first develops on your teeth, plaque is 80 percent water, 20 percent solid. Before long it develops into a hard deposit called **tartar** that settles over the enamel surface of your teeth. Eventually (and unnoticed by you because it's painless) the calcium of your teeth begins to dissolve, the gums get irritated, teeth and gums part company—and teeth are eventually lost. The only way to prevent periodontal disease from sneaking up on you is to fight off plaque every day.

The best way to begin is by seeing your dentist and having the tartar build-up removed. (Plaque that has hardened into tartar will not come off without professional cleaning.) Then begin a tooth-cleaning regimen that keeps you one step ahead of plaque. Brushing your teeth religiously isn't enough. You'll need the help of dental floss, toothpicks, and patience.

The right way to clean your teeth Every night, before you brush your teeth, take an 18-inch length of unwaxed dental floss, and wind an end around the middle finger of each hand, leaving about a 3-inch length in between. Pull the floss taut and work it up and down gently between each tooth. Then curve the floss around each tooth to remove plaque from its surface. Finally, using the rounded end of a toothpick, gently scrape the area between the gum and the tooth. You'll be amazed at how much food and gummy plaque comes off in this process. When you've finished going over each tooth, brush all the loosened matter away with your toothbrush. Brush for at least two minutes—downward for the upper teeth, upward for the lower teeth, back and forth over the tops of the molars. Use the floss routine once a day. The other times you brush, just brush as usual.

If you want to check on how well you're doing with plaque removal, you can buy plaque-disclosing tablets (some come in a kit that includes floss and a mouth mirror like the one your dentist uses). You chew a red or purple fast-dissolving tablet and swish it around in your mouth for a minute before you spit it out. Your gums and teeth will be pink, and darker spots will appear where plaque lurks. Since the dye is water soluble, it will disappear in about half an hour. While you perfect your new tooth-brushing routine you might want to use plaque-disclosing tablets every day. Later, use them only occasionally as a spot check.

Another plus to this thorough tooth-cleaning regimen is that it reduces the chances of bad breath caused by food that's trapped between the teeth, out of the reach of your toothbrush. (If, after adopting the floss and toothpick method, you still have halitosis, it could be a sign of a tooth-and-gum disease or some gastrointestinal problem that a dentist or doctor should check.)

Maybe your teeth are crooked. Or a bit buck. Maybe a couple of teeth are chipped. Or missing altogether. Maybe you're so used to covering your mouth with your hand when you smile that you don't even realize you do it—or maybe you feel awkward and self-conscious about the appearance of your teeth most of the time. Maybe you think braces are for kids and capping is for movie stars, or maybe you've never even realized that there is something you can do to have better-looking teeth.

What to do if your smile is less than beautiful

First, determine how bad the problem is. It may be that the buck teeth you think of as funny-looking are considered by other people to be a distinctive mark of your character. Plenty of people have let irregular teeth become a trademark. If, however, you decide that fixing your teeth would make you happier, here are some of the kinds of treatments you might get:

If your teeth are broken or badly decayed, you can have them capped. Your dentist will first be sure that the tooth or teeth to be capped are free from decay. Then, before it's capped, the tooth is ground down and the remaining portion fitted with a gold crown that's topped with a porcelain cap. A cap of this kind (tinted to match your natural teeth) is permanent, it will not decay, and the match you get to your other teeth will be so good that no one will be able to tell which teeth are real and which are false. If only a portion of a root is left after decay or breakage, the tooth can be saved and capped if your bone structure is good. (A metal pin can be put into the root and capped with metal and porcelain.)

If you have a missing tooth, it can be replaced by a false one. The oldest method of replacement is one that uses bridgework. The teeth on either side of the missing one are used as anchors for the false tooth. The neighboring teeth are capped, and the replacement tooth sits in the middle, connected to the capped teeth near the bottom. A newer method is called implantation. This less proven technique involves implanting a new root under your gum and attaching a false tooth to it.

If your teeth are crooked, they can be straightened with braces, or, if overcrowding is the problem, by extracting teeth so that the others have room to even out. Correction with braces may take at least a couple of years—a nuisance you may not want to bother with unless you consider your crooked teeth a real problem.

Eyes

Your eyes will look and feel their best when you're well rested, when your diet is healthy and the alcohol in it kept to a minimum, and when you've protected them from the harsh, reddening effects of sun, water, wind, and pollution. If your eyes are often bloodshot, dull, and lifeless-looking, it's for a reason. You may be under a lot of stress and not getting enough sleep; you may not be getting enough vitamin A (your mother was right when she told you to eat your spinach—it's rich in vitamin A, as are carrots, liver, and fish); you may be neglecting to wear sunglasses when you're out on bright days, or forgetting to close your eyes when you swim in chlorinated or salt water; or it may be that city soot and smog are getting to you.

Why you need your eyes checked every two years

Just as you may take good, healthy teeth for granted, so you may be totally unconcerned about your eyes—until they give you problems. One obvious reason it's important to visit your eye doctor at least every two years is that your eyes are always changing. If you've never needed glasses before, you may need them now, and the eyeglass prescription that was perfect last year may not be perfect next year. Another reason to visit the eye doctor is to be sure your eyes are free from disease. Glaucoma, for example, which is not evident to you until it reaches advanced stages, can be detected early on by an eye doctor, and if it's caught early it can be arrested. If glaucoma goes unchecked, it can lead to total blindness. Glaucoma most frequently threatens people who are over 50, but it can begin to damage your eyes as early as age 30. Cataracts, a hardening of the lens of the eye (causing partial or total blindness), is commonly associated with old age—but it can be caused at any time by wounds, radiation, or electric shock. Diseases such as diabetes, kidney disorders, and syphilis can severely damage your eyesight too.

How to choose frames for your glasses

If you've just received a prescription for your first pair of glasses, you'll soon find yourself at the optician's, surrounded by an array of frames. And the range of choices may be confusing. One pair of frames may seem too trendy—and foolish. Another pair may seem too conventional—and staid. How to choose? The right frames for you will be in a proper balance with the size and shape of your face, and will fit the image you have of yourself. (Like it or not, the kind of frames you choose will project an image.) Eyeglass frames, when they're correct for you, will be comfortable, will look and feel right. They should not:

· Sit too far above or below your eyebrows.
· Extend too far beyond the sides of your face or down on your cheeks.
· Be so big that they overpower a small face.

Contact lenses

There are many good reasons for you to switch from regular glasses to contact lenses. Contact lenses are practically indetectable. They won't get in your way when you play handball or slip down your nose when you jog. Contacts often give you better vision than glasses do (with contact lenses you're always looking through the center of the lens, so you won't get the distortion you experience with glasses). Contacts can counteract many year-to-year changes in your eyesight. And they allow a wider range of vision than glasses do, since they move with your eye.

However, not everyone can wear contact lenses, and anyone who does wear them needs time to go through an uncomfortable period of adjustment. Contacts require more care than glasses because they are fragile and because a dirty or damaged lens can hurt your eye. (You need to clean and store them in a special liquid whenever you take them out.) They are easily lost—they are so small that if you drop one into a shag carpet, for example, it's a tricky business to find it.

Hard lenses or soft?

Contact lenses are either hard (made of thin, light acrylic plastic) or soft (made of a thin, water-absorbing plastic called hydrogel). The hard ones float over your eyeball on a film of tear fluid and are slightly smaller than the average cornea. Soft lenses mold themselves to the shape of the cornea, adapting to your eye without putting any pressure on its surface.

Why choose one kind over the other? Soft lenses are easier to get used to, and can be worn for longer periods of time than hard lenses. Soft lenses may be more easily alternated with eyeglasses (if you're used to wearing hard contact lenses your vision may blur when you try to wear your glasses instead). Since soft lenses cling to your eye, they are less likely to fall out than hard lenses. Hard lenses, however, have some advantages. They last longer (six to eight years as opposed to two to three for soft lenses). They damage less easily (soft lenses are easily disturbed by wind or heat or changes in your tear flow). It is easier to care for hard lenses than for soft ones. And hard lenses cost a good deal less than soft ones.

For you, the choice may be determined by the needs of your eyes. If astigmatism is your problem, the hard contact lenses may be the only ones that are right for you. If you have difficulty adapting to hard lenses, soft ones may work just fine. It's best to discuss your own eye problems with your eye doctor and then decide which choice is more likely to work for you.

Sunglasses

Whether you wear prescription glasses or not, you'll need to protect your eyes on bright sunny days with a good pair of sunglasses. To be effective, they must filter out visible rays (brightness and glare) as well as invisible rays (ultraviolet and infrared). The best sunglasses will:

· Be dark enough to filter out 15 to 25 percent of the light.
· Have ground-glass lenses that are impact resistant.
· Have stems that are no more than half an inch wide at the temple (they'll block your vision otherwise) and are connected to the frames by a screw, not a pin.
· Have metal reinforcement that keeps plastic stems from bending or stretching.
· Have gray or sage green lenses—they'll give you the least color distortion, the best protection from glare. Yellow lenses are good for skiing in poor light or for driving in a haze. Pale or pastel lenses won't give your eyes enough protection from the sun.

A way to test sunglasses

A good way to test sunglass lenses when you buy: Turn the sunglasses over under an overhead light and let the light reflect off the insides of the lenses. Move glasses slightly so that reflection moves across the surface of the lenses. If the image becomes distorted, wiggles, or waves, the lens is faulty and may produce eyestrain. Put it back.

If you wear prescription glasses, you really should buy prescription sunglasses too. The only other solution is the clip-on kind. These provide less peripheral protection (the glare from the sides can hurt your eyes); they add extra weight; and clip-on lenses, combined with the lenses of your regular glasses, can produce confusing reflections.

A rule for all sunglasses wearers: Don't wear sunglasses indoors or at any time when they're not really necessary. You can make your eyes overly sensitive to natural light that way and literally become a sunglasses addict.

An important rule

If you have bushy eyebrows, or eyebrows that run in a straight line across the bridge of your nose, they may get in the way when you start wearing glasses. If this bothers you or if you don't like the way your eyebrows look, it's OK to tone them down by plucking them out with tweezers. (This can be done professionally, as can eyebrow removal by waxing or electrolysis, but plucking is pretty simple for you to do yourself.) To make plucking easier, you might let a moisturizing cream sit on your brows for about ten minutes or do the tweezing when you get out of a hot shower. To thin your brows over the bridge of your nose, start in the middle and work outward. Don't thin too much, or it will look unnatural. Thin the rest of your brows by tweezing from below, not from above—and leave a few straggly hairs; a clean straight line will give you an artificial look. When regrowth starts, pluck individual hairs as they appear.

It's OK to pluck your eyebrows

If you've never grown a beard or a moustache, it's probably one of those things you've always wanted to do but never found the right opportunity for. Unless you're planning a 30-day backpacking trip or windjammer cruise, growing a beard or moustache can be downright awkward. In the four to five weeks it takes to get a decent growth you have to put up with the stares and comments: "You, growing a *beard*?" or "You call *that* a moustache?" In case you decide to brave it—or have already braved it and are wearing a beard or moustache now—here are some things you should know.

Beards and moustaches

A beard and moustache can do a lot for you. Either offers terrific protection from the wind, cold, and sun. A beard or moustache or both can hide scars, add character to your appearance.

However, you must understand and pay close attention to proportions. The kind of beard or moustache you cultivate must balance the shape of your face and body or you may create an effect just the opposite of the one you're after. A lot of men, for example, try to offset a bald head with a lot of facial hair. If this isn't done with a sensitive eye for proportion, sideburns and beard can get so bushy that the effect looks bottom-heavy—and ridiculous.

It can help to consult a men's hair stylist who's seen a lot of successful—and unsuccessful—beard and moustache styles. Friends' objective opinions can also help you to determine what looks right on you. A flowing walrus moustache might add marvelous character to your face, but overgrown muttonchop sideburns might look unattractive on your wide jawline.

Will a beard or a moustache help you attract the woman of your dreams? Probably not. Some women say they love the tickle of a beard or moustache when they're being kissed; others say that beards and moustaches scratch, look messy, or simply turn them off. What's probably most true is that if a woman is going to be attracted to you, she'd be attracted whether you're wearing a beard or moustache or not.

Once you've grown that beard or moustache, you can't just ignore it.

Big Nose A flowing moustache can diminish a big nose; a thin moustache makes it seem bigger.

Narrow Face A full beard will fill out a narrow face. A long beard and flowing moustache will make a narrow face seem more so.

Square Jaw Minimize a square jaw with a soft, rounded beard. Keep sideburns in check. (No muttonchops!)

· Keep it clean. A beard will trap perspiration, and it can get smelly. You may not notice it, but someone who's nuzzling up to you will. Shampoo your beard (moustache too) every day, and keep it soft by using a hair conditioner on it.

· Keep it groomed. Comb it. Brush it. Trim it every week or so (unless you're letting it grow into a Robinson Crusoe look). You can do your own trimming with scissors and a razor, and you can thin your beard by running a comb through it and passing an electric razor across the comb.

· Keep it out of the soup. The worst pitfall to beard and moustache wearers is food. If a moustache hangs too far over your upper lip it's bound to get food on it. Bread crumbs, flecks of food, and drops of liquid will spill onto a beard. Keep busy with a napkin—you need to use it much more often than you did when you were clean-shaven.

Grooming your beard or moustache

Weak Chin To strengthen a weak chin, go for a full beard and moustache, not just the moustache alone.

Round Face A walrus moustache looks fine on a round face, but a pencil moustache looks ridiculous.

Bald Head To give balance to a bald head, keep whiskers trimmed.

Basic care   You don't need anyone to tell you that your hair is important to your looks. Men have become as conscious of their hair as women have always been.

Now that there's such a thing as men's hair styling, you may feel lost. You may still feel uncomfortable with the idea of having your hair "styled" (something you find synonymous with looking unnatural), and you probably haven't the slightest inkling of how to style it yourself. So you either go on with the get-it-cut-once-or-twice-a-month, part-it-on-the-left routine that you began in high school, or you let it grow, hoping that the unruly thatch you've created looks fine. More than likely, neither your old part-it-on-the-side style nor your haphazard home-grown approach gives your hair a chance to look as good as it could.

What a hair stylist does   A good men's hair stylist (and some barbers are just that) can give you a haircut that's natural looking, easy to manage yourself, and flattering to your face—once you're willing to get into the act and tell him what you want. It's a good idea to bring in a picture from a magazine, to ask questions, to try experiments.

You can use a hair dryer without losing your masculinity and without making a mess of things (though a dryer is not always necessary). Just keep in mind that you'll probably need to practice for a while with a dryer before you master the technique.

Some of the fancy-sounding shampoos can actually do good things for your hair, but don't expect them to work miracles. Your hair, like your skin, eyes, and teeth, won't be healthy unless you are. Good, balanced meals (see "Cook for Your Health," page 50) are the best assurance that your hair will shine. But even healthy hair will look less than terrific if you don't treat it well on the outside, too.

Proper hair care isn't really complicated. What it boils down to is simply keeping your hair clean; being sensitive to its quirks (which means knowing how to treat it if it's oily or dry, frizzy or floppy); and finding a hairstyle that looks good on you and one which you can take care of easily.

If you have to wash your hair *every* day to keep it clean, then *wash it every day.* There's no excuse for oily, stringy, smelly hair—ever. Unless you're using a shampoo that's too harsh for you (one that irritates your scalp, dries out your hair), you won't hurt your hair by washing it every day. And, contrary to hearsay, frequent washing and blow-drying will *not* cause baldness.

You have oily hair if it takes a shampoo every day or two to keep it fluffy and shiny. You have dry hair if, four or five days after a shampoo, it's dull and brittle but not oily. You have normal hair if it becomes oily three or four days after you shampoo. Oily hair should be washed every day with a mild shampoo. Dry hair should be washed as often as is necessary to keep it clean with a low-detergent shampoo that has soothing conditioners (like lanolin) added to it. Dry hair should be treated with a conditioner after the shampoo's been rinsed out. Normal hair needs shampooing about twice a week; include a conditioner in the routine every now and then to make up for the inevitable abuse of sun, pollution, and general wear and tear.

Environment also determines how often you need to wash your hair. Whatever type of hair you have, it'll need more shampooing in the moist, grimy air of a big city than in the clean, rarified air of the mountains.

Besides washing away dirt and grime, a good shampoo will leave your hair soft, shiny, and manageable. Which shampoo will work best on your hair? The only way you can find out is to test several different kinds until you find one you like. Give a product a chance (a couple of weeks) before you pass judgment. If a shampoo causes your scalp to flake or itch, if it makes your hair dry as straw or limp and oily, stop using it. Stay away from supermarket specials in favor of brands from well-known cosmetic lines. The savings you may get aren't worth it. The cheaper shampoos cost less because lower-grade ingredients are used.

Basically, shampoos consist of various synthetic detergents that will not leave a dull residue on your hair as soaps will. Besides detergent, a shampoo will contain ingredients like olive oil, coconut oil, ethyl alcohol, potassium hydroxide. A good shampoo for dry and normal hair will have conditioning agents (like lanolin, silicone, or protein) added to replace the oil and moisture that are stripped away by dirt-cutting agents. Shampoos for oily hair will contain a higher

percentage of detergents, a lower percentage of conditioners. Some of the words you'll read on shampoo labels:

Balsam—The word simply means soothing, which some balsam shampoos are. Some balsam shampoos actually contain extracts from the balsam tree—which don't do much of anything for your hair though they can't hurt it. Other balsam shampoos contain no balsam oil at all, yet have good cleansers and conditioners in them.

Herbal—Herbal shampoos smell fresh and natural. Some are actually formulated with natural herbs; others have chemical additives that smell "natural." Some are mild and soothing and do a good cleaning job too. A number of people argue that herbs and other natural ingredients—wheat germ, honey, for example—contain nutrients that are good for your scalp. Maybe. Don't expect miracles, though.

pH—The symbol pH is used to express the degree of a solution's opposite properties of acidity and alkalinity. A pH balance in a shampoo simply means that the product will not disturb the natural pH balance of your skin and hair.

Protein—Shampoos that contain protein are not going to feed your hair and make it healthier. The only protein that helps you grow healthier hair is the protein in your diet. However, protein in a shampoo's formula has conditioning effects—it can plump up damaged hair and smooth split ends so that your hair looks better temporarily.

How to wash your hair   To get the full benefit of a shampoo, be sure you:

• Massage your scalp with your fingertips before and during your shampoo. This gets your circulation going under your scalp and loosens dead skin cells and sends them down the drain.

• Shampoo in a shower. The steady beat of the shower spray is good for the scalp's circulation and a help in rinsing out shampoo.

• Draw the shampoo lather along the full length of your hair several times. Go over every inch of your head to be sure you haven't missed any spots.

• Use the right amount of shampoo. If you wash your hair every day, one soaping should be enough. If you shampoo every few days, or if your hair's very dirty (after you've been swimming in salt water or bicycling behind a bus, for example) you'll need to lather up twice.

• Rinse. And rinse. And rinse. Get out every bit of shampoo. Many men mistakenly think they have dandruff when it's actually the flaking of leftover shampoo that's dried on their hair.

• Condition your hair. Unless your hair is terribly oily, you *need* a conditioner. Use some once or twice a week, or if your hair is dry, every time you shampoo. Shake all the water out of your hair to free strands so that the conditioner can coat them more thoroughly. Spread the conditioner over the palms of your hands and run your hands and fingers through your hair. Let the conditioner sit on your hair for a minute or two, and then rinse thoroughly.

Why do you need a conditioner? If you looked at a strand of hair under a microscope, you would see that the outer shaft consists of tiny scales. These scales become damaged by sun, salt, hairbrushes, rough treatment. What a conditioner does is coat the shaft of hair and fill in the breaks in the scales (called cuticles). It doesn't *cure* hair problems, but it nicely camouflages them. It plumps the hair a bit, makes it look and feel thicker and softer. It also gives it protection from further damage.

Dandruff is a scalp problem, not a hair problem. It's what happens when your scalp sheds its outer layer in excessive amounts, resulting in flaking. Dandruff itches and is embarrassing when it collects on your shoulders and collar. Dandruff is likely to be worse in the winter than in the summer (the sun helps clear it up). Dandruff shampoos (containing ingredients like tar, sulfur, salicylic acid, or selenium sulfide) may do a good job of controlling flaking. Since you can become immune to the ingredients in one dandruff shampoo after a while, it's a good idea to switch from one brand to another. If your dandruff is really profuse or persistent, see a dermatologist.

What is dandruff?

Other products that you might find useful in caring for your hair:

Tips

Scalp massagers—There are several electric, vibrating kinds to give your scalp a rub-down, and there's the hard rubber dime-store massager with soft, bendable bristles to rub over your scalp. Many scalp specialists feel that massaging is good because it stimulates circulation under your scalp and keeps it healthy. Others warn that excessive or rough massage can cause skin cells to slough off prematurely (wounding your scalp) and can break off fine hairs just as they're growing in. If you use a scalp massager, take care not to get overzealous.

Hair dressings and hair sprays—Moderation is the word. If you need a lot of spray or hair dressing to control your hair, your cut is probably wrong for you. If you do want to use a hair cream or spray to add a little moisture or do a little taming, go easy. Never put on a hair dressing when your hair is wet—wet hair makes it impossible to tell how much you've used, and it's easy to overdo. If you use hair spray, don't point the spray directly at your scalp—hold the can at least a foot away from your hair and mist it briefly. Pay attention to scents, too. If you're wearing cologne or an after-shave that has a fragrance, be sure any hair dressing you use is unscented. Otherwise scents will fight each other, and you'll smell awful.

Cuts and barbers   If you consider your hair to be one of your biggest assets, you're either terribly lucky or very involved with getting your hair to look the way it does. If you consider your hair to be a constant problem, or if it's simply something you don't think about much, it's likely that you're not doing everything you can to get your hair looking its best.

How to get what you   Maybe you've been to a hair stylist a couple of times and were
want from your barber   disappointed with what was done to you. Maybe you tell yourself your hair is such a problem (too curly, too wispy, too drab) that it's not worth bothering with. But great-looking hair rarely just happens. To find a style that works for you and a barber or hair stylist who can help you keep it that way takes a bit of effort—effort, however, that turns out to be well worth it once the results are in.

Here's how to begin to get great looking hair:

· Decide what you want. Do you want your hair to widen your narrow face? Camouflage your big ears? Look fuller, fluffier, or just more "with it?" Are you willing to learn to style your own hair with a blow dryer after each shampoo, or is a wash-and-wear haircut a must? Take a good look at other men—friends, people you see on the street. When you see someone with a haircut you admire, go up and ask him who cut it. (Word of mouth is the best way to find a good hair stylist or barber.) Thumb through magazines. If you see a picture of a style you like, clip it out, and take it with you to the barber and ask if he can adapt it to your face and type of hair.

· Be realistic. Some things are possible and some things aren't. If your face is round, no hair style will give you a lean look. If your hair is like wire, no barber can make it like corn silk. But the right style, when you find it, can do wonders for your looks. If you've been unsuccessfully trying to flatten down thick, curly hair, for example, a barber might show you how cutting it the same length all over and *letting* it be curly can open up and relax your face.

· Be prepared to participate when you're in the barber's chair. Just sitting there passively is a sure way to be disappointed in the haircut you get. The more you can tell the barber, the more likely he'll be to give you what you want. If you have a picture from a magazine, show it to him and tell him what you like about it. If your hair has quirks (tends to curl around the ears, gets limp in humid weather, sticks out in tufts where it's gray at the temples), tell him. And listen to the suggestions he has. If they don't sound good to you, you don't have to go along with them. But sometimes a barber who's seen thousands of heads of hair can come up with an idea that will help solve a problem. Just be sure that you and the barber are in agreement and that you both understand the look he's aiming for before he takes the scissors to your hair.

· Be patient. It takes a few visits to a particular barber for him to get to know your hair and its growing patterns. If you like something he does, tell him. If there's something you'd like him to do differently, tell him that too. After two or three visits you should be really pleased with your hair—and your barber.

When you pick a haircut, consider the shape of your face, the texture of your hair, how much tending you're willing to do to maintain a style, and any physical features you want to play up or down. All are factors that should be discussed with your barber before he cuts your hair.

Drying and styling your hair

If you have a wash-and-wear haircut, all you need to do is jump out of the shower, blot your hair dry with a towel (don't rub—you can damage your hair), comb it (perhaps with just your fingers), and you're done. Quick. Easy. Simple.

You may, however, have a hairstyle that needs tending with a blow dryer. That's quick, easy, and simple too—if you know what you're doing. Pay attention to the barber or hair stylist as he blows your hair dry. Ask him to explain what he's doing, step by step, so you can duplicate the effect at home.

The right kind of dryer

What kind of dryer do you need? Best are the mallet-shaped kind that you hold in your hand, with a nozzle that forces air onto your hair.

Some blow three or four temperatures, from cool to very hot. Some have different air-flow settings. Some come with styling attachments (combs and brushes) that slide onto the nozzle. Some of the dryers you'll look at in the store will have decidedly masculine designs, while others will look more feminine—one kind will do the job just as well as the other. Just be sure the air flows hard enough and the heat gets high enough to get your hair dry fairly quickly. (You can test several kinds in the store.)

The right kind of brush and comb

If your dryer doesn't have attachments and you need a brush to style your hair as you blow it dry (a good idea if your hair is over two inches long), you can buy a round styling brush. The ones with natural bristles are kindest to your hair. The best kind of comb to have is one with teeth evenly spaced and not so close together that they yank at your hair. (The thicker your hair, the wider apart the comb's teeth should be.) Don't get rough with a brush and comb. You can damage your hair, especially when it's tangled or wet.

How to use a hair dryer

Your barber may teach you any number of tricks with a dryer. Hair tends to hold the shape it was in when it dried—if you pull your damp hair straight or curve it around a brush or styling attachment, it will retain that straight line or curve when it's dry.

Blow drying your hair will give it more body, more shape, and more manageability. If your hair is fairly short, simply blowing it dry before you comb it down will give it more body and shape than it would have had if it had dried by itself.

If your hair is longer than two inches, you'll get better results if you dry it in two stages. The first stage gets out most of the moisture. Run the dryer over your hair in a sweeping motion, leaving it barely damp. The second stage is for styling. Go over your head a section at a time, twirling the styling brush or holding the attachment around the hank of hair you're drying. Don't linger on one spot too long—you can scorch your hair, scalp, forehead, ears. When all of your hair has been dried, brush it straight back, then gently comb it into place. (If heat drying makes wavy hair too bushy, use the cooler setting at the last.) Your hair should look soft, sleek, and natural.

Hair coloring

It used to be that the only reason a man would color his hair was to hide the gray. He'd feel sheepish about it and probably try to keep the whole thing secret. Few men feel that way now, and if you want to color your hair for any reason, you're likely to say, "Why not?"

Why color your hair?

Maybe you don't like the way gray looks on you. Maybe you picked up some highlights in the summer sun and would like to keep them through the winter. Maybe you want to return to the lighter shade you came by naturally when you were younger. And maybe you're just curious to know what you'd look like with hair of a different color.

There are many different methods of hair coloring. A temporary rinse just coats the surface of your hair shaft. You put it on when you shampoo, and it lasts until you wash it out. A semipermanent coloring coats your hair shaft and also penetrates it slightly. It lasts three to six weeks. A permanent hair coloring penetrates the hair shaft and chemically alters it. It lasts until your hair grows out and you cut it.

Hair coloring can be done at a good barber shop, at a men's hair stylist, or at home. For anything other than temporary rinses, it's a good idea to turn coloring jobs over to the professionals.

Some facts about hair coloring:

· The color you see on the box won't be exactly the color you get on your hair. It's a good idea to snip off some of your hair and to sample-color it before you commit your whole head to a coloring process.
· Rinses will add some colortone to gray hair, but they won't cover it completely.
· Only permanent hair colors will lighten your hair. Semipermanent colors and temporary rinses contain no peroxide.
· Very dark hair looks strange on pale skin, and very light hair looks strange on swarthy skin. Be sure the color you pick for your hair is compatible with your skin tone.
· Patch testing will help you avoid allergic reactions. This involves dabbing a small amount of dye on your skin and waiting 24 hours to make sure you have no reaction. The colorist in the salon or the label on the box of permanent dye will tell you how (the FDA requires it).
· Experimenting can lead to disastrous results. Read directions carefully and follow them to the letter.
· Coloring dries out your hair. Be sure to use a conditioner after every shampoo once your hair's been tinted.
· Color-treated hair requires touch-ups about every four weeks. Don't put new color over the old. Be sure to touch up only the untreated roots—otherwise you'll end up with two different shades.

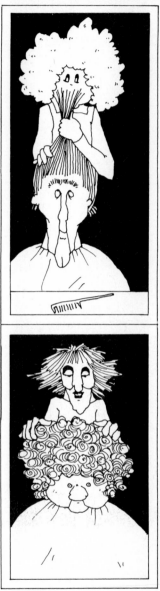

Maybe your hair is so wispy and limp that you've never been able to make it stay put. Or maybe it's so frizzy that even getting a comb through it is a major effort. You can get just as fed up with constantly struggling with your hair as women do. And if your hair is very wiry or straight and limp, having it professionaly straightened or curled may give it a texture you find more manageable.

Curling and straightening

Experiment If the idea of having your hair "permanently" straightened or curled (which means subjecting it to a process that stays with you until it grows out) seems too drastic, you can experiment with temporary measures first. If you want to try out some curls, you might use a woman friend's hot rollers or have your hair professionally water-set in a salon. Don't like the look? Wash it out. Temporary straightening can be done with a hot comb in a salon and give you results that will return to normal in about two or three weeks.

The different kinds of "permanents" you can get include: having your hair straightened; getting a body wave that adds bulk and thickness without giving you curls; getting your hair loosely waved or tightly curled (sometimes called "frizzing".)

How permanents work The process used to chemically straighten your hair is similar to the process used to curl your hair. In both methods the hair stylist will apply a chemical (such as an alkaline solution of thioglycolic acid). This chemical will "soften" your hair by breaking the chemical bond in its shaft. While your hair is in a softened state, it's either wrapped around a roller (to curl it) or combed down flat (to straighten it). When the chemicals are removed and the hair neutralized, the bond re-forms in the new shape. The curled or straightened state remains until that portion of your hair grows out and you cut it off.

A short, curly style may give you the opportunity to have a wash-and-wear haircut for the first time in your life. Straightened hair may give you a tamer look or accentuate your features in a way that pleases you. Some cautions, however: permanents can be disappointing—especially if you expect too much. The "frizz" you hoped would be fun might just seem messy. Straightened hair may seem stiff, brittle, and awkward. Chemicals can damage your hair, particularly if they are not handled carefully, or if you go for a permanent too often. And your new permanent may make your hair dry—take care to pamper it with conditioners whenever you shampoo.

Baldness and alternatives If you're getting bald, there's only one thing you want to hear: that there's a cure for it. There isn't. In a vast majority of cases men go bald because they have inherited the condition, and, to date, nothing has been found that will prevent hereditary loss of hair.

Most baldness is hereditary Natural baldness (also called male-pattern baldness) is believed to be related to aging and to the degree of sensitivity of your hair follicles to androgen, the male hormone in your system. It used to be thought that hereditary baldness was passed through the mother, but now medical experts aren't sure how you inherit baldness. It does seem that if baldness is in your family's history, it's more likely to happen to you than if everyone in your family tree wore a full head of hair right into old age. The follicles that are most susceptible to baldness are the ones on your forehead and crown. The hair on the sides of your head is less likely to fall out.

Other causes of baldness

Sometimes, temporary hair loss is caused by illness, malnutrition, or trauma. The follicles under your scalp that determine hair growth (hair itself is actually dead) are very sensitive to changes in your diet and in your nervous system. You could experience some hair loss after a trauma (a death in the family, a serious car accident) or during times of extreme stress (after the loss of a job, the break-up of a marriage). Hair loss can be caused by anemia, thyroid disorders, or various skin problems such as dermatitis, psoriasis, allergic reactions. If you suspect that any of these kinds of things might be the cause of your thinning hair, a doctor can give you tests to determine whether you're anemic or suffering from an iron deficiency, a thyroid condition, or a skin disturbance. Shots, pills, or a change in diet will set you on the right track, and your hair will grow back again.

Making the best of the situation

If, however, your baldness is hereditary—and it probably is—you *can* do some of the following:

• Take heart in the knowledge that, statistically speaking, most of your hair loss is likely to occur before you're thirty. What you have at thirty, you're likely to keep—at least most of it.
• Eat a balanced diet, avoid androgenic foods (wheat germ, liver, and kidneys, for example), and stay away from diets that may cause a vitamin deficiency.
• Use shampoos and conditioners that contain protein. Protein coats the hair shafts and makes them look thicker.
• Get rid of the notion that baldness is bad—consider that it's just another way to look.
    This last, which requires a new point of view about your hair and your looks, is the hardest thing to do. It will help if you find a hairstyle that makes the most of the way you are—bald spot and all. Hairstyles that try to cover up baldness look unnatural—they actually draw attention to the baldness and make it look like a problem, which it needn't be.

Common mistakes

Some of the most common hairstyling mistakes men with bald spots make are:

• Growing exaggerated muttonchop sideburns in an attempt to compensate for the lack of hair on the head.

• Growing the side hair extra-long and combing it up and over the bald spot.
• Teasing or back-combing the hair around a bald spot, then using hair spray to hold it in place.
• Letting the hair on the sides grow to the shoulders.
• Wearing a wig or toupee that's obviously fake.

Good ways to handle baldness

Hairstyling that works best for baldness works *with* the bald spot instead of trying to hide it. Some of the best solutions include:

• Wearing your hair shorter and fluffier all over (protein shampoos and conditioners help). Using a blow dryer adds body (blow drying won't hurt you unless you get careless and burn your scalp).
• Growing the hair around the sides to just cover your ears, curving inward to frame your face. This works best if you're fairly tall and if your face is lean. It probably won't work if you're short and round-faced—experiment and see.
• Keeping your hair well trimmed and adding a well-trimmed moustache and beard. This is especially good if you have "horseshoe" baldness.
• Shaving everything off. If your features are strong enough to carry it, a totally bald head can be very distinctive and sexy.

Some men can take hair loss and baldness in stride. Their easygoing attitude shows in their appearance and, for them, baldness really *isn't* a problem. Other men find the thought of baldness intolerable. They are the ones who'll try any gimmick and who can be seduced by any trickster who promises to get their hair growing again. "Remedies" that include scalp massages, tinctures, and sunlamp treatments are risky, expensive, and rarely if ever successful at growing your hair back. Before you attempt any treatment like that, discuss it with your doctor. Instead, consider a *good* toupee, hair weaving, or hair transplants.

If you find a bald head or a bald spot undesirable, there are several things you can do to have "hair" again. You can go to a salon for a toupee or hair weaving. Or you can go to a medical doctor (usually a plastic surgeon or a dermatologist) and have hair permanently transplanted or implanted into your bald area.

Toupees

A toupee is built from a base that's shaped like the bald area to be covered. This base (which may be made of something hard, such as fiberglass, or soft, such as nylon) is attached to your scalp with strips of double-sided sticky tape and will be covered with real or artificial hair. You take if off when you sleep, shower, or swim, and you must have it cleaned periodically (which makes owning two a necessity). A good toupee will fit perfectly, look absolutely natural, stand up to sun and rain, be easy to clean, and last for years. A bad toupee will fade or discolor in the sunlight and look unreal due to its color, texture, or fit. Any toupee you wear should stand up to the most critical scrutiny or it's not worth a nickel.

Hairweaving

The hair weaving process creates a more permanent kind of hair piece. A nylon lattice is placed over your bald spot and woven and knotted at the edges into your existing hair until it's anchored securely. Then real or artificial hair is woven into the lattice.

A good hair weaving job looks natural. It won't come off. You can bathe, swim, sleep in your new hair. However, as your real hair grows out, the artificial piece will become loose, and you'll need to visit the salon every six weeks or so to get it tightened. WARNING: salon visits are time-consuming and expensive, and the constant tugging on existing hair has been known to cause headaches and to cause more hair to come out.

Hair transplants

The hair transplant is a delicate surgical operation that involves taking plugs of hair from the back and sides of your head and transplanting them into the bald area of your scalp. Each plug includes about 12 hairs, supporting skin, follicles, and some fat. Care must be taken not to damage the follicles in transit, as they must go on living to produce hair in their new location. After a few months, the transplanted follicles resume their normal growing cycle. This process is often very successful—and permanent. However, not all follicles survive transplanting, and the process can be painful. You'll need patience too; it requires office visits over many weeks or months before the transplanting is complete.

Hair implants

Hair implanting is another surgical process; it involves putting plugs of artificial hair into the bald area of your scalp. It's permanent and natural-looking. However, since the process can cause reactions (your scalp may reject foreign bodies or become prone to infections), you'll need to make frequent checkup visits to the doctor and you'll need to shampoo often to guard against infection. And, as with hair transplants, this process can be painful.

Before you undertake hair implants or transplants, a doctor should give you a thorough checkup of your physical and emotional health. He should also fully inform you of the discomfort, inconvenience, and expense involved in receiving either kind of cosmetic surgery.

Aging attitudes   When you're in your 20s, you're likely to feel that you'll stay young forever. At one point or another the hopelessness of this point of view hits you with some impact. And whether the jolt comes at 35 or 50, the message is the same: you're getting old, and you're going to die. This jolt, part of a mid-life crisis so well described in Gail Sheehy's book *Passages,* is usually accompanied by a period of bitter self-appraisal and a feeling of lost opportunities. If you are a lawyer with a wife, three children, and a mortgage, for example, you might overlook your accomplishments and chide yourself for getting roped in. You know that the artist's life you once dreamed of will never become a reality. You'll never know the thrill of having a one-man show. And if you're an artist, unencumbered, perhaps, by emotional ties or financial responsibilities, you might look at the work you've done with skepticism and chide yourself for having no commitments, no roots, no durable emotional relationship with a lifelong partner.

When the press of time passing you by and a sense of failure are upon you, you may react in one of several ways. You might bury your feelings (they're too unsettling) and push yourself harder at work. You might try to prove to yourself that you're as young as you ever were by going to more parties, downing more drinks, or finding new (younger) women to make love to. Or you might resign yourself to getting older and give in to what you consider to be the inevitable by-products of maturity: a flabby stomach, a lowered libido, a narrowing of your interests. It's so much easier to sink down in front of the TV after dinner than to muster up interest in something new.

You may hide from reality   Burying yourself in work, frantically clutching at youthful forms of behavior, or passively giving yourself up to a sedentary existence are equally blind and limiting approaches to life. None take into account who you really are as you get older—a broader, more experienced, more fully developed human being who can continue to grow and become better, not just older.

Sound like a lot of pep talk? It's not. The common belief that emotions, sights, tastes, and smells are less keenly experienced in middle and old age is simply untrue. Getting older does not have to mean becoming dull, flabby, or unable to take on challenges. In fact, there are feelings and rewards available to you at older ages that were simply out of your reach when you were young. For example:

Some good things about aging

Your sexuality—Sex can become better. The frequency of your lovemaking may not be what it was when you were 20, but your capacity for fulfillment increases with experience. Your ability to maintain a prolonged state of excitement may be accompanied by a deep, rewarding sensitivity that you never experienced when you were younger.

Your brain and body—It has been found that the more you work your brain, the more it will work for you; and the same thing is true of your body. Doctors have discovered that diminishing capacities of mind and body are the result of disuse, not of biological decline. If, for example, you think you're too old to learn to ski, to take up the piano, to take on a new career—you will be. But what's holding you back is your point of view, not your mental and physical potential. As you get older, mental accuracy *improves*. And if you stay in shape with sensible exercise, you will actually retard the aging process.

Your appearance

Of course, time will cause changes in your appearance. As your skin loses some of its elasticity, your face will develop character lines and wrinkles. When you exercise, you'll become winded sooner than you did when you were younger, because you won't have the same amount of stored oxygen. But if you keep exercising your heart, your mind, and your muscles, they'll serve you well and afford you a much more youthful maturity than you'll have if you become mentally and physically lazy. If you choose to, you can stay trim and energetic until the end of your life.

If your attitude about yourself and your life is positive, you will feel the thrill of learning new things—always. It takes work to push through the lethargy and the subconscious attitudes that caution you to slow down, give up, take it easy. But many people find that once they give up the myth that maturity means being sedentary, they find that they are constantly discovering new pleasures—and enjoying life.

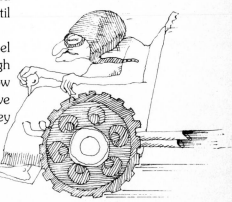

There are some simple, sensible things you can do as you grow older to keep yourself feeling good:

Some rules for healthier aging

• Stop smoking. You'll reduce the chance of getting lung cancer, heart disease, and emphysema, among other things.
• Drink in moderation. The less you drink the fewer brain cells you'll destroy, and you'll be less prone to liver disease.
• Eat low-fat, low-calorie foods. You'll reduce your chance of heart attack and diabetes, and be more energetic.
• Get regular medical checkups. Diseases are infinitely more curable when you catch them early.
• Exercise routinely. You'll look better, have more energy, stay healthier.

The idea is not to "stay young," but to be the best possible you at any age. Life is growth. If you view maturity and settling down as stultifying or as an end to future growth, you'll cheat yourself of the full value of living. You may have been taught that restlessness is childish. But the needs to question and explore that are behind restlessness are paths to growth. Be restless. Be curious. Try new things. Allow yourself to question. Dare to make changes when things don't work. Who says you can't switch careers at 45? Or that you've got to make it by 40? Expand your definitions of success. Get rid of the concept of limitations. The only limitations are the ones in your mind.

When you see life as a progressive series of renewals, failure becomes simply the end of one phase that didn't work out. Paul Gauguin didn't start painting until he gave up his banking career at 41. Charlie Chaplin was still fathering children when he was over 80. Artur Rubinstein claimed he was playing the piano better than ever when he was 80. Why? He was less afraid to make mistakes. Take note of the many astounding older people you know who have health, vibrancy, and joy. If you plan to be one of them, you will be.

The climacteric

Up until recently, no one talked about male "menopause" or even recognized that it existed. Menopause (or climacteric) was considered strictly a women's problem. And so men who encountered physical, emotional, or sexual upsets as their production of testosterone declined endured these side effects alone and confused about what was happening to them.

There's still room for a lot more research on the subject, but it is now known that men do experience a climacteric period of life (usually between ages 40 and 55) during which their physiological and psychological reactions may run parallel to a woman's experience of female menopause.

During the climacteric period your body begins to slow its production of sex hormones (testosterone). The process is usually gradual—it generally goes on over a period of years—and, except for a possible decline in the frequency of intercourse, there's no reason for the hormonal change to affect your sexual functioning. And, since your production of testosterone goes on all your life, you'll probably be able to produce sperm and father children for many years—possibly into your 80s. In 85 percent of males, hormonal decline is so gradual that changes are barely noticeable. Some men have no indication that anything's happened at all. But a small number of men experience wide swings in hormonal levels that cause enormous shifts in mood.

What are some of the climacteric symptoms?

Symptoms vary from minor to extreme. You may experience a few, or many. They may bother you a little or a lot. Some of the commonest are morning fatigue, vague pains, listlessness. Others include nervousness, irritability, depression, anxiety, frustration, insomnia, memory lapses, diminished sexual potency, loss of self-confidence, headaches, dizziness, hot flashes, chills, heart palpitations. You may have manic highs, depressing lows. You may question your marriage, your lifestyle, your career. You may dwell morbidly on death; you may lose your temper a lot.

These symptoms won't hit you all at once. You may have a few for a day or two; then they'll go away for a while. A few weeks or months later those same symptoms may return, or others could crop up. If any symptoms become severe, you'd do well to seek professional help. In an extremely depressed or manic state you may institute changes (leaving your wife, buying a new house) that you'll later regret.

Impotence is almost always temporary

Ninety percent of impotence is psychological. The kind of psychological impotence that occurs in the climacteric period is linked with anxiety, and the effect of anxiety on your testosterone level. It's now known that the male hormone testosterone varies enormously and is governed by your emotional state. And the older you are, the more likely it is that your testosterone level will be affected by anxiety. If you feel worried, insecure, or anxious, your mental state can trigger a suppression of the production of testosterone. This, in turn, will give you a temporary loss of sexual energy—but you may fear that it's not temporary, and the fact that you cannot get an erection will make you even more anxious. The more anxious you are, the longer your testosterone level stays down. It's a vicious cycle—and usually simply a temporary problem. Chances are very good that you'll breeze through male "menopause" without a hitch. But knowing that it can be a difficult time will help you take a philosophical view of it if any of its unsettling problems affect you.

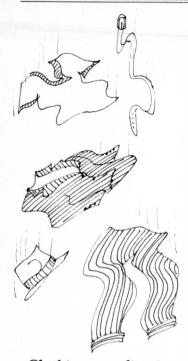

PULLING IT ALL TOGETHER

Clothing coordination

Before you can pull your wardrobe together, you must know what you already have. Set aside time for a review. Go through your closets and drawers and take out all your business clothes—suits, jackets, slacks, shirts, and ties. Lay them out on your bed in separate piles.

Try to see your suits as simply a selection of pants, vests, and jackets. In fact, you might separate them into piles. Then experiment with different combinations—try your suit jackets on as sports jackets with other slacks, for example, or try your blazer on with some light-colored suit trousers. It helps to have a full-length mirror.

Once you've found a combination that interests you, try it out on a friend. Getting a second opinion—in the privacy of your home—helps to ensure that you won't venture out in the outfit that looks casually elegant to you but absurd to everyone else.

The simplest clothes combinations are those made up of solid colors since you avoid the problem of matching patterns. Although some fashion experts say this can be a dull way to dress, it need not be. Something as basic as a navy blue suit worn with a white broadcloth shirt and a maroon silk tie can have a crisp, authoritative look.

Make sure you get the right contrast in tones. Tones that are too similar give the impression of a dull wash of color over your body. A tie that is too close to your shirt color will simply disappear.

To heighten the contrast, choose a shirt that's lighter than either your tie or your suit. Try to visualize how each element would look in a black-and-white photograph. If you don't think the colors would show up as being noticeably different, try a darker tie or a lighter shirt.

When you wear patterns, be extremely careful. Limit yourself to two, and be especially careful if the two are in the shirt and tie. A plaid shirt worn with a boldly striped tie can have an unpleasant effect.

Mixing patterns

The pinstripe pattern in suits and shirts is the simplest to mix and match because the pattern is so faint. Chalk stripe suits and shirts with heavy solid stripes have dominant patterns and should not be worn with other patterns.

When you put two patterns together, make sure that one is more subdued than the other—wear a "buffer" solid color between them—for example, wear a solid shirt with a striped tie and a pinstripe suit.

Pay attention to details—for example, socks with different colors or patterns than your suit. A pair of checkered socks could ruin an otherwise impeccable look.

Ties and lapels

Try to select ties that will highlight some hidden color in your suit or sports jacket. Something as subtle as a thin thread of red running through a gray suit will pull together a blue shirt and a red paisley tie.

Be sensitive to the way shapes work with one another. If you already have a selection of suits and ties, you probably have a mixture of different widths in ties and suit lapels. Be careful how you wear them. A narrow tie is going to be overwhelmed by a wide-lapel suit. A wide tie will look completely out of place with a narrow-lapel suit. There is, however, no hard-and-fast rule on the limits of width in either case—you have to trust your critical eye.

It is worthwhile to pay attention to window displays in fashionable men's stores and to look closely at the better-dressed men you know. Look for appealing styles and color combinations you can imitate with your existing wardrobe. The more clothes and clothes combinations you see, the more you will develop your own sense of style.

Wardrobe purges

Weed out the items in your wardrobe that you will never wear again. Your life will be simpler if you give away those ties that are too torn, too rumpled, too far out of fashion, or just too ugly. Pull out the shirts with frayed collars and cuffs. Set aside the suits, jackets, and slacks that no longer fit or that you simply don't like and give them to a local clothing drive. Then make a list of the items you need to replenish your wardrobe. (A list of basics appears on page 137.)

Periodic wardrobe purges help you to get rid of clutter and to rediscover valuable clothes or combinations you may have forgotten.

Dress for your body   Your body is part of your "wardrobe." Your shape determines what clothing looks best on you. So take a hard, objective look at yourself.

Strip to your shorts and stand about six or seven feet away from a full-length mirror. Let your body settle into its natural posture. Fight the inclination to hold in your stomach or stand ramrod stiff. You won't get a realistic picture by distorting the facts of your physique.

Fitting your physique   Consider your overall physical characteristics. Are you short, tall, fat, or thin? Be perfectly honest. If you are five feet two, for example, you are short by any standard. Accept that fact and you'll be able to choose the clothes that suit you best. For a more objective opinion, you may have to ask a friend for an evaluation.

The next step is to examine specific areas of your body. Take a look at the general shape of your face. Is it long and narrow, or short and broad? What about your neck? Is it noticeably long or short?

Scan the general symmetry of your body. Remember that there is no such thing as a perfect body—every body is out of proportion to some extent. Most people have one arm slightly longer than the other, or a shoulder or hip that rides slightly higher than the other. Check your body for these factors, and note whether your proportions are thrown off by other parts of your physique—a barrel chest, heavy muscular legs, or muscular arms. Even the length of your legs is important—they could be too short and throw off the rest of your body lines.

You should also consider your personality. If you tend to be gruff and aggressive or quiet and shy, you can change the impression you make with a different style of dress. Lighter colors will make a softer impression and tone down a gruff appearance, while darker colors will have a stronger visual impact.

Fitting your personality

Keep in mind the idiosyncracies of both your body and personality the next time you get dressed for work. Take more time than usual, stand back, and try to evaluate the fully clothed you. The process shouldn't take long—about a minute or two at the most.

How do you really look in your clothes?

Try to be as objective as possible about the man you see in the mirror. Note your first impression. Do you look confident, knowledgeable, sure of yourself? Or do you look uncomfortable? Look at specifics, starting with the fabric of your suit. Note what color and pattern do for you. Do they make you look heavier, shorter, taller, or thinner?

Next look at how the shapes and lines of your clothes interact with your body. A jacket that is cut a little too long, for example, makes a short man look even shorter; and by the same token, a jacket that is cut too short exaggerates the height of a tall man. Wider lapels and ties look fine on a tall or thin man but tend to be unflattering to someone who is short and stocky. Take special note of how your shirt collar fits. It should not appear to be choking you. Make sure it looks well and feels comfortable.

What next? Choosing the right clothes for your particular shape and size is nothing more than finding a complimentary optical illusion. A well-put-together look highlights the more attractive parts of your physique and de-emphasizes the features that throw your body lines out of proportion.

Colors, patterns, and fabrics If you are heavy or short, lean toward pinstripe suits in dark colors. Dark colors give a more compact look, and the vertical effect of pinstripes visually narrows broad dimensions. The stripes give added stature because of their strong vertical lines. Avoid bulkier fabrics such as heavy tweeds and, instead, select suits made of smooth-surface worsteds or gabardines.

If you are tall or thin, you should avoid suits with strong vertical lines. Your clothes should create an illusion of additional width. (In suit patterns, plaids do this best.) You can wear most colors successfully, but if you are exceptionally tall and husky, you should use restraint in wearing dark colors—they can make your size seem even more overwhelming.

Suits

Suit details should also emphasize the vertical if you are short or stout. A more fitted suit jacket and straight-legged, cuffless trousers will give you longer-looking body lines. Avoid double-breasted jackets and wide lapels which broaden rather than stretch you. If you choose to have your trousers "break" at the tops of your shoes, make sure the break is minimal—too large a crumple of fabric will give you a bottom-heavy look. Keep your ties on the narrow side, and use the thinner four-in-hand knot.

If you are tall or thin, you can wear double-breasted suits to special advantage. Wide lapels and wide ties worn with the bulky Windsor knot will help balance your strong vertical lines.

About collars

When selecting shirts, always pay special attention to how the collar looks against your neck and face. If you have a long thin neck, buy shirts with high collars to bring your neck into proportion with the rest of your body. Collars with a shorter rise look best on men with short necks.

Collar styles should also be chosen to compliment your face. If you have a broad face, a collar with long collar points and a narrow spread (a small space for the tie knot) will be most flattering. For a long face, the most complimentary style is a collar with short points and a wide spread.

Paying attention to these details will ensure that when you put all the elements of your wardrobe together, you'll have a total look that displays your body in the most attractive way possible.

Color co-ordination

Coordinating clothing colors is easy if you remember that all colors can be grouped into three tonal families: warm tones, cool tones, and neutrals. Reds, oranges, yellows, and browns are warm, while blues, grays, and greens are cool tones. Black and white are neutral colors.

You can comfortably harmonize colors in the same tonal family or try for contrasts using warm and cool colors. The neutrals tend to wear with either group. For example, with a brown suit try a yellow shirt and a red and yellow striped tie, or with a blue suit go with a solid gray silk tie. It's a harmonious color look. If you decide on contrast, you will find that shades of reds and yellows work best with blues and grays. With dark browns, green is the easiest cool color to use. Lighter shades of tan and beige are versatile and look fine with blues as well as greens. Because of the almost unlimited range of color shadings, it's impossible to honestly offer specific guidelines. Thoughtful trial and error with suits, shirts, and ties will tell you what the "right" and "wrong" color combinations are in your wardrobe.

Dressing for business Your wardrobe is an important part of your personal business equipment. Clothes awareness in business attire is opening up a new profession—clothes consultants for appearance-conscious businessmen. These advisors help a man choose clothes appropriate to his occupation and status in the working world. Even though you may not be able to afford the services of one of these experts, you should take the time to consider the "right" business attire for your profession. By using your powers of observation and common sense you can act as your own consultant.

About dress codes Some organizations spell out a specific dress code that covers everything from your suit color to the style of your shirt cuffs. In other instances, it may not be so simple, but you can always be sure, no matter where you work, that there *is* a dress code—the only difference between the written and the unwritten kind is that it takes a bit longer to figure out the second one.

If your organization or business has an unwritten dress code, you should make a few notes on what people around you wear. Pay special attention to the men who seem to be going places and who may have been in the business for a few years—long enough to have picked up on all the nuances of the dress code. Begin by concentrating on the suits. Note which colors (and shades of colors) are dominant, and note the dominant suit style. Most businesses favor the American-cut suit, which is looser-fitting and has narrower lapels than the European style. Note also whether two-piece or three-piece suits are generally worn, and whether any particular patterns or fabrics predominate.

Although the tradition is dying, you may still find that among men in your field the only acceptable shirt color is white. Pay attention to the other details of your co-workers' shirts. Are button-down collars favored or perhaps French cuffs? What about fabrics? Is the bulky weave of Oxford cloth or the smoother broadcloth preferred?

Finally, take a good look at one of the most telling features of dress—ties. Notice which styles *seem* to predominate. There may be good reasons why some styles are or are not worn. It's possible that your boss has a bias against the striped rep tie, and by being aware of this, you can wisely avoid wearing that style. Pay attention to other details—briefcases, overcoats, and shoes.

Your goal should not be to slavishly imitate every "company style" you see, but to use what you discover as a guide. And keep in mind which styles and colors suit you best.

Your boss You should consider another influence on your work wardrobe—your boss. One of the facts of life is that when you dress for business you have to please three people: your boss, your client, and yourself, in that order. Your boss has the power to promote you or fire you. Dressing right can only help to reinforce the impression that you're worthy of greater responsibilities.

It helps to be aware of his clothes biases. You can pick up some of these biases from observing what he wears, but it is not necessarily wise to copy his quirks of dress. The fact that your boss happens to favor French cuffs could simply mean that he prefers formal shirts. But wearing French cuffs might also be his way of setting himself apart from those under him. He might think you presumptuous if you show up flashing *your* French cuffs. You must rely on your personal knowledge of your boss to help you avoid disastrous errors.

Your clients

When dealing with business clients, you'll always be safe if you follow the dress code of your company. When you know your client's clothing preferences, however, it can't hurt to adjust your look accordingly. For the more conservative client, darker colors—navy blue or dark gray—and a more formal three-piece suit would be appropriate. For a more relaxed business situation or one in which you want to project a softer image, lighter colors—beige or light gray—might be best.

Dressing to meet the unknown

There will be times when you won't have a clue about appropriate dress. The job interview is probably the most typical of these steps into the unknown. The best course of action is to lean toward the conservative. The standard single-breasted, American-cut, dark blue suit is probably a safe choice. Wear it with a white or pale blue shirt and a tie with conservatively colored stripes or a fine print of subdued colors. Wear black or blue socks and lace-up shoes, preferably wing-tips. Do *not* wear decorations of any kind—no handkerchief stuffed in the breast pocket of your suit, no French cuffs with gaudy cuff links, no jewelry other than a plain, functional wristwatch and your wedding band, no shoes with tassels or other decorations.

Buying clothes for business wear

Never scrimp on your business wardrobe. Buy the best you can afford in suits, shirts, ties, and shoes. This does not necessarily mean spending huge amounts of money, but it does mean knowing how to invest your money in your clothes. Well-made clothes cost more, but they look better, last longer, and help your business image.

The point is that you should take your business wardrobe seriously. You can't afford to ignore how clothes can work for you. Even if you don't pay attention to what you're wearing, others do. Since many of those people will have a direct effect on the course of your career, it makes sense to make the best possible impression.

CLOTHING CARE

Care and storage

How long your wardrobe will last depends on how well you care for it. To get the best possible return on your clothing investment, you need to make sure your clothes are being cared for and stored the way they deserve to be.

In general, there are no extraordinary steps you have to take to preserve your wardrobe—just day-to-day precautions that will pay off in the long run. Taking the time to care for your wardrobe isn't being foppish or overly fastidious—just economical.

Suits

The clothes you wear for business should get most of your attention. Consider your suit. You should brush it off each time you put it on in the morning and when you take it off at night to remove lint and dirt particles. When you hang up a suit or sports jacket, you should always use a plastic or wooden "wishbone" hanger—the sloping kind that approximates the contours of your shoulders and back. You should also take all heavy or bulky items out of a jacket before putting it away, and make sure that no pocket flaps are crumpled inside the pockets. Make a wide space in the jacket section of your closet and, when you hang up your jacket, leave it unbuttoned and leave enough space around it to let it air out. Make sure the jacket's shoulders sit evenly on the hanger and that its lapels are not squeezed or crushed.

The best way to hang your pants is without a belt and with absolutely nothing in the pockets. Use a spring-loaded pants hanger that clamps onto the bottom of the trousers; laying pants over a hanger will leave a soft horizontal crease across the trouser legs.

Let your suits "rest"

Your suit deserves a rest as much as you do. Try to wear it no more frequently than every other day, and on hot or rainy days when it gets dampened by perspiration or rain, hang it in the bathroom to dry out before you put it in your closet.

Always have your seasonal suits cleaned before putting them in storage. If the suit is wool, store it in a closet with moth crystals or, even better, in a cloth garment bag. Since mothballs do evaporate, you may have to replenish them every three or four months to make sure your clothes are getting enough protection.

Shirts and ties

Depending on your available space, you can store shirts on hangers or folded and piled in dresser drawers or on closet shelves. If you decide to hang them up, use either plastic hangers or wire hangers covered with paper to eliminate the possibility of rust stains. Shirts stored in drawers or on shelves should never be piled more than four high, because the combined weight of the ones on top will flatten the collars of the ones on the bottom. To minimize squashing problems, it is a good idea to alternate the ends at which you put the collars.

Permanent-press shirts, of course, never need starch, and you should avoid using it on all-cotton shirts as well. Starch tends to weaken the fabric of the shirt and shorten its life span. Thus, if you want to get the most wear out of your shirts, tell the laundry (or whoever does your shirts) "No starch."

Ties should be hung on a tie rack with an individual spar for each one; *don't* drape your entire tie collection over a single hook. If you're running short of room, you can drape a towel over the crossbar of a hanger and hang your ties on that.

Never hang up a tie with the knot still in it, for this will put a permanent crimp in the fabric. When you remove a tie from your neck, untie the knot. Don't pull the short end free from the knot—you'll stretch and twist the fabric. Make a point of hanging up every tie after you use it to avoid such unpleasant surprises as finding a favorite tie balled up in a jacket pocket days after you took it off. Knit ties are the exceptions to this rule—they tend to stretch out if you hang them on a tie rack. They will survive better if you roll them up and put them in a drawer.

Ties can be cleaned, but not every dry cleaner has the knack for doing it. If you have doubts about a cleaning establishment, it might be wise to try them out with a couple of expendable ties before you commit one of your soiled favorites to their care.

Shoes

Shoes get more brutal treatment than any other part of your wardrobe, but with a little attention they will usually last for years. Always polish a new pair as soon as you get them, to protect the new leather, and when you're not wearing them keep a pair of shoe trees (preferably wooden) in them to absorb moisture. Make a habit of using a shoe horn, especially with slip-ons, to avoid damaging the backs of your shoes. Give your shoes a rest every other day to let them air out (even in cold weather they absorb a lot of moisture from your feet).

The shoes you wear the most should be cleaned with saddle soap at least once a month to remove surface grime and excess wax and to soften the leather. They should also be polished regularly—once a week at least, more frequently if you are rough on shoes. Shoes with a suede finish, of course, need only an occasional brushing with a stiff-bristled brush to loosen surface dirt and raise the nap of the suede, and newer patent leathers now come with a special coating that lets you clean them with a wipe of a damp cloth.

Never let the heels on your shoes get run down too far. In addition to looking unattractive, a badly worn heel can ruin the shape of your shoe by shifting the way your body settles into it. Leather heels generally look better than rubber, but they also tend to wear out a little faster. You can slow down the erosion of leather heels by having the repairman tack half-moon-shaped pieces of hard rubber on them.

When shoes get wet   You should always give your shoes first aid when they get soaked in a rain storm or take a false step into a puddle. Since water can ruin the toughest of shoe leathers, take a few special precautions in drying out your shoes. First, sponge off excess water with paper towels and slip wooden shoe trees into the shoes to maintain their shape. (If you have no shoe trees, stuff balls of newspaper into each shoe, making sure to replace them with dry newspaper every hour or two.) Let the shoes dry in an open, airy place, and under *no* circumstances put them near a radiator or any other direct source of heat. The intense heat will only shrink and crack the leather. When the shoes feel dry, slip them on your feet and wear them around the house to reshape them. A light wipe with saddle soap and a coat of polish should revive them completely. (With suede shoes, a few buffs with a stiff brush should be all you need.)

The other item you may wear daily, your belt, needs very little attention. Since belts tend to curl at the ends when they're stored rolled up in a drawer, you are better off hanging belts by the buckles from hooks or hangers in your closet. A saddle soaping once or twice a year will keep belts supple.

Coats   Your overcoats should be cared for and stored in the same manner as your suits. Hang them only on wooden hangers and, if they are wool, put them in mothproof storage during seasons when you're not wearing them. They should be cleaned when needed and just before you store them.

Raincoats should be hung only on wooden hangers, and when they get wet should be left out to dry before they are hung in a closet. Never stuff a damp coat in the closet, or the next time you take it out you will probably find yourself with a musty, wrinkled garment.

There is no set cleaning schedule for raincoats. Lighter-colored coats will need cleaning more frequently than darker ones. When you do decide to have your raincoat cleaned, read the label first. Some coats can be cleaned in your washing machine at home and still retain their water repellency, while others can only be dry cleaned. If you have a coat dry cleaned, ask the cleaner to give it a water-repellency treatment at the same time.

Sweaters

Sweaters should always be folded, *never* put on hangers. They tend to stretch out and get deformed hanging in a closet. For mothproof protection, store your sweaters in cloth bags, or in boxes with mothballs or moth flakes. If you always fold sweaters in thirds lengthwise like shirts, you might want to try another method that makes storing and packing them somewhat easier. Lay the sweater face down; fold the sleeves over on the seams at the shoulders of the sweater; and bring the bottom hem of the sweater up to the collar. This makes the folded sweater much wider, but it is flatter and easier to stack.

If you find that a wool sweater has stretched or shrunk a bit, you can return it to its original shape by taking it to a cleaner for *blocking*. This is a reshaping process that expands or shrinks a wool sweater to a different size. Essentially, it is nothing more than laying a wet sweater on a steam board and pressing and manipulating it until it is shaped to the size you want. Crew-neck and turtleneck styles are the ones most likely to need this kind of treatment.

Leather garments

Unless you are rough on leather garments, they should last for years with only a minimal amount of attention. Leather apparel comes in two finishes—smooth and suede—and each requires a slightly different kind of attention.

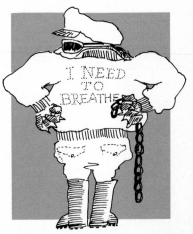

Always hang leather jackets and coats on wooden hangers, and when you store them cover them with paper or cloth to keep them dust-free and to let them "breathe" at the same time. *Never* store them in plastic garment bags, and hang them well away from direct sunlight and heat to keep them from drying out.

You can give most leather a once-a-year at-home cleaning for maintenance, but garments with special spots and stains should be taken to a professional leather cleaner. To clean a garment at home, all you need is a damp cloth and a mild soap or detergent. (This will only work on leather, not suede.) Lay the leather garment on a flat surface, wipe it lightly with the cloth, and pat it dry. Never let damp or wet leather dry near a radiator; put it in a well-ventilated room away from any source of direct heat.

To remove wrinkles, hang a leather garment (or, indeed, any other tailored garment) in the bathroom while you're taking a shower; the steam should eliminate most wrinkles. More persistent ones you can iron out: put your iron at a rayon setting, use no steam, and place a layer of heavy brown paper between the iron and the leather for protection. Press the *outside* of the garment, using quick, light strokes to avoid burning a shine into the leather.

Clothes made of shaggy-textured suede or split leather (heavy cowhide turned inside out) should be brushed regularly with a clean terry-cloth towel to remove some of the leather dust (or *crocking*) that new suede sheds, as well as dirt that may have settled into the surface.

Have suede cleaned at least once a year. You should be able to take care of most small stains and spots yourself. Whenever suede becomes water-spotted, for example, hang it up to dry and then give it a good brushing with a towel. You'll find that you can remove most other small stains with a soft gum eraser, or a chalk cleaner (available in stick or aerosol form in most department stores).

Heavily stained suede or leather that has been discolored by grease or perspiration should be handled by cleaners who specialize in cleaning these materials. If you are tempted to send one piece of a two-piece suede outfit out for cleaning, don't—send *both* pieces, because leather does change color during the cleaning process, and you will want to retain the match in your outfit.

Laundry and cleaning

The person who makes the biggest difference in the way your clothes look is the one who cleans them. That could be anyone from yourself to the man who runs the laundry around the corner—but whoever it is should be giving your clothes the care and attention that they deserve.

If you're like most men, you don't have the time to do your own laundry and will have to leave it in someone else's care. As you look around your neighborhood, you will probably find that there are two kinds of laundries: those that do all their washing on the premises, and those that send your clothes on to a central plant, where they are cleaned with thousands of other laundry loads. Although they usually cost a little bit more, the ones that do the work on the premises are better bets. The problem with the industrial-scale laundries is that they use hotter water, hotter drying cycles, and harsher detergents than most local laundries. Repeated exposure to this kind of treatment takes its toll on fabrics and eventually shortens the life span of your clothes. In addition, mass-production laundry procedures make it more likely that you'll lose some of your wardrobe sooner or later.

Choosing a good laundry

Among local laundries, the hand laundry is probably the most expensive—and the best. Laundries of this kind pay more personal attention to a customer's laundry. Next come the Chinese laundries, which are noted for the mild detergents they use. Cheapest of all are the coin-operated laundries, which charge you by the pound for washing and folding a load of clothes. For ironing they charge you by the item.

One problem you may have with *any* laundry is getting the right amount of starch in your shirts. One way to get around this problem is to buy nothing but permanent-press shirts, which need no starch. Another alternative (and a good one) is to forget about starch altogether and just have your shirts pressed. It can be to your advantage to do this, since starch not only weakens fabrics and shortens the wearing life of your shirts, but also clogs up a shirt's pores and won't let it "breathe," making it suffocatingly hot to wear in the summer (or in an overheated office).

If you are determined to have your starch, make a point of complaining if it's not right, and take the time to bring in a shirt that is over- or under-starched and explain the change you want made. If they still don't get it right, change your laundry, or start buying permanent-press shirts.

Doing your own laundry

Or you can do your laundry yourself. In spite of the array of dials and settings you see on washers and dryers, doing your own laundry is not a tremendously complicated task. To begin, sort your clothes into two piles—one for colored things and one for all-white items. If you have doubts about how to wash a particular garment, read the label—washing instructions should be there. When you wash, make sure that the wash-cycle dial is set for the appropriate fabric. Items that tend to shrink a great deal or bleed should be washed in lukewarm water.

If you plan to use bleach, never pour it onto the dry laundry—and never use it on nylon or other totally synthetic fabrics. The best time to add it is when the tub has filled with water and the clothes are wet.

Use shorter drying cycles for permanent-press garments, since too much dryer heat may permanently fix wrinkles in the fabric.

Clothes that have "wash by hand" instructions on them can often be dry cleaned, but if you have the time, you can do just as good a job at home. For your sweaters, for instance, all you need is a good cold-water soap, a towel, and some cold water. As you wash and rinse these garments, be careful not to wring or twist them, but *squeeze* them to work the soap through the fabric and later, when rinsing, to remove excess water. After one or two washes and rinses, shape the garment on a towel to dry. Never hang it up, or it will stretch from the weight of the water still in the fabric.

About dry cleaning   When you take clothes to a dry cleaner's, take them to a place that does its work on the premises. As with laundries, there is less chance with the "on-premises" place that they will lose any of your clothes, and you will probably get better service as well.

Clothing labels should tell you what to dry clean, and common sense should tell how often. Light-colored suits will probably need more frequent cleaning than dark-colored ones, and suits worn in the summer and in the grimy air of big cities will also tend to get dirtier faster. In general, you should take your suits in for a cleaning every time you feel it's necessary. Unless you are extremely hard on your clothes, don't err on the side of cleaning much more often than this—frequent cleaning will shorten a suit's life span.

Before sending any of your clothes off to the cleaner's, empty the pockets of *everything*, even the lumps of lint you find. Brush any large pieces of lint from pants cuffs, and carry a suit to the cleaners carefully folded. Balling it up might damage some of the reinforcing fabric in the shoulders and lapels.

For best cleaning results, point out stains that should get attention, and tell the cleaner the cause of the stain as well as the type of fabric that has been stained. This will make his job of selecting the right stain removal strategy much easier and increase the odds of your getting a spotlessly clean garment. Don't expect the cleaners to perform miracles with stains that have had weeks or months to set. Attend to them as soon as possible.

When you pick up your clothes, check to make sure everything was done. A well pressed suit or sports jacket should never have creases in the sleeves. Jacket lapels should have a smooth roll to them, and not be pressed flat against the jacket. Trousers should have no double crease. On double-knit trousers, the crease should be a definite one rather than a knife edge. If you asked for your raincoat to be freshly waterproofed, pour a little water on the sleeve and see what happens: if the water beads up, you've got rain protection, but it it soaks into the fabric, you've just paid for something that wasn't done. Make as many clothing checks as you can while you're in the cleaning establishment. Any deficiencies you find should be corrected before you leave. If they refuse, find another cleaner's.

It's a sure sign that you have found a quality cleaning establishment if they are willing to do a few extras for you. Although the tradition is disappearing, some cleaners will sew on buttons that came off during the cleaning process, make minor repairs on jacket linings without charge, or even stuff the sleeves of your suit jacket to retain their shape. If you find a cleaner like this, he's worth whatever you're paying him. Hang on to him at all costs.

Time may heal all wounds, but it also sets all stains. For that reason, you should attack all stains soon after they occur. Regardless of what's caused the stain, the first step is always to blot up or scrape off as much of it as you can. What you do after that depends on a number of variables.

Removing stains

You should be able to cope with most stains at home, but there are certain instances in which stain removal should be referred to a professional. If you don't know what kind of material the stained garment is made of or the substance that caused the stain; if a stain or stains are spread over a large area; if the material is silk, satin, leather, or suede—take your problem to the cleaner's. If the stain was caused by paint, fingernail polish, or any medicine, or if it's a blood or egg stain that has set, also take it to a professional to be on the safe side. Any stain problems other than these you should be able to handle yourself.

As a general rule, before you use any stain-removal concoction on a fabric, always test it on an inconspicuous part of the garment—the tail of a shirt or an unexposed inside seam, for example—before going ahead and treating the stain. If you find that there is some damage to the fabric or that the colors run, take your problem to the cleaner's.

You will find that all stains are of three general kinds: greasy, nongreasy, and combination stains that have both greasy and nongreasy materials in them. Appropriately enough, there are also three stain-removal strategies: dry for greasy stains, wet for nongreasy stains, and a dry/wet combination for combination stains.

The dry technique for greasy stains gets its name from the fact that it uses no water, but cleaning fluids or powders instead. Powders are sprayed or sprinkled over a stain, preferably while it is still wet. Let the powder sit awhile to absorb the stain and, once it has dried, brush it off; more than one application may sometimes be necessary. There are many powder cleaners available in drugstores and department stores.

Greasy stains

When you use cleaning fluid, you'll need a white towel to put under the stained fabric and a sponge or some absorbent material to apply the fluid. Place the fabric inside out on the towel. Barely dampen your sponge with fluid, and work from the center of the stain to its edges to avoid forming rings in the fabric. It is best to go over the stain several times, using just a little bit of fluid each time, to ensure that you won't leave any traces of fluid in the material. If either the white towel or your cleaning pad pick up some of the stain, make sure to change them to avoid restaining the material by accident.

Nongreasy stains   For nongreasy stains, such as those from alcoholic beverages and fruits, warm water and a gentle soap should be all you need. On washable fabrics, wash the spot with cold water first and then lightly rub with a cloth dampened with a detergent solution and rinse the fabric. For tannin (vegetable matter) stains like coffee or liquor, ammonia solutions work well while for albuminous (animal matter) stains like blood and egg yolk, vinegar solutions are more effective.

Combination stains   In attacking a combination stain, such as lipstick, always try the dry method first and then the wet one. When you are working on any stain, be extremely careful not to leave telltale rings behind. (This can be a real problem with solid-color or smooth-finish fabrics.) Try to blend your cleaning ring with the surrounding fabric by sponging the edge of the stain area with the fluid or detergent. In some cases, you'll find that a powder cleaner will also wipe out the edges of rings.

Other tips   If a stain is deeply set in a heavy fabric, you may be able to break it up by rubbing the area, using short, light strokes, with the edge of a stainless steel spoon. If the fabric is delicate, dampen the stained part of the fabric with cleaning solution and roll it between your thumb and forefinger.

Another tactic you can use with hard, crusted stains is to put a towel under the stained area of the fabric and place an absorbent pad soaked with the appropriate cleaning solution on top. Let it sit and soak until the crust begins to soften, and occasionally pick at the edge of the stained area lightly with your fingernail to help break it up.

A cleaning tool that may help in treating stains is one of those small, round-headed brushes used to apply shoe polish. Get one with a wooden handle so it won't react to chemicals, and with nylon bristles that will stay stiff even when wet. This kind of brush can be used effectively on stubborn stains that have soaked into smooth-surfaced, closely woven fabrics. Spread the fabric over a hard surface and hit the stained area lightly with all the bristle tips, with the same force you use in tapping home a tack. Do this very lightly with delicate fabrics.

When treating stains, you should take the precaution of laying the fabric on something that is not likely to be affected by cleaning fluids and solutions. Covering a table top with aluminum foil, or laying the fabric over a heavy glass dish, is a good way of protecting your household effects.

You don't need an arsenal of exotic cleaning fluids to cope with most stains and spots. Having a few special-purpose fluids or solvents on hand will help, but generally you can get by with ordinary household chemicals. You will be very well equipped to deal with stains if you have:

- A liquid dishwashing soap or mild cold-water detergent.
- A bottle of household ammonia that has no color or added fragrance.
- Peroxide bleach. (Always spot check peroxide bleach on an inconspicuous part of the garment.)
- White vinegar.
- An enzyme presoak.
- A powder cleaner.
- A liquid grease solvent.

You will also need a large bowl, a white towel, a sponge or clean cloth, paper towels, a stainless steel spoon, and one shoe-polish brush. Thus equipped, you're ready for the attack.

For the sake of your clothes, always use the utmost caution when working on stains. Make it a matter of routine to spot-test your cleaning solutions. Even though you may know what caused the stain and what kind of fabric the stained garment is made of, it is still possible that the dyes in the fabric will run, creating a bigger mess. When using the combination cleaning method, always let the cleaning solvent fully evaporate from the fabric before proceeding with the wet part of the cleaning; otherwise you could create another stain. Read carefully all instructions and warnings on presoaks and commercial cleaning solutions before using them on your fabrics, and never smoke around flammable substances such as grease solvents. The following chart should give you some idea of how to tackle the common stains you are likely to confront. Since different strategies are often necessary with washable and nonwashable fabrics, the chart has been divided accordingly.

There are a few recipes you should know before tackling a stain. A "detergent solution" refers to half a teaspoon of detergent diluted in one quart of warm water. An "ammonia and detergent solution" is the same thing with a tablespoon of ammonia added, and a "vinegar and detergent solution" is one that has a tablespoon of vinegar added. Unless otherwise indicated, an "enzyme solution" is a quart of warm water with one tablespoon of a presoak added, and peroxide bleach is usually diluted with an equal amount of water before use.

Stain removal at a glance

Home guide to stain removal

Stain	Washables	Nonwashables
Alcoholic beverages (beer, wine, whiskey) and soft drinks	Daub with plain water if stain is fresh, but if spot resists your cleaning efforts try a detergent solution. If spot still persists, then try a detergent and ammonia solution and use peroxide bleach for any remaining stain. For beer stains, soak 30 minutes in enzyme solution. Note: Some fabrics, such as silk, can be permanently discolored by alcoholic beverages. In these cases there is simply nothing you can do.	Daub with vinegar and rinse.
Perspiration	Try plain water first, then soak or sponge thoroughly with detergent and ammonia solution. Peroxide bleach applied with an eyedropper may remove final traces of stain. Note: If the color of the dye has changed in the stained area, daub a one-to-one solution of ammonia and water on the stain and rinse. This is safe for delicate fabrics such as wool and silk.	Apply a few drops of ammonia and rinse.
Ballpoint ink	Daub with solvent. Rub with soap and wash if stain remains.	Daub with solvent. Send to dry cleaner's if stain remains.
Blood	Proceed as for perspiration.	
Butter, margarine	Daub with dry solvent and let dry. Wash.	Daub with solvent.
Candle wax	Scrape off excess. Sponge remaining stain with cleaning solvent.	
Catsup	Daub with dry solvent first, let dry. For the remaining stain try a detergent solution and, if stain persists, a detergent and ammonia solution.	Dampen area with a solution of half a teaspoon of presoak and a half a cup of warm water. Let stand and rinse with cool water.
Chewing Gum	Scrape off excess and daub with cleaning solvent. If stain persists, send to the cleaner's.	
Chocolate	Proceed as for catsup	

Stain	Washables	Nonwashables
Coffee, tea	Proceed as for alcoholic beverages.	
Cosmetics (including lipstick)	Daub with cleaning solvent	Send persistent stains to cleaner's.
Cream	Proceed as for perspiration	
Egg yolk	Proceed as for perspiration. If stain has set, send to the cleaners.	
Fruit juices	Sponge area immediately with cold water. Daub with white vinegar if the stain has dried. Then…	
	Presoak and wash.	Send to the cleaner's.
Grass stains	First daub with solvent and let dry. Then soak in a detergent and vinegar solution. Use hydrogen peroxide for stubborn stains.	Sponge with cleaning fluid and let dry, or use cleaning powder.
Gravy	Use the combination cleaning method (see page 000).	
Grease, oil	Use the dry cleaning method (see page 000).	
Mayonnaise	Use the combination cleaning method (see page 000).	
Mildew	Launder thoroughly and use hot water and a strong bleach if the fabric permits. Where stain remains, moisten with a mixture of lemon juice and salt. Spread in the sun to dry and rinse.	Send to the cleaner's
Mustard	Scrape off excess mustard carefully and daub with cleaning solvent or powder. Where stain persists daub with a detergent and vinegar solution.	
Pencil marks from lead or colored pencils.	Rub gentle with a soft eraser to remove marks. If marks persist.	
	Dampen stain with soap then rinse. Repeat this using a few drops of ammonia for really stubborn stains.	Send to the cleaner's
Shoe polish	Daub with dry cleaning solvent and send to cleaner's if stain persists.	

Ironing   There may come a time when you suddenly discover that you forgot to send one of your all-cotton dress shirts to the laundry or that the press in your permanent-press shirt is no longer permanent, and you have no time to send it out. When this happens, you need not panic as long as you have access to an iron and some kind of flat surface on which to iron.

For best results, take shirts right out of the washer and iron them while they're still damp. If a shirt is already dry, you can dampen it with one of those pump-spray misters used to water plants. Use a dry iron—no steam—and use whatever setting is appropriate to the fabric.

An ironing board is always a convenient thing to have, but an acceptable substitute is any flat area covered with a towel (for padding) and then with a sheet (to create a smooth ironing surface).

When you do your ironing, start with the yoke of the shirt and go from there to the collar, doing first the inside of the collar and then the outside, always pulling it taut as you iron. Do the back, the sleeves, and then the cuffs, ironing the latter in the same way as the collar.

The front comes last. Start on the button side of the shirt, and be careful to iron *around*, not over, the buttons. There are usually grooved indentations on either side of the toe of the iron that accommodate the edge of a button and allow you to iron under it. As you do the buttonhole side of the front, take special pains in pressing the placket—that strip of fabric in which the buttonholes are centered. When you do the front of the shirt, iron from the collar on down.

For a slightly crisper look with all-cotton shirts, use a little bit of spray starch on the front of the shirt. To avoid scorching the starched cloth with an iron that may be too hot, put it at one setting lower than the one recommended for cotton.

Wrinkles in suits   Minor wrinkles in a suit will usually steam out if you hang the suit in the bathroom while you take your shower. Ordinarily you should leave the wrinkles that persist to a professional, but if you are pressed for time, you can do some emergency ironing on a wool jacket or a pair of wool slacks yourself.

You will need an iron and a pressing cloth (anything from a clean towel to a piece of a sheet). Set the iron for wool and for steam or—if you do not have a steam iron—dampen the pressing cloth first. Always use some kind of protective cloth when ironing wool to keep the fabric from direct contact with the hot iron. If you don't have some kind of buffer between the two, you may very well singe the wool and leave a telltale sheen behind.

Don't iron by leaning on and pushing the iron. Instead, lightly lower the steaming iron over the wrinkled spot. Move along the surface of the wool, following the grain of the fabric, gently raising and lowering the iron over the wrinkles. Let the steam, not brute force, do the work. When you're finished, you may not have a suit that looks as though it's just come from the cleaner's, but it should be an improvement over the prune-textured garment with which you started.

Sewing on buttons

Sewing on a button is a simple and basic repair skill. You should learn it—because, like it or not, there will be times when you'll face the problem.

Basic equipment is very simple. Almost any small sewing kit available in the drugstore or the five-and-dime should contain everything you need—a selection of needles and a variety of threads in the most common colors. Or simply buy a package of needles and some individual spools of thread. White, navy blue, black, and brown may be all you'll need.

It's always best to sew a button back on a garment as soon as possible after it pops off. At the very least, drop the button in an envelope and mark where it belongs. If you don't, there's a good chance you will either lose the button or forget where it goes.

To do your sewing, choose a needle about an inch and a half long with a medium-sized eye. Select a thread of approximately the same color as that on the remaining buttons of your shirt, jacket, or coat. Unroll about a foot of thread, cut it, and lick one end to a point. Poke the thread through the eye of the needle and continue pulling it through until you have a double thread hanging from the eye. Tie the two ends together with a loop knot.

Shirts

Starting from the back of the fabric, poke the needle through one of the holes where the original thread was. Pull the needle through, and string the button on the needle and thread. Make sure the correct side of the button, the concave side, is facing you. As you stitch on a four-hole button, cross the needle over to the hole that is *diagonally* opposite. Make three or four stitches across the diagonal with the last stitch ending behind the fabric. Then make the same number of stitches across the opposite diagonal. The stitches should form a small X. This will anchor the button securely to the cloth.

After you have made the X, push the needle through the button without drawing it through the fabric. Wind the thread three or four times around the stalk of threads connecting the button to the shirt. Then push the needle on through to the back of the fabric. Draw it tight, make two tight knots, and cut it.

Jackets and coats

Sewing on a jacket or coat button is only slightly different. Use a stronger, heavier silk thread, and pull it only a little way through the eye of the needle so that you essentially have a single strand of thread.

Knot the long end. Make four or five runs through each of the button's holes, this time making stitches that parallel each other. Before finishing the last stitch, hold the button away from the fabric and wind the thread around the base three or four times as you'd do when sewing on a shirt button. Push the needle through the fabric, make a securing knot in the back, and then snip the thread. *Voilà!* Your button is back where it belongs.

Care of specific fibers

To do an intelligent job of caring for any garment, you must first find out exactly which fibers have been used in its composition. An astonishing variety of natural and manmade fibers and fiber blends are used in clothes today and it's worth your while to have at least a passing familiarity with the techniques for handling each of them.

Start by reading your clothing labels. These will tell you not only the fiber content of the garment, but also how to care for it. By law, nearly every piece of wearing apparel sold must have a care label which indicates the best way to clean it. Instructions vary from a terse two or three words to an elaborate, step-by-step guide to laundry care. Legally, no label may recommend dry cleaning for a garment that can just as easily be machine washed at home. But labels in garments made of colored or printed fabrics are *not* legally required to warn you against using chlorine bleach on the clothes, because it's assumed that most people know not to do this. (In fact, whenever you plan to use chlorine bleach it is a good idea to spot test it first on inconspicuous parts of your garments.) This goes to show that you must pay attention to what labels don't say as well as to what they do.

A garment made of a fiber blend should be treated as if it were made of the blend's most delicate fiber. When you wash a shirt made of a cotton-and-polyester blend, for example, avoid using bleach—polyester is sensitive to bleach, though cotton is often not. When drying and ironing this shirt, use moderate heat; pure cotton will withstand intense heat, but polyester will wilt or even melt at high temperatures.

Making sense of the variety of names given to clothing fibers is not as complex a task as it may at first appear. Many of the labels you see on synthetics, for example, are just manufacturers' trade names. There are only two basic kinds of fibers: natural and manmade. All manmade fibers can be further divided into two groups: cellulosic—produced from the plant fiber cellulose; and "pure" synthetics—fibers such as nylon that were born in laboratory test tubes. Every fiber falls into one of these categories.

Natural fibers

Cotton is probably the most common and most versatile of all the natural fibers. It is durable, cool, and comfortable to wear, and a 100-percent-cotton garment with good color retention can be machine washed with hot water and bleach. Since it wrinkles easily, cotton also needs a high-temperature iron setting.

Linen, made from the stem fibers of the flax plant, is an excellent fabric for summer jackets and slacks because it is cool and highly absorbent. Unfortunately, it also wrinkles very easily, and it is losing some of its popularity to less cool but wrinkle-free synthetics. Linen can be machine washed like cotton, but dry cleaning does a better job of retaining its shape.

Silk, the elegant, lustrous fiber, is more popular for its looks than for its practicality. Although it is usually simpler to dry clean silk, some silk garments can be washed by hand *if* their labels say so. Use a gentle, cold-water detergent, and *never* twist or wring silk garments when washing or rinsing—always squeeze. You can have a professional cleaner press silk after you've washed it, or you can do it yourself with a dry iron set at a medium temperature. Iron silk on the wrong side of the fabric only—and be careful—silk is very delicate.

Wool comes in two general forms: woven woolens, as in suits, and knitted woolens, as in sweaters. Woven woolens should be dry cleaned unless the label indicates otherwise. Knitted woolens may be either dry cleaned or washed by hand in cold water. Wash knitted woolens as you would silk garments, and shape them down on towels to dry. *Never* use chlorine bleach on any washable wool garment.

Manmade fibers—cellulosic

Acetate is made from cotton and wood pulp. It is woven into fabrics to make them soft and fast-drying. Sometimes used in shirts and slacks, acetate is usually dry cleaned, although there are a few instances in which acetate garments may be hand washed in warm water and then ironed on the wrong side with a cool iron. You may see it under the trade names Acele, Celaperm, Celanese, and Estron.

Rayon is a silken fabric often used as a material for linings, for ties, and, blended with polyester, for suits and pants. It is a delicate fabric that is usually dry cleaned. Hand-washable rayons should be hung on

Manmade fibers— synthetics

a plastic hanger to dry and should be pressed while still damp with a moderate iron on the wrong side of the fabric. Rayon goes under the trade names Avril, Enka,, and Zantrel.

Triacetate is a variation of acetate that is usually machine- or hand-washable and must be ironed at a high temperature. It is highly wrinkle-resistant and is often used in blends in flannel, jersey, and sharkskin fabrics. Arnel is its trade name.

Acrylic is a soft, featherweight fiber that, when knitted, has the look and texture of wool. For that reason, it is often used in sweaters and socks by itself or in a wool blend. More delicate acrylic garments should be washed by hand. When you machine wash acrylic garments, use warm water and low drying temperatures. Never hang acrylic garments up to dry because the fiber stretches when wet and can never be made to regain its former shape and size. The most common trade name for acrylics are Acrilan, Creslan, Orlon, and Zefran.

Modacrylics are synthetic fibers commonly used in fake furs. Modacrylic furs should either be dry cleaned or fur cleaned. Dynel is the modacrylic trade name.

Nylon is the oldest manmade fiber, and one of the most versatile. Most nylon articles can be machine washed in warm water and machine dried at low temperatures. A warm iron setting will press out the wrinkles. You'll find it under a variety of brand names, including Actionwear, Antron, Enkalure, Monvelle, Qiana, and Ultron.

Polyester is another adaptable synthetic that is highly durable and wrinkle-resistant, and thus it is often blended with cotton. It is also often blended with wool fibers for suits to give them a smooth finish and durability. Tailored polyester clothes should be dry cleaned, but other garments can usually be machine washed in warm water and dried at moderate temperatures. (Remember that this synthetic is quite sensitive to heat.) Common trade names for it are Avlin, Dacron, Kodel, Fortrel, and Trevira.

Spandex is an extremely soft, lightweight, and elastic synthetic often found in bathing suits, ski pants, and support hose. It can be washed by hand or by machine in lukewarm water, but should never be machine dried and may only rarely be ironed because it is so heat sensitive. You may know it under the names Lycra and Lastex.

A primer on fabrics and weaves

It is always to your advantage to have some knowledge of fabrics and fabric terms—if only so you can describe to a salesclerk what you want and/or ask intelligent questions about clothing material.

Knowing a few basic facts about fabrics should also help you to make some sense of the variety of names and terms you hear used so often. The simplest way to sort out fabrics is to remember that they are usually either *knits* or *wovens*. Knits are materials formed from interlocking loops of yarn. Wovens are materials formed when two lines of threads heading at right angles to each other are joined by being run over and under each other. Among knits, there are two general kinds: weft knitting and warp knitting. **Weft knitting** is a machine version of hand knitting in which a single strand of yarn runs across the width of the fabric, forming a horizontal row of interlocked loops. In **warp knitting,** the interlocking loops run the length of the fabric. All knits are variations of one of these two.

Similarly, there are only three basic ways a fabric may be woven: with a plain weave, a twill weave, or a satin weave. The **plain weave** is the most basic. In it, the horizontal thread, or *filling* yarn, runs under or over each vertical thread, or *warp* yarn. In the **twill weave,** the filling yarn goes under and over two or more of the warp threads at a time, giving the fabric surface a distinct texture of diagonal lines. The **satin weave** is similar to the twill weave in that the filling yarn also skips over and under two or more warp threads at a time. It raises the warp threads from the surface of the fabric and gives it the distinctive luster that satin has. All fabric weaves will be variations of one of these three.

In addition to being described by the types of knits or weaves of which they are made, fabrics may be described according to their surface textures. The chart that follows, while hardly all-inclusive, will acquaint you with some of the more common fabric terms and give you a brief description of each.

A guide to fabrics and weaves

Fabric	Appearance	Use
Batiste	Sheer, finely woven cotton or cotton blend fabric.	Shirts
Broadcloth	Tightly woven cotton or cotton-blend fabric with a fine, ribbed texture.	Shirts
Challis	Named after the American Indian term "sha-lee," meaning soft, this is an extremely soft, plain-weave fabric with a faintly ribbed texture. Woven from fine wool or cotton thread.	Ties, shirts, sweaters
Denim	An extremely sturdy twill-weave fabric of cotton or cotton blend with a solid color warp and a white filling yarn.	Jeans, shirts, suits, jackets
Double-knit	A weft-knit fabric made on a machine that uses two sets of needles. The result is a fabric that looks the same on both sides.	Suits, jackets, slacks, shirts
Faille	A lightweight fabric of silk, polyester, or rayon woven in a variation of a plain weave that has a slightly ribbed effect.	Ties and lapel facings on tuxedos
Flannel	Any smooth-surfaced fabric with a slight nap to it concealing the weave. Usually wool, a wool blend, or cotton.	Suits, slacks, jackets, casual shirts
Foulard	A twill weave of a lightweight silk or rayon; usually a patterned fabric.	Ties, handkerchiefs, scarves
Gabardine	A compact twill weave of wool, wool blend, cotton, cotton blend, or synthetics such as polyester and rayon.	Suits, jackets, topcoats, raincoats
Harris tweed	A trademarked woolen material spun, dyed, and woven by hand by islanders in Harris and other islands of the Outer Hebrides, Scotland.	Suits, jackets, topcoats
Herringbone	A distinct woolen twill weave in which a zigzag effect is created by alternating the direction of the twill.	Suits, jackets, topcoats
Hopsacking	A basket weave of wool, cotton, or other fabrics; copied from the burlap sacks of hops pickers.	Jackets, slacks

Jacquard	An intricately knitted or woven fabric with a raised motif of figures.	Shirts
Jersey	A weft-knitted fabric with a plain, not a rib, stitch; may be of a variety of materials, including wool, cotton, acrylic, silk, polyester, rayon.	Sweaters, shirts, underwear
Oxford cloth	A modified basket weave of cotton or cotton-and-polyester blend. May be all white or may have a colored warp and a white filling yarn.	Shirts
Poplin	A tight plain-weave material with a ribbed or corded texture; of wool, cotton, silk, polyester, fiber blends.	Suits, jackets, top-coats, raincoats
Seersucker	A cotton or cotton-blend fabric with a puckered finish created by alternately loosening and tightening warp yarns.	Suits, jackets, slacks
Serge	A twill-weave, smooth-surfaced fabric made of a smooth, sturdy worsted yarn of wool, cotton, or fiber blend.	Suits
Shantung	A plain-weave silk with an irregular nubby texture. It gets its name from Shantung, China, where the weave originated.	Suits, jackets, ties
Sharkskin	A smooth-surfaced material made of a twill weave of two tones of yarn; usually with a faint luster. Used in worsted wool for suits and topcoats, in acetate and triacetate for sportswear.	Suits, topcoats
Tricot	A warp-knitted fabric using a rib stitch and usually made with synthetics such as nylon and polyester, and manmade fibers such as rayon.	Beachwear
Twill	A general name for any fabric with a distinct diagonal cord in its texture. The best-known example of this is cavalry twill, an extremely rugged fabric used in trousers.	Suits, jackets, slacks
Woolen	A fabric term used to describe garments made of coarse wool fibers that give the fabric a fuzzy nap. Tweed is a typical woolen fabric.	Suits, jackets, slack, ties
Worsted	A general term for yarns that are tightly twisted and extremely smooth. It is also used to describe fabrics made from these yarns and is used to differentiate smooth-textured wool suits from the shaggier woolens (see above).	Suits, jackets, slacks

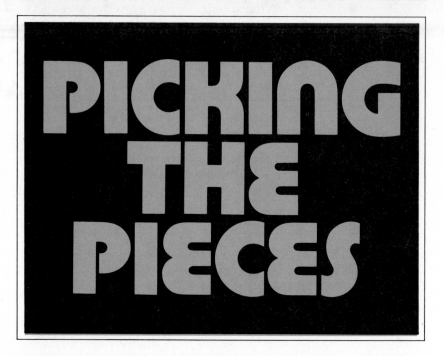

PICKING THE PIECES

Wardrobe necessities

A good wardrobe is adaptable. By leaning toward the more consistent styles and relying on what have become men's fashion classics—items such as the blazer and the trench coat—you'll end up with a selection of clothes that can survive fashion's shifting trends.

A heavyweight suit is an example of an item you don't need in a basic wardrobe. Offices are so well heated that heavy tweeds and other wools are unnecessary. When you have occasion to go outside in winter weather, you'll always have your overcoat to keep you warm.

You should also avoid double-knit suits. All but the most expensive tend to bag at the elbows and the knees. If you already have a basic suit wardrobe and want to add to it, you'll be better off buying a suit made of natural fibers or a natural fiber blend.

Many major elements of a good wardrobe can be used interchangeably. For example, a blazer—probably one of the most versatile wardrobe items—can be worn with the pants from a year-round gray suit or lightweight poplin suit. The fully cut jacket of a tweed suit can double as a sports jacket and, for that matter, the jacket of a navy blue blazer-style suit can itself be used as a blazer. Other elements, such as a vest, may also be added or subtracted for a formal or informal effect. How you use the pieces will really be limited only by your imagination and sense of style.

The following list is a guideline to clothing that can form the foundation of a businessman's wardrobe.

Suits—all single breasted
Priority purchases
1 Solid navy suit, lightweight, with blazer-style jacket
1 Medium gray flannel suit, lightweight (it has great mix-and-match possibilities)
1 Poplin suit for warm weather wear
Optional purchases
1 Dark blue three-piece pinstripe suit in tropical worsted or polyester blend for more formal occasions.
1 Medium weight tweed suit for winter wear

Sports Jackets
1 Lightweight navy blue blazer

Slacks
1 Pair of gray flannel slacks
1 Pair of tan summer-weight slacks
Optional purchases
1 Pair of tan cavalry twill slacks
1 Extra pair of summer-weight slacks, preferably gray

Shirts
2 White shirts (one broadcloth, one Oxford cloth)
4 Blue shirts (broadcloth and/or Oxford cloth)
2 Pinstripe shirts (one blue stripe and one maroon stripe)
2 Yellow shirts (broadcloth and/or Oxford cloth)
Optional Purchases
2 Shirts in the patterns of your choice (plaids or bold stripes)

Ties—one for every shirt; they should offer a good mix of:
Solids (at least two—blue and maroon)
Small polka dots (at least one)
Paisleys
Stripes

Shoes
2 Pairs of lace-up shoes (one brown, one black)
2 Pairs of slip-ons (one brown, one black)

Socks—all over-the-calf
4 Black
4 Navy blue
4 Brown

Coats
1 Camel's hair or blue wool overcoat
1 Tan trench coat

Shopping for suits

The American cut (top) and the sleek European cut.

Regardless of how big or small your wardrobe is, the single most important element in it will always be the suit. Whether you like it or not, the suits you wear are part of your outward personality. Other people scan them to get a fix on everything from your status and attractiveness to how competent you are professionally. The suit is a powerful and eloquent article of clothing, and for that reason buying one is something that demands some special attention on your part.

Before you ever set foot in a clothing store, you should work out as specific a picture as possible of the kind of suit you will want. If you already have a working wardrobe, the chances are you plan to replace a suit that you're ready to retire to the Salvation Army. In this case, the decision process is fairly simple—you already know the color, style, size, and material of the suit you'll need. If you're in the process of building a wardrobe, you may have a specific notion of the color and pattern you want but be undecided about the kind of styling you're after.

Whatever your situation, you have a choice of two general suit styles: the American cut and the European cut. The American cut is distinguished by sloping natural shoulders, a loose-fitting jacket, and moderately wide-notched lapels, so called because they have a V-shaped indent where the collar meets the lapel. The European cut is a more dramatic fit with higher, tighter armholes, padded shoulders, a jacket that narrows in at the waist, and peaked lapels, lapels that flare out at the tips. In either style, you will have the choice of single- or double-breasted models.

Suit material is available in stripes—either thin pinstripes or the wider chalk stripes; plaids; solids; and tweed patterns such as herringbone. Fabrics typically used are wool, wool-and-polyester blends for lighter-weight suits, synthetic double-knits, and cotton and linen (for summer wear.)

Suit jacket styles: a two-button, a three-button, and a double-breasted jacket.

Do you want a vest? If so, do you want one with five buttons or six? Do you want trousers with or without cuffs? These are all things to consider before you venture into a store. You also have a choice of a variety of pocket styles on your suit jacket. Most common are flap pockets; if you want no flap, there is the less common *besom* pocket. On European-cut suits you may have a choice of either patch pockets, pieces of cloth sewn to the outside of the jacket to form pockets, or hacking pockets, flap pockets tilted at an angle. There is also the sporty look of the bellows pocket, which has folds on its sides and bottom to make it expandable. This was adapted from the roomy pockets of shooting jackets.

To get the most out of your suit investment, your best bet is to be conservative in both color and style. For example, you may find that that stylish double-breasted suit you bought can be a real nuisance to wear because it only looks good when it's fully buttoned—thus you look fashionable in it but you're hot and uncomfortable as well. If you select a suit with a moderately conservative cut, the odds are you'll be able to wear it long after this year's latest fashion is out of date. If you're tempted to take the high-fashion plunge, stop a moment and remember the Nehru jacket.

Once you've sifted through the possible style alternatives and decided what you want in a suit, the next step is to get dressed up for your shopping trip. Put on your best-fitting suit and the shoes you expect to wear with your yet-to-be-bought new suit. Wear a belt or carry one with you, and make sure you take all the items—pencils, pens, datebook, wallet, eyeglasses case—that you ordinarily carry in your suit when you go to work. If you usually wear shirts with French cuffs to work, wear one on your shopping trip; and put on the kind of tie you envision yourself wearing with your new suit. Dressing up like this will serve two purposes. It will probably get you better service than if you walked into a clothing store wearing jeans, sneakers, and an old shirt. And it gives you something to compare the fit and feel of a new suit with.

Tell the salesperson in the store *exactly* what you're looking for in a suit—size, style, color, weight—everything that is important to you. This will make it easier for him to wait on you and will keep you from wasting time looking at suits you don't want. After the salesperson takes you to the rack of suits that are your size, ask to be left alone. This way you can go through the suits at your own speed, without the distraction of sales chatter. If, after a thorough check of the store, you see nothing you like, leave immediately. That way you remove yourself from the temptation to buy something you don't really want.

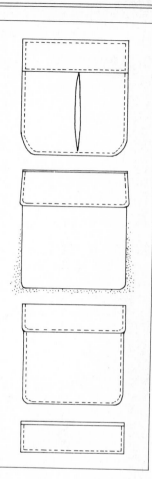

Different pocket styles (above) let you vary the look of your jacket. When you're wearing a vest (below), leave the bottom button undone.

Doing a quality check

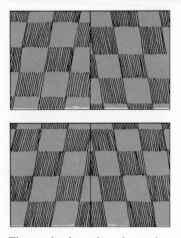

The mark of good workmanship in a patterned suit is the match along the seams. In poorly made suits (top) this detail will be ignored, but in a quality garment (below) the pattern is carefully matched at the seams.

When you do find what you like, do your own personal quality check on it. Turn up the collar and examine the stitching joining it to the rest of the suit. Nice even stitches indicate that the suit is machine sewn. Slightly uneven or irregular stitches are a sign that it is hand sewn and of slightly higher quality. There are other signs to look for. Check to see whether the buttons are bone or plastic and whether they're sewn on securely. Look at the inside of the jacket. Better jackets are fully lined, usually with rayon or silk. Examine workmanship where the sleeve lining joins the body of the jacket at the armpit. A good job of stitching here means the lining won't be hanging in rags within a year.

Now take a good look at the outside of the jacket. Squeeze the lapels and see if they spring back to their original shape without a wrinkle—if they have enough interlining they will. Turn the jacket around and examine the vent or vents in the back. Vents should be properly aligned and hang even with the edge of the jacket.

If the jacket is made of a patterned material, check the way the suit pattern is matched on the seams. Nothing will scream "cheap" more clearly than a sloppy match of fabric pattern; it indicates that the suit-maker was more interested in scrimping on fabric costs than on making a suit well. If you spot this defect put the suit back on the rack and forget about it, no matter what else it may have going for it.

After you've examined the jacket, take a close look at the trousers. There should be enough excess material to let out the crotch if necessary. Roll the waistband between your fingers—you should be able to feel some reinforcement in it. Reinforcement will keep the band from rolling over the top of your belt when you're wearing the pants. The trousers should also have a second button tab inside the fly, just below the waist button. This will give you more support, a better fit, and take some of the strain off the waist button. Finally—a small point—the fly zipper should be plastic, not metal, and should be in a color that matches the suit.

There is one last test that you may prefer to do when a salesperson is not around, since it can be a real heart-stopper for him. Take a sleeve of the suit in your hands and twist it hard for about a dozen seconds or so, then release it. If the sleeve springs back without a wrinkle, consider buying the suit. If the fabric stays puckered and twisted, put the suit back on the rack and quietly leave the store. You have just saved yourself a few hundred dollars in cleaning and pressing bills.

Trying on a suit

When you come upon a suit you like, try on the jacket while you're still out on the showroom floor. If you wear French cuffs you may discover that the sleeves of the suit are too narrow to permit you to stick your arm all the way through. You may also find that your usual suit size does not fit you in this particular style. This sometimes happens with different cuts—you shouldn't hesitate to go one size up or down to get the correct fit. Once you find a jacket that fits and you like what you see in the mirror, ask to try on the pants in the fitting room.

One thing to remember while you are having *any* clothing fitted: let your body relax and settle into its natural posture. That's the way you'll be wearing your clothes, and that's the way you should be fitted. Unless your normal posture is ramrod stiff, do not stand up straight no matter what the tailor says.

Once you're in the fitting room, the pants come first. After you pull them on, put your belt on and transfer into the pockets everything you normally carry: loose change, car keys, and so forth. Put on your shoes. You're ready for a fitting.

The correct fit for the waist of suit pants is fairly high up on the body, slightly below your navel. Unaltered, the pants should hit you at about this point. If they ride way above or below that general area, get out of the suit. No amount of tailoring will ever make it fit you correctly.

As the tailor fits the pants, make sure he pins alterations in place rather than just marking them with chalk. This will give you an immediate feel of how the pants will fit. Check the waist. It should be snug but not so tight that you have a difficult time slipping the flat of your hand between you and the trousers. The seat should lie smooth and flat without feeling too tight. And if the crotch is too baggy have the tailor pin in the alteration, making sure to tell him on which side you "dress"—that is, near which leg your penis hangs. You will need a little extra fabric there to be comfortable.

Pants bottoms are the last part of the fitting. Whether you choose plain or cuffed bottoms is strictly up to you. As guidelines you might want to remember that cuffless bottoms look better with heavier fabrics and give someone who is on the short side a longer, sleeker look. Cuffs, on the other hand, help a lighter material keep its press and hold the shape of the leg. If you decide on no cuffs, have the pants tailored so that they hang one-half to one inch longer in the back than they do in the front. There should be only the slightest break on the shoe. Cuffs should hang perfectly straight all around and just brush the top of the shoe.

With the alterations set, give your pants a workout. Stoop, sit, walk around a bit, and see how they look in the mirror. When you are satisfied that they hang and fit well, try the next part of the suit, which will be the vest if there are three pieces.

You'll get a much better fit if you wear a shirt of the same thickness

Suit Glossary

Notched lapel
Conservatively cut lapel with a V-shaped indent where the collar meets the lapel

Peaked lapel
Usually found on double-breasted blazers and some European-cut suits, this lapel flares out dramatically to two sharp points

Suiting
The fabric out of which a suit is made

Flap pocket
The most common kind; this pocket is inside the suit with a flap of suiting material covering the opening

Hacking pocket
Essentially a flap pocket set at an angle to accentuate the lines of the suit. Copied from hacking jackets, hence its name

Besom pocket
An inside-construction pocket that has no flap. It makes for a cleaner, sleeker appearance

Patch pocket
A pocket made by stitching a piece of cloth to the *outside* of the suit

Bellows pocket
A pleated pocket that can be expanded to hold more. Adapted from the cartridge-carrying pockets of shooting jackets

Custom-made suit
A suit fitted one piece at a time to the body of its prospective owner

Semicustom-made suit
An entire suit made up from someone's measurements and later altered to a correct fit

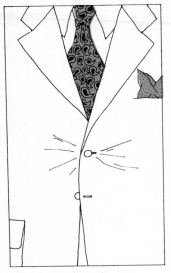

A distinct X-shaped crease in the front of your buttoned jacket is one sign of a fit that's much too tight.

you would ordinarily wear with a vested suit. When the vest alterations are done, check to see that the vest does not sag when you sit or stand.

Last comes the suit jacket. If the trousers and vest are all bunched up with pinned alterations, take them off and put on the suit pants you wore to the store. Put on the jacket, making sure to transfer to its pockets all the items you usually carry around. If the tailor objects to the bumps and lumps these items cause, simply tell him to take those shapes into consideration as he alters the jacket.

The first item that will get attention is the collar. Step in front of a three-way mirror and, without twisting or straining your neck, notice how the collar sits. It should lie flat against the back of your neck and allow about half an inch of shirt collar to stick up.

Any lumps or wrinkles in the collar will have to be corrected, and since this can only be done by removing and reattaching the collar, a difficult tailoring job, your fitter may object. He may suggest simpler alternatives—a nip here, a tuck there. Insist on the collar change. Those nips and tucks will probably do nothing but produce more bumps and lumps. Suggest the tailor use a temporary basting stitch in fixing the collar so that if further adjustments are necessary in the next fitting, they can be done without much difficulty.

Moving down from the collar, check the fit of the jacket in the chest and back. Too loose a fit will make the lapels sag in front and create a vertical crease up the middle of your back. Too tight a fit in back will create a distinct horizontal crease.

Next, button your top button if it's a two-button suit, the middle one on a three-button model. Radiating out from this button will be a faint crease in the form of an X. A sharp, definite X crease means that the jacket fits too snugly around the middle. As another check for fit, sit down and see if the jacket bulges or pulls anywhere.

Length of the jacket is crucial. To find out if it's right, let your arms hang straight by your sides and curl your hands. The bottom edge of

Signs of a well-fitted suit are (1) a collar and (2) cuffs that reveal no more than half an inch of shirt collar and shirt cuffs; (3) pants that break slightly at the shoe, (4) a jacket hem that settles into the curl of your cupped fingers.

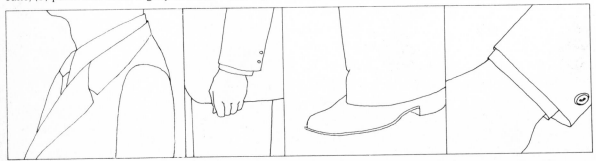

the jacket should settle snugly into that curl. If the hem is noticeably above or below the curl, start looking for another suit, because this one will never look right on you.

Finally, check sleeve length. The sleeves should stop roughly five inches from the tip of your thumb and allow about half an inch of shirt cuff to show, regardless of whether you wear French cuffs or barrel cuffs. Showing more cuff than this may make you look like a Mississippi riverboat gambler.

It should take at least one more fitting to get the kind of tailoring you want. Even if they have your suit neatly boxed and ready to go when you return to the store, insist on trying it on. This will give you the opportunity to see if they made all the alterations you requested and did them to your satisfaction. It will also give you the opportunity to evaluate the suit with a keener eye and possibly turn up some finer alterations that need to be done.

Do the second fitting the same way you did the first. Start with the pants, looking at the waist, seat, crotch, and the way the cuffed or cuffless bottoms settle. Make sure the vest fits snugly, and check the collar, chest, back, length, and sleeves of the jacket.

No matter how minor the adjustment—even if it's just sewing on a loose button more securely—ask that it be done before you accept the suit. If the store is reluctant, insist on it. If they still balk, get your money back and leave them with the suit. Their job is to provide you with a suit that fits. If they cannot or will not do that, they don't deserve your business.

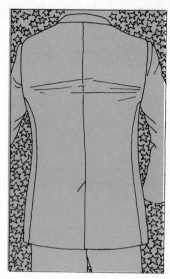

Distinct horizontal ripples across the back of a jacket indicate that the fit is too tight. Definite vertical ripples, on the other hand, indicate a loose fit.

Custom-made suits

It may happen that for one reason or another, you are one of those people who just cannot get a decent fit with an off-the-rack suit. If appearance is very important and you have a lot of money to spend, you may want to consider the custom-made or "semicustom" suit. The difference between the two is in price and quality.

The custom-made suit is the most elegant and expensive option. The process is long—the suit is fitted piece by piece to your body—and expensive—costs typically run from $500 to $800. Since it is an option very few people can afford, this is all we will say about it.

Less costly but still expensive is the semicustom-made suit. You go to a tailor, leaf through a book of fabric swatches, and choose one for your suit. The tailor then takes all your important suit measurements and has an entire suit made up in his shop. Several fittings later, you will have your semicustom-made suit at a price that may range from $350 to $600. For those who have spent fruitless years in and out of men's clothing stores looking for the perfect fit, this is probably the only alternative.

Sports jackets   Give a little thought to how you'll be wearing your jacket before you go shopping for one. Choice of fit, style, and fabric will all be influenced by whether you plan to have a jacket do business and social wear duty, or plan to restrict it to one of the two. In most situations a sports jacket is considered too informal for business wear; if it is considered acceptable in your particular line of work, your best bet is to lean toward the conservative look in both style and material. If you have casual plans for your sports jacket, you're going to have more latitude in your choice of color and material.

Whatever you end up choosing, the same criteria for quality and fit that you use in buying a suit apply. Check the workmanship of the garment and, after putting it on, the fit of the collar and chest, making sure the lapels lie flat and smooth. Look for the telltale creases of a loose or tight fit in the back; check the length of the sleeves and the overall length of the jacket.

As you did when trying on suit jackets, load up your pockets just before the fitting with what you expect to be carrying in them. If the jacket you are shopping for will be worn casually with a sweater, be sure to wear that same kind of sweater to get a fit loose enough to accommodate it.

The kinds of styling and details in a sports jacket are essentially the same as those of a suit. Generally there will be the looser, natural-shoulder fit of the American style and the more closely tailored look of the European cut. For comfort's sake you might want to choose a single-breasted jacket, although the double-breasted may be all that is available in certain styles and fabrics that you particularly favor.

When you're shopping for a patterned jacket, wear the trousers you hope to wear with it. This may save you the added nuisance and expense of shopping for a new pair of trousers if you get the jacket home and find that it doesn't quite match.

The classic blazer   A blazer is the most versatile jacket you can buy. It probably should be your first choice if you don't already have one. It can be worn the year round if it is a lightweight wool-and-polyester blend. And it can be used as informal evening wear and in less formal business situations. Although blazers are available in various colors, the traditional navy blue model with gold or silver buttons is the one to get.

The blazer has remained a classic since it was designed in 1850 by the captain of the H.M.S. *Blazer*. The captain, a man with a sense of style, was dissatisfied with the motley appearance of his crew's various outfits. To correct this, he ordered that blue serge jackets with gold buttons be made for each man. The blazer went from there to become a favorite wardrobe item of the yachting set and has since passed on to the general wardrobe.

Next in popularity and versatility is the standard single-breasted tweed jacket. It comes in a variety of patterns, such as herringbone and plaid. Again, the more quiet colors will blend in best with the business look in a wardrobe if that's your intended use. The one big limitation with these is, of course, a strictly seasonal one. Fall and winter will be the times this jacket can be frequently worn, a factor you may want to consider if you are rounding out your basic wardrobe.

If you've decided to use your tweed jacket strictly for casual wear, you'll have a much wider range of styles to choose from. One of the more common ones is the hacking jacket, modeled along the lines of the English riding jacket. Usually made in a houndstooth check wool, it has European-style fitting, is nipped at the waist, and has a high single vent in the back. To complement its lines, its flapped pockets are inserted at an angle, giving the jacket a distinct flair. As a touch of authenticity the better copies come completely equipped with a wind tab behind the left lapel, which is meant to be folded over and buttoned with the tab in foul riding weather. If you're not a member of the horsey set, this jacket will make you look as if you are.

The Norfolk jacket is an item designed for the lord of the manor. The name comes from the Norfolk district of England, where the Earl of Leicester was the first to wear the jacket (at around the turn of the 20th century). Although there are variations, the basic design has a yoke of fabric on the shoulder, a long vertical pleat on either side of the front, and a third pleat down the middle of the back. A belt of the same material as the jacket buckles in front.

The Earl had pleats built in to give him a lot of freedom of movement as he hunted grouse and pheasant on his 43,000-acre estate. The belt he found handy for making the jacket fit tightly around the middle and keeping out the damp and chilly early morning air. Now this design has been modified so that one pleat is still found in the back and the belt is just a band of fabric around the middle of the jacket.

For a real splash of color you'll have to return to the blazer and some of the extravagant fabrics and colors available for turning it into a strictly casual jacket. You can get it in kelly green, red, and even snow white linen. There are also blazer jackets in startling patterns of Indian madras, and in shantung silk, lush velours, soft supple suede, camel's hair, cashmere, and Ultrasuede®. If you choose one of the more colorful versions, always remember to wear it with quieter colors to enhance its stunning effect.

Tweed jackets

Glossary

Hacking jacket
A tight-fitting tweed jacket, usually a houndstooth check, modeled after the British riding jacket.

Norfolk jacket
A casual tweed jacket usually featuring a yoke on the shoulder, a pleat down the middle of the back, and at least the suggestion of a belt around the middle.

Slacks

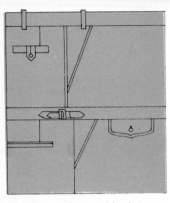

A clean, uncluttered look in pants details is preferable.

Color is the secret to getting the most out of the money you invest in slacks, especially those you plan to buy for dress. Basic solid colors in muted shades of gray, blue, and tan will blend best with your wardrobe. Simplicity is also important in determining a style that will last. Pants featuring gimmicks such as buckles, zipper pockets, or embroidered designs will usually not make it through the fashion year, and will leave you right where you started in building your wardrobe.

Although some slacks can be used interchangeably for either dress or casual wear, there are some slight differences between them. For one thing, dress slacks are traditionally fitted like suit pants—high on the waist, with the waistband circling the body just below the navel. They also tend to have more conservative details, such as the vertically cut pockets (called onseam pockets) also typically found on suit pants, and pleated fronts (which add a fullness to the front of the pants; this looks appealing on pants worn by thin-waisted men).

The same fitting procedures that apply to suit pants apply to dress slacks. Request that all alterations be pinned so that you can make some kind of judgment about how the trousers will feel. Once the alterations are set, do your pants-testing exercises—walking, sitting, stooping. Wear to the fitting the shoes that you plan to wear with the slacks in order to make sure the pants hang properly at the bottom. Again you have the choice of cuff or no cuff, and the suit rules for fit apply here too.

None of us would ever have to concern himself with the detail of cuffs if King George V of England hadn't been so concerned about getting his pants dirty. It seems that the king, who was a trend setter in his day, had been invited to speak in a park. His approach to the speakers' platform was blocked by an enormous puddle, and the only alternative open was to walk through it. To keep the bottoms of his pants from getting soiled, George turned them up and then waded to the platform, where he duly gave his speech. As he forgot to turn the bottoms of his pants legs back down before approaching the podium, his audience noticed the upturned trouser bottoms, thought they looked quite smart—and before long, they had become part of men's fashion lore.

Colors and patterns

If your new pants are to be worn with a certain jacket, wear the jacket when you shop. You'll be taking too much of a chance if you try to match colors or patterns strictly by memory.

The traditional fabrics for dress slacks are the loose, soft flannels; the tightly woven gabardines; and the crisp cavalry twills. Double-knit synthetics are also coming into their own as an alternative group of pants fabrics.

For a more casual touch for your slacks, you might want to eliminate the belt altogether and replace it with a cloth tab in the front and side tabs to adjust to your waist size. In fact, with slacks that will be worn strictly for casual living, the features you can choose will be much more numerous. As with the sport version of the blazer, you have a wide choice of fabrics: madras, suede, velours, cashmere, camel's hair, corduroy, denim, just about anything. If it's possible to make a pair of pants out of any fabric, there's a good chance someone already has.

With casual slacks, the fit will be lower and closer to the hips, and the styles of the pants legs themselves will become more varied. Generally, casual slacks styles will come as straight legs, as flares (in which the leg gets somewhat wider toward the bottom), and as bell bottoms (the more exaggerated version of the flares). Taller and thinner men usually benefit more from the horizontal emphasis bell bottoms and flares give their body lines, while short, heavyset men look better in the straighter leg styles.

Another detail that deserves some of your attention is pockets. Some of the tighter-fitting European-styled slacks, for example, come with only one rear pocket—or none at all. Other pants pick up the western-style front pockets and the rear patch pockets found on jeans. And then there is what could be called the fatigue look, which features flapped and buttoned patch pockets in the rear and two similar pockets attached to the front of each pants leg just above the knee.

What have without question become the favorite of all casual pants are blue jeans. What were once good tough work pants made of a cheap, heavy blue cotton have now become a fixture in casual wear. The baggy blue pants are gone and have been replaced by a wide variety of tight-fitting, well-tailored styles that many people would not dream of dirtying by wearing for doing manual labor. The jeans look has influenced the cut and style of just about all casual pants, and jeans themselves have gone from being part of the counterculture uniform to being the preferred weekend and vacation wear of just about everybody.

Getting a pair is no longer a simple matter of heading on down to your local Army-Navy store and buying whatever they have on the shelf. Most of the major jeans manufacturers have their own stores that sell nothing but jeans and jeans-style pants. Now when you walk into a jeans store, you'll have to choose among different weights and blends of denim, denims exposed to a variety of fading and preshrinking processes, and dozens of variations on the old blue jeans

Glossary

Gabardine
A tight weave of smooth cotton or wool.

Cavalry twill
A heavy weave of cotton or wool with a diagonal texture.

The fit of casual slacks

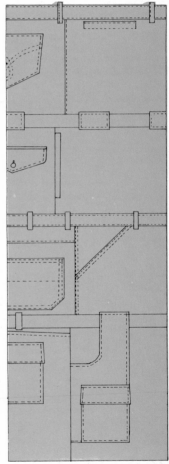

style. For help in finding your way through this fashion maze, you will find a chart on page 174.

Shirts

Since your shirt size can change long after you've stopped growing, shirts can sometimes be a little tricky to buy. All ready-made shirts are sized by the circumference of the collar and the length of the sleeve measured from the nape of the neck to the tip of the cuff. As you gain or lose weight, or even as you grow older, your collar size in particular may change. For that reason, you should be measured for your shirt size at least once a year.

Collar size is usually measured on the neck at a point just below the Adam's apple; sleeve size is measured from the bony bump at the base of your neck to the point where your wrist joins your hand. Once you've found your right size, how a shirt will fit will depend largely on the style you choose. With standard, looser-cut shirts there should be three to four inches of extra play around your waistline. If you choose the tapered look of the European-styled shirt, there will be much less looseness—these shirts closely follow the line of the torso all the way down to the waist. They look good on slim-waisted men but tend to look a little strained on heavier men.

Another detail that influences both comfort and appearance is the number of buttons. Look for shirts with seven buttons running down the front. The bottom button should fall far below the waistline to help keep your shirt tucked in and to keep the shirt from spreading open just above the belt line.

As far as fit and style go, the collar is probably the most important part of the shirt. Generally, it should fit close to the neck but not so close it looks as if the shirt is choking you, and certainly it should not fit so loosely that it looks as if your collar and tie are dangling from your neck. The slope of the collar—how high it sits on your neck—will also make a difference in how well or poorly the shirt looks on you. High-slope collars look best on men with elongated features and long necks, while low-slope collars are more complimentary to the man with a thick neck or a large, round face. The third style, medium, suits the average man just fine.

The style of collar you choose should be influenced by the shape of your face and neck, the style of knot you prefer in your tie, and the cut of your suit. Basically, there are five shirt-collar styles to choose from.

The **standard collar** is the most common design. Its point (measured from the collar tip to the neckband) is usually about three inches long. This is the most adaptable design, and it looks best with a tie with the standard four-in-hand knot. Equally versatile is the

Glossary

Collar slope
The height of the collar on the neck; there are three variations: low, medium, and high.

Long-point collar
A long-lapeled collar that goes well with Continental suits and large. round faces.

French-style collar
A short collar well suited to large tie knots such as the Windsor.

Point
The distance from the neckband to the tip of the collar.

Spread
The distance between the collar tips.

Barrel cuffs
Cuffs that button; they fit more snugly than French cuffs.

French cuffs
Double-folded cuffs that require cuff links for fastening.

Broadcloth
A tightly woven, smooth-surface shirting fabric.

Oxford cloth
A rough weave of fabric that uses alternating white and colored threads.

Batiste
A light, sheer fabric ideal for warm-weather wear.

button-down collar. It goes well with just about any suit style, any face shape, and any knot you care to tie.

The **long-point collar,** which usually measures four to four and a half inches long, goes best with the extravagant lapels and the dramatic cut of European-style suits. Because of its elongating effect, it looks flattering on men with large or round faces. Those with elongated features should avoid it. Because of its relatively small spread (amount of space between the tips of the collar), it looks best with a four-in-hand or half-Windsor knot.

A collar that is complimentary to the man with elongated features is the **French-style collar,** which has short points and a large spread that will accommodate the bulk of the large Windsor knot.

The last style you will commonly see is the **tab collar,** given that name because the collar tips are pinched behind the tie knot by two snap tabs or a collar pin. While this is not for the man with a short thick neck or a large face, it is suitable for all others.

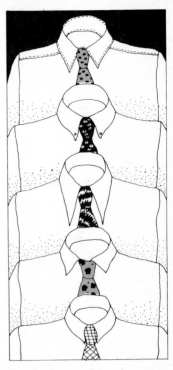

Regular, button-down, long-point, French-style, and tab collars (top to bottom).

Another feature to check for in a shirt is cuff style. If you prefer barrel cuffs—that is, cuffs that button—make sure that there are two buttons to give the end of the sleeve a smoother look. For a dressier appearance, you can chose French cuffs, double-folded cuffs fastened with cuff links.

Removable collar stays are another handy shirt feature. If you buy a shirt with these, make sure that you remove them before sending the shirt to the laundry—otherwise they'll be melted permanently to the fabric by the heat of the iron.

It is generally best to stick to solid colors when buying shirts. White and blue are the most popular, and, on occasion, a pale yellow will make a pleasant change. For more variety you can also buy stripe patterns, preferably pinstripes, and plaids—the fainter the better. Your shirt should be simply background for your suit and tie, so try not to let the colors and patterns get out of control.

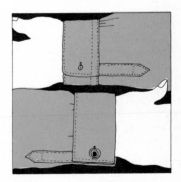

The barrel cuff (top) and the dressier French cuff.

Shirt fabrics may be natural, manmade, or blends. Natural fibers such as cotton are extremely cool and comfortable, but wrinkle very easily and can cost their weight in laundry bills. Synthetic shirts stay neat, but they tend to be too hot. Polyester-and-cotton blends are the best choice since they offer some of the coolness of cotton as well as the wrinkle resistance of the synthetics.

You'll find that the most common kinds of shirting fabrics are broadcloth—a tightly woven, smooth-finish fabric with a suggestion of ribbing in its texture; Oxford cloth—a rough basket weave of alternating white and colored threads (commonly used in button-down shirts); batiste—a sheer, lightweight fabric ideal for summer wear; and knits, usually of cotton and polyester, which have a soft look to them.

Ties   People habitually take sociological readings from the clothes you wear, and they pay special attention to your ties. They will look at your tie for clues to what kind to taste you have, how fastidious you are, how sophisticated you are, even what kind of personality you have. What the well-chosen tie does is give off nothing but positive readings. You control these, for you can assure that your ties are flattering to you. It's worth your while to spend a little time shopping for ties—and, since you're the one who will end up wearing them, you should always choose them yourself.

When it comes to choosing ties, follow this rule: buy conservatively for business, buy what you want for sports wear.

As you are giving a tie a quality check, look for a feature called the bar tac, a horizontal tacking stitch on the back of the larger end of the tie. This is put there to keep that end from spreading open, and it should be neatly stitched, with no material pulled or bunched. Inside the small end of the tie look for slip stitching—this was used to shape the tie after it was reversed. (All ties are made inside out and then reversed.) If you can't find this, chances are it isn't properly made.

Another quality check is to hold the tie at midpoint and see how it hangs. If it doesn't hang straight but swivels slightly, it's usually an indication that the outer fabric is too tight for its lining. Since it is a defect that cannot be corrected, don't buy a tie that does this.

Finally, check how the tie knots. If it is made of a thin fabric such as a lightweight silk or polyester, it should have enough lining to give it bulk so that when you tie it you don't get a tiny little knot. If the salesman will let you, and a salesman in a good store should, try an experimental knot in a tie that you suspect may be a little bit too thin.

Most ties range in length from 54 to 56 inches, and they will fit differently on your body depending both on your height and on how much fabric you need to knot your tie. Once it's knotted, the tip of your tie should just hit the top of your belt line. The simplest way to find your length is to carry along a tie that fits and measure it against those you are considering.

Width is another feature that will merit your attention. Ties currently measure from four to four and a half inches at their widest points. The right width for you will depend on your build and the style of suit you wear. The narrower tie widths look better on short men and with suits with moderate to narrow lapels. Wider styles are suitable for tall and

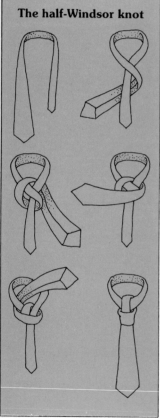

The half-Windsor knot

husky men and with suits with wider or extravagant lapels.

When you go tie shopping, the basic tie fabrics you will have to choose from are silk, silk-and-polyester blend, polyester, acetate, rayon, cotton, and wool. If the tie is rayon or acetate, reject it out of hand. These synthetics tend to pucker and wrinkle after just a little bit of wear and are seldom worth the money.

The best tie material is silk because it is easy to knot, and it looks luxurious and rich. Since a good silk tie is expensive, some good alternatives are silk-and-polyester blends or good polyester ties that look like silk.

Silk and silklike ties come in a variety of fabrics; the most common is foulard, a featherweight weave of silk that usually requires a substantial bit of interlining to give the tie enough bulk to make a good knot. Foulard is usually found in patterned ties only.

There is a heavier regular weave that is used in solid-color silk ties and is usually the kind of material that has a faint sheen, which adds a tone of richness to the tie. Since it is a heavier material, it is easier to tie than the foulard tie—and it can also be a little more expensive.

Other fabrics that may use silk in them include shantung, which is made of irregular yarns that give the tie's surface a nubby, irregular texture; grenadine, a loosely woven fabric of lightweight silk with an irregular surface; and faille, an extremely soft fabric with a faint ribbing effect in its surface texture. There is also the silk crochet tie (usually reserved for relatively formal wear); this features a bulky machine-made or hand-knitted fabric.

Wool is probably the next best choice for tie materials, and it commonly comes in two kinds of fabrics: challis and woven fabric. Challis is a lightweight material usually found in both patterns and solids. It is so closely woven that it is sometimes mistaken for a silk tie. Of a slightly coarser texture is the woven wool tie; this is a more seasonal item, since it goes best with the bulky look of winter tweeds.

For summer and warm-climate wear, cotton ties are usually a good choice, especially if you want the lighter, summery colors. These are relatively inexpensive and, of course, should be chosen to coordinate with your lightweight suits.

The general selection of patterns for ties for business wear include solids, stripes, regimental stripe or rep ties, club ties, Ivy League prints, polka dots, paisleys, and plaids. Solids are usually a safe buy, especially if you've taken care to buy well-made, expensive (or expensive-looking) clothes. Although some fashion experts recommend against it, wearing a solid tie with a solid suit and plain shirt does

Glossary

Bar tac
Horizontal stitch used to keep fabric in place at the large end of a tie.

Slip stitch
Shaping stitch used in small end of a tie

Foulard
Lightweight weave of fabric commonly used in silk ties

Shantung
A weave of irregular yarns that gives the tie fabric a coarse, nubby texture

Faille
A soft, faintly ribbed weave often used in silk ties

Challis
A tight, closely woven fabric used in fine lightweight wool ties

Rep tie
Any tie with diagonal stripes that is made of a rib-weave fabric

Regimental stripe tie
Once distinct from the rep tie, but now practically the same thing; originally a striped tie carrying the colors of a British gentleman's old army regiment

Paisley
A colorful design that looks like ornate microbes swarming over the fabric; adapted from an Indian print pattern

Club tie
Generally, a blue tie with repeated patterns of heraldic devices or sporting symbols

Ivy League tie
A tie patterned with a small geometric pattern that may be simple or very detailed

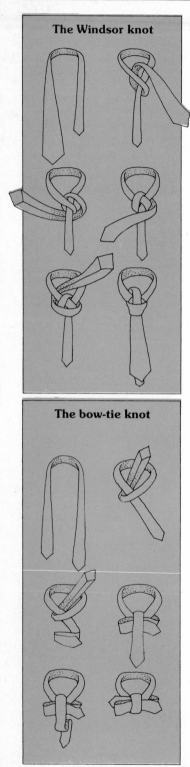

The Windsor knot

The bow-tie knot

give you a crisp, pleasant appearance. If you are just starting your tie wardrobe, basic solid colors such as blue and a dark rich red are always good buys. Don't buy black unless you are going to a funeral, and avoid white ties—they soil too easily.

Among patterned ties, the diagonal stripe is probably the most common. It is variously known as the rep tie (so named after the distinct diagonal weave of the fabric it uses) and the regimental stripe tie. The regimental tie has been copied from the English, who wore the colors of their old army regiments on their ties.

In choosing a striped tie, pick one that is subdued in both the width of its stripes and its colors. It should have at least one color in it complimentary to your suit, which is the color leader of your wardrobe. For example, a green, blue, and brown tie could be worn in pleasant contrast to a gray suit; a tie with a reddish brown stripe could be used to pick up that brown thread of color running through your suit.

Another common tie pattern is the club tie, traditionally a repeated pattern of insignia (such as small heraldic devices) against a solid field. As with the regimental tie, this once was a kind of badge of membership among an exclusive group of men—in this case, members of the same club, whose insignia was stamped on the tie. Now there are more club ties than clubs, and the patterns are usually a repeat of some sporting symbol that can be anything from crossed polo mallets or tennis rackets to tiny pictures of your favorite breed of hunting dog. In general, the smaller the design, the better the look—and the more versatile the tie. This kind of tie goes best with solid shirts or shirts with extremely subdued patterns.

More conservative than the club tie is what is sometimes called the Ivy League tie, a pattern of small, evenly spaced geometric shapes sometimes with internal designs of their own. Usually printed on silk, the pattern gets its name from that part of society steeped in the family tradition of Ivy League schooling. Regardless, you'll find this an attractive and adaptable item to have in your wardrobe. When matching it to your suit, take your color cue from the dominant background shade of the tie.

Equally conservative and attractive is the polka-dot design. Remember that the smaller the dots, the more conservative and elegant the look of the tie. Larger dots should be avoided, since they tend to verge on op art and get a little too overwhelming.

For a slightly sportier but still acceptable look, try a tie with a paisley pattern—but *keep it subdued*. Although the pattern gets its name from Paisley, Scotland, where it was first mass-produced on cloth, the ornate little squibs of color originated in Kashmir, India, where the women used the repeated pattern on their shawls. Although this kind of tie might be a little too colorful for an extremely formal business meeting, a dark paisley print, preferably on silk, is acceptable for routine business wear. The variety of colors in it make it an excellent tie investment—it may go with several of your suits—and it can also be worn on more casual occasions.

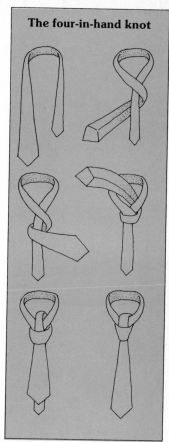

The four-in-hand knot

The last category of patterns you will find in ties are plaids. For winter wear they come in heavy woolen woven ties, and for summer, cotton is the preferred fabric. Because of their bold effect, plaids go best with the subdued look of gray flannel in winter and the lighter-colored solids of summerweight suits.

When it comes to buying a specific tie, it is usually a good idea to have on the suit you plan to wear it with. While there are no ironclad rules as to what tie to wear with what shirt and suit, you are generally pretty safe wearing solid ties with patterned shirts or patterned suits, and patterned ties with solid shirts and suits that are either solid or have just faintly visible patterns. Once you get a sense of your style and taste, you can make your own rules.

You have a choice of three knot styles for your tie: the Windsor, the half-Windsor and the four-in-hand. The **Windsor** knot is used to fill the space between wide-spread collar points, and you need lots of fabric to tie it. Make sure you buy the longer ties if you favor this knot. For standard-spread shirt collars, the **half-Windsor** is more appropriate; it should also be used with lighter-weight foulard silk ties to add bulk to the look of the knot. For heavyweight fabrics and for small-spread collars like the tab, the **four-in-hand** is ideal. If you have a heavy face, to give a more streamlined look to your neck and collar area, avoid the bulkier tie fabrics as well as the bulky Windsor and half-Windsor knots.

Because it is such an odd piece in a man's tie wardrobe, the bow tie deserves a section all its own. It is a most schizophrenic item of neckwear—in the daytime it is considered strictly casual wear, usually not for business, but at night it is the required item for formal occasions. For reasons that could form the basis of a sociological study of attitudes about ties, people seem to have a definite aversion to a man who wears a bow tie as part of his business attire. If you do buy one for casual wear, the rule of thumb is to make the bow as wide as the distance between your eyes.

The formal bow tie is an elegant piece of cloth usually made of black satin, crepe satin, or velvet. This bow is available in a clip-on model or a tie-it-yourself model, and the latter usually looks better. Unless you frequently go to formal dinners, the bow tie will not be a significant part of your wardrobe.

Belts   The simplest thing to remember about buying a belt for your business wardrobe is that if you think it is going to be noticed at all, don't buy it. The belt should be an inconspicuous, functional part of your attire, not a focuspiece by itself.

No one should wear a belt two inches or wider for business—this goes double for stout men. A wide strip of leather just draws attention to your middle, while a big fancy buckle not only looks out of place with a business suit, but tends to interfere with the fit of the vest of a three-piece suit, causing the vest to bunch up at the bottom or to get caught behind the buckle. Some men have problems with *any* belt they wear with a three-piece suit. If you are one of them, you may want to take the drastic step of removing your belt altogether and replacing it with a pair of suspenders. They will be covered up by your vest and give you a smooth fit around the waist.

Shopping for belts   Every good belt will have five holes; the size of the belt is measured from the middle hole. Since a pair of heavy pants or a heavy shirt and pants combination can add an inch or two to your normal waist measure, always try a belt on the pants for which you are choosing it. The only other thing you have to worry about is whether the belt fills the loops of your pants comfortably. Too tight a fit will eventually start tearing them out. Too loose a fit will mean that the belt will slide up and down your waist when you wear it.

Sport belts come in a variety of materials and colors. Most common these days, at least with jeans, are the wide, big-buckled belts made out of tough, long-lasting saddle leather. A more ornate variation on them are the western, or cowboy, belts with fancy designs tooled into the leather, and perhaps silver and turquoise buckles.

For resort wear, there are lighter versions such as the "rope" belt, a rope-textured elastic cord with leather ends; woven straw belts, which compliment the cool whites and tans of summer clothes; and the sportier look of the colorful nylon elastic belts that go so well with tan trousers.

There is one other style that has become very popular in recent years. For lack of a better name it could be called the "golfer's look;" this is a white vinyl or leather belt usually measuring two inches wide or more. It is usually worn with brightly colored trousers of the kind favored by many professional golfers. The only men who should observe fashionable precaution in wearing these bright white belts are those who have large waistlines—that is, 36 inches or more. Since the brightness and the width of the belt tend to highlight a man's middle, it looks best on men with slim waists and broad shoulders.

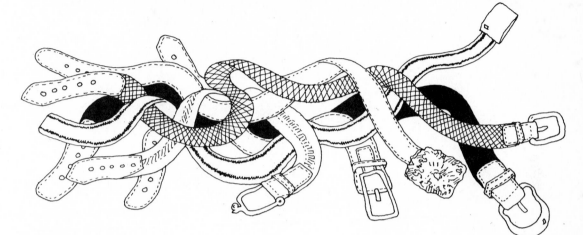

Shoes

Your feet are complicated examples of bioengineering. Each one is made up of 26 bones and a network of muscle tissue, nerves, and blood vessels—all of which has the job of carrying around your whole body weight for the duration of your life. In fact, experts estimate that in the lifetime of the average person, his feet will carry him a distance that is roughly equivalent to two trips around the world. For that reason alone, your feet deserve the best you can give them in footwear.

Ensuring a proper fit

Common-sense preparations will help you get the kind of fit and look you want in a shoe. To ensure a proper fit, wear socks of the same thickness you plan to wear with your new shoes. Also remember that feet tend to expand during the day as you walk around; this is especially true if you wear looser-fitting loafers or slip-on shoes. Therefore, don't wear slip-on shoes when you go shoe shopping (*unless* that's the style you plan to buy), or you may wind up getting shoes that will be a little bit too big. It is, however, a good idea to plan your shopping trip for later in the day when your feet have expanded to their normal daytime size.

Whatever you wear or whatever you're looking for, always make sure to ask the clerk to check your size. A person who spends a lot of time on his feet as part of his job sometimes finds that his foot size increases by as much as one whole size over the years.

Finding your size abroad	
Shoes	
American and English	**Continental**
7	40
8	41
9	42
10	43
11	44
12	45

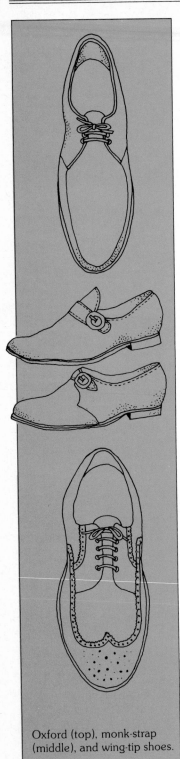

Oxford (top), monk-strap (middle), and wing-tip shoes.

When you get the shoes, put both on and as you take them for their trial spin around the shoe store floor, notice the general feel of them. Trust your instincts. If they feel at all tight or uncomfortable, don't buy them. If you're *tempted* to buy them, think of that not-quite-right pair of shoes you may have gathering dust in the back of your closet at home.

The fit is whatever is comfortable for your foot. Henry VIII had his shoes made twelve inches wide in the toe for relief from his painful spells of gout. Toe room, in fact, is critical to a good fit. Your big toe should be at least half an inch from the tip of the shoe, and there should be ample room to wiggle your toes comfortably. Your small toe should feel snug in the shoe but not cramped. (Your heel should have a similar feeling of snugness, without the sensation that the edge of the leather is cutting into your tendon.)

As you walk, notice where the shoe creases on the top. If the crease is too far back from the base of your big toe, this could mean blisters in the future. With higher-heeled shoes and boots, the weight of your body will force your foot deeper into the shoe with each step, so make sure, as you walk, that you have enough toe room.

If you are in doubt about the fit but really do like the shoes, take them home for an overnight test—but make sure to restrict your walking to carpeted areas where the soles won't get scuffed.

Because heel heights often vary, it's not a bad idea to wear the pants you plan to wear with your new shoes when you go shopping. If the heels of your new shoes turn out to be lower than those you usually wear, the bottoms of your pants may swallow up your foot and drag on the ground; if the heels are higher, your pants bottoms will dangle unattractively somewhere around your ankles.

You should consider getting leather heels on your shoes, since the leather heel is more attractive than a block of black rubber. Unfortunately, leather heels also wear more quickly, an economic factor you may want to consider.

Follow your instincts when it comes to shoe style. If they don't look as good on your feet as they did in the window, try a different style or a different shoe store. You can always come back for a second look.

For business wear, you should stick to conservative lace-ups. Among lace-up shoes, the most common style is the plain-toed oxford (so called because it was once the favored footwear of students at Oxford University in England). This is essentially a plain, round-toed shoe with three or more eyelets for the laces. It comes in a variety of leathers and textures, the most common of which is the **cordovan**

shoe, made from the heavy, almost indestructible leather that comes from the rump of a horsehide.

The **brogue** is the next most common lace-up style. It is a heavy, sturdy, low-heeled shoe that usually has an additional piece of perforated leather covering the toe in the approximate shape of a bird's wings. Commonly known as the **wing-tip,** it is now a standard part of nearly every businessman's wardrobe.

The slip-on shoe is generally considered to be too casual for work, but one accepted slip-on style is the **monk-strap shoe**—essentially a plain-toed shoe that fastens across the instep with a buckle and strap. There is also a slip-on that comes with elastic sides that give a snug fit. This often mimics the toe design of the oxford or the wing-tip shoe and blends in with business wear fairly easily.

A current business status symbol is the Gucci-style loafer. Created by the Italian shoemaking firm of the same name, the shoes are elegant, thin-soled loafers with a moccasin-style toe, crafted out of soft leather. The trademark of the genuine Gucci loafer is a distinctive brass decoration on the front of the shoe. The style has been much copied and is quite popular in the larger metropolitan areas of the country. In more conservative business circles, however, the style is considered something of an affectation.

Generally speaking, the businessman's footwear should come in one of two colors—black or brown—and should be free from gimmicks: no exaggerated high heels, no fancy decorations, no dazzling two-tone designs.

You should *always* wear black shoes on formal occasions. If you own your own tuxedo and attend a lot of formal affairs, you might want to take the fashion plunge and get a patent-leather version of the Gucci moccasin or, for even more elegance, thin-soled patent-leather pumps with a cloth bow on the front. These are designed for evening wear only. Short of these, any pair of well-shined black shoes will do.

What you wear on your feet after work will in large part be determined by how you spend your leisure time. Slip-on styles are a big favorite, because they are looser fitting and, therefore, a bit more comfortable

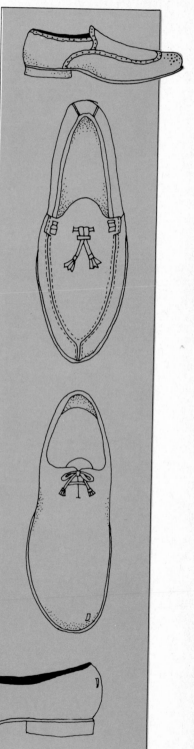

Slip-on shoes, such as the two shown at the top, may be worn for business. For formal evening wear, patent leather lace-ups or pumps (bottom) add a touch of elegance.

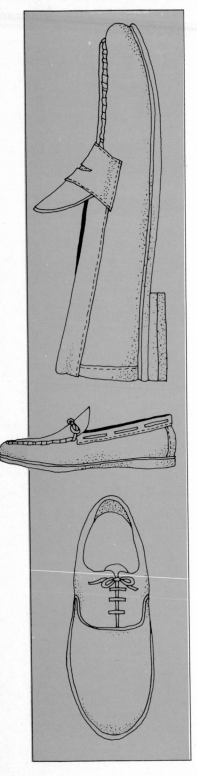

than lace-up shoes. A classic in the slip-on department for casual wear is the **penny loafer,** which gets its name from the tradition of putting a penny inside a slit in the leather band that runs across the instep. There is a modified version of this with tassels on the band. Either version is a highly adaptable casual shoe that can be worn with jeans or with slacks and a sports jacket and look equally appropriate in both cases.

Much more casual is the **moccasin,** usually a thin-soled copy of the Indian design, which can be worn around the house as a slipper or, in harder-sole models, outside. This is a strictly casual shoe. A variation of this design, a boating moccasin, is quite comfortable without socks.

The **espadrille,** a canvas, rope-soled shoe, is cool and comfortable for summer wear. A big favorite along the Mediterranean, this shoe is light and extremely comfortable and is designed to be worn without socks. It is perfectly appropriate as summer footwear for casual social gatherings.

An old standby among lace-up shoes for summer wear is the **white buck** or **white suede shoe** with a red rubber sole. The buck shoe also comes in a buff color; this version is appropriate for informal wear with a jacket and tie in any season.

The **saddle shoe,** a two-tone shoe that comes in black and white or brown and white, slips in and out of fashion. Its name comes from the "saddle," or strip of dark-colored leather, that is sewn over its instep. When it is in fashion, it is a favorite shoe for fall wear.

One casual shoe that always seems to remain in fashion is the **desert boot** or **chukka boot.** This is a high-cut shoe that extends slightly above the ankle and is usually made of a soft calfskin or suede. Always fitted with a cushy crepe sole, it is a comfortable walking shoe.

The **negative-heel shoe** is still something of a novelty item of footwear. In this style, the sole is roughly in the shape of a wedge, with

the thicker part being in the front, not the back, of the shoe. The effect of this is to shift your body weight from the balls of your feet to your heels, and the idea is to duplicate what is believed to be the healthy effect of walking barefoot on soft ground. It takes a while to get used to this shoe, and there are in fact people who, for a variety of reasons, never make the adjustment. If you have particularly short or inelastic Achilles tendons this may not be the shoe for you. People who do adjust, however, claim the shoe does everything from improving their posture to eliminating backaches.

Although in times past the **jogging shoe** might have been called a sneaker, it is not called that now. For one thing, it is definitely out of the price range of the average canvas-topped, rubber-soled sneaker. It is also—unlike the sneaker—built to give your feet maximum protection and efficiency while you're running. It has such features as a specially designed sole pattern, a padded toe and an elevated and padded heel, and extra cushioning inside the shoe on the tongue, sole, and around the heel. The jogging shoe is so comfortable that it has been adopted by nonrunners for casual wear. It comes in a variety of materials, colors, and designs, but the most common is the white leather shoe with three colored leather stripes angled across the instep.

The **Chelsea boot,** popularized by the Beatles in the 1960s, is a leather boot that hugs the ankle. It comes in two general designs—black with elastic side panels, or black or brown with a zipper up the side. The toe is usually rounded, and the boot has heels that vary in height but are always higher than the average shoe heel. This style is appropriate for casual wear and is also acceptable for business wear if, in your line of work, dress codes are fairly liberal.

The classic version of America's original contribution to footwear, the **cowboy boot,** has metal toe and heel guards to minimize wear, a pointed toe to make it easy to slip the boot into a stirrup, and a high heel to keep the foot from sliding through the stirrup. These boots now come in three common toe designs—pointed, squared, and rounded—and in heights that vary from mid-calf to knee high. They may be cleft at the top or cut straight across, stovepipe style, and some have elaborately tooled and stitched leather. For cold-weather wear, they are a perfect complement to another casual standby, blue jeans.

Boots

Casual footwear—the desert boot, classic penny loafer, moccasin, and saddle shoe (opposite page, counterclockwise), and the negative-heel shoe (top) and the cowboy boot (bottom).

Underwear

Clark Gable dealt a nearly fatal blow to an industry when he took his shirt off in the 1930s film *It Happened One Night* and revealed that he had no undershirt on underneath. Within weeks of the movie's release, undershirt sales plummeted—American men had decided that bare was better. Since then, underwear manufacturers have been trying to keep abreast of men's fashions and to start a few trends themselves. Thus, the standard white cotton undershirts and underpants you knew as a boy are often crowded off the shelves by a rainbow of dazzling colors and designs. If you like to dress colorfully but as a rule can't do it on the job, now you can satisfy that urge without anyone's being the wiser.

If you wear undershirts, you have a choice of two basic styles: the T-shirt and the tank top, or athletic shirt. The T-shirt most commonly comes in a crew-neck style that fits tightly around the throat and the open V-neck. Many men prefer the V-neck as an all-around undershirt, for it can be worn with an open-necked sports shirt without any underwear showing. If you don't wear T-shirts with your sports shirts, this won't be a problem, but if you do, buy the V-neck when you shop.

Many men like wearing undershirts but don't like the smothering feeling of the T-shirt under their shirts. For them, the sleeveless athletic shirt with the U-shaped neck opening and shoulder straps is a better choice. Like the V-neck, it doesn't show under sports shirts.

Undershirts are sized two ways—in inches by chest size, and as small, medium, large, and extra large. They are now made to fit more closely than they did in the past so that they can be worn under the popular tapered shirt designs without bunching up and creating lumps and wrinkles.

In recent years both undershirt styles have come out from under to succeed by themselves as items of casual dress. The T-shirt has made it as a walking billboard, often carrying just about any political, personal, or commercial message you care to display on it; the tank top has made its fashion mark as beachwear and as part of the overall casual summer wardrobe.

Underpants

While you can choose to wear or not to wear an undershirt, and may in fact never buy one, sooner or later you will have to replenish your supply of underpants. You have three style choices: boxer shorts, briefs and very briefs, and bikini-style pants.

Boxer shorts got their name from those the prizefighters wear. They are loose fitting, come with an elastic waistband, and have a fly that may be open or closed with snaps or buttons. Although they are cut much slimmer and shorter than they used to be, they've lost some

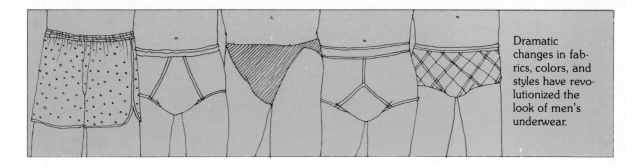

Dramatic changes in fabrics, colors, and styles have revolutionized the look of men's underwear.

of their popularity because they tend to bunch up under today's jeans and tighter-fitting pants. Like all underpants, they are sized according to waist measurement.

If you have a mixed wardrobe of boxer shorts and briefs, one thing you may want to remember when you get fitted for a suit or for dress slacks is to wear your boxer shorts if you plan to wear them with the suit or slacks. Since there is a little more fabric in boxers, your pants may have to be tailored a bit more loosely for a comfortable fit.

More popular these days are the **briefs** and **bikini-style** underpants. They have a snug, smooth fit that suits the tighter pants styles of today. Most briefs have an elastic waist and leg bands and are made of stretchy knits for a supportive fit. Among the variations on the brief style is the slimming brief—basically the male version of a girdle. These are almost totally elastic, they "slenderize" by compressing everything they cover.

For those who like to travel light, there are briefs made of sheer lightweight nylon that can double as swimming trunks. And for the minimum in underwear, there are bikini-style pants copied from the equally minimal European swimsuit. These cover the bare essentials and are usually made of highly elasticized material for a tight fit.

White is no longer the typical color in men's underwear. You have a choice of tops and bottoms that come in pale blue, electric blue, sunshine yellow, blazing red, and a variety of wild patterns. There are even variations in the fabric used. One major underwear manufacturer has tops and bottoms that come in a fishnet weave of a cotton blend.

In most cases, underwear will be of a knit or weave of pure cotton, or of a cotton blend. Some styles are made completely of nylon. Cotton is probably the most comfortable fabric because it "breathes" and absorbs body perspiration as well. Cotton blends are a little less absorbent but more durable. Nylon is the least practical fabric—it is hot to wear, does not "breathe," and sticks to the body in warm weather.

Glossary

T-shirt
Short-sleeved underwear top with a tight-fitting crew neck or a V-neck

Athletic shirt
Sleeveless underwear top with a U-shaped neckline and shoulder straps

Boxer shorts
Loose-fitting underpants that are copies of boxers' trunks

Briefs
Tight-fitting underpants with an elastic waist and leg bands

Bikinis
Skimpy, snug-fitting underpants modeled after the abbreviated look of European swimsuits

Slimming brief
A completely elasticized pair of underpants that are essentially the male version of a girdle

Lisle
Fabric made of a fine cotton thread; commonly used in better ribbed socks

Clock stitching
Small design embroidered on the side of a sock

Links and links
Cable stitching design used to ornament socks

Socks

For business wear, the only length sock you should consider is one that fits over your calf or reaches as high as mid-calf. The lower-slung model, called the anklet, should be reserved strictly for sports wear. It is considered poor taste to allow any part of a pale, naked leg to peek out from under the edge of a hiked-up trouser cuff—high-rising socks prevent this.

With today's elasticized, stretchy fabrics, most socks fit all sizes and will not come crumpling down around your ankles. Wool and nylon are the most common sock materials, and the better socks are a blend of the two, giving you the comfort and absorbency of wool and the durability of nylon. Another popular and comfortable fabric is cotton lisle, a high-quality cotton yarn used in making many ribbed socks. Although there are socks made of pure synthetics, they tend to be too hot and not as comfortable as pure natural fibers or natural-fiber blends.

When shopping for your business socks, concentrate on getting solid colors. Black and navy blue are the most versatile colors, but you may also want to get some brown or even some subtly patterned socks to break the monotony. When wearing patterned socks, remember that one noticeable pattern is enough for a day's outfit—if you are wearing a patterned suit one day, for example, don't wear a pattern on your feet as well. Whatever colored or patterned socks you buy should be keyed to the colors of one or more of your suits.

Even with subdued solids, you can add a little variety to what you wear, for there are some subtle differences in the stitching of dress socks. The most common sock pattern is the **ribbon stitch**—alternately raised and lowered ridges of fabric running the length of the sock. There is also **clock stitching**—small designs embroidered into the sock—and there is the decorative look of **links and links**—a cable stitching that runs up and down the side of the sock. For formal wear, there is the sock woven from sheer silk; this is usually worn only with a tuxedo.

When you do your shopping, check to see whether the socks you plan to buy have had some kind of antistatic treatment. Those that haven't tend to pick up lint, and when you're wearing them static electricity tends to build up to the point where it makes your pants cling unattractively to your lower leg.

If your shoe size is:	then your sock size is:
8	9½
8½	10
9	10½
9½	11
10	11½
10½	12
11	12½
11½	13
12	13½

What you wear to bed is strictly your business. But pajamas, if you wear them, *are* part of your wardrobe, and it's worth thinking about them just a bit.

The standard style is the loose-fitting **coat style** with button-front top (which may or may not have a collar) and bottoms with an elastic or tie-cord waist. For warm-weather wear there is a short-sleeved, short-pants version of this.

In colder weather, you may want to wear what are sometimes called **ski pajamas**—close-fitting pajamas in a heavy cotton knit. These have a pullover top and elastic cuffs around the wrists and ankles to hold in body warmth.

More fashionable just now is the **karate-style** pajama. This is modeled after the loose-fitting exercise suits karate students and teachers wear. It has loose-fitting sleeves and legs, and the top is a short, wraparound robe with a sash to hold it in place. This is often stylish enough for loungewear as well as sleepwear.

The **night shirt,** a large, loose-fitting, knee-length shirt that may come with long or short sleeves and may have an open neck or a three-button one, has been with us for generations and may well outlast all other pajama styles.

The best material to get in pajamas is cotton or a cotton blend; your body gives off moisture while you sleep, and for that reason you will be most comfortable in pajamas with the breathability of cotton.

Bathrobes

The standard bathrobe design is a single-breasted, knee-length style with a sash at the waist. It may come in a formal dressing-gown look complete with lapels and breast pocket, or it may have the more casual look of a wide-sleeved, karate-style wraparound that could be knee length or a shorter thigh length. A style that has become popular in recent years is the caftan, copied from the Arabs' djellaba—this is an ankle-length pullover robe with a hood.

How you use your robe will determine the kind of fabric you choose. Lightweight velours, cotton, synthetics—or, if you can afford it, silk—are ideal for relaxing, while the bulky, absorbent terry-cloth model is probably your best bet if all you want is a bathrobe.

Sweaters

As you build up your sweater wardrobe, you'll find that you have a choice of two general styles: the pullover, named after the way it is put on; and the cardigan, named after the man who led the Charge of the Light Brigade, the seventh Earl of Cardigan.

Pullover sweaters

Pullover sweaters are the more versatile of the two, and they come in a wider variety of models. The most common is the **crew neck,** which fits one to one half an inch below the collar line. The neckband, cuffs, and bottom hem of this sweater are made of a ribbed weave that is slightly elastic and is different from the rest of the sweater. You'll probably find this the most useful style to own, since it can be worn over a shirt with jeans or with a sports jacket and slacks for a slightly dressier look.

Glossary

Crew neck
Round-necked sweater that fits tightly on the throat about an inch below the collar line

Boat neck
Sweater which has a horizontally slashed neck opening running from shoulder to shoulder

Cardigan
Button-front sweater with a V-shaped neckline

Shetland
A light, fluffy wool from sheep raised in the Shetland Isles of Scotland

Mohair
A shaggy, silky wool taken from Angora goats

Cashmere
Fabric made from the hair of the Kashmir goats raised in the Himalayas of India

The **V-neck** style is the next most common. For casual dress it is sometimes worn as a warmer substitute for a vest with a jacket and tie. There is a sleeveless version of the V-neck, called the sweater vest, that has become popular in recent years and may be worn with or without a jacket. Wear it with a shirt, always. The V-neck shows more of your chest than most people want to see. Probably the most distinctive V-neck model is the tennis sweater, which has become a classic—it is a white wool sweater with a cable-stitch pattern knitted into the front and distinctive red and blue stripes bordering the neckline and the cuffs.

If you want to look a little more dashing, you might invest in a **turtleneck** sweater, sometimes called the **polo neck** because it was once an indispensable part of polo attire. This has a long tubular knit neck that folds over on itself for a tight, high-necked look. A variation of this is the **mock turtleneck,** which duplicates the turtleneck look without using an extra fold of fabric. This sweater style tends to look best on men with long necks and elongated features. Heavier men with shorter, thicker necks sometimes look as though a turtleneck sweater is swallowing them up. The turtleneck sweater has become tremendously popular as a more comfortable alternative to a shirt and tie for informal social occasions.

Strictly for sports wear is the **boat-neck** sweater, which has a horizontal slash at the neck opening that runs from shoulder to shoulder. Unlike those previously mentioned, this sweater just won't go with a sports jacket.

The cardigan sweater comes in one basic style with some variations in its look. It is a button-front sweater with a V-shaped neckline. How deep the neck will be depends on the number of buttons in front. This is a strictly casual sweater that is usually worn without a jacket. The style has become a big favorite with golfers, who wear cardigans with loose blousy sleeves that will keep them warm but not inhibit their swing. Many nongolfers favor the cardigan because it is easier to put on and take off than the pullover and because the button front lets them adjust to changes in temperature more comfortably.

The cardigan sweater

Whatever style you choose, you will find that all sweaters are sized in one of two ways: by chest measurement in inches, or as small, medium, large, or extra large. The kind of fit you get will depend on how a sweater is designed to be worn. Some turtlenecks, usually the heavier ones, are cut looser and fuller to fit over a shirt, while others, made of a lighter knit, are designed to replace the shirt and fit close to the body. Most of the crew necks, V-necks, and cardigans are made to be worn over a sweater or a shirt and are loosely cut.

Size and fit

When trying on a closely cut sweater, make sure that it fits in the shoulders without binding under your arms and that the sleeves don't stop short of your wrists. The overall fit should be snug but not oppressively tight. Sweaters are supposed to be comfortable so if a sweater doesn't feel right on you, don't buy it. With a loose style, you are in danger of buying one that is too baggy. The easiest way to check the overall fit is to make sure that the bottom of the sweater doesn't hang appreciably lower than your crotch. In either case, look for a sweater with a nice tight-fitting cuff. All cuffs stretch with wear, and in some cases the cuffs get too loose, making the sweater look baggier than it is. The tighter the knit, the less likely it is that this will happen.

If you're just starting up a sweater collection, buy a few crew-neck sweaters before you get anything else. These are appropriate in any situation in which a sweater can be worn. Avoid wild patterns or designs, and build up a good selection of neutral tones that will blend in with the rest of your wardrobe. Colors such as beige, heather, navy, and gray are good starters.

Sweaters are commonly made of pure wool, wool-and-synthetic blends, and pure synthetics. Wool or wool blends are the best investments. They look better than synthetics, keep you warm, and are usually softer and more comfortable. (Wool blends offer warmth and the look of wool with the durability of a synthetic.)

For a light, soft look and feel, try to find sweaters made of Shetland wool, a fluffy, warm material taken from sheep raised on the Shetland Isles off the coast of Scotland. Even softer is lamb's wool, which comes in the same light, fluffy knit as Shetland wool. For a bulkier look there is mohair, a shaggy, shiny wool taken from the coats of Angora goats. The most luxurious of wools is cashmere, an extremely soft and silky material that may be used by itself in expensive sweaters or in combination with other wools. It usually comes in a tighter, smoother weave than other sweater materials.

A good sweater is a durable piece of clothing. It should give you years of good wear and, if handled properly, a good fit as well. But because it is made of loosely knit materials, a sweater *will* stretch and expand with normal wear. Therefore, although fit is not too critical in loosely fitting styles, careless yanking off of pullovers (the crew necks and turtlenecks especially) is ill advised, for it will eventually ruin the fit and shape of the sweater. Be a little careful and you will extend the life span of your clothing investment.

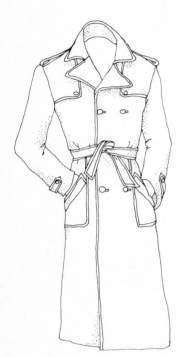

The trench coat style is a standard look in rainwear and in overcoats; the variation shown above features patch pockets. Classic coat collar designs (left to right): the shawl collar, the notched collar, and the plain collar.

Coats Next to your suits, the biggest single clothing investment in your business wardrobe will be what you wear over them—your topcoat or overcoat. There are good reasons for taking some care in making

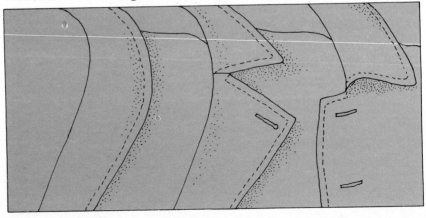

your selection. One is that a coat will be a conspicuous part of your dress and should project the same kind of image as your suits—one that is studied and tasteful. Another is that a coat is a substantial investment and is likely to be around for quite a few years. If you make a mistake in your coat choice, you not only have to pay for it, you have to live with it.

Fortunately, the choice is not difficult. You can have a perfectly adequate coat wardrobe by owning one heavy coat for the cold months and a raincoat for the rest of the year.

When you go coat shopping, dress for the occasion—wear the bulkiest suit you are likely to have on underneath the coat; that way you can get a fit for all your suits.

An overcoat should fit as well as the suit it protects, and that usually means that you're going to need some alterations.

When you try on a coat, button all the buttons and tie or buckle the belt if there is one. Check for telltale horizontal or vertical wrinkles in the back, clues that the coat is too tight or too loose. Look at the sleeve length as your hands hang by your sides. The coat should extend about half an inch beyond your shirt cuff. Length is also important—for looks as well as for protection from the weather; the bottom hem of the coat should hit you below the knees. Finally, if there is a belt, it should ride at about the same point on your midsection as the waistline of your suit pants. If it is above or below that point, have the tailor lower or raise the belt loops.

Always choose a conservative color or pattern. A dark tweed is a good choice. Navy blue is even better, since you can wear a navy blue coat with formal evening wear. If you prefer a lighter color, choose a coat in a fabric such as camel's hair. As a general rule, solid colors are a better choice—they are less likely to clash with patterned suits you may wear underneath your coat.

In coat styles you will have a choice between single-breasted and double-breasted models, with or without belts. The **Chesterfield coat,** a classic, is designed with a slightly fitted waist; it comes in either a single-breasted or a double-breasted model. It is generally made in a number of fabrics, from wool to camel's hair to cashmere. Probably the best-known version of the Chesterfield is a formal black model with a velvet collar.

For a looser fit there is the **Balmacaan,** a single-breasted coat with full raglan sleeves (loose sleeves the seams of which run up to the neck of the coat). This is an extremely comfortable coat, and its lines have also been adopted for single-breasted raincoats.

The Balmacaan coat (above) has become a classic. The wraparound style (below) enjoys periodic comebacks.

Finally, there is the **British Warm,** a copy of the military coat worn by the British army in World War I. This has a slightly pinched waist, a flared bottom, epaulets, and pockets inserted at an angle.

If you have no real style preference but want a coat that will last, a Chesterfield coat is probably your best buy. It's a style that has never gone out of fashion in the past and is not likely to in the future.

Rainwear

The trench coat, sometimes called the officer's coat, is a classic in rainwear. What has been the movie uniform of the spy and the foreign correspondent got its fashion start in the trenches of World War I, where it was worn by the officers of the British army. Many models today still are outfitted with the accessories that appeared on those officers' coats—the gunflap that appears on the right shoulder was to help cushion the recoil of a rifle; the adjustable straps on the sleeves were to keep out the weather; and the brass D-rings hanging off the belt were originally used to carry such gear as grenades, canteens, and ammunition.

Since these accessories give the coat a certain flair, they are preserved in today's models. However, the fabric has changed. The original trench coat was made of water repellent gabardine; today tightly woven poplin, poplin-and-synthetic blends, and even knits are the most common materials.

Something else that is new is the zip-out lining for cold-weather wear. There's also a choice of various colors and patterns, but the most versatile color remains the classic tan.

If you don't happen to like the trench coat, your raincoat alternative is a plain, single-breasted model with raglan sleeves and either a fly front (with buttons concealed under a flap of fabric) or a button front. This style is roomy and comfortable and has clean, simple lines. Although this too comes in different colors and patterns, your best choice again is a neutral shade of tan or beige.

About waterproofing

Don't expect too much from any raincoat you buy. All raincoat fabrics have been treated so that they are water-repellent or water-resistant; but what this means, in practice, is that they will not keep you bone dry if you stand out in a downpour. Water-repellent and water-resistant treatments eliminate some of the natural absorbency of the fabric so that it sheds more water than it absorbs. The disadvantage of this is that if you stand out in the rain long enough in *any* raincoat, you are going to get wet. The advantage of this is that the raincoat fabric still "breathes," making the coat more comfortable to wear. The only time that a coat (or any garment) is guaranteed waterproof is when it is made of a nonporous material such as rubber or vinyl. This will definitely keep all water out—but, since it doesn't "breathe," it will also keep your body heat and moisture in, a feature that could cause a lot of discomfort on warm rainy days.

Formal wear

One day in 1886, a young dandy, tired of the white tie and tails that were the standard formal evening wear in his day, decided to create his own outfit. He had his tailor make a brilliant red copy of the traditional English smoking jacket, satin lapels and all. Wearing this, he appeared at the exclusive Tuxedo Park Ball in Tuxedo, New York. His daring new jacket created an instant fashion sensation, and that evening the tuxedo—or, as the French call it, "le smoking"—was born.

Since then the tuxedo has eclipsed other styles as the preferred mode of dress for formal wear. The red worn by that innovative dandy has been replaced by the more subdued look of black, but the touches of satin on the lapels have remained. This revolution in formal wear is now so well established that today it would be the man wearing white tie and tails to a formal event who would cause heads to turn.

Although your only contact with the tuxedo may so far have been on a rental basis, it could be in your interests to buy one. The obvious advantage to having your own is that you will look and feel better in a tuxedo tailored to your body—no rented tux can duplicate your own custom-fitted one. And there can be financial advantages—if you find that you need a tuxedo or a dinner jacket more than three times a year, it's worth it to buy one. (If, on the other hand, you get to a black-tie affair less often, keep on renting.)

The basic tuxedo design has changed little over the years. If you buy a good one and take care of it, there's no reason it shouldn't last ten years or more.

In choosing a tuxedo the two things to remember are conservatism and comfort. If you want something you can wear to a formal affair five years from now without embarrassment, ignore all trendy, flashy styles. In recent years there have been some particularly outrageous variations of "le smoking;" some of them have included flame red velvet dinner jackets worn over shirts with waves of ruffles and lace cascading down their fronts. They never last long.

Buying a tuxedo

Although tuxedos come in both single- and double-breasted models, your best bet is one that is single-breasted and features a moderate lapel style. A double-breasted tuxedo can be hot at a formal affair which includes a lot of dancing or is just plain stuffy. What's more, you can't unbutton it and still look neat—something that is no problem with a single-breasted model. And by choosing a moderate lapel width, you should be able to survive most fashion shifts without looking out of date.

Glossary

Studs
Removable button substitutes for wear on formal shirts; they are usually made of gold or dark semiprecious stones

Grosgrain
A tightly woven silk usually reserved for ties and clothing decoration

Modified straight bow
A narrow bow tie with very little flare at its tips

Butterfly bow
A wide-tipped bow tie that looks best with larger faces

Cummerbund
A satin, pleated waistband worn as part of a tuxedo; pleats always face *up*

Waistcoat
A backless formal vest that can be worn as a substitute for a cummerbund

Cutaway
Formal day coat with knee-length tails in the back and a short, jacketlike front that is never buttoned

Stroller
A formal day coat that looks like a gray blazer and is worn by the groom at formal weddings

The standard black tuxedo with satin-faced lapels and a strip of satin running down the outer seams of the trouser legs is the one to wear. If you think you may be attending a number of formal events in the summer, you may want to add a white dinner jacket. Otherwise, you can get by quite nicely with just the dark jacket and trousers.

Linen, wool, and silk are the fabrics most commonly used in tuxedos. (Another that is becoming popular is velvet.) Choose a lightweight or, at the heaviest, a medium-weight fabric for the most comfort. (In this regard, you might want to rule out velvet.)

Ruffles and bows   Simplicity is important in choosing a **dress shirt.** All you need is a basic white shirt with a subtle decoration of vertical pleats. If you'd like a little color, you can get a shirt in pale blue for more relaxed formal gatherings, but nothing else. Stay away from shirts with outlandish puffs of ruffles and lace, as well as those that come in offbeat colors like green or brown.

Formal shirts have French cuffs, but it will be up to you whether or not you want buttons or holes for studs—removable buttons—in the front. Buttons are easy to fasten and unlike studs, which often get lost, are always there when you want them. Studs, however, do look handsome, and they can be changed to give some variety to your shirt front. Standard stud designs are dark stones or plain gold. If you wish, get a set that matches your cuff links.

Standard dress-shirt material is a finely woven cotton that is well starched to give it a crisp, fresh look. If you have more luxurious tastes, you might choose a dress shirt made of a cream-colored silk for a touch of understated elegance.

The formal **bow tie** is traditionally black, and is made either of black satin or of a closely woven grosgrain silk. You can deviate from this norm a bit by wearing a tie of black velvet or a colored bow in subdued, dark shades of blue, green, or maroon. Avoid anything brighter.

Do be sure to wear a tie that suits the proportions of your face. Ties come in two general styles—the narrow modified straight bow and the broader butterfly bow. Bow widths range from two inches to two and three-quarter inches. Men who are short and have small features should go with the narrower widths while the larger butterfly bows look fine on larger men.

At one time the **cummerbund** served to catch whatever crumbs a gentleman might drop in the course of a dinner, and, in commemoration of that, it is still worn with those crumb-catching pleats facing *up*. The standard color for this part of the formal wardrobe is black, although the more adventurous dresser will occasionally wear a cummerbund made of green or maroon silk or even a needlepoint cummerbund for variety's sake.

If you find the cummerbund restrictive and uncomfortable, replace it with a **waistcoat,** or false-back vest. Since the waistcoat has no back, just a small strap to hold it in place, it is much easier to wear than a conventional suit vest. Most are made of black satin and come with two watch pockets in front.

To round off a formal wardrobe, you need a pair of **suspenders.** (Black again is the proper color, but since your suspenders will be out of sight you might want to experiment with something a bit livelier.) **Stockings** should always be black, preferably of sheer silk and designed expressly for formal wear. Any pair of well-shined black shoes will get you by, but for the truly formal look, patent leather pumps—low-slung slippers with bows—or elegant four-eyelet lace-ups are considered the thing to wear.

Full dress

Unless you move in high diplomatic circles or in the upper echelons of society, you will probably never have an occasion to wear the more formal alternative to the tuxedo, the white tie and tails. This differs from the tuxedo in that the jacket has a cutaway front that doesn't button and a pair of long, split, knee-length tails in the back. The shirt has a raised, wing-tipped collar and it may also have a false front and a highly starched, detachable collar. The tie is always white and is usually piqué. The rest of the outfit—satin striped pants and patent leather pumps with silk stockings—is identical to tuxedo dress. As one last bit of formality, white gloves and a top hat are sometimes worn.

Dress for weddings

You may be asked to wear similar attire if you are one of the wedding party at a very formal wedding. On such occasions the men wear gray jackets with cutaway fronts and tails and striped trousers. The shirt has a wing collar and is worn with an ascot tucked into a pearl gray vest. (According to the rules of dress, the ascots of the groom and his best man should be different from those worn by the ushers.) Gray or white gloves and top hats are sometimes worn.

For a slightly less formal wedding, dress for the groom is a gray stroller coat and striped pants. The stroller is similar to a gray blazer and is worn with a matching waistcoat or vest, a white shirt with a regular turned-down collar, a gray and black striped four-in-hand tie, and black shoes.

Proper attire for a guest at a formal wedding held during the daytime is a dark suit. If the wedding is in the evening—any time after 6 P.M.—black tie is the dress for both the guests and the wedding party when indicated.

Coats for formal wear

In cold weather any dark overcoat will do to cover your formal attire, although a black Chesterfield coat with a velvet collar is considered the most appropriate look. In wet or warm weather the classic trench coat is fine. You can always add a little bit of flair when you wear an overcoat by draping a silk scarf, preferably cream-colored or white, around your neck.

The rules of formal dress

Fortunately for men today, the rules on what constitute proper formal dress have become more relaxed. Accessories that were once considered necessary are seldom worn these days—years ago no man was considered formally dressed unless he had a silk top hat; likewise, no gentleman would think of going out for a night on the town without a cape and one of his dressier canes. Every so often there is a pang of nostalgia in men's fashions and there is a brief revival of the cape, for example, as evening wear. These revivals seldom take hold, and today a man got up with cane, cape, and top hat is no longer the picture of a gentleman in proper dress, but of a magician on his way to work. All you need to look like a well-dressed man about town these days is your tuxedo.

In casual wear the emphasis these days seems to be on utilitarian clothing. Just looking good isn't enough; clothes must have a sturdy, no-nonsense air about them. The rule today seems to be if it's not practical, don't wear it.

Sportswear

Blue jeans probably are the best example of this utilitarian shift in fashion. For years denim was the fabric of workers, not of suburbanites. It was a cheap, sturdy fabric that originated in Nimes, France. (In fact, the cloth gets its name from that city, denim being a variation of *de Nimes*, meaning "from Nimes.") It was a popular fabric for making work pants for French farmers and sailors and, once it crossed to the United States, for cowboys and miners. That was the extent of its popularity until the 1960s, when jeans became the uniform of the college student. Fashion hasn't been the same since then. Blue jeans have become standard items in the leisure wardrobe. And because so many people had adopted the work pants of the American cowboy, it wasn't long before they started wearing the rest of his clothes—the boots, the wide belt, the close-fitting shirt. The western look was born.

In addition, the popularity of backpacking and hiking in the deep woods has had an effect on what people are wearing on city streets. People came to appreciate the sturdy, practical clothes designed for roughing it—and the rugged style they had. As a result, people who have never hiked any farther than across the backyard to the garbage can have adopted the backpacker look—parkas, down vests, sturdy pants. This trend toward no-nonsense sports clothing has also popularized tweedy English-style sportswear. Once again men are appreciating the classic qualities of hacking jackets and heavy cardigan sweaters.

Attire for active sports is changing too. Tennis players have dethroned the all-white look that was the uniform of that game by wearing blue and yellow shirts out on the courts. The colors acceptable for golf wear seem to get wilder and brighter by the year, and ski styles change almost every season.

All these fashions and trends shouldn't overwhelm you. Just rely on common sense in your clothes buying and approach the task of building a lesiure wardrobe with the same logic (and following the same general fashion guidelines) that worked in building your business wardrobe. Do take your sports and casual wardrobe seriously—it can work for or against you. Establish what your priority clothing needs are. Plan your purchases. Avoid the outlandish in whatever you buy and, when in doubt about style, always go for the classic look.

The Jeans Scene

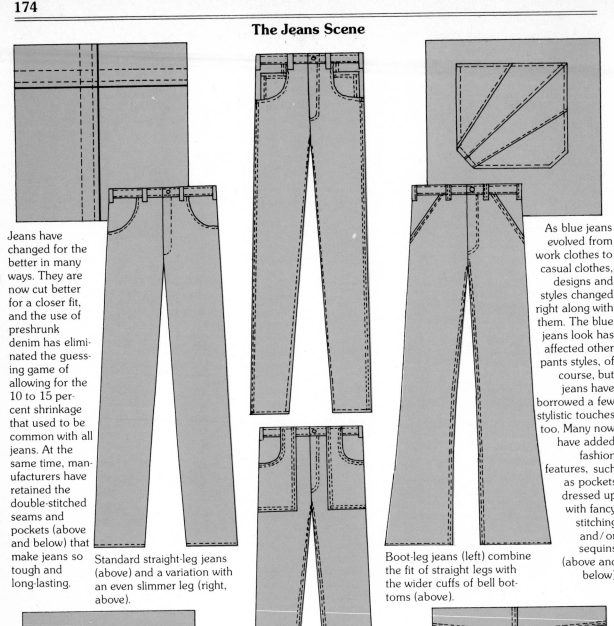

Jeans have changed for the better in many ways. They are now cut better for a closer fit, and the use of preshrunk denim has eliminated the guessing game of allowing for the 10 to 15 percent shrinkage that used to be common with all jeans. At the same time, manufacturers have retained the double-stitched seams and pockets (above and below) that make jeans so tough and long-lasting.

Standard straight-leg jeans (above) and a variation with an even slimmer leg (right, above).

Boot-leg jeans (left) combine the fit of straight legs with the wider cuffs of bell bottoms (above).

As blue jeans evolved from work clothes to casual clothes, designs and styles changed right along with them. The blue jeans look has affected other pants styles, of course, but jeans have borrowed a few stylistic touches too. Many now have added fashion features, such as pockets dressed up with fancy stitching and/or sequins (above and below).

Jeans

Blue jeans, easily the most popular and versatile piece of casual clothing, have come a long way from the baggy blue denim work pants that Bavarian immigrant Levi Strauss first sold the prospectors who passes through San Francisco in the mid-1800s. When you visit a jeans store today, what you find is wall-to-wall denim on floor-to-ceiling shelves and endless stretches of racks stocked with what looks like an overwhelming variety of styles.

Take a close look at the dozens of different styles. More often than not you will find that the differences are largely superficial. Some jeans have no front pockets. Others have no back pockets. Some can be worn with belts while others can't. There are jeans with patch pockets in the front, zipper pockets, pleated pockets, embroidered pockets. In some cases the difference is just a matter of the amount of decoration or some fancy stitching here and there.

With or without all these pockets and decorations, you are only going to have a choice of three basic styles: straight legs, boot legs, and bell bottoms (with some variations on each style).

Straight-leg jeans, the classics, are exactly what their name says: the trouser leg is the same width from the top of the leg down to the cuff. There is a tighter-fitting variation of this, sometimes called pencil leg jeans, that can only be worn well by people with long, thin figures.

Boot jeans fit like straight legs on the top but flare out slightly from the knees down to accommodate the bulk of a boot fitting under the pants leg.

Bell bottoms are wide-bottom jeans with cuffs that range in size from moderate flares to great flapping bells of denim.

Let your body be your guide in picking a style. Tall men look better in jeans with the fuller leg silhouettes of bell bottoms, while shorter men look best in the straight-leg look. Of course, if you like to wear cowboy boots, the boot jeans will be a natural choice.

The fit of jeans

All jeans are cut to fit close to the body. Just how close, though, is strictly up to you. For example, there are expensive French jeans designed to fit so tightly that in the stores where they are sold, it sometimes takes the combined strength of two clerks to zip a customer into a properly fitting pair. You no doubt will want a pair that one person can put on by himself. Fortunately, jeans fitting is a little simpler than it once was; people had to buy jeans one or two sizes large to allow for shrinkage. Now most denim used in jeans is preshrunk, so you can feel fairly confident that the size that fits just right in the store is the size you should buy.

You should try to find the brand that fits your body best. Different manufacturers cut their jeans in different ways. As you go around making test fits, you'll find that some are too loose and others too tight. When you get to the just-right pile, always make it a habit to try on at least three pairs of jeans in the model and size you want. More often than not you will get three different fits. Take the one that fits the best. Since in spite of preshrunk fabrics jeans still tend to shrink somewhat in the length, make a point of buying them a little long. Once you've found the brand and the style that fits you best, memorize it so you'll never have to go searching through racks and shelves of jeans again.

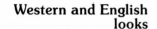

Western and English looks

If, when you sort out your taste in casual dress, you decide that the backpacker look is not for you (or at least not all the time), you will probably find that you are drawn to one of two other styles of casual attire. One could be called the western look; typically it has as its important elements jeans, boots, a wide leather belt, and a close-fitting, tapered shirt. The other style is the English look; its fabrics are tweeds, bulky wools, and corduroy, and its look is dressier than the cowboy look. The kind of images you project when you adopt one or the other of these styles vary tremendously, and it might help to see what the differences are.

The distinctly American style of the "cowboy look" is definitely the more casual of the two. Everything in it—the boots, jeans, and shirt—is copied from the practical, tough work clothes cowboys still wear today. It's a limited style because it's usually considered to be a look for younger men—except, of course, in the parts of the country where it is standard wear for everyone. It's also limited because its long lean look goes best with long lean bodies. Men who tend to be heavy and on the short side usually don't carry it off well.

If it's the look that suits you, though, get yourself a snug-fitting pair of boot jeans (see "Jeans," page 174), the best boots you can afford (see page 159), a well-made saddle leather belt (see page 154), and the cowboy shirt of your choice. Cut close to the body, these shirts usually come with a stylishly cut yoke of fabric on the front and back of the shoulders, two flapped breast pockets, and close-fitting cuffs with two or more snaps on them. They come in every conceivable fabric from wool to silk and come in solids or—the most popular look— ginghams.

If your taste and inclinations in fashion are more conservative, the English look is probably for you. The advantages of it are that men of many different ages and sizes can wear this style. It fits in more easily on informal social occasions when jackets and ties may be worn, and, best of all, you can borrow pieces of your business wardrobe to put it together.

The tweed or corduroy jacket is the heart of the English look. It could be a brand-new hacking jacket you just bought for casual wear, or a jacket salvaged from a tweed suit that is too worn to make it any longer as part of your business wardrobe. Leather elbow patches, suede side out, will not only cover up the worn parts of your coat but give it an even more sporty flair.

Wide-wale corduroy or tweed trousers, preferably straight legged, go with this look. (In the summer, a comfortable pair of tan cotton slacks will do.) If it gets very cold, slip on a Shetland crew-neck sweater or, for a dressier look, a turtleneck sweater, under your jacket.

To complete the look wear a pair of comfortable, high-cut shoes such as desert boots, and wear a soft Irish tweed hat—good protection from cold and wet. For the ultimate in the English look for cold weather, get a loose-fitting toggle-button coat or duffel coat.

Outdoor gear

Even if you don't do much backpacking, hiking, or mountaineering, you'll find that many of the clothes designed for these activities are good investments. They're tough, well made, and have a rugged style all their own. They usually last for years and never go out of fashion.

No outdoor wardrobe is complete without one wool shirt, preferably in a red and black plaid. Get one that is made of a wool-and-synthetic blend so you can be sure it will last a long time. Models that are cut full with long tails are the most versatile. In milder weather you can wear them as light jackets with the tails out and, when it gets colder, you can tuck the tails in for warmth.

Some people don't like the feeling of wool against their skin; if you're one of them, you can still get the comfort and warmth of wool in a shirt that's made of chamois cloth. This is a tough, heavy cotton flannel used to make solid-color outdoor shirts. It gets its name from

the fact that it has the soft, velvety feel of chamois leather. Like the wool shirts, these usually come with two roomy, flapped breast pockets; they can also double as jackets in mild weather; and they have the advantage of being machine washable.

To go with your rugged shirts, get a pair of backpacker pants. These are straight-legged, cuffless slacks that are distinguished by the fact that they have two button-flap pockets in the back and two extra ones in front on the upper part of each pants leg. They're dressier looking than jeans, and come in wrinkle-free cotton-and-polyester blends for warm-weather wear and in worsted wool or corduroy for chillier weather. They look good whether you're out on the trail or just sitting around relaxing on a weekend.

If you need a really versatile all-weather jacket, you might also want to take a look at the backpacker's parka, which, these days, is seen as often on city streets as out in the wilds. This is a hip-length, hooded, multi-pocketed jacket with a drawstring waist, Velcro fastenings on pockets and cuffs, and a zipper or snap front. Made either of cotton or a cotton blend, this parka is windproof and water repellent. If you buy one, make sure it fits loosely. The backpacker's parka is designed to be worn by itself or, in cold weather, as a wind shell over other layers of clothing.

For an extremely lightweight sweater substitute to wear under the parka, get a down vest. This is a sleeveless version of the puffy down-filled jackets seen so often these days. The advantage of the vest is that it will keep you as warm as a heavy sweater, but it weighs only ounces and leaves your arms much freer than a sweater. Before you buy one, check to make sure it's filled with goose down, which is warmer than the cheaper duck down; that it has an insulated collar that can be closed to cover the lower part of your neck; and that it is cut a little longer in the back for added warmth. The beauty of the vest is that when you're not using it you can squash it into a ball not much bigger than your fist and tuck it away in one of your parka pockets until you need it again.

How to shop   The best way to shop for the outdoor look is not store to store but catalogue to catalogue. Some of the best outdoor gear sold these days is available from mail-order houses. Send for every catalogue you can and start looking them over. Before long you'll find yourself wanting outdoor equipment you never knew existed. You may even end up out on the hiking trails with everyone else.

Clothes for active sports   Fashion and style play a part in your sports clothes. Leisure activities are often social occasions, and for that reason you'll want to look your best on the courts, the links, or the slopes—and appearance can be especially important if you mix business with pleasure when you engage in sports. Take a little care with your sports wardrobe. It can only help.

Colors are more and more accepted on the courts, but if you stick with the traditional all-white look for tennis you won't go wrong. The classic tennis look starts with the shirt—a short-sleeved cotton or cotton blend shirt with a soft collar and a three-button neck. There are no other choices; this is the only style. Do make sure you get one made of cotton or a cotton blend. The natural fibers of cotton will absorb your perspiration and "breathe" to keep you cool. Synthetic shirts will suffocate you.

Tennis

Wear white tennis shorts that fit trimly in the waist but fit high on the thigh, leaving you plenty of leg room for running and moving around. Beltless shorts that use buttoned cloth tabs on the waistband are the most comfortable. A good feature to look for is a rear pocket to hold that second ball while you're serving. Not all tennis shorts have one, so make sure to check.

The classic tennis shorts were once made of wool, but cotton, cotton-and-polyester blends, and pure synthetics are just as common these days.

If you are tempted to wear color in your tennis clothes, keep it simple. Avoid patterns and wear only light solid colors. But remember that the all-white look isn't just a matter of pure snobbism; it has its practical side too. White will reflect more sunlight off your body than any color, and this can make a difference if you're playing in the heat of the day.

For maximum comfort, wear all-wool, all-cotton, or synthetic-blend socks. The better tennis socks will have elasticized tops to keep them

from crumpling down around your ankle and thick cushioned soles to absorb perspiration and make your foot more comfortable.

At one time, standard footwear for tennis was a pair of ugly black leather shoes with spikes on the bottom. Now there are feather-light white sneakers with canvas, nylon, vinyl, or leather tops and thick rubber soles with everything from specially engineered ridges of rubber to miniature suction cups to give better traction. These usually come with built-in arch supports and padded collars, tongues, and inner soles. Make sure the fit of your tennis shoes allows for about half an inch of space between the tip of your toe and the end of the shoe for the best in comfort and a blister-free game.

Optional accessories that are fairly popular include the tennis visor, a topless baseball hat with a white brim, adjustable hat band, and green lining under the brim to minimize glare from the sun. For more head cover there is a round tennis hat of soft white cotton that has a narrow brim (also lined with green). And this comes in a terry-cloth model that makes a good towel substitute. (If you don't like hats, you might like a terry-cloth sweat band that goes around the forehead and fastens in the back with two Velcro tabs.) In cooler weather, you might want to have a tennis sweater, a white wool V-neck with a cable-stitching pattern on the front and red and blue trim on the neckline. It's a classic design that has never gone out of style and one that you can incorporate into your summer wardrobe for off-the-court casual wear.

Golf

In the 1920s and 1930s no well-dressed golfer would dare go out on the course without putting on his knee socks, knickers, long-sleeved white shirt, and tie. Some even preferred to top all this off with a sports jacket. Today a pair of comfortable pants, a loose-fitting short-sleeved shirt, and, for cooler weather, a cardigan sweater are all a golfer needs to be properly dressed.

In buying golf clothes, the basic rules still apply: keep it simple; don't mix patterns with patterns; coordinate your colors; and let one wardrobe item be the center of attention. Now, if you feel that putting together a good-looking outfit from the burnt oranges, cherry reds, and electric blues that are sometimes found in golf clothes is beyond you, don't bother. You can't go wrong by staying with the basic summer colors—white, tan, navy, and red—and you'll probably look better in them besides. That's an especially important point if you're going to be conducting some of your business in your golf clothes.

For golf shirts it's hard to beat the three-button pullover polo shirt. For coolness and comfort make sure to get a cotton or cotton blend, and for a loose and easy golf swing you might want to get the golfer's polo shirt that has stretchy insets at pivotal points under the arms.

Any lightweight, light-colored slacks tailored to a comfortable fit are fine for golf. Knit slacks are extremely popular because the way they fit close to the body makes them look good, and the way they stretch and give with body movement makes them feel good. For cool-weather golfing you'll find that slacks made of corduroy or medium-weight wool are good.

In cooler weather take along a loose-fitting cardigan sweater with blousy, full sleeves that won't interfere with your swing. For a little rain protection, buy a golfer's windbreaker, a waist-length jacket with insets of loosely knit, stretchy fabric under the arms to give you full freedom of movement.

The last item on your golf clothing list is a pair of spiked golf shoes. Typically you'll find plain brown or black oxfords, two-tone saddle-shoe styles, or oxfords with a distinctive fringed tongue hanging over the top. To make it easy on yourself and the rest of your wardrobe, buy a pair of plain brown shoes. They go with just about everything and relieve you of the bother of fussing about what you can or cannot wear with the fancier models.

Skiing

Skiing is one sport in which both the fashion and the technology are changing at a dizzying rate. It's easy to get caught up in keeping abreast of this year's look in parkas or ski pants, but the fact is that last year's pants and parkas work just fine. In some cases, following the fashions can have dangerous consequences. One year the fad in parkas was the wet look—a slick, vinyllike surface on parkas. The smooth surface on the jackets offered almost no friction resistance to snow, so that when people wearing them fell on the slopes, they continued their runs down the mountainside on their backs or bellies, often at breakneck speeds.

Your priorities in buying a parka are function first and fashion second. Any parka you buy should be filled with either goose down or polyester fiberfill—both are extremely light and efficient insulators. Your ski parka should be close fitting and made of nylon to minimize wind resistance as you go streaking down the slopes. To hold in body heat and keep out the cold, it should have elastic knit cuffs and a drawstring in its waist or bottom. The collar height varies from one parka to the next, but it should cover your throat when it's turned up and be insulated as well. Finally, take a close look at the nylon fabric. If it has a grid of thick threads woven into it, it is ripstop nylon. Should you accidentally tear or rip the jacket, these reinforcing threads will keep the gash from getting bigger. Ripstop nylon is an indication that the parka will be sturdy.

Parkas come with or without hoods and are usually in waist lengths and hip lengths, with or without belts. Waist-length models give you more freedom of movement, but hip-length ones are a little warmer. It

always pays to invest in a good parka, because when you are not on the slopes you can still get a lot of wear out of it as a warm and comfortable winter jacket.

Ski pants are definitely worth buying if you plan to do a lot of skiing. Most today are made of a tight-fitting, stretchy synthetic like Lycra Spandex. Like the nylon parka, these minimize wind resistance and shed moisture. More versatile pants are knickers made of heavy wool or corduroy. Worn with a pair of heavy wool knee socks, they're ideal for downhill skiing, cross-country skiing, hiking, bicycling, or simply for adding a jaunty look to weekend wear. If you don't want to buy any pants just yet, you can get by quite well with a comfortable pair of jeans.

Get a good pair of insulated ski gloves or mittens for your hands. The gloves should fit snugly but still be flexible enough to let you wrap your fingers around a ski pole easily. A densely knit wool ski cap will keep your head warm; on balmier winter days, you can wear a ski band, a wide band of stretchy wool that will cover your ears but leave the top of your head exposed.

The secret of dressing warmly for skiing is to do it in layers to hold your body heat. The bottom layer should be long-john style open mesh or waffle-knit underwear; this forms thousands of heat-trapping air pockets. Over this go your ski pants and a cotton turtleneck jersey. The feet get the same layer treatment, first with a pair of lightweight cotton or wool socks and then with your heavier ski socks. Now you're ready for the slopes.

Since the top has come off the man's bathing suit, swimwear fashions have been primarily a matter of how much or how little should be worn on the bottom. You have a choice of four standard swimsuit styles: Bermuda-length trunks, boxer trunks, tank shorts, and bikinis. Bermudas are long and loose fitting, hitting just above the knee. Boxer trunks fit much tighter and stop at mid-thigh. Tank shorts are tighter still and fit low on the hips and high on the thigh. Last, and least, are bikinis, which put as little between you and the water as possible.

In and on the water

Boxer shorts and Bermudas are probably the most popular styles; most men find them comfortable to wear and a little more colorful than other styles since, unlike the solid-color bikinis and tank shorts, they come in a wide selection of stripes and patterns. If you can't find a bathing suit you like, do what a lot of people are doing these days—recycle an old pair of jeans by cutting off the legs at the length you want.

The most comfortable outfit you can come up with for sailing is a cotton-knit polo shirt and washable white shorts made of duck or a sturdy cotton-and-synthetic blend. For protection against wind and water, a hooded, waterproof slicker is ideal. You can get them in rubber, vinyl, or lightweight coated nylon; they come in both zip-up and pullover styles. When the weather gets cooler, a pair of jeans and a heavy sweater will keep you comfortable.

For occasional boating just about any pair of sneakers is fine, but if you plan to do a good deal of sailing, it will be worth your while to invest in a pair of boating sneakers or shoes. They have a sole design of closely spaced ripples of rubber that run across the width of the shoe. This gives you good traction even on slick wet surfaces. The sneakers come in a variety of different colored, canvas-topped models, and the equally comfortable boating shoe comes with a water-resistant leather top.

Hats, gloves, and handkerchiefs

The test of any accessory is how well it blends. Accessories are subordinate wardrobe items that give your clothes a touch of individuality—they should never be noticeable in and of themselves.

Hats

One accessory that has become optional for business is the hat. There was a time when it was considered as much a part of proper business dress as the suit and tie. This is no longer the case. Hats are worn today more as protection against the weather than anything else.

If you want a hat, you'll find that the standard look for business is the snap-brim style—in which the brim is turned down in the front and up in the back. This is a plain felt hat with a band of silk (or similar material) about two inches wide running around it. Its crown can be steamed into a variety of shapes—usually a crease down the middle or two dimples pinched in the front. A subdued color—dark brown, gray, or blue—is the most versatile.

The homburg, which has a tapered crown and a brim that is curled on the sides, is usually worn with formal evening wear. This hat is made of soft felt and comes in black or dark blue.

For warm-weather wear, you might try the boater, or sennit—the round, flat-topped straw hat made famous by vaudeville entertainers. Usually decorated with a colored ribbon hatband, the boater makes periodic comebacks as a sporty summer hat. An equally cool and lightweight alternative is the planter's hat, copied from a standard style worn by plantation owners in the tropics. Usually made of coconut palm or a similar light material, it has a flat-topped crown, a curl on the

edge of its brim, and is usually decorated with a brightly colored *puggaree,* or hatband. Finally, there is a summer classic: the Panama hat has long been a favorite because it is cool, light, and durable.

While hats may be fading from favor for business wear, they are holding their own in casual and sportswear. One popular style is the cloth hat—basically a snap-brim wool hat in a plaid or checked pattern. Perhaps the best-known version of this is the Irish tweed hat, which has a high, bucket-shaped crown and a narrow round brim, and is usually made in solid color or Donegal tweed.

The Tyrolean hat, modeled after those worn by legendary Swiss yodelers, usually comes in the snap-brim style and has two or more cords twisted about the base of the crown. It also has a small brush stuck in the cords as a decoration. It can be made of anything from felt to suede or velours, and is equally suitable for the woods or downtown.

For golfing or fishing, you might want to get a poplin porkpie hat—so called because its round, flat-topped design makes it resemble a pork pie. Usually made of water-resistant fabric, this soft cloth hat can be rolled up and tucked into the compartment of a golf bag, your tackle box, or a raincoat pocket. Although tan is the most popular color, you can also find it in reds, blues, and yellows.

Gloves

Pigskin or deerskin is probably the softest and most comfortable glove leather, and dark brown is the most versatile color. For milder weather, a lining of silk or a thin knit of wool might be enough, while a fur lining or a heavier thermal knit is more comfortable for cold weather. Unless the weather turns brutally cold, bulkier gloves (those with suede finishes and furry or sheepskin linings) should be reserved for casual wear.

One slightly less practical accessory is the pocket square, worn tucked into the breast pocket of your suit jacket. Unlike the pocket handkerchief, the pocket square is strictly for show. If you have to sneeze, use a handkerchief and keep it tucked away in some other pocket out of sight. This 20-inch square of cotton, linen, or silk can be used to brighten up the front of your suit. Pocket squares come in solid colors, patterns, plain white, and white with the owner's monogram. If you wear one, let it stand by itself. Don't overdo it by wearing a pocket square *and* a boutonniere, for example—that will look overdone. Furthermore, if you choose a solid color or patterned pocket square, be certain it complements your tie. *Never* wear a pocket square and tie made of identical patterns. The total effect is much too pat to be elegant.

Folding your handkerchief

There's more to wearing a pocket square than just stuffing it in your pocket. You can choose one of four basic ways to fold it and wear it.

The first is the triangle. It is best suited for monogrammed handkerchiefs. Simply fold the handkerchief in half diagonally so the monogram is at the apex of the triangle. Then fold in the sides and fold up the bottom so that it fits into the pocket with just the monogrammed point protruding.

A variation of this is a petal fold, which works best with a light silk square. Fold the square in half diagonally and continue folding it into triangles one or two more times. Tuck it in your pocket so that the tips of the triangles spill over the top.

For a slightly irregular look, simply grasp the square in the center and tuck it into your pocket center first so that an irregular cluster of handkerchief corners spills over the top.

For a neat puff of fabric, again grasp the square in the center and, still holding it there, tuck it into your pocket corners until about an inch of the slightly rumpled puff of fabric is poking above the pocket.

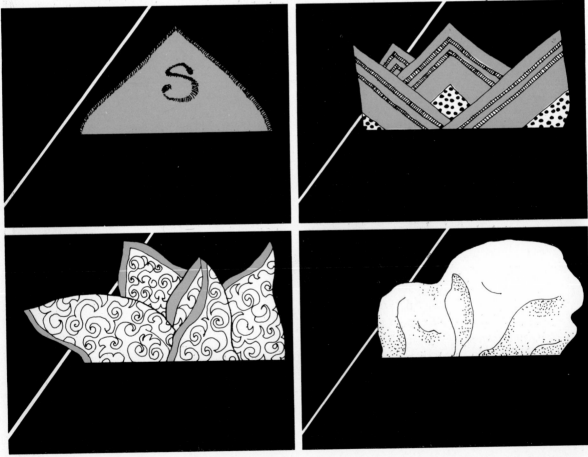

Your attaché case is probably the most important business accessory. **Leather goods**
It is as much a part of your business look as your suit, and it can
enhance your professional image. Although cases today are made of
a variety of materials, the classic leather case still looks the smartest.
Buy the best leather case you can afford. Dark brown or black is the
most useful color. A case with excessive decoration—flashy metal bits
or designer initials—will look pretentious.

The style you choose is purely a matter of practical considerations **Attaché cases**
and good taste. The amount of paperwork you carry routinely will
probably be the biggest factor. The rule of thumb in business seems to
be that as you move up the corporate ladder, your load of paperwork
becomes increasing less.

There are two basic attaché case styles. One is the hard-sided box
type that is hinged on one side and looks like a small suitcase; the
other is the soft-sided case with two handles on the top and a zipper
that runs around three sides. If you carry a lot of paper, the hard-sided
case may be more practical—it has a little more room.

If you carry a handful of papers, you might prefer a zippered
envelope case. Less cumbersome than an attaché case, this is better
looking than a manila envelope. Make sure it's durable leather, not
vinyl.

The shoulder bag, once considered a fad, is here to stay—basically **Shoulder bags**
because it is practical. The shoulder bag first became popular when
closer-fitting European-style suits came into vogue. Men who wore
them found they couldn't get more than a wafer-thin wallet and car
keys into the pockets without making unsightly bulges. A small
shoulder bag became a useful item.

If the shoulder bag suits your personal or business style, you can
select one in either vinyl, canvas, or leather. Since leather lasts longer,
the extra expense is well worth it. Alternatives to the shoulder bag are
the well-made canvas and leather hunting bags, or an army surplus
shoulder bag. While these bags may be of limited use for business—
the shoulder bag has not replaced the attaché case—you will find them
indispensable as overnight bags, flight bags, or general-purpose
catchalls.

Wallets   You may never wear a shoulder bag, but it will be a rare moment when you won't be carrying another leather accessory—your wallet. This is often the forgotten item in your wardrobe. Long after you've replaced a worn-out pair of shoes or a suit, you may continue to carry a shabby, dog-eared, bulging wallet. Not only is a fat wallet unattractive, it can ruin the lines of your suit when stuffed into a jacket or hip pocket.

Wallets come in two general styles: the hip-pocket style and the taller pocket secretary style that is usually carried in a jacket pocket. If you have no preference, you should consider the pocket secretary type. It is a little more stylish looking, and the ease with which you can get to it when you need it is a definite plus. Few things look more awkward than a man hunched over trying to wiggle free a wallet that is stuck in his hip pocket. Furthermore, most pocket secretary wallets hold at least as many credit cards as the hip-pocket styles and still lie flat in your jacket pocket. Whatever style you choose, get one with slots in it for storing credit cards, *not* one with plastic fold-up strips with pockets. The slots let you stagger the cards and minimize the bulk.

Better wallets are made of a soft leather such as calfskin, and are usually fully lined with leather. The less expensive ones are lined with silk or rayon or have no lining at all.

Jewelry   Jewelry looks best if it's simple and understated. This is especially true when dressing for business, where the trend these days seems to be toward less jewelry.

Tie clips and studs   Tie clips are no longer a necessity, and tie tacks are used much less frequently than they were in the past. Now the style is to let your tie hang loose and unchecked.

French cuffs are also worn much less frequently these days, except in conservative companies and on formal business occasions. If you decide to wear cuff links, keep them as plain and unassuming as possible. Simple gold cuff links are the best. You can get them with a matching set of studs if you wish to wear them with a tuxedo.

Watches   A plain gold or silver wristwatch, the slimmer the better, is your best choice. Wear it with a dark leather strap or a matching metal strap. Avoid wristwatches that are novelty items. These tend to be cumbersome, distracting, and short-lived.

If you habitually wear a three-piece suit, you can wear a gold or silver pocket watch with matching chain. A watch chain draped across your vest may be just the right touch of understated elegance. But make sure you really feel comfortable with it—otherwise, it will seem like a self-conscious affectation.

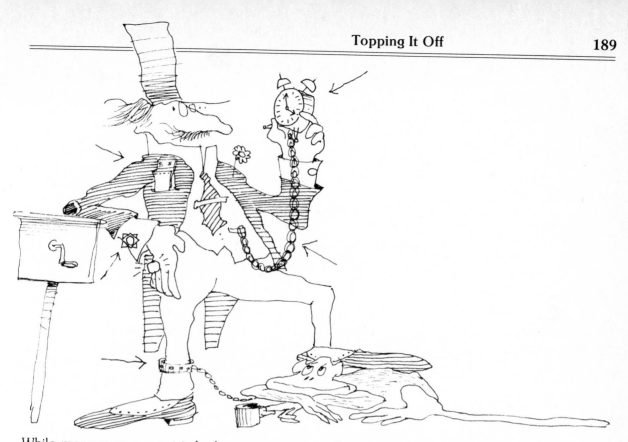

While many men wear strictly decorative rings, such as pinky rings, they rarely work well with a business wardrobe. These rings often use large stones or decorations to keep them in proportion to the size of a man's hand. These decorations and stones, especially if they are diamonds, are often overwhelming and become distractions.

Other jewelry

Obviously, you're going to have more latitude in the jewelry you wear casually, but the same general guideline applies: keep jewelry simple and understated. One item that has become popular is the neck chain—a gold or silver chain that fits close to the throat and is worn with an open-necked shirt. Limit yourself to one chain at a time. Wearing two or more chains of different lengths around your neck will just create a cluttered look.

For casual wear

If you wear a chain with an ornament, make sure the ornament is not overwhelmingly large. A huge pendant will look cheap even if it is made of solid gold. The important thing to remember in using *any* jewelry is not to wear it to excess.

When you are not wearing your jewelry, store it in something with a soft lining to keep it from getting scratched. Accessories made of silver will tarnish and will need periodic cleaning with a good silver polish.

Care of jewelry

Make yourself happy   When asked if there were any characteristic common to all of mankind, H. G. Wells replied, "Every one of these hundreds of millions of human beings is in some form seeking happiness." The *need* for happiness is universal; the *nature* of happiness, however, is singular. And because each of us has an individual definition of happiness, each of us must search for happiness in an individual way. No matter how helpful external influences are, your own happiness will be found only within your own self.

Your worst enemy   Being happy is widely considered our most natural (i.e., our healthiest) state of consciousness. Why, then, is this state so often difficult to attain? Well, if you're like most people, there's someone in your life who's been effectively sabotaging many—perhaps all—of your efforts to achieve happiness. No, it's not a disgruntled business associate or a still-angry ex-lover. Want to see the face of this dedicated saboteur? Just walk into the bathroom. Turn on the light. And look in the mirror.

Hard to believe? Think it over for a minute. Do you remember the time you talked yourself out of asking the boss for that raise? Or the night you were sitting next to that beautiful woman but couldn't work up the nerve to say anything to her? How about those school exams for which you never bothered to study because you just *knew* you weren't going to pass? Or those jobs for which you never applied because you didn't feel qualified? If any of these situations sounds familiar to you, you're not alone. Everyone has, at some time or another, been assaulted by self-doubt. It's not an easy assault to repel, either. Self-doubt attacks from within. At best, it can lay siege to your ego, blockade your goals, and disperse your ambitions; at worst, it can force you to become your own worst enemy. Reinforcements are needed. Fortunately, you have a natural ally—and he may be closer than you suspect.

Your closest friend

Keep looking in the mirror. Smile. Wave hello. That person staring back at you doesn't have to be a foe. Instead, he can be changed into your most essential friend. The secret ingredient in this transformation is TLC—Tender Loving Care. You must be kind to yourself. Learn to value your uniqueness. Nourish your self-esteem. In order to be happy with what you attain, you must first learn how to be happy with what and who you are.

Peace with the past

In a sense, being happy means being free of your own personal history. Have you ever struggled toward some cherished goal only to compulsively throw it away at the very moment it's finally won? Often this is not so much as act of self-destruction as it is an act of self-*punishment*. To be human is to be imperfect—there's not a person on this planet who hasn't done things he's later ashamed of having done. And because it's painful to face our "sins," we tend to suppress all memory of them. Like ghosts, these memories haunt our lives, compelling us to hurt ourselves in a continual cycle of guilt and atonement. By acknowledging the sins, we exorcise the ghosts. To paraphrase Santayana: Those who cannot remember past mistakes are condemned to repeat them.

This is *your* life   Any truly comprehensive examination of one's life will, of course, require several years of intensive analysis, usually supervised by a professional counselor. (See "Getting Loose," pages 37-38.) However, as this type of treatment is not always necessary or accessible, psychiatry has devised a less elaborate form of analysis known as the "Life Review." Based on the principle that self-help is generally the best help, this relatively new method has already proved remarkably effective in increasing awareness of our past actions. Some of the major advantages are:

· **Availability.** The Life Review offers a means of coming to terms with the past without having to commit years of your future to the process. All that's needed is a little notebook, a few hours each day for approximately a week, some rudimentary knowledge of meditative procedures, and the desire—and the will—to make yourself happier than you now are.

· **Objectivity.** The problem with self-examination is that it often, far too often, leads to self-pity. Blaming yourself for an action is a common experience. Say that you've just fouled up at work. Ideally, you should try to *understand* why you made a mistake, not *accuse* yourself. Self-accusation increases both your insecurity and the possibility that you'll make the same mistake again (and again and again). On the other hand, reviewing the past puts considerable distance between your actions and your self. Thus you'll be able to correct mistakes unhampered by feelings of inadequacy.

· **Patterns.** Rarely does an action exist by itself. More likely it is just one link in a long chain of actions stretching back to childhood. These chains, or patterns, are often extremely self-destructive. For example: Your relationship with your lover has been steadily improving. Suddenly, for no apparent reason, you feel driven to say or do something that disrupts, perhaps even ends, the affair. By utilizing the Life Review, you can chart the course of previous relationships. If you discover a series of similar incidents, then you've also discovered a self-destructive pattern. (You can sometimes even trace it back to the very beginning. One hypothetical example: At age 15, you badly hurt your first girlfriend, and have, ever since, been using other women to hurt yourself as a form of penance.) Recognizing past patterns of self-destruction liberates you for future patterns of self-*construction*.

First day—Preparations   Before you start the Life Review, devise a week's schedule that allows two hours of free time each day (if possible, during the same period each day). You'll need either a composition or loose-leaf notebook. Lay out all facing pages in the following manner:

Because the Life Review is, basically, a free-form exercise in memory, it requires an uncluttered, noncritical, responsive mind. In order to enhance this state, it will help if you acquaint yourself with the fundamental principles of meditation. (See "Getting Loose," pages 35-36.) If done correctly, meditation will begin to clear your mind of all debris. Spend your first Review day practicing until you feel empty of tension and concern.

Second day—Decisions

Meditate. Let your mind run free over any choices that you've faced in your life. Decisions are the mirrors that reflect our sense of self; what we decide to do is a fairly accurate measure of what we decide we want. And since we don't always want what we need, examining past decisions is an essential step toward achieving more complete happiness.

Write down everything that memory presents to you. Some of the decisions you'll remember may seem insignificant, but if it's important enough to appear in your mind—especially when you're in a meditative state—then it's important enough to appear on your list. (How you spent your allowance ten years ago, for instance, may be considerably more important than you think.) Leave yourself open; don't be critical. At this point, the one limit you should impose is that of time—include only those decisions made at least a year ago, and spend only the allotted two hours concentrating on them. To do otherwise is to solicit self-pity, and self-pity seldom refuses an invitation.

Third day—Alternatives

Meditate. Are there any further choices you've thought of since yesterday? If so, add them to the first column. Now turn your attention to the notebook section marked ALTERNATIVES. Every decision situation has at least two built-in options, and now that time has passed you judge whether the option you selected was a good one. Don't forget that the Life Review is not only a means of dealing with the past but also a way of identifying and terminating existing self-destructive patterns. Match the decisions on the list with all the alternatives you had when you made those decisions. A word of caution: By now, no matter how hard you've tried to ward it off, a little self-criticism is probably creeping in. Fight it; it's vital you remain open-minded.

Fourth day—Controls Decisions are also influenced by *external* or *internal* controls. An external control is anything, or anyone, that affects your decisions from the outside ("I didn't marry Jane because my mother didn't like her"); an internal control is, conversely, a motivation that springs entirely from within ("I didn't marry Jane because I didn't love her"). Meditate on controls. If you made a choice because you hoped to please someone else or were responding to a dictate you didn't believe in, mark it "external." If the choice was based only on your own wishes, mark it "internal." Again, avoid as much self-criticism as possible.

Fifth day—Results By "results" we do not mean the chain reaction of cause and effect that a decision often initiates, but rather whether that decision made you more happy than not. Since considering results will require an examination of your past values, it's now necessary to let at least some self-critical judgments into your consciousness. Meditate on the values that created the most conflict. However, instead of being specific ("Was the money I gained on such-and-such an occasion worth the pain it directly caused so-and-so?"), try to generalize ("Is gaining money for myself worth causing pain to others?").

Sixth day—Strained Interlude All right, you're going to feel a little depressed today. Regardless of how closely you've followed the instructions, the Life Review is a harrowing experience. Meditate, but not on the columns of your notebook. Just go with the flow. You've earned the right to rest.

Seventh day—The Review Open your notebook again. If you've been honest, you've created a rough sketch of your previous actions. Study the decisions that didn't make you happy. (If this is a recurring pattern, it's time to reevaluate your goals.) Next, consider the alternatives you selected. (If you consistently rejected more attractive options, you've been acting self-destructively.) Don't forget to tally up your controls. (If the majority were external, perhaps you haven't assumed enough responsibility for your own life.) Finally, confront those terrible ghosts. Chances are there aren't as many as you thought and that you haven't caused nearly as much damage as you've been blaming yourself for. Chances are, in fact, that you've hurt yourself far more grievously than you've ever hurt anyone else. Still, there's no denying you have caused others some pain. So now that you've faced that, what do you do?

Forgive yourself.
Forget the past.
And begin again.

PAST
FI

The past haunts us, the future taunts us, but the present seems to constantly elude our grasp. Consider:

The best of the present

It's vacation time—two full weeks of sand and surf. Each day you walk down to the ocean, stretch out on the beach, and bask in the sun. But are you enjoying the heat, the lassitude, the sensual pleasures of total relaxation? Oh, no; you're far too busy thinking how your friends are going to admire that great tan. But when you return home, are you going to enjoy your friends' admiration? No again; you'll be too busy wishing you were back on the beach.

Simplistic as it is, this example can be viewed as a metaphor for the way most of us approach life. We spend so much time brooding about what was, and worrying about what will be, that we lose sight of what is. But you can't be happy living in the past or the future; you can only be happy in the present moment of existence. If you use that moment for regrets or anticipation, you're wasting it. The key to unlocking the secret of happiness is one word, and that word is *now*.

Don't throw away that notebook you used for your Life Review. Not yet, anyway. It's list time again.

How to take account of yourself

When psychiatrists talk about change, they're not referring to transformation of, but rather improvements in, personality. Having a poor (i.e., self-destructive) personality trait is somewhat like being an alcoholic. The Alcoholics Anonymous party line—and most doctors agree with it—is "Once a drunk, always a drunk." But if alcoholism can't be eradicated, it can be restrained. Likewise, although a harmful character trait cannot be erased, it can be identified and either completely controlled or, at the very least, acceptably modified. Before you can begin to improve yourself, you have to know the elements of your self that need to be improved. Keeping an account of your traits will allow you to emphasize the good and diminish the bad.

Let's start with the good. List all those traits in which you take pride. Use your own happiness quotient here; don't be swayed by any values other than your own. If you consider yourself gentle, for example, do not pay any attention to a society that demands that men be rough 'n' tough. If you're happy with your gentleness, it's most definitely an asset and should be thus recorded. If you enjoy the company—and a variety—of different lovers, don't let a monogamous world henpeck you.

Assets

Be as honest as you can, but also be as kind to yourself as you can. If a characteristic seems only marginally beneficial to you, put it down as an asset anyway. The primary rule for self-happiness is: Always give yourself the benefit of the doubt.

Deficits   Next, list the traits you consider to be your bad ones. By now you've learned something about the importance of remaining objective. Even so, proceed with caution. Remember that this is only a list; don't let yourself give in to those old "if only I was this instead of that" regrets. This kind of thinking invariably leads to our old nemesis, self-pity. Stick to the facts. If your temper's on so short a fuse that it's cost you friends and/or jobs, it's definitely a deficit; if you worry so much about your temper that it's ruining your sleep, worrying is a deficit too. Nothing is too small to be recorded—even bumming cigarettes, if you do it often enough, can end in misunderstandings and unhappiness.

Good/bad traits   Some personality traits can be both good *and* bad. Aggression, for instance, can be a most helpful trait when applied to your career, and a most damaging trait when applied to your love life. Make a third list of your good/bad traits. Any characteristic that seems double in nature should be included here.

There's no way you'll be able to do a self-appraisal without some subjectivity creeping in, so the help of a friend is required. Show your notebook to a friend you can trust and ask for an audit. There'll probably be additions to the assets list and—if your friend's a *good* friend—there'll be some additions to the deficits list as well. (If you're feeling particularly courageous, show the lists to an *ex*-friend. Not only will you probably get a more candid—if somewhat less tactful—appraisal, but you may also find that the act of sharing your private self will create enough intimacy to renew your friendship.) Once all the entries are in their proper place, you're ready to begin actively correcting your faults.

One step at a time   Don't try to do everything at once. Concentrate on one trait at a time. It's not enough to simply cancel out deficits; you should search out means to convert them into assets. If you've discovered that you talk too much, don't just stop talking—start listening too. If you have a habit of borrowing from everyone in sight, spread your largesse around. If you proceed correctly, your list of assets will increase as the list of deficits dwindles. And, not so incidentally, your happiness will increase too.

How to love yourself   Don't be afraid of the term "self-love." It may seem to be a pejorative, but it is, in fact, a major element in the quest for happiness. Contrary to popular belief, self-love is not limited to the garden-variety Narcissus who spends all day, each day, reminding everyone how wonderful he is. (Indeed, this type of compulsive behavior is generated more by fear and insecurity than conceit, and our Narcissus probably spent all night, each night, trembling in bed with the covers over his head.) Self-love means treating yourself with respect and esteem. This is not always easy—but it is always necessary.

By now you should realize that you're a far better person than you've credited yourself with being; it's time—it's long *past* time—to start acting in a manner that reflects, and supports, that realization. What follows is a series of simple exercises designed to reinforce your sense of worth and help enhance your sense of value. This series is by no means inclusive. As you become more comfortable with the concept of treating yourself well, you'll be able to add more exercises of your own devising.

· Flatter yourself. Why not? You're quick enough to shoulder the blame—how about a back pat when you do something right? Most people don't compliment themselves enough; many don't compliment themselves *at all*. If you've just performed a difficult job, congratulate yourself on it. And keep on congratulating yourself until you can accept the fact that you succeed at what you do because you're good at what you do.

· Reward yourself. If the job was a particularly hard one, buy a treat for yourself. Go to a restaurant, say, and feast on some lobster. Or go to a clothing store and buy that pair of jeans you've had your eyes on. Or go to a liquor store and stand yourself to a bottle of champagne. Or do all three. Don't worry about the price. You're worth it.

· Treat yourself. On second thought, why wait for an important occasion before you get yourself a present? You don't need an excuse to be nice to yourself. Do it any time you feel like it.

· Accept accolades from others. If someone praises you, don't dismiss it with an embarrassed shrug and a modestly muttered, "I was

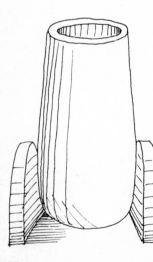

lucky." Luck has nothing to do with it. Of course, courtesy—not to mention sanity—forbids you to leap up into the air, click your heels together, and shout, "Yea for me!" whenever you receive a compliment. So just respond by saying "Thank you." The point is to acknowledge to both yourself and others that the applause is well deserved.

· Give affection. Don't keep your private feelings private. The next time you're with someone you love, say it loud and clear: "I love you." Your love will make your friend happy. *You* will make your friend happy.

· Explore new experiences. A great portion of your time is reserved for life's duties. Relax. Begin to enjoy some of life's pleasures. (Besides, if you spend more time with the things you want to do, you won't feel so resentful of the time spent on the things you *have* to do.) If you believe in yourself, no activity is beyond your scope. Climb out of that rut. Sample new foods. Meet new people. Take an unplanned vacation. Deliberately do something silly like wading barefoot through a park fountain. Try a new hairstyle. If there's an organization you'd like to join, join it. If there's a sport you'd like to learn, learn it. By choosing to indulge in pleasures, you are choosing to love yourself.

· Rid yourself of jealousy, whether it's sexual or social. If you care enough for yourself, you won't need external influences—that is, the love and/or approval of others—to provide you with a sense of worth. All right, so your lover's gone off with a new friend, or that promotion's been handed to a coworker. So what? Tell yourself that someone's choosing another is not a reflection on your own value, but rather a reflection of that person's own particular needs. If may be hard to banish the green-eyed monster, but it's considerably harder to suffer its torments all the time. In reality, jealousy is a put-down of self; by allowing yourself to be jealous of a person, you're admitting that he or she is better than you are.

· Stop blaming yourself. Facts are facts. It can be a cold, cruel world, and you're not always going to win. If you should happen to fail in a social or business situation, resist the litany of self-accusation. "It's all my fault" is most definitely *not* the way to deal with setbacks. Instead, put some distance between you and the catastrophe. Be objective. If, indeed, it was your fault, examine what you did wrong; this way you can avoid the same mistake in the future. Often, however, you'll see that it wasn't your error—at least not completely. But if you automatically shoulder all the blame, others are going to automatically blame you too.

How to present yourself

Self-doubt often compels us to wear external masks that hide our inner selves. Afraid that we're not strong enough, or smart enough, or aggressive enough to deal with the world, we force ourselves to present the image (rather than the reality) of who we are. As a matter of fact, there are many schools of thought—notably, assertion therapies—that actively encourage this sort of public concealment. The guiding principle seems to be: There are sharks in the water, and the only way to fight them off is to become an even larger shark. Unfortunately, this attitude encourages you to cut other people off from your feelings. Worse, it cuts *you* off from your feelings. If carried to an extreme, the mask becomes indistinguishable from the face; indeed, the mask *is* the face.

There is, however, an alternate approach. Instead of repressing emotions, express them. Constantly strive to present yourself as you really are. After all, you'll never be happy if you're uncertain of your ability to be publicly accepted. Basically, there are two rules for self-presentation:

1. Don't fool yourself. To be a man in this society is to be constantly tempted by the macho ideal. The strong, silent male is not only an attractive role—it's also a safe one. By never showing emotion, you'll never be vulnerable, right? Of course, you'll also spend a great deal of time alone and miserable, but that's the price of masculinity. Right? Wrong.

The attempt to live up to the male stereotype interferes with friendships, changes sports from pleasure to compulsion, elevates competitiveness and diminishes tenderness, discourages love or even affection, and reduces sex to mechanics. There's no ready-made way to combat machismo; it requires honesty, self-esteem, and—above all else—a sensitivity to your own needs. You might begin by taking your emotional temperature whenever something unsettling occurs. Ask yourself how you feel. Don't lie; don't hedge; don't put on that old mask of stoicism and nonconcern. If you've just been fired from your job, it's absurd to dismiss it with an airy "Who cares?" Dammit, *you* care. Allow yourself to express pain. And don't, *don't* be embarrassed to cry over hurts. You're not only a man but a human being—and one of the most unique qualities of humans is the ability to weep.

2. Don't fool others. Once you've learned how to reveal your feelings to yourself, start revealing them to other people. If they do something that affects you, let them know it. Are you angry? Then say so. Don't fall into the trap of sublimating it—you'll only end up taking all that anger out on yourself. Whenever you meet someone for the first time, assume the best. Trust the person. Listen to him/her. If a new acquaintance does turn out to be a shark—well, it's simple enough to just keep out of his/her way. It takes two to play power games; if you don't play, you can't lose.

Games people *should* play

These are sensory exercises designed to increase your sensitivity to both yourself and others. When done properly, they will help you get into a state of mind in which all of your attention is directed toward the here and now.

Body Awareness. Sit up straight in a chair and plant your feet firmly against the floor. Feel the pressure of your feet against the floor and the pressure of the floor against your feet. Concentrate on your toes, one at a time. Then your ankles. Then the muscles in your legs, front and back. Slowly move your concentration up along your body. When you reach your head, move it slowly back and forth so as to feel the sensations at the back of your skull. Touch the skin on your face, your lips, your cheeks, your forehead, your ears. Listen to the rhythms of your breathing. If you do this for thirty minutes, you'll experience a great sense of relaxation with yourself.

Eye-to-Eye Contact. Find a partner—the more intimate, the better. Sit opposite each other at a comfortable distance (two to four feet). Now look into each other's eyes for about three minutes.

Don't talk. At first you may both be anxious, then embarrassed, but as you continue to stare at each other you'll start feeling more and more peaceful. When this feeling of peace peaks, you will have achieved the state of "now"—that is, you'll be existing in the act of merely recording and acknowledging what you see.

Palm-to-Palm Contact. Again, you'll need a partner. Hold one hand, palm out, against your partner's palm. Close your eyes. Don't talk. The resulting feeling is similar to the one you achieve in the eye-to-eye exercise, except that your sense of intimacy, peace, and closeness will be even more heightened.

The Blind Walk. Close your eyes and allow your partner to lead you around the room by your hand. Your partner will choose certain objects for you to explore with your fingers. (Any objects—a chair, a mirror, the wall—will do.) When you've finished, open your eyes and share the sensory experiences with your partner. This enhances trust and communication.

How to express yourself   Considering how much talking we all do—researchers estimate that the average person will utter as many as 12,000 sentences each day—it's amazing how little we actually seem to say to each other. Although language's function was, is, and always will be communication, many people have subverted it into a weapon, or a protective camouflage, or a defensive shield. But the way you choose to speak is a direct statement of your personality, and no amount of filibustering is going to conceal you. You may think you're being clever by using evasive, long-winded, or petty talk to cover up your inner self, but actually you're merely indicating that you're timid, boorish, or small-minded. So, since you can't hide behind a verbal barrage, you might as well learn the do's and don't's of straight talking.

First, the don't's:

Don't use cliches. The employment of platitudes is a sure sign of a noncreative mind. Also, although slang can often be a particularly supple and expressive form of language, don't overdo the jargon.

Don't use unnecessary interjections. Stop peppering your sentences with all those useless phrases, you know, that make you sound so dull, you know, and worse, you know, make your listener, you know, want to, you know, reach over, you know, grab your neck with both hands, you know, and *throttle* you. You know?

Don't use words with which you're not comfortable. Those eight-syllable words aren't going to impress anyone—especially if you mispronounce them.

Don't try to match your words to the person you're addressing. Regardless of whom you're talking to, college professor or high-school student, remain true to your own personal speech patterns. Talking down—or, for that matter, talking up—to someone is a not-so-subtle form of patronizing him, and (as any first-year psych student will tell you) patronizing other people is a sign of deep insecurity.

Don't use new-speak. Thanks largely to politicians, there's a sublanguage that's become more and more prevalent in this country of late. Phrases like "primary objective" and "that statement is no longer operable" have already done more than enough to drain speech of its meaning and grace. Don't compound the damage. And a sentence like "Let's run it up the flagpole and see who salutes" may be acceptable in the boardroom. But use clichés like that in the local singles bar and they're going to laugh you right out into the street.

Now for the do's:

Do use, whenever possible, simple and straightforward speech. Uncluttered language is a singularly powerful way to get the message across. An overabundance of adjectives, too many figures of speech, a purple tinge to the rhetoric—all these are devices that conceal rather than reveal. No matter what your literary taste, read any page from any book written by Ernest Hemingway. There's no better instruction in how a simple sentence can carry a complex thought.

Do learn a second language. There are many advantages to knowing a foreign language. For one thing, it can be a definite plus in your career. Even more important is the way studying a foreign language can make you more aware of the structure of your own.

Do explore the wonders of nonverbal language. We all do as much communicating with our hands and facial expressions as we do in speech. Learn to listen with your eyes as well as your ears. Buy some books on body language—not just the popular best sellers but some anthropological studies too. You can discover some fascinating facts in these tomes. For example, did you know that showing your teeth in a smile was originally a gesture of agressive threat?

Do use speech aids. Buy a few primers on grammar and bone up on the fundamentals. A tape recorder can be handy, too; by listening to yourself speak, you'll be able to identify and correct your more blatant speech errors.

Organizing yourself   Living in the present is composed of a complex stream of people, obligations, and events. How efficiently you are able to deal with this barrage discloses more about you than your résumé ever could. Everyone admires people who are creative, efficient, and responsible with their resources, and who seem to lead cohesive, organized lives. But most of us believe that *we* could never be that kind of person. The fact is that you *can* be that kind of person.

No one was ever born organized. Becoming organized is a process of imposing order on the chaos of day-to-day life, and that process must be carefully developed and continually refined. But becoming organized is neither difficult nor painful. It doesn't require that you lead a structured existence or that you sacrifice the excitement and spontaneity in your life; it just requires that you think a little bit.

When you *are* organized you deal more efficiently with your time and money. Directions in your life emerge as your goals are defined, worked toward, and achieved. Making important decisions is no longer a major trauma because information that bears on problems is *there*, concise and available. In short, you spend less time worrying and more time enjoying life.

Your time   In order to begin organizing your time, you must first come to grips with two simple, often ignored, facts of life.

1. There are a limited number of hours in the day in which to accomplish what needs to be done.
2. Because time is limited, you can't possibly get *everything* done today. Therefore, you must plan ahead and then have a system for keeping track of the plans you've made.

Aids   There are several items which will make planning and monitoring your time much easier. They are:

· A watch. It doesn't have to be expensive, but it must work.
· Calendars. Get one for the house and one for the office. Make sure that there is enough room on each to make several notations per day.
· A "pocket organizer." This consists of a calendar that can be read a week at a time and a notepad, and will fit into a vest pocket.
· A book in which to note addresses and phone numbers.
· A pen. This is perhaps the most important item. Get into the habit of always carrying one with you .

Monitoring your time   The best way to remember any information is to write it down. And the best way to remember where you wrote it down is to get into the habit of using your calendars and address book.

When a date or time of day must be remembered, note the fact on your calendar. Try to keep the office calendar for work-related information, and the one at home for social obligations.

Be sure to note *all* of the necessary details, such as the nature of an event and the time and place at which it's to be held.

At the end of each week, transfer the information on your business and social calendars to next week's calendar in your pocket organizer.

Anyone with an address or phone number worth remembering gets noted immediately in your address book.

Set specific goals for yourself. They can be small, like "get to work on time," or large, like "paint the house," but make sure they're well defined. Many vague, major tasks can be broken down into manageable undertakings. For instance, "clean the living room" is clearer and more manageable than "do the household chores."

Realistically estimate the time involved in any task, and then allow for complications. Remember that almost everything will take longer than you originally estimate.

Separate your projects into those that can reasonably be accomplished in the course of a normal day (such as cleaning the living room), and those that will require periodic attention over a number of weeks or months (such as painting the house).

Budget your time. Work your projects into your day-to-day schedule, but remember two things: you won't want to work for eight hours at home after returning from the office, and projects that overwhelm you become ex-projects. Allow yourself time to relax, eat, and sleep.

Planning ahead

Thoughts on time use

Be punctual (use your watch). Not only is it courteous, it also keeps your schedule intact.

Persevere. Once you have set aside time for a specific endeavor, use *that* time for *that* task.

Remember that "getting there" takes time. Don't assume that you can leave the office at one o'clock and be across town at ten past.

Almost all jobs have specified starting and stopping times. Adhere to both. Starting time because you have to; stopping time because you have things to accomplish outside the office, and because, if you don't, you'll end up hating your job.

Paperwork

Much of the paperwork you do needs to be retained for future reference. Managing this collection is frequently annoying and confusing. It doesn't have to be. Organizing this facet of your life is relatively easy—but first let's consider some of the items you'll want to keep, and why they're important.

Insurance policies. Insurance requirements vary with the individual. Your policies should be tailored to your needs, so locate a competent agent. When you find one you're happy with, you should consider the following types of coverage:

• Automobile. Most states will not let you license an uninsured vehicle, which answers the question "Do I need it?" The extent of your coverage will probably be dictated by your financial situation. Keep in mind that it is better to be slightly overinsured than to have to cover the costs of an accident out of pocket.

• Renter's. If you rent, you may not be covered under your landlord's insurance policies. Many insurance companies now offer coverage for fire, theft, and personal liability to those who rent. Check with your landlord. If you aren't covered, you may want to investigate this type of coverage.

• Medical. If you aren't covered by some form of medical insurance, you're running the risk of financial disaster should you require medical assistance or hospitalization. The cost of medical care is substantial; consequently, the cost of medical insurance is high. There are a variety of coverages to choose from. The most common are hospitalization, surgical, general medical, major medical, income protection, and comprehensive. Many businesses, unions, fraternal organizations, etc., arrange less expensive group coverage for their members. If you're eligible for this kind of medical insurance, it's your best bet. If not, see your agent and have him determine the best plan for you.

• Life. If you're a young, single man, why would you want to consider life insurance? For one thing, it's less expensive and easier to obtain coverage now, when the odds of your passing away are slim. And to be perfectly grisly, the cost of funeral arrangements and estate settlement can be exorbitant. There are three basic kinds of life insurance: term, whole life or cash value, and endowments. Have your agent explain the benefits of each.

Once you and your agent have established your needs and you have your policies, you will need to periodically review your coverage, because as your position in life changes, so do your insurance needs. Having your policies handy makes this process easier. You'll also need to refer to your policy should a question arise concerning premium payments, the extent of your coverage, or beneficiaries.

Tax returns. The IRS can audit your returns from one to three years back, so keep your copy for three years—and keep *all* your expense receipts.

Titles. Titles for your car, house, boat, etc. should be kept handy—they are your only true proof of ownership. Also, you may at some point wish to sell one of these items, or pledge them as collateral for a loan. If you do, you'll need the title for transfer.

Bank statements. Checking account statements should be reviewed for errors each month and then retained to help in preparing your tax return. Having the canceled checks also comes in handy when you have to prove that payment for an item *was* made. Savings account statements are a help in financial planning, and you'll need them to report interest income on your tax return.

Your will. It may seem an inopportune time to consider the possibility of your dying unexpectedly, but it does exist. It's fairly inexpensive to have a lawyer help you draw up a will, and it does make estate settlement easier should something happen.

Other items you may want to keep are: a copy of your lease, receipts for major purchases and services; documents explaining your veteran's benefits (provided you're a veteran); a copy of your birth certificate; warranties and owner's manuals for your car, stereo, appliances, etc.; your passport; copies of important correspondence.

Keeping track

Fortunately, keeping track of these papers is not as difficult as acquiring them was. The simple and best thing to do is to purchase an expanding file (inexpensive—get one at the stationery store), consolidate the material you wish to keep, file it in some order (alphabetically is easiest), and then place the file in a convenient spot so that you will be able to find it when you want it. Filing all your papers won't help if you can't locate the file.

There may be certain documents, such as stocks, bonds, deeds, or even some of the abovementioned items, that you will want to keep in a more secure spot. If so, check with your bank about renting a safe-deposit box. For a nominal fee you receive your own private corner of the safe. *Don't* keep your will or the deed to your cemetery plot in your safe-deposit box. If you should die, your family must obtain a court order to open the box, and this can take several days.

Some rules

Be discriminating when setting up your files. Only keep the pertinent information. The whole purpose of this file is to be able to locate *important* materials quickly.

As new material comes in, make sure that it finds its way into the file right away. Don't stack things on top of the refrigerator figuring you'll get around to them later; you won't. The same rule applies for anything that's removed from the file—put it back as soon as you're done.

Periodically weed out your files, removing anything that you no longer require.

Your money   Money is what you use to convert the time you spend on the job into the products and services you require. Money management deals with a flow: money is obtained, earmarked for specific uses, and then spent or invested. In order to make management efficient and effective you must control this flow, not let it control you. Organization can give you that control. And by organizing—that is, developing strategies for planning and monitoring your financial situation—you will be able to arrange for financial growth and economic stability.

Sources   Before you can organize your finances, you must understand the sources of the money you use.

In essence, the only money you can spend is the money you have earned, inherited, or been given. However, by borrowing or buying on credit, it is possible to spend tomorrow's income today.

Credit, in any form, is simply using someone else's money when you haven't got the cash necessary for a purchase. Credit can be a blessing or a hindrance. Without credit, it would be almost impossible to purchase a house, car, or any other major asset, but the indiscriminate use of credit can lead to financial disaster. Here are some things to think about when you're considering the use of credit:

· Don't use credit if it's not necessary. Ask yourself whether you would purchase the item if you had to pay cash.
· Obligations should never exceed 25 percent of your take-home pay. Ten to 15 percent is a more manageable figure.
· You should never become so indebted that illness or layoff would make repayment a hardship.
· You should never borrow to pay off existing debts—that only compounds the problem.

Always shop for credit. Credit isn't a favor, it's a service, and you are charged for the use of the money you borrow. The charges are called interest, and the rates of interest charged vary (the Federal Reserve Board and individual state governments determine the rates that may be charged for different types of credit), but the Truth in Lending law states that you must be notified of the true annual interest charge any time you use credit. Take the time to see what's available—interest rates do vary.

Getting credit   The following is a list of the most common places you can get credit, the types of credit they offer, and the relative interest rates.

Insurance companies. If you have a "cash value" life insurance policy, you may be able to borrow against the existing value of the policy. These loans are inexpensive and repayment is at your leisure.

You are billed monthly for interest charges; *you* determine when to pay back the principal (original amount borrowed). The only problems are that you cannot borrow more than the cash value of your policy, and borrowing will decrease the amount your beneficiaries will receive if you die before repaying the loan.

Savings banks and some savings-and-loan associations. The loans you can get from these organizations are like the loans obtained from life insurance companies in that you must be a customer and you cannot borrow more than you have in your savings account. Loans are of the installment variety (you make monthly payments), and interest rates comparatively low. (If you are wondering why you shouldn't simply withdraw your savings, consider which you are more likely to repay—a loan, or your savings account.)

Credit unions. Credit unions are cooperatives set up to handle their members' savings and borrowing needs; many businesses and trade unions have them. To borrow you must be a member. If you are eligible to join one, first make sure the management is responsible (usually members take turns running the union), and then *use* your credit union—loans are inexpensive.

Commercial banks. These institutions offer rather expensive installment loans of two basic varieties: secured (they hold the title for the item to be purchased, such as a car, until the loan is repaid in full); and personal (unsecured—you need a good solid, well-established credit rating to get this type). Commercial banks are good places to establish a credit rating because you don't have to bank there to qualify (although it can help).

Retail or commercial credit. This kind of credit is available from department stores, gasoline companies, airlines, etc. They will either let you make purchases "on account" or issue you a credit card. Normally if you settle your account within 30 days, there is no interest charge. After that, rates are fairly steep. If you plan to make a major purchase at a store and plan to take more than a month to pay it off, you should investigate a less expensive type of loan.

Other credit cards. There are basically two other types: bank cards (Visa and Master Charge are the best known), and "private" cards (Carte Blanche, Diner's Club, and American Express are the best known). Again, if you pay within 30 days there is usually no monthly charge, but after that this kind of credit gets expensive, so pay attention to the terms of your contract (on your application form or printed on the card itself). If you qualify for these cards, they are worth having—they can be a great asset when you're traveling—but it's not a

Important:
If problems should arise and you find that you are unable to meet a repayment schedule, *contact your creditors.* In most cases an alternate schedule can be arranged, and silence only makes them nervous.

good idea to run up so many charges that you can't pay them off in a month or two.

Finance companies. These companies advertise "quick and easy" credit terms. Short of loan sharks and pawnbrokers, finance companies are the places where you'll pay the most for the money you need. Avoid them.

Money management

In order to take control of your financial affairs you will need three basic tools. They are a workable budget, a checking account, and a savings account. It is also very useful to make a periodic determination of your net worth.

A budget, to be comfortable and therefore useful, must be simple—and tailored to *your* lifestyle. To go about developing a budget, proceed as follows.

1. Determine your short and long-term financial goals (maybe a vacation this summer, a new car in five years), and determine how much you will have to set aside each month to achieve them.

2. Estimate your monthly income.

3. List your fixed expenses and determine how much you will need each month to meet them. Fixed expenses are those that will not change in the short run, such as rent, utilities, insurance premiums, transportation costs, installment payments, union dues, taxes, savings toward a reserve fund for emergencies.

4. List your variable expenses. These are expenditures over which you have a fair amount of control, such as clothing, furniture, recreation, household expenses, food, car maintenance, newspaper and magazine subscriptions, entertainment, personal luxuries (cigarettes, for instance). You may have to keep track of these for several months and then average your expenditure to come up with accurate estimates of how much you must spend (or how little you can get by spending) on these things.

Now total your monthly expenses and compare this total to your monthly income. With any luck you'll have a surplus of income that can be tucked away in savings. If this isn't the case and your monthly expenses actually exceed your income, you'll have to make some difficult decisions on where to cut back. Remember that expenses must be brought into line with your income, not the other way around. The easiest place to make adjustments, obviously, is in the variable-expense category.

Budgeting is an ongoing process. As your obligations, income, and personal needs change, so should your budget. In order to monitor your needs, get a notebook and, at the top of each page, note an expense ("clothes," "phone bills," etc.) and the amount you've allowed for it. Then, as you spend money on that category, mark it down. If you find that you're consistently overspending in one area, you may want to up your allowance in that area—but remember that this will mean taking something from another area.

A checking account makes paying bills much easier and provides you with an accurate record of the majority of your major financial transactions. You should have one, and you should be careful to use it properly—always write down the date, payee, and amount of each check. Keep canceled checks and those you void with your important documents for taxes and financial review.

Your bank accounts

Commercial banks currently offer a wide variety of checking accounts. Some offer free checking if you maintain a minimum balance; others guarantee protection against having your checks bounce. Discuss the matter with a bank representative and settle on the kind of account that suits your needs.

A savings account is usually a person's first exposure to capital investment—that is, letting someone else use his money while he collects interest. Savings accounts vary—some allow you to deposit and withdraw at will; others (paying higher interest) set restrictions on when you can withdraw your savings. Again, talk to a banker and determine the type of account that's best for you. You may find that you want to put your savings for long-term goals into an account that pays higher interest while keeping your emergency fund and other savings into a type of account that's more flexible. In any event, once you've opened an account (or two) make sure you use them.

Net-worth computations are normally done once or twice a year by corporations. You can borrow the technique and use it to follow and plan your financial growth. Computing your net worth is done by listing your assets and liabilities. (It's usually most convenient to do this at tax time when you have most of your financial material out and the figures are fresh in your head.)

Determining your net worth

Assets are items like cash on hand (include your savings and checking accounts), automobiles (at current market value), furniture, appliances, life-insurance policies (at cash value), any stocks or bonds (at their current market value), jewelry, and your television, stereo, etc. Remember that items like stereos and furnishings are devalued over time, so be realistic when you appraise their worth.

Liabilities are any outstanding bills at the time of computation. For instance, if you haven't paid this month's rent, it should be included as a liability, but you wouldn't include next October's. Be sure to note all the money owed on installment purchases, auto loans, credit-card purchases, etc.

Now simply subtract the total amount of your liabilities from the total amount of your assets—the figure remaining is your net worth. If it happens to be negative, you need to do some major restructuring of your spending habits—otherwise, you're bound to get into serious financial difficulties sooner or later.

Checking your net worth not only lets you see your overall economic growth, but also lets you monitor specific areas (such as savings, household furnishings) to make sure you're maintaining them satisfactorily.

The last word Once you've established a comfortable budget and begun saving money regularly, once you've begun (with the help of your checking account) to really keep track of where your money goes—and once you've gotten some idea of your real net worth—you'll be in a position to make financial decisions without fear. No longer will you need to worry about whether you can afford a certain course of action—all you'll have to do is check your records to *know*.

Addressing the future Most of us will spend approximately half our waking hours at work. It is therefore obvious that being happy in that work is vital to being happy in—and with—ourselves. A routine job that no longer offers any opportunity for challenge or growth quickly becomes both creatively and emotionally numbing. Perhaps this numbness wouldn't be so terrible if it were restricted to your career time, but chances are it will eventually affect your private time too. The only solution to this kind of problem is change. And as any suitable employment change requires six months to a year of active searching, it's never too soon to begin making plans.

Time for a change How do you know when it's time to look for a new job? Ask yourself the following questions:

When was the last time I received a promotion or raise? If it's been more than two years, the moment's come to move on. In fact, even if you have advanced on a regular basis (once a year is standard), you might consider making a change. Today, employers like to see several different jobs within the same field on a prospective employee's résumé. Just don't overdo job hopping—more than three jobs in five years is considered the mark of an unstable personality.

Is there anything left to learn? If you don't feel there is, you've reached the point of diminishing returns.

How many superiors are over me? If you've been at a job for a reasonable amount of time and there are as many people above you as there were when you were initially hired, you might as well get out (you're certainly not going up).

Have I been passed up? If you were due for the promotion that's been awarded to someone else—or if your company has a promotion-from-within policy but still hires someone from the outside to supervise you—start looking for another job immediately.

Do I like my coworkers? Feuding with fellow employees often leads to intolerable working conditions. Also, a change in management sometimes results in a sudden lack of appreciation of your proven talents. If you're having problems—move on.

Does my present work satisfy me? This is the million-dollar question. Dissatisfaction with a job is an excellent—perhaps the most excellent—reason for changing positions. If the dissatisfaction is with your entire career, try to switch fields.

As a job seeker, the most useful tool you'll have is your résumé. It must be neat, orderly, and easy to read. (Don't permit any sloppy typing, poor punctuation, misspellings, or grammatical errors—they will be counted against you.) It must be objective and specific about your employment record. (Don't misrepresent any past jobs.) It must give precise information and keep all descriptions of work to an absolute minimum. (Don't provide any irrelevant materials and don't elaborate—let the facts speak for themselves.) It must *not* include personal references, salary requirements, or photographs, or use the first-person·pronoun. The basic ingredients of a good résumé are:

Your résumé

· Personal data. At the top of the page list your full name, home address, birth date, telephone number, marital status, number of dependents, and sex.

· Career objective. Most guidance counselors agree that this is a very important part of the résumé. The objective must not be stated as a future goal ("To eventually become chief accountant in a major corporation") but as an immediate goal ("To become an accountant in a corporation that allows advancement"). Try to state your objective in a way that's specific yet nonlimiting. ("To become fiction editor" is wrong; "To become an editor" is correct.)

· Work history. Start with your most recent job and work backward. List each job title, company, company address, and length of employment separately. ("Accounting Clerk, Delta Chemical Company, Omega, N.J., June 1968 to January 1971.") Describe specific duties only if they cannot be assumed from the job title. Describe any special accomplishments—"Limited expenditures to $8 million of $10 million budget"—if they place you in a particularly good light. If you're seeking a managerial spot, mention the number of people you've supervised.

• Education. Start with your highest academic degree and work backward. Identify each school you've attended. (Don't lie; employers tend to check on school histories.) If you've taken any other courses—especially those that are work-related—be sure to add them. An extensive academic background is always a strong selling point.

• Additional personal information. Community activities, military experience, knowledge of foreign languages, membership in professional organizations, articles published—list anything you think will demonstrate your abilities and ambition. Do *not*, however, include such irrelevancies as your hobbies or favorite sports, even if you are excellent at them.

The great job hunt   Never leave one job before you've found another. The pressure is just that much greater when you're unemployed. You may, in fact, be forced to accept a less-than-desirable position just to pay for the groceries. When you're already working, you can be more particular about what you choose. And don't be so impatient that you accept the first job that comes along.

Take your time; explore all alternatives; track down all leads. The best sources for these leads are:

Want ads. Old Faithful. Don't restrict yourself to the Sunday papers. Check the employment section each day, paying particular attention to the job description and the salary offer. You may also want to try to get hold of copies of some of the larger corporations' own magazines—they're referred to as "house organs"—because they sometimes list openings. Most employers who run want ads will ask for your résumé before setting up an interview. Be sure to send a covering letter with the résumé stating your interest in working for that particular company.

Employment agencies. Some charge fees, some do not. Many are now designed to serve specific fields—one agency may be exclusively for publishing, another for accounting—so it's best to check their credentials before you make an appointment. The advantage of private agencies is that they want to place you as badly as you want to be placed (they don't earn any money for good intentions). The disadvantage is that they just might try to convince you to take a job that's wrong for you. (Use your own discretion.)

State employment agencies can't devote as much time to you as private agencies, but they can provide useful job information. There are more than 2,000 offices nationwide, and most are hooked up to a computerized job bank. They also keep a national register for certain occupations, keep track of job openings among companies that have not listed those openings with private agencies, and publish local, state, and national labor-market information. No fee is involved with these services.

Executive recruiting firms. Sometimes known as "headhunters," these agencies specialize in industry, banking, merchandising, sales, or public-relations work. Usually they operate at a "don't call us—we'll call you" level, but it won't hurt to approach them anyway.

School placement offices. An excellent service, but one that is almost always restricted to students and alumni of the school in question.

First impressions are lasting impressions. Be on time. Be prepared— read up on the company beforehand; if this is impossible, try to talk to people who've worked there. Bring an additional copy of your résumé, and any other documents you may need (school transcripts, published books, samples of previous work, etc.).

The job interview

Keep the interview businesslike. Let the interviewer control the discussion. Answer all his questions as completely—and succinctly—as possible. Don't exaggerate your qualifications. Don't volunteer any personal information (and if you think *his* questions are too personal, don't be afraid to tell him so). Don't criticize former employers. Dress modestly; if you dress too formally you'll seem overanxious; if you dress too informally you might be violating the company dress code. Never take anyone with you to the interview. Don't smoke unless you ask first if it's all right to, and *never* use the telephone for personal calls. If you're not offered the job at the interview, ask the interviewer when you should call him for his decision. If he asks you to return for a second meeting, make sure you write down the date, time, and place. If he says he can't use you, ask him to suggest another employer.

If you are offered the job, ask your prospective employer the following questions before you accept: In what way has the position been handled in the past (and how can you fill it more satisfactorily)? What are the current duties of the position? Can it grow in responsibility? How important is this position in the overall structure of the company? Is this a position with a sharply defined scope, or can it be expanded? Will you be involved in decision making? What authority will you have over others? What will this position be worth (in money and prestige) in a year? Where can you move next from this position? Don't be afraid to bring all these points up. Concern for the future is a mark of the professional.

When to accept

GOOD FORM

Keeping afloat in a sea of change

A man is not judged by the cut of his suit or the trim of his beard alone. It's not just how you look and feel that count, but how you behave as well. This is where good form comes in. Good form is knowing how to behave whenever you find yourself with other people, which is most of the time. It is as important for the active sportsman as for the high-powered businessman—and as simple as helping others feel comfortable when they're with you.

Your behavior should display the side of you that you want the rest of the world to see. Like a carefully chosen picture frame, it influences the way that people look at you. If you have attained inner peace, your actions must reflect it if the world is to find out about it; if you haven't, there's no reason for anyone else to know. Besides, peace of mind is not attained in a vacuum—most people find their self-fulfillment in the company of others.

In these changing times, old-fashioned etiquette may seem out of place, and, indeed, good form does not have to mean slavishly following trivial rules dreamed up by etiquette writers of the past. In today's rapidly changing world, the best behavior is that which allows you to remain at ease while helping others remain at ease as well. Today's "etiquette" is a tool to help you steer through unfamiliar situations, to make your path through the world of other people easier.

A new simplicity has been injected into our day-to-day relationships. Many of the old forms are out of favor, and correct behavior no longer has to be a struggle. Without prescribed rules of behavior to follow, good form can be as simple as applying everyday common sense to your social life. No etiquette guide can tell you how to behave in *every* situation; at best, it can merely outline the underlying principles of common courtesy.

Strive for a natural elegance and charm, free of affectation. An affected mannerism is no more than a transparent sign of insecurity and is more likely to draw a smothered giggle than the admiring glance it is pleading for. Remember, the point of good form is to be considerate of others, not to show yourself off.

Sincerity and self-discipline

The basic rules of modern etiquette are to keep your heart in the right place and your head screwed tightly onto your shoulders. Whenever you make a blunder—and everyone makes them at one time or another—let it be on the side of excessive thoughtfulness rather than of unintended rudeness. If need be, make a simple apology rather than belaboring the point of your good intentions. (If your intentions really were good and your heart was really in the right place, that will be clear enough without an extended explanation.) A little sincerity can go a long way.

The other half of etiquette is self-discipline. Hold back that sarcastic aside, no matter how well deserved; casual putdowns and sly gossip make you look small-minded, not clever. Everybody suffers from impatience and fatigue at the end of a long day, but there's no excuse for making somebody else suffer for it.

Changing customs have been accelerated by the politics of liberation. The idea of liberation—that we are free of the bondage of traditional social conventions—has swept through our society like a prairie fire and left a social revolution in its wake. This can be a mixed blessing to the man who must cope with the new forms of liberation. Caught in a bind between today's politics and the rules you grew up with, you may now find it harder than ever to get through an entire day without insulting anybody.

The etiquette of liberation

The women's movement can be as liberating for men as it is for women. It is a social and cultural reality. Virtually everyone in the United States today is affected by it, whether he (or she) admits it or not. No longer must you race to a door to open it for a woman, or carry matches even if you don't smoke so that you can light women's cigarettes. If she gets to the door first, let her open it herself, and if she still wants to smoke, knowing that you don't, let her light her own cigarettes.

In larger cities, nearly every woman you meet will consider herself liberated. Just what that means can vary widely from woman to woman. One will consider it demeaning if you open a car door for her or help her into her coat, while another will enjoy the "old-fashioned" courtesies. In smaller towns, a woman may not refer to herself as being "liberated" because of the negative image she thinks this raises

in many men's minds, but she may be every bit as independent and self-sufficient as her big-city sisters.

The best way to deal with liberation, and with women's liberating themselves, is to approach the subject with an open mind. Try to understand what women are going through. Forget all the bad-taste jokes and learn enough to draw some intelligent conclusions of your own. You need not join a men's consciousness-raising group; you can learn through reading. If you lack the time for books, take the trouble to ask a few questions next time you're with people discussing women's liberation. Remember that while for some women's liberation is just one more weapon in the war between the sexes, most take it seriously as something that is improving their lives.

The new etiquette of liberation allows you to behave in the ways that are most comfortable for you. It does not mean that anything goes, but that there is now a broad range of accepted behavior instead of yesterday's specific forms. Eyebrows will no longer be raised when a woman orders the meal at a restaurant. But if you want to retain the chivalrous courtesies, that's all right too—if you do it with elegance and without affectation, you can mark yourself as someone special. (Besides, a few lingering touches of chauvinism may present an intriguing challenge.)

Language and the way we use it has also been changed by liberation politics. The word "committeepeople" no longer draws a laugh, and "chairwoman" is no longer read as a misprint for a British cleaning lady. The most common change has been in the use of the words "girl" and "woman." Where a man once referred to a "girl" in either the office or at home—even if the "girl" was old enough to be his mother—the use of "woman" is now preferred. The new language is not necessarily any more logical than the old; depending on who's speaking, any female past the age of puberty may now be called a "woman." If you're unsure which to use, say "woman."

If you're occasionally confused about how to behave in these liberated days, you're not alone. Men and women are still feeling their way through the unfamiliar manners of change. The important thing to keep in mind is that liberating your behavior means being considerate to other people. The etiquette of liberation is no different from any other etiquette. Behaving with courtesy and respect, and keeping your heart in the right place will more than make up for even the biggest blunders.

A note on gay liberation   Rudeness to anyone is more a reflection on yourself than on the object of your slurs. The subject of someone's sexual preference is not a topic for conversation unless it is brought up by that person—and then it should be discussed openly and objectively, without innuendo. And remember that it's unnecessary to defensively emphasize your own preference.

Conversation

Conversation is a craft, not an art. The hard-earned skills of creating an exchange of ideas are what make a good conversationalist; no one is born with a gilded tongue. This is one area in which a man can turn etiquette to his advantage and develop a natural elegance and ease of manner. You should not be afraid to speak your mind at the risk of provoking, but you should not go out of your way to offend. You can be at the center of a conversation without being its subject.

Half of communication is in what's left unsaid. A wink of an eye can speak volumes, while hours of talk may say nothing. Much of the time you spend communicating is used for more than just making a point. Formalities of phrasing, courtesies of introduction, significant pauses, and even silences are all part of the art of conversation. If these little things are ignored, you'll never get across the big things you're trying to say.

You should know how to listen. Pay attention to what other people are saying instead of trying to think of something to say next yourself. Encourage them to say what's on their minds instead of jumping on them for the most trivial disagreement with your opinion. And, most important, figure out what you enjoy hearing others talk about. That's the best guide to knowing what they'll enjoy hearing when it's your turn to speak.

Starting a conversation

The most difficult part of a conversation is not, as many people think, what to say first. It is, rather, what to say *first* that will cause someone else to say something *second*. Bulldozing your way across a crowded cocktail-party floor to ask that woman you've been admiring what time it is is unlikely to start any conversation longer than "Five-thirty." . . . "Thank you." On the other hand, too artificial an opening remark is more likely to provoke embarrassed silence than meaningful exchange. What you say to a stranger only has to indicate that you want to start a conversation.

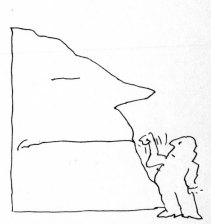

Choosing a subject is getting to know someone. To suit a conversation to a partner, you have to know something about that person. The act of finding out is the way to get into a conversation. Try asking a few safe personal questions, such as how long he or she has lived in your town or what he or she does to earn a living. If you want the conversation to be more personal, start with your own life before probing into the other person's. Asking a woman if she's married is not the recommended method of fishing for a topic, but being open about your recent divorce is a good way to find out about her marital status.

Sex and obscenity

In this day and age, there are no subjects intrinsically off limits; only if you treat a subject as though it's impolite does it become unfit for polite conversation. Any subject—even sex—can be broached if you do it with tact. Tact is the part of etiquette that calls for keeping your head screwed tightly onto your shoulders—so think before you speak.

Obscenity is a rather different matter. Few people will bat an eyelash at the occasional "hell" or "damn," but rank obscenity is unfit for most social occasions.

Humor

Humor is the key to pacing a conversation. Forced comedy or slapstick is out of place in polite conversation, but an easygoing wit and a sense of timing can miraculously relax all present. (Tease an old friend's choice of tie, but don't trip the waiter.) Even puns have their place if they're not overdone. Remember, though, that forcing a joke into that awkward pause is unnecessary; silence too has its place in conversation.

When new people enter a conversation, make sure that everyone knows who they are. If you don't know this new person yourself and no one else introduces him or her, ask his or her name bluntly, as in, "Hi, I'm Bob. Who are you?" If you don't feel the need for introductions in an informal conversation, refer to the newcomer by name without interrupting the flow of conversation. One rule of etiquette that hasn't changed is that men are always presented to women, as in, "Susan, this is my old college buddy, Jack," not, "Jack, this is Susan." In a large group, simply list everyone's name.

Forgetting a name need not be a disaster. A simple apology will elicit the needed information and save you the embarrassment of asking days or weeks later. To save others embarrassment, always introduce yourself.

When you've been introduced to someone, stick to a simple, "How do you do?" or "Pleased to meet you." Save the "How are you?" for those you already know—it's a question that won't be answered honestly anyway, so why ask it? Get out of your seat for a woman, and shake a man's hand. The best handshake is somewhere between a wet-fish clasp and wrestler's bone crunch—use your judgment and be natural. Don't kiss a woman the first time you meet her. Shaking a woman's hand is increasingly acceptable, but let her offer her hand first. In many foreign countries, be prepared for frequent handshakes and kissing on both cheeks. Aside from that, don't try to imitate Continental manners.

Finally, you should know how to get out of an unwanted conversation gracefully. The trick is to make the other person want to end it. In this regard, remember that taking a hint is as important as giving one. If you begin to feel that someone is tired of talking to you, excuse yourself and go away.

Writing and telephoning

Not all communication can be done in person. Your conversational skills will have to play second fiddle when the time comes to write a letter or make a phone call. But the general principles of communication are the same in every medium—a modicum of politeness and consideration for the other person is always called for.

Personal phone calls

The opening lines of a personal phone call should always follow the standard form: answer the phone with a simple "Hello." Avoid the too abrupt "Yes" and the too informative "So-and-so speaking." If it's that persistent bill collector or salesman on the phone, you may regret revealing yourself so quickly. (For information on dealing with business calls, see "At Work," page 224.)

If you're placing the call, identify yourself as soon as you hear the word "Hello." How you give your name depends on who you're calling and who picks up the phone. If the person you're calling won't need your last name, you don't have to use it, but don't take a chance if you're not sure. There's nothing more embarrassing than being asked, "John who?" If a child or a parent answers the phone, use your last name whether your friend will need it or not. And don't ever ask an unfamiliar voice who it belongs to until you've identified yourself, even if you're phoning your best friend.

When a person calling you doesn't identify him or herself immediately, it's not impolite to ask who it is. Stick to a courteous, "Who is this, please?" or (if the call is for someone else) "Who should I say is calling?" If the caller was rude enough to start out with "Hello, who's this?" then you're justified in shooting back with "Who's *this*?" before answering the question.

A few telephone rules

If you reach a wrong number, state the number you were trying for and ask if you've reached it. *Don't* ask, "What number is this?"—it's none of your business.

When you're making a personal call, you needn't state the purpose of your call until after concluding the social pleasantries. It's equally impolite, however, to chat for half an hour and then add before hanging up, "Oh, by the way, the reason I called is..."

Avoid getting into a long conversation unless the other person has indicated that he or she has time to chat. Always pay for your calls if you're a guest in someone else's house. And if you're called away from the phone, don't keep the other party waiting long—especially if you made the call. When you're inviting a friend over or asking a woman for a date, be specific with your invitation instead of asking, "Are you busy Saturday night?"

Your correspondence

Ideally, personal letters are written by hand, but a typewritten letter is equally acceptable in informal correspondence. The idea is that a typed letter lacks the personal touch, but it is certainly preferable if your writing is unreadable or if you would never get around to writing otherwise. After all, the point of a letter is that it be read and understood, not admired for its aesthetics.

For your personal correspondence you should choose a stationery to fit your personality. Conservative colors are the safest, but if you're not the conservative type, there's no need to repress your personal tastes. Whether you choose sturdy, unadorned paper or go for a more elegant style is up to you, but avoid ostentation. The most useful size stationery for general letter writing is seven inches by ten or slightly larger. You may decide to leave it unpersonalized; engrave it with your entire name, address, and phone number; or stick to simple printed initials, as you prefer.

Many men find it useful to have printed social cards (approximately four inches by four) in addition to their personal stationery and business cards. These cards can be used with gifts and for invitations, replies, and announcements. (You'll also find these cards handy for short letters—if you use a card you won't have to worry about filling an entire page of stationery.) Your card should be engraved with your name and title ("Mr." unless you're a medical doctor, clergyman, or army officer). Your address is not necessary but is probably helpful; your phone number, however, is out of place. If you're living with a woman, you may want her name included as well, and if you're married, don't forget that your wife has a first name too.

Don't try to be formal

A personal letter should be written in your "speaking tone." It's not necessary to be more formal on paper than you would be in person. On the other hand, just because you have poor speech habits doesn't mean you have to imitate them in a letter. Try to strike a casual note.

You need not include your address when heading a personal letter, even when the information is not printed on the stationery—but don't forget a return address on the envelope. Including the date is mandatory—write it out in the upper right-hand corner of the first page. The salutation, "Dear So-and-so," is the best, followed by a comma. The closing may be whatever you feel is appropriate: a simple "Love," "Yours," "As ever," or the more formal "Yours truly" or

"Sincerely yours." Sign your name in the form you use in person with your correspondent. As in personal phone calls, last names are necessary only if the person you're writing to may not recognize you as just "Bill."

Thank-you notes should be sent when you've received a gift or been an overnight guest, and on every occasion when people have gone out of their way to be hospitable or kind to you. Thank-you notes need not be elaborate; a simple "thank you" is sufficient as long as it specifically mentions the gift or occasion that inspired it. Printed thank-you's are all right too, as long as a few handwritten words are included to personalize them.

At work

Keeping your head above water in the business world calls for more than good intentions. While the basic principles of etiquette are as true in business as in your private life, it's more important here to use your head. The difference between social and business etiquette, as the *Esquire* etiquette guide pointed out 25 years ago, is that while social manners are based on equality, the working world is a hierarchy.

The business world has gone along with the loosening of etiquette in the last 25 years, but has not completely accepted the new informality. In the business world there are still those who give orders and those who take them. Those who take your orders may be called by first name, but until you're told otherwise, you must still address those who give them to you by their titles. The difference the last 25 years has made is that the title may now be "Ms." as well as "Mr.," "Mrs.," or "Miss".

Knowledge of office etiquette is more important at business meetings than anywhere else. The top-ranking participant always opens the meeting. If the conference is held at a long table, participants are usually seated in rough order of their rank, with the highest-ranked at the head. Even if the meeting was called to discuss a junior member's idea, the senior member opens the meeting, briefly explains its purpose, and introduces the junior member. After that, anyone may speak whenever he has something to say, as long as he doesn't interrupt. Do remember that the decision is made at the top—address your remarks in that direction.

Outside the office

Outside the office, hierarchy is less important. A boss may seem more human to those who work for him over a drink or two at the end of the day. Last names are too stuffy for a bar or a cocktail lounge, so don't raise your hackles if you hear your given name spoken out loud for the first time by an employee. The same goes for office parties. However, revert to normal procedure back at work the next day.

When you do have a drink with your coworkers, stick even more

firmly than usual to the rule against getting drunk. And remember that whoever's highest up the ladder picks up the tab.

Keeping your private life separate from your office life is safest. Talking shop with colleagues can be fun over drinks, but tight friendships at work often lead downhill. Maybe you can't avoid being a sympathetic listener, but don't get embroiled in the problems of office friends unless you want to be sucked down with them. Keep out of office politics, or at least make it appear that you're doing so. Gossip at the office is best kept one-way—pay attention to everything you hear, but be very careful not to cut yourself off from your sources of information by gossiping.

A final important consideration: always respect your boss's position. When you're bucking for that promotion, don't bypass him for his superiors.

Business phone calls

When you're using the telephone for business, you *must* state your name immediately when another party answers. This can't be overemphasized. Unless you're asked, you don't have to state your business until you're connected to the party you're trying to reach (although doing so may expedite matters). When you are finally connected, make the purpose of your call the very first thing you state. If you want to ask about the other person's family, wait until you've concluded the business at hand. (This isn't necessary for personal calls. See "Writing and Telephoning," pages 221-222.) In any case, keep the social pleasantries to a minimum; even if you have time to waste, it's a good bet the person at the other end doesn't.

A businessman doesn't have to worry just about his own manners on the phone—his secretary's voice is an extension of his own. If you don't trust your secretary to screen incoming calls, ask to be connected with all your callers. And if you asked your secretary to place a call for you, be ready to pick up the phone immediately so you won't keep the other party waiting.

Business letters

Business letters should always be short and to the point. There's no need to go on after you've said what you want to say. If you know the correspondent personally, you needn't treat him as a stranger (addressing him as "Dear Sir," etc.), but except for an occasional short postscript, save the personal news for a personal letter.

Your name should be typed in full below your signature even if you're signing with a nickname. If you're using a company letterhead, your title should be included below your name.

Sports and games

When Grantland Rice wrote that how you play the game is more important than whether you win or lose, he wasn't talking about

contemporary America. Nowadays, it seems that winning is everything. Under these circumstances, the mark of a good sportsman is
being able to win and still leave his opponent smiling. And since for
every winner there must also be a loser, a good sportsman makes the
winner look good by wearing a smile *even* when he loses.

   Although rules and manners vary from pastime to pastime, there
are a few guidelines to keep in mind no matter what the name of the
game is.

· Learn the rules and play by them. Ignorance is no excuse for an
embarrassing mistake that will make all the players have to start all
over again. And cheating is frowned upon in most sporting circles.
· If you're playing for money, pay up promptly and uncomplainingly. If
you haven't learned to control your losses, don't bring more money to
the game than you can afford to lose. *Never* play on credit.
· If you're not having a good time, don't let your glum spirits be
contagious. Let your companions keep enjoying themselves. Complaints and excuses will only bring your friends' spirits down to your
level.

Tennis

As tennis grows in popularity, more and more players enter the courts
ignorant of the game's long tradition. Unless you can play like Jimmy
Connors or Ilie Nastase, you haven't earned the right to behave like
them. In short, pay attention to the sport's common courtesies. Offer
your opponent either the best court or the first serve. Change courts
after the odd games. Don't call for your ball from the next court until
they've finished their point—nor should you return a ball across their
field of play. When you're playing doubles, call attention to your
partner's mistakes politely or ignore them altogether; there's no need
to get angry in a friendly game. Likewise, effusive apologies are out of
line when you're the weaker half of the team. (Better yet, don't get into
a game—any game—with players you can't keep up with.)

Skiing

When you finally leave for the long-awaited ski weekend, have yourself
prepared. To avoid delaying your companions—as well as yourself—
make sure both your equipment and *you* are ready for the slopes. If
you're a top-notch skier, don't *schuss* mockingly past the neophytes
on the beginner's slopes; similarly, don't block the narrow expert trails
if you've just buckled on your first pair of ski boots. Get on the ski lift
quickly, without holding up those in line behind you.

Golf

On the golf course, play quickly enough to give others a chance to
finish their game, and leave the fairways in as good condition as you
found them. Wait until others are out of reach before hitting the ball,

and if you don't know your own strength, don't forget to yell "Fore!" No matter how sure you are that you have the answer to the other player's problem, save the lesson for the 19th hole unless he specifically asks for your advice. Do *not* decide to make that witty remark just as your opponent is beginning to swing. And when you find your partner's lost ball in the rough, don't pick it up and wave it just to prove your point.

Card games   If you like to relax with a deck of cards and a six-pack, make sure the "friendly game" you've been invited to is actually that—don't get caught as an afternoon player in a room full of card sharks. At the poker table, stick to the basic forms of the game when it's your turn to deal. Serious players aren't interested in playing with half the deck wild. When you're playing bridge, do your opponents a favor and be nice to your partner, even if your partner is your wife and she's just trumped your ace. Sit quietly in your seat when you're dummy, and, while it's okay to look at the other player's hands, you should keep your brilliant finesses to yourself.

Clubs   If someone invites you to spend a day at "the club," it's OK to ask a few questions about club policy. There's no need to be shy. Hardly any two sport or country clubs share the same rules and regulations, so it's perfectly acceptable to ask your host beforehand about clothes, tipping, or anything else you don't know. You are generally expected to bring your own special equipment with you—don't count on being able to rent or borrow things.

On smoking   Though smoking may have meant high status when you started sneaking those first few puffs behind the barn or at school in the boys' room, you aren't 14 anymore, and smoking no longer makes you the big man in the schoolyard. Nowadays, that person approaching you as you light up is less likely to admire your style than to reprimand you for infringing on one's right to clean air. The word for smokers to remember today is *discretion*.

As nonsmokers get more militant, the plight of smokers becomes greater. Smoking is now forbidden in an increasing number of movie theaters, and smokers are no longer guaranteed seating in the smoking section of an airplane. If you don't want to end up in the uncomfortable position of being told to put out your cigarette, pay attention to a few basic rules of smoking courtesy.

· The most obvious hint is a "No smoking" sign. It may seem clear that whoever puts up these signs sincerely doesn't want you to smoke, but some people go ahead and ignore them anyway. Obey the rules when

you're with people who could be offended by your thoughtlessness.
• If you don't see any ashtrays at a party, ask for one before you light
up. Requesting permission to smoke is never a bad idea in someone
else's home or office, even if you're sure the question is unnecessary.
• If you're out with someone, offer a cigarette each time you light up. If
they don't smoke, ask whether they mind if you do. And if you ask the
question, be prepared to accept a negative answer.
• Don't smoke while others are eating, or between courses. Even
leaving a cigarette burning in the ashtray can be annoying to your
companions, so make sure those butts are completely out.
• In a restaurant, if there are no ashtrays on the table and you don't
see anyone else smoking, ask the waiter for an ashtray, and if smoking
is forbidden, he'll let you know.
• Be clean. Don't spill ashes all over your clothes or the host's carpet.
Scrub your fingertips free of nicotine stains. Try to get rid of stale
tobacco odors on your breath and your clothing.
• Put out your cigarettes in ashtrays, not in dinner plates or potted
plants. Don't throw them out car windows or grind them underfoot on
somebody else's lawn.
• Take the hint graciously if your neighbor on a train or in a restaurant
asks you not to smoke. After all, you really are polluting the air.

Cigars are for gambling men, because smoking a cigar means taking a
chance on the people who are around you. People either love them or
hate them; there's rarely any in between. A cigar will be seen as a sign
of sophistication by some, but it's equally likely to cause others to ask,
"Where is that smell coming from?" as you walk by.

Be sure you do *smoke* cigars, not chew them. A soggy, chewed-up
cigar butt is smelly and disagreeable, and in any case the acids
released by masticated tobacco will ruin the taste of your cigar. Don't
leave your cigar butts in someone else's ashtray—put them out
completely and then throw them in the garbage. Use a cigar cutter on
the tips of those high-quality, uncut cigars instead of slicing them with
a penknife or biting them off

With pipe smoking, you have the chance to turn an otherwise
disagreeable habit into a social asset. Handled with flair and grace,
smoking a pipe can be an easy way to build an image of gentility and
sophistication.

A pipe should be considered part of your personality and should be
chosen with the same care you take with any of your other
accessories. When you're buying a pipe, don't be too bashful to look
into a mirror: a good pipe will have a complete, unseamed body and

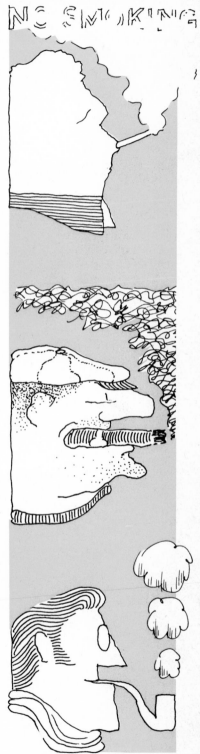

an attractive grain if it's briar, *and* it should enhance your general appearance.

Tobacco should be chosen on a trial-and-error basis—don't try one and then stick grimly with it—and a good tobacconist will try to blend a tobacco to suit your particular taste. Tobacco should also be chosen with your neighbors in mind—if your favorite blend is offensive to your friends or coworkers, smoke it in private and find one with a more pleasant aroma for social occasions. You'll be surprised how much favorable comment can be provoked by a pleasantly aromatic tobacco.

Quitting smoking

Of course, the day may come when you get tired of having to catch your breath after every flight of stairs, or you want to be able to finish a tennis match without having to stop for air. That's when you start engaging in America's favorite form of organized masochism: trying to quit smoking. There are as many different methods of quitting smoking as there are smokers. When the time comes, contact your local health council or the American Cancer Society for free advice.

Try to quit smoking without driving your friends crazy, and be especially considerate of friends who still smoke. When you quit smoking, *don't brag about it.* Don't discuss your withdrawal symptoms and relapses unless a friend expresses real interest in hearing about them. When your old smoking partner absentmindedly offers you a cigarette, refuse politely—don't make a production out of it. If the smoker on the next bar stool is blowing his smoke in your face, quietly slide his ashtray away from you. He'll get the message; there's no need to broadcast it to the far corner of the room.

Drinking and drugs

Alcohol can be a curse or a blessing, depending on how it is used. It can encourage social interaction, or it can make you completely unsociable. If you don't let it destroy you, it can become a positive addition to your social personality, because it can bring out your social side. However, you may end up unable to function socially without it, and that's bad. Use it; don't let it use you. (See "Getting Loose," page 38-40, for information on the physical effects of alcohol.)

The etiquette of drinking is the etiquette of informality. The courtesies of the afternoon may safely be forgotten on the evening's bar stool—and would probably be forgotten by the third drink, anyway. The point of social drinking is to relax people and to break down social barriers. Nearly everyone suffers from tension during the day, and it's no crime to feel that you need a drink to help you unwind afterward. But after you've unwound with that first drink or two, be careful that you don't get *too* relaxed. Maintain a certain level of decorum; no one likes a sloppy drunk.

Maintaining that level of polite behavior is most important when you're drinking at a private home. While an occasional Dionysian revel is permissible in the anonymity of a bar, a social visit to a friend's home is neither the time nor the place to become more than cheerfully high.

If you're drinking in the company of nondrinkers, don't make them ill at ease by drinking too much or telling drinking stories. Respect their right to remain nondrinkers, and *don't try to convert them*. (That goes for other drinkers who may decide to turn down a drink, too—don't push anybody into having a drink when he or she doesn't feel like it.) As long as you observe those basic rules of courtesy, there's no need to feel uncomfortable about drinking with non-drinkers. You're entitled to your pleasures, even though they may not be shared. If nondrinkers don't care to serve you alcohol when you're a guest in their homes, however, respect their wishes and don't complain about the lack of alcoholic hospitality.

In this day and age, alcohol is not the only drug you may encounter at social get-togethers. The growing use of marijuana and other mild narcotics has made them acceptable in an ever-widening array of social settings. Whether you indulge or not, you need to remember a few basic things when you're among drug users. (See "Getting Loose," page 40-41, on the effects of these drugs.)

About drugs

· Morality lectures are uncalled for among users of the so-called soft drugs, such as marijuana. You are free to make up your own mind whether to use drugs, and so is the next person. What you may consider a well-intentioned remark on the evils of drug use will only guarantee that you won't be invited to the next party.
· If you don't want to be present where illegal drugs are being used, excuse yourself politely and leave. If asked, explain straightforwardly that you don't want to break the law. There's no reason to make those who stay uncomfortable with transparent lies.
· You needn't let yourself be pressured into using any drugs that you don't want to use. Just because friends are getting high doesn't mean *you* have to. If your friends won't stay friends if you don't join them, find new ones. (Likewise, don't try to pressure anybody else into doing something they don't want to.)

If you don't use drugs

· When you're with strangers, don't be the first to produce any illegal substances. No matter how much they *talk* about their drug use, let them be the first to back up their words with action.
· You need to know the law, too. If you choose to break it, know what you're doing and what the possible consequences are in your state.

If you use drugs

And remember, decriminalization is not the same as legalization. Decriminalization means that the penalties for use of a certain drug have been reduced to a fine, but the drug remains illegal.

• At social gatherings, be moderate. If you're using drugs to relax with friends, don't get high beyond the point of sociability. And *don't drive.*

Rites of passage

As individuals, we all pass through different stages in life, from infant to child to man. In 1908, the term "rites of passage" was coined by anthropologist Arnold Van Gennep to describe the ceremonies marking the transitions from stage to stage. While they differ markedly from culture to culture, all societies have them. In modern American society, the most prominent rites of passage are birth ceremonies, religious initiation ceremonies, graduations, weddings, and funerals. Each of these rituals has its own etiquette.

Birth ceremonies

As a man, you're unlikely to be invited to a baby shower, nor are you in a position to lend maternity dresses. When friends have a new child, however, a card or small gift is a thoughtful gesture. For a first baby, ask the new parents what would be helpful. All new parents have to buy a wide array of gear for the baby and they won't be offended by questions about what they may need. (A gift for the mother is another option.)

If you're invited to a christening or circumcision ceremony at a church or synagogue, you have no obligation other than to behave as you would at any other religious ceremony. But if you've been asked to be godfather, be prepared to give the child special attention until he's grown. An appropriate initial gift would be a bond, trust fund, or blue-chip stock that will grow with the child.

Religious initiation ceremonies

Religious initiation ceremonies are holdovers from earlier times, when they marked a youth's passage into manhood. Nowadays, manhood (and womanhood) is postponed until after adolescence and these rituals have purely ceremonial significance.

A Catholic first communion and a Protestant or Catholic confirmation are strictly religious, and the gifts should be of an appropriately religious nature. A Jewish bar mitzvah is a joyous social occasion as well. In any case, when giving a gift, bear in mind that even a symbolic initiation calls for a gift appropriate for an adult, not a child.

Graduations

Today's genuine initiation into the society of adults often comes at graduation. Although graduates may expect major gifts from their parents, others are not expected to give more than a token of their affection. Let your personal relationship with the graduate be your guide.

Remember that at most schools and colleges the graduates are strictly limited in the number of guests they can invite to the ceremonies, so don't feel insulted if your name is left off the list. If you receive a graduation announcement, treat it as what it is and not as a pitch for a gift. (Frequently announcements are sent because of the limit on invitations).

If you're inviting parents or other guests to your own out-of-town graduation, make hotel reservations for them, but expect them to pay their own bills. If you invite a date, however, you should pay for her hotel room.

Weddings

In almost everyone's life, the most important rite of passage will be his wedding. As a friend of the bride or groom, you're not expected to provide for any of the couple's major household needs, but a gift that is both aesthetic and functional is often appreciated more than something that simply sits in a corner and looks pretty.

At the wedding, jokes about the high divorce rate and the groom's last chance to change his mind are out of place (and hackneyed besides). On the receiving line, confine yourself to a few brief remarks appropriate to the occasion; the wedding party is certain to be tired and eager to sit down. If you've been seated at a table with strangers, introduce yourself and explain your relationship to the wedding. A brief "Thank you" to the host is in order before you leave, but don't expect any special attention from the busy bride or groom. (For information on how to dress for a wedding, see page 172.)

The duties of the best man vary from wedding to wedding. If you've been asked to be best man, check with the bride or groom to confirm your exact role. Generally, you'll be responsible for getting the groom to the wedding, holding the wedding rings and handing them to the groom during the ceremony, and making the first toast at the reception. If there's a bachelor party before the wedding or if there's to be a quick getaway afterward, you're responsible for making sure it goes smoothly. If you're asked to be an usher, ask the best man what to do.

Your own wedding

If you are getting married, you'll be responsible for getting the marriage license and paying the clergyman; for choosing, outfitting, and giving small presents to the best man and the ushers; and for smiling a lot. At the reception, try to be polite to every wedding guest, but if you're less than effusive in your conversation, it's understood that you're feeling a little bit overwhelmed. If you're planning to whisk your bride off after the wedding to a plush hotel or exotic resort, order the flowers, champagne, and dinner in advance.

Funerals

The rite marking a man's final passage is his funeral. In the unfortunate event of a friend's or relative's death, you should ask the family if there's anything you can do to help—in person, if possible. You may wish to pay a sympathy call on the family at their home or at the funeral home.

If you're asked to be a pallbearer or usher, the funeral director will tell you your duties. At the funeral, you're not required to view an open casket if you find the prospect unpleasant. If you decide not to attend the funeral of an acquaintance, or are unable to, a card or a letter of condolence is the appropriate gesture.

Being a guest

Whether it's a casual dinner or a weekend at the beach, the responsibility for a pleasant visit to a friend's place lies with the guest as much as with the host. While an efficient host will do everything he can to provide for his guest, a considerate guest should both minimize the host's efforts and make them seem appreciated. The mark of a successful guest is an invitation to return—whether he wants to or not.

Start your visit off on the right note by bringing a gift and giving it as soon as you arrive. Some people like to send their gifts afterward, but that makes the gift seem like an afterthought. Bring whatever seems appropriate—candies to a dinner party, something for the house to a house party—and remember that a gift is supposed to be just a way of saying thank you, not a proof of your generosity. A bottle of wine fits nearly any situation, but don't be insulted if the host sets it aside for future use and uncorks the bottles he's already selected for the occasion.

Arriving too late or too early

Sometimes it's impossible to avoid arriving too late—or too early. Unless a host has told you "No later than nine o'clock" for a 7:30 dinner, try to come reasonably close to the scheduled time. If it's the local custom to arrive 45 minutes late and you show up promptly at eight to find the host or hostess still wrapped in a bathrobe, you've arrived too early—but you had no way of knowing, and you'll simply have to remember to be later next time. On the other hand, the fact that in your circle everyone always shows up 45 minutes late doesn't mean that a new business acquaintance expects the same when he invites you to meet his wife and friends.

If you can't avoid being late, call your hosts so that they won't be wondering about you; and even if you have to walk around the block several times first, don't show up before the appointed hour. If you were asked to the country house for the weekend and no specific time was mentioned, call before you leave town to let your host know when you'll be arriving—and to make sure this time is convenient.

If you don't want to sit through a formal dinner in jeans or a clambake in a tuxedo, find out beforehand what kind of party you're going to. After you arrive it's too late to correct your error, so don't be too shy to ask your host what is expected of you. If a written invitation doesn't indicate how to dress, call up and ask. ("Black tie" or "formal" means a tuxedo, "semiformal" means a suit, and "informal" means use your imagination. For more detail, see the section on "Formal Dress" beginning on page 169.)

What to wear

It has been said that a guest's only obligation is to have a good time. While having a good time is indeed important, you must not interfere with everyone else's right to have the same. And "everyone else" includes the host as well as any other guests there may be—just because a friend has invited you to his home doesn't mean he wants to sacrifice his own life to slaving over you day and night. Make his job as easy as you can.

Be a considerate guest

Knowing when to leave is like knowing when to arrive—it calls for a well-trained sixth sense. The basic idea is to leave before you get kicked out, but not to cut short a promising party by walking out just as it gets going. The problem, of course, is that a big gray area lies between the extremes, and no book can be of much help to you here—you just have to apply common sense (and your instincts) to each situation as it arises. When you do overstay your welcome and are asked to leave, keep your apologies short. Just get out.

Knowing when to leave

If you think that servants are the exclusive province of the rich, you may be surprised on your next visit to someone's house to find a smiling butler or maid ushering you inside with a flourish. Servants still do exist in this democratic era, and they're not found only on palatial estates. Though it may seem an unlikely prospect at the moment, you should be prepared for the day when you find yourself in their presence.

Servants

The main thing to keep in mind is that while servants are there to serve you, they are not *your* servants. Thus, while you should *not* treat a servant as though he's just another guest by shaking his hand and having a conversation with him, since you are not his employer, don't order him around either; he already has his instructions. Simply let him take care of your needs, and keep in mind that all you need to say to him are simple courteous hello's and thank-you's.

A note on tipping: while it's considered rude to tip servants at a dinner, overnight guests are expected to leave a few dollars for every servant who gave him personal service.

THE ENTERTAINER

Civilization may not have arrived the day men first shared bread, but it couldn't have been very far away. Nothing, rhapsodized the poet Aeschylus, is "more pleasant than the tie of host and guest." He wrote that 2,500 years ago, and what was true for ancient Greece is just as true for modern society. So if you're preparing to entertain friends with a dinner party, congratulations—you are about to enjoy one of our oldest, happiest, and most cultivated traditions.

Hosting

What is a host? Well, to begin with, he's a realistic man. There's considerably more to this hosting business than simply picking up the tab. First, the preliminaries: determining your budget *and* selecting the guests *and* deciding where you'll have dinner *and* scheduling a time convenient for all *and*...The details can be as inexhaustible as they are exhausting. Then comes the party itself: the conversation has to be kept brisk, the mood high, the wine flowing. Finally, the aftermath: it's essential that everyone exit as cheerfully and—for those whose moods may be a little *too* boisterous—as safely as possible. In short, the good host must be logistics expert, economist, social director, mother hen, master of ceremonies, and magician.

What isn't a host? Selfish. You can reap all kinds of rewards by throwing a successful party—personal satisfaction, romantic involvement, business advancement—but private motives should never get in the way of public responsibilities. Consider the case of Petronius, perhaps the most famous host in history. Ordered by Nero to commit suicide, Petronius invited the leading citizens of Imperial Rome to a mammoth farewell feast. For days he regaled them with exotic foods, dancing girls, and an endless stream of dirty jokes (he was famous for that, too). He was so skilled at keeping his company amused that no one noticed when he slipped away to obey the emperor's edict. In fact, according to contemporary accounts, Petronius's last fling lasted a good 24 hours longer than Petronius himself. Moral? A true host never lets *anything* interfere with his party.

No matter how informal the gathering, there's always one member of the group who seems to have a natural gift for taking charge of the festivities. But in truth, there's nothing "natural" about it all. Good hosts are made, not born, and in the following sections you'll learn how to make yourself one of the best.

To quote Billie Holliday, *"It ain't jelly if it don't gel."* A party is the sum of its parts. This does not mean, however, that all the parts are equally important. You can spend days, weeks, months in feverish preparation, you can hire the most expensive restaurant or caterer in town, you can supply enough liquor to float an armada—but it's people who will ultimately make (or break) your party. As host, you must take extra-special care in the selection and treatment of your guests.

Handling guests

Probably the greatest advantage to holding a large party (i.e., 16 or more people) is that you don't have to worry too much about matching up the guest list. At such gatherings, people can more or less choose their own companions. Still, there are a few basic rules with which you should become familiar.

· Only invite people you care about. This may seem too obvious to mention, but many hosts feel compelled to place far too many "pay-back" guests on the list. Asking people you don't particularly like to your party simply because they have asked you to *their* parties is a dull custom. Worse, it makes for a dull party.

· Make sure each guest knows at least two other guests. This handy little formula protects a guest from walking into a room in which everyone else is a stranger, and also offers him an escape route should the strangers prove to be boring.

· Arrange a good mix. This does not mean merely providing the conventional one-to-one man-woman ratio. Be creative: try to establish as many interesting contrasts—via age, occupation, hobby, marital status, income—as possible.

The guest list for smaller parties needs a somewhat more delicate, tactful touch. The guiding principle here is *tension*. Not the tension generated by mutual antagonism, but rather the considerably more pleasant and stimulating tension that occurs when people who share common interests meet for the first time. Too little tension, and your party will sink to an irretrievably bland level; too much tension, and your party will quickly escalate into a heated debate. The trick is to strike just the right balance.

• Invite people who complement each other. They needn't be friends—indeed, it's preferable that at least half of them will never have met before—but they should be united by some natural bonds. If the friends you invite are all approximately the same age, have some similar interests, or earn roughly similar incomes, you can be more than reasonably sure that they will enjoy (or, at worst, tolerate) one another's company. On the other hand, selecting people on the basis of too *much* shared interest can be dangerous. Thus…

• Do *not* invite people whose interests are too similar. If all your guests are married, or parents, or sports enthusiasts, or politically active, or working in the same field, the conversational range will dwindle to shop talk. Nothing—repeat—*nothing* is more fatal to a party than insulated complacency. Put yourself in your guests' position. Would you want to spend the evening with a group of people who speak, act, and think in exactly the same manner as you? Of course not. You might as well stay at home and talk to yourself.

Other considerations

Take particular pains with seating arrangements at dinner parties, where people have no say in choosing their table-mates. If you're entertaining a group of unpaired singles, there's no problem—just seat them in a man-woman, man-woman pattern. If some of the people are married and some are not, place the couples in such a way that they're near enough to help each other out in sticky situations yet far enough away so as not to inhibit their conversations with different guests. (A little common sense comes into play here; you won't, for instance, want to put the wife of a particularly possessive man next to the town lecher.) Try to seat people together who are *simpatico* in some nonprofessional way: golfer with golfer, say, or football buff with football buff. There's a twofold advantage to this—not only do you provide table-mates with an immediate topic of conversation, but you also protect your other guests from a blow-by-blow account of last Sunday's game (or whatever).

If your party will be at home and you suspect it's going to be noisy, invite the neighbors. Most people tend to get a bit feisty when there's a lot of late-night noise in the vicinity—especially when they're not making any of it. Whether they accept or not, asking the neighbors to your party is a surefire way to keep them from complaining. In the event that you can't stand your neighbors and don't wish to invite them, at least give them 24 hours' warning.

Invitations

Unless you're planning an elegant gala, party invitations can be extended by a handwritten note, a telephone call, or in person. If time allows, invite your guests two weeks in advance. If you're inviting a married couple, courtesy demands that you address the wife. If your space is limited or for some reason it's important for you to know how many people will attend your party, add an R.S.V.P. to your invitations or tell friends you'd like to know beforehand if they'll be coming. On the other hand, you may want to tell guests they're welcome to bring their own friends. In this case, be prepared to entertain up to twice as many people as you actually invited.

Regardless of its form, the invitation must include the following information: *place* (with precise directions if necessary); *date; time; party type* ("supper" refers to a buffet, "dinner" a sit-down meal at a set time, and "cocktails" a more casual affair at which snacks may or may not be served); *the guest of honor*, if any; and *appropriate dress*, if any. It may also be necessary to provide certain people with more specific information; if, for example, separated or divorced mates are both invited—a potentially volatile situation that should be avoided at all but the largest parties—they must each be forewarned.

Your duties as host

A few simple rules of etiquette must be kept in mind no matter how informal your party. Not only must you always greet and bid good-bye to all of your guests, but you must make a point of engaging each one of them in at least a few minutes of conversation. (Any guest not treated to these ceremonial niceties is going to feel justifiably slighted.) You are also responsible for introductions. Remember that a man is presented to a woman; a younger person is presented to an older person; and the person being presented is the one mentioned *second*. If some guests bring gifts, don't open them in public—you'll embarrass the guests who didn't bring anything. If someone is late for dinner, start without him—you'll embarrass him by making *everyone else* wait.

Doing too much is as bad as doing too little. *Do* show all your guests where the food is; *don't* force-feed them. *Do* point eligible singles in each other's direction; *don't* play matchmaker. *Do* see that everyone receives his/her first drink; *don't* keep pushing liquor.

As a matter of fact, don't push at all—nudge very, very gently. Is the conversation flagging? Nudge it back to life. This is not your cue, however, for that favorite hour-long anecdote. Avoid the limelight; encourage other people to talk. One good opening gambit: "Joel was telling me something amusing the other day. Do you remember, Joel?" Has an argument reared its ugly head? Nudge it back underground again. If you can't cool off the two combatants, take one by the elbow and lead him to a neutral corner of the room for a nice chat or a bite to eat. Are people beginning to form cliques? Nudge everyone back into the center of things. (The easiest way to do this is to unobtrusively rearrange extra chairs more strategically.)

Think of yourself as a troubleshooter. Throughout the party you should be constantly on the alert, ready to quash any problem at a moment's notice. Like full moons, parties seem to bring out otherwise hidden weirdnesses in people. As host, you'll have to be prepared to deal with any guest hit by the party crazies. Just don't overreact. Tact and subtlety are prerequisites here. Remember: a good host never insists—he suggests.

Some problem guests

The wallflower: Contrary to most opinions, wallflowers are not exclusively women—men are equally prey to this debilitating condition. Nor, contrary to just about *everyone*'s opinion, are wallflowers easily identified by a dowdy appearance—the flashiest exterior will often hide the shrinking violet inside. The only real clue is the eyes—if they're darting back and forth like frightened fish, chances are they're reflecting a likewise frightened soul. Talk to them. Compliment them. Encourage them to tell funny stories, and then laugh at their punchlines. Sometimes giving them little chores (helping to set the table, rearranging the flowers) will draw them out of their self-conscious panic. Offer to introduce them to other people, but always allow them the option of refusing.

The drunk: Be firm but friendly. Get them to eat roughage and starchy products (vegetable and whole grain products, for example). Eject a drunk only as the last resort. Most important of all, make sure that he or she is not planning to drive home. If need be, take the person home yourself.

The bore: Unfortunately, bores come in all shapes, sizes, and sexes. The bore could be anyone. Just make sure it isn't *you*. Short of downright rudeness, there isn't much you *can* do to shut bores up. Just keep them circulating, and pray that they run out of stories before you run out of guests.

The Don(na) Juan: Any relatively young, good-looking person is going to emanate a sexual aura (thank God). What we're talking about here are people who *advertise* their bodies. Look for tight pants and shirts open to the navel, and sheath dresses or peekaboo blouses, plus lots of jewelry, lots of teeth, lots of bare skin. Wink at minor indiscretions, but keep an *eye* out for potentially disruptive situations. Don't protect your other guests unless asked (and they probably won't ask), but do remember that wives, husbands, dates, etc., must be considered.

If you're planning a full-course, sit-down meal and your culinary talents are limited to boiling water, the most palatable solution is the restaurant. There are three basic characteristics that *every* good restaurant must have, and, lots of propaganda to the contrary, you will find that choosing a good-to-excellent dining spot is as easy as—well—as A,B,C.

Dining out

Ambience: The most difficult characteristic to define, ambience includes those nuances of courteous service, pleasant decor, attractive atmosphere, and special features (dancing, live entertainment) that are so essential to dining out. When you go to a restaurant, you're buying more than space and food—you're buying *style*. And the best way to check out a restaurant's style is to pay it a preparty visit. If this is impractical, ask your more knowledgeable acquaintances. (Word-of-mouth is a generally reliable means of discovery.) Also select a restaurant that matches your party's mood. If it's to be a romantic evening, for example, a quiet, discreetly dim café is best. If it's to be a sentimental occasion—wedding anniversary, birthday party—find a spot that has some personal meaning to the guest of honor.

Banquet: A restaurant's bill of fare should offer not only quality but quantity. After all, it's unlikely that your guests will all share the same food and drink preferences. Again, the safest bet is to sample the menu before you invite your friends. However, there are also useful restaurant guidebooks available in most cities. Incidentally, it might be a good idea to find out, if you can, what your guests *don't* like. When it comes to choosing an appropriate restaurant, *every* tidbit of information helps.

Convenience: Don't pick a restaurant that's terribly out of the way; select a centrally located one that's easy for all to get to. If possible, make sure beforehand that seating arrangements, lighting, heating (or air conditioning), accessibility of rest rooms, and so forth are acceptable, especially if any of these things are likely to be a problem for any of your guests. (Older people, for example, may not be able to sit on the floor at a Japanese restaurant.) As host, it's your duty—not the restaurant's—to see to your guests' comfort.

For some reason, many people find eating out a rather unsettling experience. They complain about the maître d's haughtiness, the wine steward's superiority, the waiters' insolence. Although it's true that restaurant personnel can be snobbish—especially when they sense uncertainty on the part of the customer—there's a simple way to deal with them. The secret? *Don't allow yourself to be intimidated.* As a patron, you have every right to demand that the restaurant fulfill its obligations. You should expect:

· **Cleanliness.** Spotted glassware, dirty silver, stained napkins, or untidy tablecloths are absolutely out of order. Don't accept anything but the most immaculate table settings. If anything seems to you less than clean, ask a waiter to replace it immediately.

· **Courtesy.** Restaurant personnel are required, by the very nature of their jobs, to serve you. They should be instantly willing to obey any reasonable requests. If they refuse, don't make a scene; simply ask to speak to the manager. They should not challenge you. If you say that soup spoon is dirty, then it's dirty, period. They should be attentive to little things. If you have to constantly ask the waiter for more rolls, butter, or ice water, he's not doing his job. (Demonstrate this to him by reducing the amount of his tip.) They should also be instantly available. The *only* proper way to call for a waiter is to lift one or two fingers in a summoning gesture. If you have to shout, whistle, or break a plate to gain his attention, it's no pleasure. Finally, waiters are never to remove any dish before everyone has finished. Be adamant about this. Hasty personnel may embarrass slow eaters—protect your guests. One reassuring postscript: none of these problems is likely to occur if, at the outset, you make it clear, pleasantly but firmly, that nothing short of complete satisfaction will do.

· **Good food preparation.** When the meal arrives, it should have been cooked to your specifications. If you receive a rare steak even though you ordered medium, don't hesitate to return it. If it's too hot, or too cold, or out-and-out inedible, do the same. On the other hand, if you neglect to alert the chef to your special tastes (as "Light on the seasoning"), you are not justified in refusing what you're served—always state your preferences *before* the food is prepared.

· **Leisure.** The restaurant is obliged to allow you to finish your meal in comfort and at your own rate of speed. Tables are not rented by the hour; if you wish to linger over coffee and dessert, or savor a good smoke, then by all means do so. (Of course, you should also be considerate of other people; if there are many people waiting for tables, it's only fair not to linger *too* long.) A not inconsiderable part of dinner is relaxing as you let it settle. You're buying the prerogative to do this from the restaurant.

The worst thing you can do when dining out is to allow yourself to become intimidated. However, there's no excuse for coming on like a storm trooper, either. Don't make unreasonable demands. You should not expect:

· **More for less.** The restaurant has the right to show a profit. Don't **What not to expect** expect to get more than what you're paying for. The most you can ask of any dining spot is that it offer quality to parallel its prices—and don't forget to take into consideration the fact that prices reflect not only the actual cost of the food but also the markup (to pay for transportation, preparation, and overhead) and the margin of profit.

· **Courtesy for rudeness.** If you're gruff, insulting, or abusive, you have no reason to expect courtesy in response.

· **Extraordinary services for ordinary returns.** It is not, generally, a good idea to order off-the-menu items. This makes life a great deal more difficult for the staff—especially during peak hours. If you insist upon having a dish prepared especially for you, be prepared to dish out some extra gratuities.

Reservations should be made the evening before your party. Allow **How to make** one or two days' extra time if you're hosting a particularly large group **reservations** at a popular restaurant. Tell the maître d' the date, time, and exact number of guests, and mention anything additional—a choice spot near the window, music, or floral decorations—you might care to have arranged. (If you want to provide your own flowers or place cards, deliver them yourself a few hours before the party begins.) Always book reservations in your name; this way, any latecomers will know whose table to ask for. If the restaurant is "booked full," pay a personal visit to the maître d' or manager, and offer him some monetary inducement ($5 should be enough at all but the most expensive retaurants). It might not work, but faint heart never won fair meal.

It's the policy of most restaurants not to present the menu until you **How to order** ask—this is to allow you to relax first over cocktails. If menus *are*

presented before they're asked for, just return them to the waiter with an explanation that you're not ready to order yet. Once you do solicit menus, open them immediately.

As host, it's your responsibility to ask about any house specialties not listed on the menu, any last-minute deletions, and all ambiguities concerning the various foods. You also handle the actual ordering, after first asking each person his or her preference. In any group exceeding six people, this can prove a very complicated process. The alternative is to order the meal ahead of time. Your guests will be pleased and flattered by the advance preparations, and they will be spared any embarrassment regarding how much (of your) money they can spend on dinner.

An absolute rule of entertaining: *never* discourage anyone from ordering an expensive dish—if you can't afford the restaurant's prices, you've got no business being in the restaurant. It may spare your guests some anxiety and make budgeting easier if you choose a place that has a table d'hôte menu (where the entire dinner, regardless of how many courses are requested and served, comes at a fixed price). Guests will not have to worry about your pocketbook, and you'll know what you're expected to pay before you're presented with the bill. If the restaurant doesn't have this kind of menu, estimate about $10 to $12 per person (except in those cities, notably New York, Chicago, and Los Angeles, infamous for their high prices).

How to pay When everyone, and only when everyone, has finished—not only the dinner, but the dessert, the coffee, the last drinks, and all topics of after-dinner discussion—the host asks for the check. *Check the check.* For the uninitiated, it can seem as cryptic as ancient hieroglyphics. Don't be shy about asking questions. Restaurants, even the very best of them, have been known to make mistakes—and those mistakes are rarely in the customer's favor. (Being charged for two bottles of wine when you've only ordered one is typical; so is being charged for an extra dinner.) Total the bill yourself—waiters aren't required to be expert mathematicians. If the total seems wrong, *ask*. If there are any unidentified surcharges, *ask*. If you can't decipher the writing, *ask*. (One point: don't argue with the waiter in front of your guests. Ask him to accompany you to the desk.) Only pay when you are completely satisfied with the correctness of the check.

If you have a credit card, use it instead of cash—that way, your guests never have to know how much the dinner cost. Better yet, arrange to pay away from the table. Under certain circumstances—on a Dutch date, or when two couples are dining on a 50-50 basis—you may be obliged to share the payment of the bill. Even so, as host (and making the reservations automatically designates you the host), you should be the one to actually pay the check. Any settling of the bill comes later, in private. Sitting at the table and discussing who ordered what is not a pleasant experience and will often leave a bad taste in everybody's mouth.

How to tip

Fifteen percent is considered a standard tip for the waiter(s); tip 20 percent if the service has been exceptionally good, 10 percent if the service has been pedestrian. The tip is placed on the check tray. If you know what the food tax is—8 percent in New York City, 5 percent in Chicago—you can save yourself some calculations by multiplying it (by two, or three, or whatever) to come up with the correct tip.

If you've also been served by a wine steward, he receives 10 to 12 percent of the wine bill. It's up to him to make himself available for payment when you're getting ready to depart. The bartender is given 15 percent of the bar tab upon presentation.

The maître d' is tipped a dollar as he shows you to the table and may be given a more substantial tip—from $2 to $5—as you leave, but only if he was helpful during dinner.

The fee to the checkroom attendant (and, by the way, the host collects the coats) ranges from 25 to 50 cents a garment. The parking-lot attendant gets a dollar; this is the only tip for which your guests are responsible.

Name your restaurant

Man cannot live by bread alone. If you want a little variety in your life, choose a specialty restaurant. (However, first be sure that all your guests are willing to comply with your choice.) The following is a compendium of the most popular types of eateries, with comments on price, atmosphere, dishes you can be relatively sure of ("safe"), dishes you might want to be wary of ("sorry"), and helpful comments. Keep in mind that this is a generalized overview only; for specific analysis, you'll have to sample specific restaurants.

French

Price: Moderately expensive to just plain expensive. It is generally agreed that there is no such thing as a good cheap French restaurant.

Atmosphere: Quiet elegance.

Safe: Especially recommended are the pâté maison, omelette *aux foies de volaille* (an omelette including chicken liver), vichyssoise, and *fromages* (cheeses).

Sorry: If there's any French food you should watch out for, it's crêpes. This is because Americans seem to be excessively fond of them. The result? Some French restaurants tend to get a little sloppy about the preparation. Also veal and lamb. When cooked correctly, French veal is superb. However, there are chefs who will drown this meat in sauce to conceal deficiencies in flavor. Also avoid frogs' legs. For the untrained palate, they'll taste like chicken laced with garlic.

Comments: The biggest problem is the use of rich French sauces to cover burnt or undercooked meats. If the menu doesn't provide English explanations of French dishes, ask the waiter. If *he* can't speak English, ask for an interpreter.

Italian

Price: Inexpensive to moderate. It's a rare Italian restaurant that has really high prices.

Atmosphere: Two types—family and intimate.

Safe: Minestrone soup, (hot) antipasto, scaloppine *di vitello* (or *ala Marsala*), rollatini, braciole (fillet of beef rolled around a pork filling), and, of course, spaghetti.

Sorry: Lasagne, fettucine, cannelloni—not because they're not delicious, but because they're laden with calories. Also, don't order shrimp dishes unless you're exceptionally fond of garlic.

Comments: Italian restaurants differ according to regional influence. Southern cooking is prepared with olive oil, and is light on meats and heavy on rice supplements. Northern cooking uses lots of butter and eggs, and offers more of a variety of meat dishes.

Chinese

Price: Inexpensive to moderately expensive.

Atmosphere: In the 50s it became quite popular for Americans to take their families out to the local Chinese restaurant for Sunday dinner. Our habits have changed, but most Chinese dining spots have retained their family-oriented decor.

Safe: Dim sum (dumplings), any fish, sweet and sour pork and/or spareribs, duck (especially Peking style).

Sorry: Szechuan dishes usually have a particularly hot sauce. Be careful if you have a tender palate.

Comments: Regional specialties—Cantonese, Mandarin, Szechuan—differ greatly. The first is relatively mild; the latter two are relatively hot. If you don't know how to use chopsticks, learn; they add greatly to the general flavor of the meal. People dining together should never order the same dishes—instead, order different things and encourage everyone to sample each.

Price: Moderately expensive to expensive.

Atmosphere: Boisterous.

Safe: Rare or medium-rare steaks and lobster.

Sorry: Well-done steaks; pork chops; lamb chops.

Comments: Steak houses usually offer the very best beef—porterhouse and filet mignon are particularly good cuts. But American cooks tend to burn meat unless you specifically ask for less than well done. Keep in mind that, for some reason, medium is interpreted as well done, and medium rare as medium. If you really want a rare cut, ask for very rare.

American Steak House

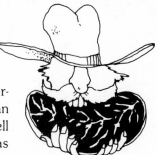

Price: Moderate.

Atmosphere: Casual.

Safe: Chef's salads, omelettes, hamburgers.

Sorry: Just about anything else—pubs aren't really equipped to prepare more elaborate meals.

Comments: Pubs can be used well for business lunches. There are a couple of basic rules here: order drinks immediately, don't start the business chat until after the first few sips, arrange for lunch to arrive unobtrusively so as not to interfere with discussion, finish the talk before the coffee arrives. Also, pay the bill away from the table—this way, there won't be a struggle over who pays the check.

Pub

Price: Cheap.

Atmosphere: Unbuttoned.

Safe: Eggs (any kind), hamburgers, French fries, malteds.

Sorry: Steak (too bland or tough), seafood (usually undercooked).

The Greasy Spoon Diner

Comments: The American diner can be a wonderful trysting spot, especially after an all-night party. There's something uniquely romantic about watching the sun come up while sipping coffee in a diner booth.

Dealing with specific foods

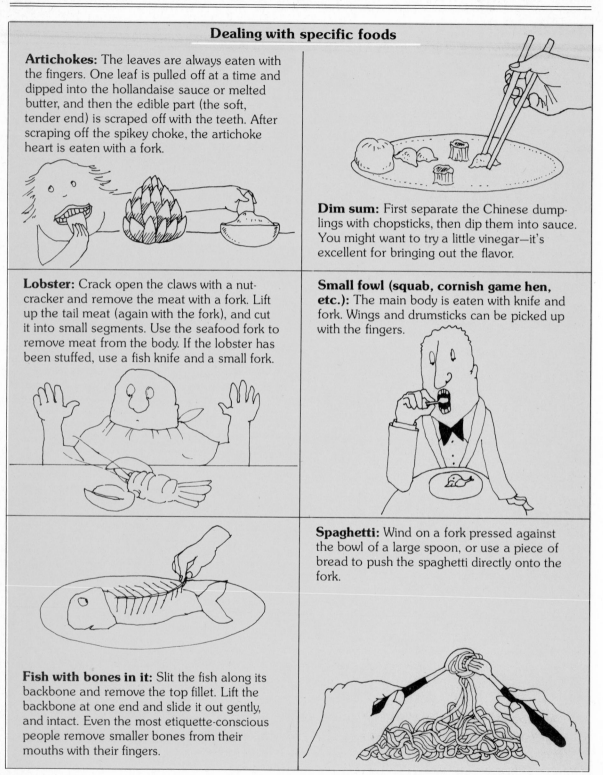

Artichokes: The leaves are always eaten with the fingers. One leaf is pulled off at a time and dipped into the hollandaise sauce or melted butter, and then the edible part (the soft, tender end) is scraped off with the teeth. After scraping off the spikey choke, the artichoke heart is eaten with a fork.

Lobster: Crack open the claws with a nutcracker and remove the meat with a fork. Lift up the tail meat (again with the fork), and cut it into small segments. Use the seafood fork to remove meat from the body. If the lobster has been stuffed, use a fish knife and a small fork.

Fish with bones in it: Slit the fish along its backbone and remove the top fillet. Lift the backbone at one end and slide it out gently, and intact. Even the most etiquette-conscious people remove smaller bones from their mouths with their fingers.

Dim sum: First separate the Chinese dumplings with chopsticks, then dip them into sauce. You might want to try a little vinegar—it's excellent for bringing out the flavor.

Small fowl (squab, cornish game hen, etc.): The main body is eaten with knife and fork. Wings and drumsticks can be picked up with the fingers.

Spaghetti: Wind on a fork pressed against the bowl of a large spoon, or use a piece of bread to push the spaghetti directly onto the fork.

There have been innumerable books written on the subject of wine—its varieties, its history, even its aesthetics. The aura surrounding wine can be mystifying. Take a pragmatic view; don't approach wine as a religion, but rather as a pleasant way to enhance your evening.

Wine basics

If you're entertaining at an unlicensed restaurant, you're required to bring your own bottle(s) of wine. (Be prepared to pay a corkage tariff. It depends upon the elegance of the establishment.) Chances are, however, that the restaurant you've chosen offers its own stock. There are three basic kinds of wine: sparkling, fortified, and table. Sparkling wines, so-called because they are bubbly, are bottled before the second fermentation is complete. This is a time-consuming practice, which explains why they're so expensive. Champagne is the best-known sparkling wine. Fortified, or dessert, wines are either very dry (aperitifs) and served before the meal, or very sweet (cordials) and served afterward. Table wines may be red, white, or rosé. As your final selection of a table wine will depend on the final selection of food, wait until everyone's ordered dinner before asking to see the wine list.

Choosing wines

Now, steel yourself—even in less elegant restaurants, the wine list may be long and complicated. Often, it will be presented to you by the sommelier, or wine steward. If this is the case, take advantage of him. Don't be afraid to ask his advice—knowledge of wines is his specialty. Lists vary in detail, but, generally, they all supply the same information: year, region, country, type, price (usually fairly high—the cost includes overhead and profit margin), and producer or distributor. When selecting—and take your time—three major points must be decided upon.

Ordering table wines

Type. The rule is red wine with red meats, white wine with white meats (poultry, fish), and rosé with either. Pork and veal are borderline—white or red depending upon how they're prepared (consult the sommelier); and rosé is nice with baked ham. If your guests order both white and red meats, consider half bottles.

Country. The second decision is whether to order domestic or imported wine. If you're a beginner, it's best to stick to domestic. California wines have a particularly excellent reputation—the labels are comprehensive (more about labels shortly), and the prices are relatively inexpensive. If, however, you have a taste for foreign wines—or want to make an impression on a very special date—you'll probably opt for an imported wine. Although wine *aficionados* seldom agree on *anything,* most think that Germany and France produce excellent whites. (There are Liebfraumilch from Germany and Burgundies and Bordeaux from France. Note that these are *kinds* of wine, not brand names.) Some fine reds come from France (Burgundy) and Italy (Chianti, Bardolino, and Valpolicella). Rosés from Portugal are a safe bet, as are most—if not all—champagnes from France.

Year. The vintage of a wine—i.e., the year the grapes were harvested—is only important to the true connoisseur. If you have any doubts about vintage, however, discuss them with the sommelier.

Just a few footnotes: Never take it upon yourself to order the wine without first consulting your guests. (It's polite, thoughtful, and a wonderful way to get a conversation started.) If you want to order an elaborate wine, practice with different wines at home first—it's a cheaper way of discovering which wines you really enjoy. Finally, most restaurants offer glasses and/or carafes of "house wine"—these are usually jug wines from California, Italy, or the south of France. They are tasty and inexpensive and should not be rejected out of hand.

The presentation of wine   Request that the wine be served prior to the meal. When the sommelier brings you the bottle, he should present it to you *unopened*. Read the label to verify that the wine coincides with its description on the wine list. Basically, you'll be checking the vintage, type, grower, and/or shipper. Domestic wines are named for their grapes (Cabernet, Pinot Noir); imported wines primarily for their region (Burgundy, Bordeaux, Moselle). Remember: the more specific the place designation, the finer the wine.

Next, check the temperature and method of presentation. White wine should be kept chilled at the table in a bucket of ice. Red wine is served *chambré*—that is, at room temperature. (If it's been stored in a

cool wine cellar, wait briefly for it to warm.) Old red wine is presented in a basket; the bottle is angled to let the sediment settle.

Only after you're satisfied that you've received what you've ordered do you ask that the wine be opened.

One of the most enjoyable things about wine is the wine-tasting ceremony. A ritual dating back centuries, it is all too often dismissed as a mere form of etiquette. In truth, however, tasting the wine before accepting it is very important. The ceremony is divided into several distinct steps. As host, you are expected to understand each.

First, the sommelier will sniff the cork. Then he'll hand it to you. At this point, you can do one of two things—stare at the cork (wrong), or duplicate the sommelier's performance (right). Even the best wines occasionally turn vinegary—if the cork dries out, air seeps into the bottle and the wine sours. What you're doing with the cork is checking to see if it is still moist and if you can detect the aroma of vinegar.

Once both you and the wine steward are satisfied that the wine has not turned, he will pour about an ounce into your glass for the actual taste test. Now, pay attention: wine is tasted with the eyes, the nose, and the mouth. Lift the glass by the stem and hold the wine up to the light to see if the wine is clear. Swirl it to release the bouquet. Sniff, again on the alert for a vinegary smell. If there is none, take a small sip and roll it to the back of your tongue. Let it rest there for a moment before swallowing. Wait for the aftertaste. Then—and only then—should you indicate whether the wine is worthy of your guests. If the wine is off, invite the sommelier to sample it before you ask for another bottle.

Wine is never rejected because it is disappointing; return it only if there's something specifically wrong with it—too bitter, vinegary. Once you approve the wine, have the steward fill everyone's glass.

Tasting wine

No matter how well-appointed the decor, no matter how tasty the food, no matter how courteous the service, a restaurant is basically an impersonal setting for a party. Entertaining in your own home invites a great deal more intimacy. Unfortunately, it also invites a great deal more work. If you do decide that the rewards offset the demands, you will probably give one of the five most common types of at-home parties.

Entertaining at home

The cocktail party. The briefest, least expensive, and—most hosts agree—the easiest way to entertain, the cocktail party requires a lot of liquor, a moderate amount of preparation, and very little food (usually dips and/or canapés). The mood is informal, but the time limit is strict—two hours, usually from five to seven or six to eight.

Open house. Actually a more informal variation of the cocktail party, the open house is usually given on Sundays and holidays. You hold this party earlier (afternoon to dusk) and it can be somewhat longer (three to four hours), but in all other respects, it's identical to a cocktail party.

The dinner party. The formal, black-tie dinner party is, beyond a doubt, the most difficult kind of affair to host. Unless you are, or have, a master chef, command complete comprehension of all the nuances of etiquette, and possess nerves of steel, you'd be best advised to make reservations at the most elegant restaurant you can find. The informal, soup's-on dinner, however, is another matter entirely. Small (six to eight people), casual, and more often than not impromptu, it is uniquely suited to the modern style of entertaining. Besides, feeding your friends is one of the true joys of civilized living. Dinner hour is, typically, eight.

The buffet supper. The buffet supper is the most practical way to deal with groups larger than about eight. The food—usually supplied by a caterer—is placed on a side table, and the guests help themselves. There are no seating arrangements to fuss with (guests eat off trays balanced on knees or chair rests); the bill of fare is comparatively simple (nothing on the menu should require a knife—too difficult to manipulate); and your duties as host are blessedly limited to making sure that seconds and refills are readily available. By ten o'clock, the buffet should be cleared away to make room for drinking, dancing, and whatever.

The tête-à-tête. Literally, "head-to-head," the tête-à-tête is the most intimate of all social occasions. You're pretty much on your own here, but a few general suggestions might help: flowers, candles, music, and an early dinner. Also, don't drink too much during dinner; save the imbibing for after.

Space—the last frontier

Before you decide on the size of your party, appraise the size of your home. If you live in a private house, you should have room a-plenty. If you dwell in an apartment, however, you already know space is at a premium. Don't despair. Even a studio can comfortably contain a surprising number of people. Examine your floor, seating, serving, and storage areas. There are several ways to expand them.

First, in order to seat as many guests as possible, remove all nonessential furniture from the main party space. You can also transform some of that furniture—low coffee tables, for instance—into improvised couches and chairs; just cover them with colorful pillows and mats. Although the bulk of entertaining will most likely be done in the living room, the kitchen, bedroom, and entrance hall can easily be turned into part of the general party area. (Incidentally, don't use the bed for coats and purses. This will severely cut down your overall space. Instead, utilize your largest closet, the hall *outside* your apartment, or even the bathtub.)

Protect your guests from your home—and themselves. Unless they're skidproof, throw rugs should be thrown out of sight. Valuable bric-a-brac should be safely packed away. And furniture should be so arranged that both it and your company can get through the evening intact. (Barked shins and scratched woodwork are damaging comedowns.) For larger parties, it's best to push all the seating against the walls. The results may resemble a dentist's waiting room, but—for the knowledgeable host—space always comes first.

The 14-day checklist

In one sense, a good party is like a good military battle: both require carefully plotted campaigns. Give yourself two weeks. Any less, and you might be caught short; any more, and you might end up with a bad case of combat fatigue. What follows is a general plan of action.

Day 14. The guest list's been organized, the party type's been identified. All systems are go. Now's the time to send out the invitations. Take a deep breath. It's the point of no return.

Day 13. Do not rush around buying anything and everything that pops into your head. Sit at your desk. Pour yourself a drink. Now, draw up your master shopping lists. Food—if you're cooking yourself; clothes—if you're planning to buy yourself a new outfit; party tokens—if you can afford to spend money on flowers, candles, etc.

Day 12. If you're going to have live entertainment at your party, contact the group involved for scheduling; if you're planning recorded music, make selections that will offend no one's sensibilities.

Days 11, 10, 9. All your guests have replied. If any have bowed out, this is the time to select replacements. If you're planning to use the services of a catering organization, contact them now. Explain the nature of your party as precisely as you can. Even though you know exactly what you want, remain open to suggestions—after all, they're experts.

Days 8 and 7. It's general cleanup time. There's no way you're going to get out of this with a token dusting. Grit your teeth and plunge in. Pay particular attention to bathrooms, kitchen, and windows. Two days will be sufficient for even the laziest person.

Day 6. Revise your shopping lists; by now, you should be calm enough to add all those items you forgot before.

Days 5 and 4. Now you start buying. Clothes, first; next, all the miscellaneous sundries; then, liquor (see next section for details); finally, the food (however, perishables—vegetables, fruit—should only be purchased the day of the party).

Day 3. Take care of last-minute details *before* the last minute. Check to make sure you have enough ashtrays and wastebaskets; arrange your storage space; plan parking facilities.

Day 2. Cook everything that's cookable, and carefully freeze. Also double-check that you have all the necessary gear—paper plates, forks, glasses, etc. Now's the time to do last-minute dusting and vacuuming.

Day 1. This is it. Prepare your space: clear out all unnecessary objects and bring in chairs. Set out the flowers, candles, fresh towels, and napkins. Dust once more for luck. Get the food ready. Allow lots of time for a relaxing bath and shave. Dress. Have a drink (just one). Now answer the doorbell.

No one expects you to whip up a frozen banana daiquiri. However, everyone does expect you to provide the basics: an acceptable variety and quality of drink, enough mixes to last the evening, and all the proper bar equipment. Unless you've hired a bartender, or are attending bartender's school yourself (not a bad idea, incidentally, for the serious entertainer), this section is must reading. Do not gulp it down in one glance; sip slowly, and savor.

Everyman's bar

A well-stocked bar offers a selection of vodka, gin, various whiskies—Scotch, Bourbon, Canadian or Irish, and rye—rum, and brandy.

Basic liquors

Brandy. Distilled from a fermented mash of grapes or other fruits (apples, apricots, cherries, and ginger are the most common), brandy is the perfect after-dinner drink. Cognac is the finest; California brandies, more modestly priced, are also considered quite good.

Gin. As every producer uses his own special recipe, only through experimentation will you discover the gin you prefer. We suggest, at least for starters, London dry gin (this is a generic, not a brand, name). It's not as sweet as other forms, and it mixes well with colas and fruit drinks. All gin is distilled from grain.

Rum. Taken from the fermented juice of sugar cane, cane syrup, or molasses and aged in uncharred barrels, rum is a very, *very* potent drink (never bottled at less than 80 proof). Rum is an acquired taste; the light-bodied variety is easier on untrained palates.

Vodka. At the moment, vodka is Number One in America. Virtually tasteless and odorless, it is the most versatile of all liquors. Vodka, it seems, mixes with *anything*. In Russia, its point of origin, it's distilled from potatoes. However, American vodka is distilled from grain (usually corn and wheat) and then filtered through activated charcoal.

Whiskies. Bourbon, mostly derived from corn, seems to be the most popular whiskey; Scotch, which is a blend containing both malt and grain whiskies, seems to be the most traditional. Canadian whiskey is lighter-bodied, and Irish heavier-bodied, than American blends. Rye, which actually contains only about 51 percent rye (the rest of it comes from a wheat and barley mash), is the heaviest of all whiskies.

In addition to the above, there are also *aperitifs* (most often strong fortified wines) that can be served before dinner to whet the appetite, and *liqueurs* (sometimes called cordials) that can be offered with dessert and coffee. There is such a wide variety of each, that only time and practice will allow you to choose the most appropriate ones for your guests.

Basic facts about liquor

Basic equipment
You will need the following basic bar equipment:

Jigger measure (with a scale of half and quarter ounces)
Shaker (or mixing glass)
Bar strainer (wire, not silver)
Teaspoon
Glass stirring rod
Corkscrew and can opener
Paring knife (for cutting fruit)
Ice bucket (with tongs)
Wooden muddler (for mashing mints, herbs, and fruits)
Lemon-lime squeezer
Large pitcher
Variety of mixers (dry and sweet vermouths, sodas, fruit juices, milk or cream)
Lemon and lime peels
Pearl onions
Cocktail olives
Glassware (two types: stemmed wine glasses for drinks served without ice, so that the heat of the hand holding the glass will not warm the drink as it's being consumed; and on-the-rock glasses for drinks—what else?— on the rocks)

When it comes to vodka, there are only subtle differences between the least and the most expensive kinds. Rums don't differ much in price, and—as previously noted—California brandies are a delightful (and delightfully inexpensive) substitute for cognac. Whiskies, however, are more difficult to calculate. It seems that just about everyone becomes an instant connoisseur when brand names are compared. The safest solution is to select a mid-level—not too cheap, not too expensive— assortment.

Over the years, a great many complicated formulae have been devised to help calculate how many bottles of liquor you will need in the course of a party. Don't trouble yourself with any of them; there's a much easier way to compute the bottle problem. The average number of drinks per person is four; the average number of drinks per fifth of liquor is 16.

You'd be surprised how many people are confused by the word "proof" (feel better?). Proof designates the percentage of alcohol multiplied by two. Thus, if a bottle is marked 100 proof, it contains 50 percent alcohol. A bottle marked 200 proof is all alcohol.

When mixing drinks, *always* go by the book. Don't be inventive; too light or heavy a mix will ruin the brew. Put in the cheapest ingredients first—if you make a mistake and have to start over, at least it won't cost as much. When mixing drinks containing fruit juices or sweeteners, the liquor is added last. Prechill glasses, either in the refrigerator or with cracked ice (which should be emptied out before making the drink). Mixes involving clear liquors and carbonated ingredients should be stirred. (Gently, please; too much stirring melts the ice and dilutes the drink.) Mixes involving fruit juices, sugar, eggs, or cream should be briskly shaken. Strain all cocktails before serving.

A basic basic   When you're drinking, know your limit, and never exceed it—at least not at a party you're hosting. Remember: a good host is good company, but a drunken host is just a drunk.

Some special drinks

Martini

Traditional:
1½ oz. dry gin
¾ oz. dry vermouth

Medium:
1½ oz. dry gin
½ oz. dry vermouth
½ oz. sweet vermouth

Dry:
1⅔ oz. dry gin
⅓ oz. dry vermouth

Extra dry:
2 oz. dry gin
¼ oz. dry vermouth

Sweet:
1 oz. dry gin
1 oz. sweet vermouth

For vodka martinis, just substitute the vodka for the gin in any of the recipes; serve with olive in each instance.

Manhattan

Traditional:
1½ oz. blended whiskey
¾ oz. sweet vermouth

Stir with ice, strain into cocktail glass, serve with cherry.

Dry:
1½ oz. blended whiskey
¾ oz. dry vermouth

Stir with ice, strain into cocktail glass, serve with olive.

Old-Fashioned

2 oz. blended whiskey
cube of sugar
dash of Angostura bitters
teaspoon of water

Stir with ice; add lemon twist; decorate with slice of orange, lemon, and cherry; serve with a swizzle stick.

Cuba Libre

2 oz. rum
juice of half a lime
lime rind
cola

Put the juice and rind in an on-the-rocks glass. Add rum. Fill with cola and ice cubes.

Bloody Mary

1½ oz. vodka
3 oz. tomato juice
1 dash lemon juice
1 tablespoon
  Worcestershire sauce
2– drops Tabasco sauce
pepper and salt to taste

Shake with ice and strain into old-fashioned glass over ice cubes. Lime peel optional.

Help!   As you've probably gathered by now, entertaining guests involves work. And the more guests there are, the more work there is. If you think your party may be more than you can handle alone, it's time to send out an SOS.

Unprofessional help   You can't, of course, ask friends to act as maids or butlers. You can, however, ask them to help you with the food, the arrangements, the decorations, and the shopping. Actually, "ask" is the wrong word; instead, drop a few well-chosen hints about how exhausting the whole thing's become. If they volunteer their services, accept gracefully. If they don't, accept that gracefully, too. (Your party is, after all, your responsibility.) Under absolutely *no* circumstances are you to *ever* approach anyone for assistance who's not on your guest list.

Professional help   Any sit-down dinner for more than eight people requires some additional help. Even if you're doing the cooking yourself, you're still going to need someone to help serve. If the party is for 12 to 16 people, you'd be wise to hire two people—one to help cook the dinner and one to serve it. If it's to be a cocktail party or a buffet for more than 20 people, a professional maid is essential. A bartender wouldn't hurt, either, although this is one role you *may* ask friends to assume.

There are many reputable temporary-help agencies; make a few inquiries. An alternative to this is hiring a catering organization. Not only will they prepare and deliver the food, but most will also arrange for members of their staff to act as waiters and barkeeps. A second alternative: restaurants occasionally will prepare, deliver, and set up full dinners (including service personnel to help you dole it out). Call the restaurant association or Chamber of Commerce in your city for details.

If you've never hired help before, there are a few points worth discussing first. Don't wait until the last minute to contact the agency; they're often booked weeks in advance. Ask that the help be on the scene a few hours before the party is scheduled to start. This will allow sufficient time for all the necessary preparations and instructions. Remember, too, that those instructions should be as explicit as possible. Good maids and waiters are attentive—they are not telepathic. If any minor mishaps occur during the course of the evening, ignore them—no one's perfect. If the mistake is so large that you *have* to speak to someone, do so in private. Berating the help in front of guests is as boorish as it is ugly. Don't forget to be polite at all times. Never be officious, bossy, or rude. Don't ask them to do anything they weren't contracted to do. If there's one unalterable rule when it comes to dealing with hired help, it's this: they're no less human, and no less deserving of respect, than you.

The party's over

But your duty as host is not. Not yet, anyway. The evening should end with as much style as it began. Once guests have made the first moves toward leaving, you're required to help them find their coats, lead the way to the door, and wish them a very good night. If you live in a house, walk them out to their cars and wait until they drive off. If you live in an apartment building, watch from the door until they enter the elevator. If a woman is going home alone, see if you can arrange a lift with another guest, or call a taxi for her.

The stragglers

For some, the party's never over—not while there's still a drink left in the bottle or a joke left to be told. It's a delicate situation to handle. You could try making oblique references to your busy morning schedule, or, better yet, *their* morning schedules. If they don't get the hint, accept the situation with as much good grace as possible. Prodigious yawns, closing down the bar, appearing in the living room in your pajamas—all these ploys are strictly *verboten*.

Do *not* allow any of your friends to drive home if they're drunk (or, for that matter, stoned). Call taxis and, if necessary, prepay the drivers; find sober drivers for the drunks' cars.

If friends offer to stay and help clean up, thank them profusely (they've earned it) and send them home. Guests are guests, and cleanup duty is cleanup duty, and never the twain shall meet.

The morning after

Stare at the lipstick-caked glasses, the cigarette holes in your favorite carpet, the scratched furniture, the dirty ashtrays, the scuff-marked floors, the food remnants on the coffee table, the dishes piled high in the sink, the broken cups and saucers, the torn drapes, and the mess in the bathroom. Now ask yourself whether it was worth it. If the answer is yes, you're a natural entertainer. Welcome to the club.

THE TRAVELER

A kindly old gentleman left his native Maine, for the first time, for a brief sojourn in New Hampshire. When he returned, the townsfolk asked his impressions. "I discovered," he said, "that the world is a lot bigger than I thought." And indeed it is.

Travel, however, can be more than broadening. It can also be maddening, frustrating, disappointing—but if you know what to expect before you start planning your trip, you can minimize the chances that something terrible will happen.

Before you go

The essence of vacation, for most of us, is change—busting out of the year-long routine. Experiencing a different culture, hearing a different tongue, sampling different foods—all make for change. But then there's the matter of taste. In choosing a vacation spot, the biggest mistake you can make is to buy on price or reputation alone, without pausing to ask, "What do I enjoy?" Here are some questions to ask yourself:

• Do I want city avenues or beach sand? Desert? Farm? Jungle?
• Hot? Cold? High life? Low life?
• Would I rather dance and drink at a resort or talk with fishermen? Gamble at the roulette wheel or climb a mountain?
• Is fine dining important? Scenery?
• Will I be happy relaxing in one or two areas, or will I be invigorated by whirling through a long itinerary?
• Do I prefer a luxury hotel, an old inn, a tent in the woods?
• Would I enjoy visiting museums and historic sites? Would I like tennis round-the-clock?

One of the most basic questions—possibly the first—to ask is, "Do I want to travel independently or with an escorted group?" The travel industry offers a range of group packages, from the unstructured to the minutely controlled. Their biggest plus is economy—prices can be excellent. Furthermore, letting someone else handle logistical hassles is for many the only way to have a true vacation: preplanned, prepaid, and carefree. A good group vacation, then, is cheap and easy.

But in the more structured packages—the complete prefab vacations—you travel in packs nearly all day, every day. A group personality is helpful. Not that you must be super-sociable, but on a group trip the truly introverted may feel very left out—it might be better to go solo so the contrast won't be so evident. On the other hand, if you don't meet people easily on your own but do react well when thrust into a social situation, you'll do fine with this kind of group travel.

Investigate packages. You'll find thousands of offerings, from cheap weekends to month-long extravaganzas to special-interest deals for hang gliders and would-be French chefs. The choices are mind-boggling, and the brochures must be combed in detail. Make sure about hotels and meals—are tips included? Also find out whether the escort-freedom ratio is to your liking, and what guarantees there are. Generally, if not enough people sign up—and this applies to simple fly-together-only deals as well as escorted groups—the whole thing is canceled. Your best help in choosing is a strong recommendation from a friend—one who's traveled on a particular plan *recently*.

Travel agents

The do-it-yourself instinct, strong as it may be, may find itself pushed into a corner when an alphabet of special fares, deals, and destinations begins to make your head whirl. Then it's time for a travel agent. Like group travel, agents, in theory, should save you money and trouble. A good travel agent helps you know your own mind and needs. How can you tell a good one? First off, the agent interviews *you*. He asks not a simple, "Where do you want to go?" but makes a thorough, searching inquiry into your likes and dislikes. A good agent will help you to discover tastes you didn't know you had. An agent who just makes a pass at your wishes and then begins to push the Special of the Month should be left sitting alone at his (or her) desk.

A good agent will read brochures with you and answer questions from firsthand knowledge. If he/she hasn't been to the spot in question, he/she asks a colleague, not trusting brochure propaganda any more than you should.

Does a travel agent cost you money?

Unless you ask for special arrangements, you don't pay a travel agent any fee—not for walk-in consultation, not for actual booking. The agent earns a living by commissions—he/she gets from 7 to better than 20 percent, depending on the item. This is nice, except that it puts the travel agent in a league with insurance men and stockbrokers—it's

Temperature conversions

Degrees C.	Degrees F.
0—	32
10—	50.0
20—	68.0
30—	86.0
40—	104.0
50—	122.0
60—	140.0
70—	158.0
80—	176.0
90—	194.0
100—	212.0

To convert a Fahrenheit temperature to its Centigrade equivalent, subtract 32 from the Fahrenheit temperature, multiply by 5, and divide by 9. To convert a Centigrade temperature into Fahrenheit, multiply the Centigrade temperature by 9, divide by 5, and add 32.

to the agent's advantage to sell you more. By saving you cash, the agent cuts his/her earnings, an unfortunate paradox. Still, again in theory, the truly wise agent will forego the immediate pleasure of a higher commission in hopes of the delayed reward of a satisfied, lifelong customer. If you find an agent who seems to be interested in saving you money, you have found such a prudent businessperson; if not, get out.

Until you have established which type you're dealing with, take agents' recommendations with a grain of salt. Some veteran travelers, in fact, do enough homework to make all their own choices about where to go, what to do, and even what prices to pay, and then let an agent handle the details. It's like investors who make all their own picks and expect their brokers simply to execute the orders. Why an agent in such cases? To cut down telephone work and because sometimes a fairly busy agent *does* carry some clout with airlines, hotels, and so on. For you, there may be no openings; for an agent who brings in a lot of business yearly, there may be just one last spot.

The giants of the business, agencies such as American Express and Thomas Cook, get you no better deals and don't necessarily carry more weight than a busy independent agency. And they do pose the risk of your being one of a faceless mass of customers. Agents who operate short-lived one-man shops out of their spare bedrooms are generally not the safest pick, either. In between are a mass of busy local agencies, at some of which you're bound to find honest, helpful agents. Watch for the emblem of ASTA, the American Society of Travel Agents. It doesn't prove excellence or reliability, but at least the national organization has a code of ethics and a Consumer Affairs Committee for complaints. Also, look for an agency of some years' standing—proof that *someone* likes its work—and rely mostly on word of mouth. If your friends don't travel much, ask your lawyer, your banker, or businessmen around town.

Research Agent or no, read about places you might visit. When you've chosen an itinerary, really work at learning about where you'll be going. Find friends who have been there; check libraries and bookstores. Find out about sights and activities, history and people. This way you can turn a trip into a real experience.

The United States Travel Service operates a toll-free telephone service that's a good starting point for information on vacations in America. For information on many foreign destinations, start with the Manhattan telephone directory, available at large public libraries or the phone company office. Foreign tourism offices are listed here (look under both the noun and adjective form of the country's name—France and French, for instance), as are the various consulates and missions that dispense information on visas, vaccinations, and other necessities.

Planning is half the fun, folks say, but not when you get to the stuff of which governments are made. Serious preparation for any major foreign trip starts at least one month in advance. **Be prepared**

Unless you're going to Canada, Mexico, or certain nearby islands, you will need a current passport. To obtain one you'll need a birth (or naturalization) certificate, an ID (like a driver's license) with your signature and physical description on it, and two identical photos of yourself (*not* from a vending machine) that are two and a half to three inches square and feature a light background. Apply to a regional passport office or ask at your local post office or county courthouse. Expect to wait a few weeks, although rush service is available if you show air or boat tickets. Record your passport number and the date and place issued, and carry this record with you during your trip—*not* with the passport. Carry your birth certificate too. **Passport**

Some governments insist on clearing you before you cross their borders—you need a visa. Every country has different rules, so it's up to you—or your travel agent—to find out who demands what. Just be sure to find out *before* you go. **Visas**

For foreign driving it's often required, and always smart, to have an international driving permit. Your local chapter of the American Automobile Association will help you obtain one. You need a valid U.S. license and two passport photos. **International driver's license**

Be careful about taking foreign-made items out of the country with you. When you try to return that Japanese camera or English sports coat you bought at home, the U.S. Customs inspector could accuse you of having picked it up abroad. Register these articles with U.S. Customs as you leave. **Your own goods**

If you're a full-time student, regardless of your age, buy an International Student Identity Card from the student travel service of the Council on International Education Exchange in New York. It brings special travel rates of all sorts and is recognized in most frequently-traveled countries. You'll need to send the name of your school, last semester's transcript showing full-time credits, or a letter on school stationery, including the school seal, that confirms your full-time status; a small recent photo; and your birthdate. **A bargain for some**

Dollars and sense Before you go, convert some money to the currency of your first destination; include small change for a call to the hotel, taxi or bus fare, etc. Communist-bloc countries usually set a minimum per day that you must convert and spend; check with your travel agent or travel line about applicable countries and minimums. Ask your local commercial bank where to get foreign currency, or, if you're flying out, change money at the international airport. Also, take 20 or 30 U.S. one-dollar bills. You'll need them on your way back. When you need money changed overseas, go to a bank; hotels, restaurants, airports, and shops charge premium exchange rates. In some countries black-market money changers will approach you with tempting rates. Black-markets *are* illegal and you can end up in trouble, so don't take the chance.

Strive to understand the currency of the lands you visit; don't just hold out a handful of cash and say, "Take what I owe you." Know equivalents—if there's no convenient multiplying or dividing factor, memorize the equivalent of a quarter, a dollar, five dollars, and ten.

Traveler's checks It's safest to keep the bulk of your money in traveler's checks, in this country or abroad, since they will be replaced if lost or stolen. (Always carry receipts separate from checks.) Most traveler's checks are sold for 1 percent of the value of the checks; however, there are companies offering free traveler's checks. Your bank may also give free traveler's checks to customers. Shop around. If you have doubts about acceptability of specific checks where you are going, ask the company issuing the checks.

Credit cards Using a credit card abroad means you don't actually pay for several weeks, until the slips come across the ocean. However, if you lose them, to avoid liability you'll have to phone or cable (collect) all the home offices (carry the numbers and addresses with you). One major credit card should suffice.

Insurance If you are nervous about flying or cruising you may want to obtain some life insurance. If you will be carrying valuables, either from the start or purchased en route, or if you simply want to protect your luggage, you may feel better with coverage for theft. Insurance is inexpensive and readily available. Your travel agent can arrange for coverage, or you can purchase insurance from one of the counters or vending machines located in most airports. Several of the major credit-card firms also provide life coverage for cardholders. Before you leave, determine whether you are covered by any existing policies.

Your health Shots are no longer required for travel to most popular destinations, but it's smart to keep your smallpox, tetanus, and other shots up to date. Your local health department, the U.S. Public Health Service, and airline and cruise offices can fill you in on requirements around the world. Don't wait until the last minute; some shots take a while to become effective; others may hurt your arm or knock you out for a short time.

Here's something to take and hope you won't use: a small package of **Medical kit** medical supplies. Everyone should carry aspirin, antiseptic, a few bandages, an anti-diarrhea medicine, and a Red Cross first-aid booklet. If you're going far off the beaten path, you should take an antibiotic such as tetracycline, an antihistamine, and halazone tablets for water purification. Take an extra pair of glasses (or your prescription). If you carry any drugs, keep them labeled and carry the prescription as well to avoid any inspection troubles. If you have a serious physical condition, carry an ID tag or card describing it, and join the International Association for Medical Assistance to Travelers so you can get its list of English-speaking doctors throughout the world.

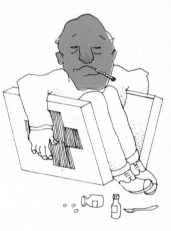

   It's a good idea to have a thorough medical checkup before you go—and make sure your doctor's phone number is included in your address list. And if you haven't seen a dentist in a while, go before you leave. Nothing is worse than an abcess in a foreign country.

Flying through time zones is hard on your body. Flying from the **Jet lag** United States to Europe, for example, you gain five or six hours, but your biological clock doesn't know this. Some people adjust better than others, but everyone is somewhat affected. Best advice: For eastward travel, stay up an hour later than usual the third day before you go, two hours later the second day, and three hours later the day before. Go to bed progressively earlier for westward travel.

· Dress in loose, comfortable clothes.   **A few in-flight tips**
· Don't eat heavily or drink much coffee or alcohol.
· Drink plenty of water.
· Wash your face before landing.
· Take it easy the first day.

Japanese tour groups are often seen doing exercises *en masse* in airport transit lounges; it's a good idea to get some exercise both before and after a flight.

Don't go off without a list of addresses—friends, friends of friends, **Advance planning** business contacts, American embassies, your hotels, recommended backup hotels in case something falls through, "must" restaurants.

Also take your own postcard list. Mailing cards while you're on vacation is one of those traveling traditions that's hard to ignore.

Mail from home   You can use American Express or Thomas Cook Travel as a mail drop in many major cities of the world. You may be asked to prove that you're a customer of the company in question; carrying a single $10 traveler's check of theirs will do. Generally speaking, in high season the lines at Cook are shorter; American Express offices, especially in popular spots like Paris and Athens, tend to turn into "Young Americans Abroad" social clubs. You can also receive mail virtually anywhere through the local equivalent of our American general delivery (*poste restante*, the French term, is widely understood)—inquire at the national tourist office of the country in question here before you go. And be sure that any stateside correspondents post their letters in plenty of time—a week or more for most overseas destinations.

Speaking their language   "Everyone knows English," you've heard. It's not so. Especially in small towns or nations with little tourist business, you will find no English at all. What to do? Take a phrase book. Forget most of the minutiae and esoterica. (Why learn, "Porter, will you please raise the left window an inch and a half?" when you can raise it yourself?) Memorize at least the key words: *yes, no, please, thank you, I don't speak———, hotel, room, water, excuse me, how much?* It's smart also to learn to count to ten. Knowing how to say "Beautiful!" (and using it frequently about your host country) will make you immediately welcome anywhere. And don't forget to learn the most important word of all in any language: *toilet.* Sign language just won't do for that one.

Take a two-way pocket dictionary for best coverage. When you have a communication gap, look up the English word on the spot and point to the entry (where the word will appear in the other language) if necessary. Language hassles can be an amusing way of breaking the ice with people you encounter.

Packing   Old traveler's rule: Lay out everything you really need—only the bare essentials. Then put back half and pack the rest.

Why? Freedom from porters, from taxis, from aching arms, from incessant rearranging of your worldly goods. Take lots of luggage on cruises and on auto trips, where it doesn't matter. Otherwise, travel light. Smart travelers, in fact, make sure their bag isn't really full, so there's room for acquisitions. It may mean extra laundry if your stay is a long one, but it's worth it.

Airlines usually allow a carry-on bag if it'll fit under your seat (which usually means its length, width and depth must total less than 45 inches). The trick is that you can generally stow a hanging suit bag in a plane closet as well. If you limit yourself to these two and perhaps a small shoulder tote, you gain the greatest freedom of all: no baggage wait. Just grab your things and run.

Unless you're going on business or to a lot of parties, you can get along with one suit *or* jacket-and-tie combination for weeks. Who's going to see you twice? And if you stain the lapel you can find a cleaner. And if you can't, you must be in an area where you don't need a suit anyway.

OK, so take a suit *and* a jacket, but no more. Pack two ties, two pairs of slacks, a pair of jeans, four shirts, four sets of underwear and socks, a sweater, a decent pair of shoes and a pair for kicking. (You'll be wearing part of all this when you leave.) If it's cold where you're going, you'll want to wear (or carry over your arm) a heavy coat and pack a sweater, scarf, and gloves. If the climate will be warm and wet, take two bathing suits. Maybe you should take a light raincoat, which can double as a bathrobe if your hotel shower's down the hall. And bring soap, shaving kit (plus converter if your razor is electric), toothbrush and paste, shampoo, deodorant, hairbrush, medical kit (*see* "Be Prepared," page 263).

Stick to dark clothes when possible (they show dirt less) and pick colors that go with each other. Wash-and-wear always: it takes just a few minutes to wash underwear and socks at night if you want to cut down on laundry bills. In most cities, people dress citylike, not beachlike; do likewise.

Smart optionals: rubbers, a collapsible umbrella, washing powder, two handkerchiefs, suntan lotion, shoeshine pads, stick spot remover, an alarm clock, a styptic pencil, a travel clothesline and clothespins. Things you might not think of: binoculars, corkscrew, laundry bag (for both laundry and loot). Take some small plastic bags for soap, wet bathing suits, and to use on picnics and a dozen other ways.

Chic, matched, initialed, stiff, hand-rubbed leather luggage looks nice. Unfortunately, that's all. First, fancy bags invite prying, lock picking, and theft. Second, they're heavy even when empty. Third, they're not as flexible as soft luggage or the newer soft-walled bags, which have shaped frames but stretchable sides. Go soft. Look for strong-looking seams and handles that are reinforced with big patches. If you add a hanging suit bag, as suggested, you'll be surprised at how much you can pack. If you'll be roughing it with little gear, consider the standard youth bag—the backpack. Once you're used to it, it's surprisingly comfortable, and your arms are freed for other tasks.

Finding your size abroad

Suits/Overcoats

American and English	Continental
36	46
38	48
40	50
42	52
44	54
46	56

Shirts (collars)

American and English	Continental
14	36
14½	37
15	38
15½	39
16	41
16½	42
17	43

Shirts (sleeve lengths)

American and English	Continental
32	81
33	84
34	87
35	89
36	92
37	94
38	97

Sweaters

American	English
Small	34
Medium	36–38
Large	40–42
Extra Large	44–46

Continental
44
46-48
50-52
54-56

How to pack

Pack large items at the bottom of your suitcase—suit and/or jacket, unless you have a hanging bag for those. To fold a jacket, pull up the collar; put your hands in the armholes and fold the shoulders together, backward, evenly; pull the collar behind the shoulders, turning the jacket inside out; lay it on a bed and reach in to straighten the sleeves; fold the whole thing at the middle for the suitcase. A good method for a suit is to stretch trousers out on a bed; spread your jacket, buttoned and arms straight, across them, shoulders to seat; fold pants legs up; fold coattails up. To fight wrinkles, slip plastic cleaner's bags into the folds. (Otherwise, try the steam-in-the-shower-room technique at your hotel.) Make sure pocket flaps and lapels are smooth.

Shirts go front-to-front, alternating collars. Shoes go in plastic bags. Underwear and socks go rolled into scrolls or folded for filler—in your shoes, in your shirt collars, in corners. Roll neckties, starting at the narrow end, to avoid wrinkling. An extra belt, if you take one, should be wrapped around the inside of your suitcase, not coiled tight. Anything spillable goes into plastic bags, twisted shut. Anything breakable goes between layers of clothing.

If you're checking any luggage, get rid of old destination tags on your bags—they're a nice badge of the well-traveled man, but they confuse handlers. Attach a name tag (with your address on the reverse, so that sharp-eyed people can't spot you leaving, note where you live, and steal everything in your house). Put a business card or another name-and-address tag *inside* your suitcase, with the address you're headed for and dates of stay written on it; that way, if your bag goes astray and falls into the hands of an honest soul you'll get it back. Attach something unusual—a ribbon, a rope, a huge colored-tape "X"—to your suitcase so you'll recognize it from afar. Finally, note the maker and model of your suitcase and inventory the contents on a piece of paper to carry with you.

To pack a suit or a jacket and slacks, lay the trousers down first on your bed or any flat surface. Place the jacket, fully buttoned, face up on the pants so that the shoulders of the jacket cover the top half of the pants as shown below. Next fold the trousers over the front of the jacket so that it covers the upper chest area. Lastly fold up the bottom of the jacket to cover the pants.

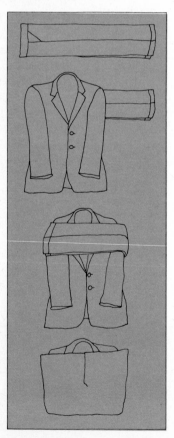

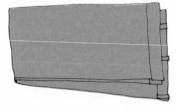

In packing slacks alone, you can fold them as shown above, or roll the legs in thirds from bottom to top. Make sure you keep the seams square.

Avoid overstuffing. It wrinkles your clothes and strains your luggage.... and embarrasses you at airline security and customs checks when you have to sit on the case to close it. Coming home with more than you brought out, you'll probably stuff a laundry bag and jam little extras into your pockets.

Keep it with you

Passports, important medicines, eyeglasses, tickets, crucial papers, ID's, cash, checks, and other valuables should always be in carry-on luggage. Never stow them in a bag that will leave your side. Keep a shirt change handy, too.

Airlines

"When you let a machine take you up that high," Jack Benny once told Hollywood writer Irving Brecher, "you're taking your life in your hands." Brecher agreed. "Even birds don't go that high," he said pensively. "And flying is their *business!*" For the fearful, getting there is never half the fun when a plane is involved.

Should you fly?

No matter that in a commercial jet you're statistically 15 times safer per passenger-mile than in a car. No matter that American pilots, at least, are top professionals checked out twice a year for proficiency and health. No matter that even conservative insurance companies don't think flying is so dangerous—they don't charge pilots any more for insurance than they charge the earthbound. Flying can still produce fear.

In a recent British book called *Destination Disaster*, the world's big airlines were surveyed for safety records over 25 years. American carriers came out on top. Bringing up the rear were Cubana, JAT of Yugoslavia, CSA of Czechoslovakia, IAC of India, Cruzeiro of Brazil, THY of Turkey, PAL of the Philippines, Egyptair, Avianca of Colombia, and Tarom of Rumania. Avoid those if it'll make you feel any better. Otherwise, breathe deeply to relax, distract yourself with conversation or a book, and don't look out the window when things get choppy. Admit it—flying is the best way to go far fast.

The best deal

Finding out who flies where is easy enough—look at the *Official Airlines Guide* in an airline or travel agent's office, or just read the ads. Figuring out the best deal is much tougher. "The day may come," *Business Week* magazine once said, "when a customer walks into an airline office, international and domestic, and is offered a choice of one or two fares, without having to swear he's a member of The Friends of Pipe Organs, or having to make ground 'arrangements' including a free bus ride around the Municipal Reservior. But don't bet on it soon." A choice of one or two fares? Not yet. You can pay full fare or one of a dozen excursion, standby, or charter fares.

Charters, incidentally, are no longer limited to members of special groups and tours; anyone can join if he's willing to book and pay far in advance. Savings are significant, so, for many, "Charter is smarter." If you back out, though, you usually lose your money—but travel agents sell inexpensive insurance policies that pay you back if a doctor says illness forced you to cancel.

Airline prices change with season, day of week, time of day, length of stay. It's confusing—but at least deals don't really differ from line to line most of the time. Figure out where you'd like to go. Either see a travel agent, who should be able to unravel the choices, or make at least three calls to an airline and balance the information. Be patient on the telephone—clerks are sometimes as mixed up as you are.

Getting seated   First-class air travel is for the expense-account set—its advantages include more room, more service, peace and quiet, free drinks, better food, quicker on and off. Coach (also known as economy) fares are much cheaper; this class of air travel is for most of us. Don't get any ideas that you'll be able to sneak into first class if the section isn't full the way theatergoers can upgrade to orchestra seats. You won't.

Tips   Reserve your plane seat this way:

• For smoke-free air, get a seat deep in the no-smoking section, far away from smokers. There's no wall between sections, so in the nonsmoking area right near the dividing line smoke gets into your eyes.
• For a quiet and smooth ride, get a seat over the wings (avoid rear seats).
• For safety, get a seat near an exit (but not over a wing).
• For leg room, get a seat near the emergency doors—aisle seats preferred.
• For peace in a 747 or DC-10, get a double seat, not one of the four-abreast seats in the center of the plane.

Other things to consider when you're booking a flight:

• Even if you're not sure when you want to come back, always book a return flight. It's easier to change it than to be stuck.
• Most airlines offer special dietary food. Some travelers say kosher meals are better than the mass-produced variety. Make your special orders in advance.
• Flying times do differ—ask, "How many stops?"
• Often you can make free stopovers in cities en route to your destination—ask, "Any stopovers allowed?"

And, when it's finally time to leave   • Even if you hold a ticket, confirm two days before departure.
• Before you leave for the airport, phone to check on delays. And if a

delay is announced while you're in the terminal, you'll get the best information on how long it'll be by telephoning the airline rather than asking in person. If a long holdup seems likely, check other airlines' schedules—you can usually transfer if the second airline has a seat free on a flight that will depart earlier than yours. (There's trouble defecting if you've already checked baggage, however.)

· The airlines say you should appear 30 minutes ahead of time for domestic flights, 60 minutes ahead for international travel. If you come late, though you can bypass the check-in counter and go straight to the gate. Do leave at least 15 minutes.

· If cabin pressure on landing hurts your ears, don't sleep. Swallow a lot, chew gum (or chew the air), force yawns.

· Never tip on an airline.

Cruises

Probably the most widespread wrong idea about travel is that going by boat is cheaper than flying. In fact, it's usually more expensive, no matter what the accomodations. So why go on a cruise? You're afraid to fly. Or you like the notion of a relaxing, preplanned, prepaid, comfortable vacation—no constant packing and unpacking, no worries about reservations and food, no taxi hassles, no waiting, the same bed every night. Or your're turned on by the whole atmosphere at sea.

Particularly aboard cruise ships, which account for most floating tourist travel, things are at once serene and lively. Serene, because you're away from it all, being generously fed and rocked by the waves. Lively, because cruise ships are really floating resort hotels, overflowing with saunas and pools, movie theaters and discothèques. With few exceptions, party atmosphere prevails. Then, too, there's shopping at various ports of call—and no problem with the weight of the booty.

Who shouldn't go?

The nervous, the claustrophobic, and the weak of stomach should not go on cruises. Ship stabilizers do reduce *mal de mer*, and simple wonder medications are available to prevent seasickness, but a rough storm can still be hell.

Choosing a cruise   If you're thinking of taking a cruise, read the ads, see a travel agent, talk to friends. There are plenty to choose from leaving from several American ports besides the obvious New York and San Francisco. Consider itinerary and cuisine (eating is definitely the number-one activity on cruises). Be alert for special-interest cruises for singles, music lovers, star-gazers, bird-watchers, etc. If nightclubs are your thing, watch for cruises featuring big-name entertainers fresh from Las Vegas.

You can find everything from a few days for a few hundred dollars to Around the World for 20 Grand.If an agent or a friend touts ship A, make very sure he or she has been on ship A for more than a bon voyage party. You'll be paying $50 to $100 a day or more, and it's difficult to change cruises if you feel that you're stuck.

Tips   The longer the cruise, the richer the clientele. Therefore, if you're looking to meet single passengers, the more eligible will probably be on the modest voyages. Incidentally, if you are a single in search, tell the ship staff—every cruise has a paid matchmaker. And always choose the later dinner sitting—early meals are for families and older people.

You pay more for a porthole, more for a high deck. Try for a midship cabin to avoid engine noise and sleep smoothly.

Most cruise passengers like to dress up. If you don't, don't go on a cruise.

Freighters   For far-off ports without luxury, hop a freighter; this kind of travel isn't as uncomfortable as it sounds. Accommodations are more than ample, in fact, but you'll find only a dozen comrades, no partying, crazy schedule changes midstream, dinner with the crew. Travel agents can help.

Trains, buses, and other ways of moving   "Ever since childhood, when I lived within earshot of the Boston and Maine," wrote Paul Theroux in *The Great Railway Bazaar*, "I have seldom heard a train go by and not wished I was on it." Romantic, perhaps, but that's the reason some travelers—from hoboes to princes—choose trains. Others like trains because they like the price, the sociable atmosphere, the nonhighway scenery, the convenience of arriving in midtown. America's trains are improving, Europe's are good right now, Japan's are mostly topnotch. Don't names like the Orient Express, Le Mistral and the Trans-Siberia Railway impress you?

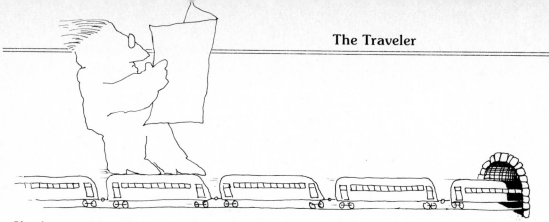

· Check timetables. If you want speed, local trains can be deadly.   **Train advice**

· If you'll be doing a lot of traveling on the Continent, explore Eurailpass, a card you buy at home that's good for unlimited first-class fares in 13 countries. See a travel agent or any office of the Swiss, French, Italian, or German rail systems.

· If you're touring the U.S.A., Amtrak also has special rates for 14, 21, and 30 day passes.

· If you're not traveling with a special pass, always check the difference between first- and second-class seating; there often isn't enough to justify the price spread.

· Arrive in time to choose a seat on the aisle. The view is skimpier but the ride is smoother. Don't sit over a wheel.

· Expect no bargains in the dining car. The European custom on long train trips is to take along half a pantry's worth of supplies, including bottled water.

· Night travel by rail may not be popular here, but elsewhere it's done all the time. You can't watch the scenery, but you sleep inexpensively.

In the United States, airplanes and railroads serve fewer than a   **Buses**
thousand cities. Intercity buses hit some 15,000 towns! And so there will probably always be people who travel by bus. When it comes to major destinations, when there's a choice, buses are popular with those who don't mind minimum comfort, or those whose wallets tell them they have no alternative. One trip teaches you to keep away from the rear of the bus, where the engine noise and heat are bad.

Buses are convenient in places like Canada, England, Italy, parts of Central and South America, and elsewhere. In Europe, Eurailpass holders can get discounts on certain bus routes. In the United States, Continental Trailways and Greyhound sell similar single-fare passes for 15, 30, or 60 days of unlimited travel. These can be a good deal.

Plenty of hardy souls have seen the world by motorcycle. It can be   **Two-wheelers**
done. Gas bills are way below auto fuel bills—you pay even less for gas for mopeds. Best bet for Europe: Buy a cycle there, ride it, sell it. Bicyclists may prefer their own familiar machines. Best for plane

shipping is the clear plastic bike bag some airlines sell for a few dollars—there's no dismantling involved, and your bike's visibility encourages careful handling. The International Bicycle Touring Society guides members on two-wheel vacations. On any two-wheeler, be conservative in judging miles per day, and be prepared to get damp.

Renting a car

Mileage and Speed Conversions	
Mileage	
kilometers	miles
2	1.3
5	3.1
25	15.5
40	25.0
100	62.5
300	187.5
500	312.5
Speeds	
kph	mph
10	6
30	19
40	25
50	31
60	37
80	50
100	62

More convenient than a locomotive, more comfortable than a bus, safer than hitching....it's renting a car. People choose the drive-your-self way for the freedom of it. Whether you reserve in advance through one of the huge international firms or book locally when you get where you're going depends on how secure you need to be. One advantage of the big American-based outfits: If there's bill trouble, you can continue the argument at home.

If you plan to cover a lot of ground, make sure the company has a network of offices wherever you go, in case of car trouble; otherwise you're getting no bargain. If you reserve, get written confirmation. Always specify automatic transmission if you need it, since lower-priced models abroad are usually stick shift. If you'll be in rough mountains, ask about four-wheel drive cars. If you'll be driving from Western Europe to the Iron Curtain countries, pay extra and rent the most unusual Western car you can find. Sports cars and such make fantastic ice-breakers there: people appear from nowhere to ask about them.

Airlines offer some good "fly-drive" packages—flight to and auto rental there—but always check to be sure you can't do better independently.

The business of it

If you don't have a credit card, you'll have to go through credit clearance (this will take up to three days) and still plunk down a huge deposit to rent a car. If you work for a big company, you may qualify for a business discount, even for a pleasure trip. Try to estimate how many miles you'll drive and do the arithmetic with various rates offered; there can be a substantial difference. The optional zero-deductible collision coverage is a good deal for a few days' trip, but not for long hauls. Check for dents and a full tank, and jot down the odometer reading, on your own, before you leave.

On the road

Renting a car abroad isn't necessarily costlier than it is at home. Buying gas usually is—it costs three or four times as much in many places (although you'll probably get more miles per gallon). Some countries, like Italy, offer high-discount gas coupons to tourists. Outside very developed areas, it's smart to refill your tank at the half mark. Learn how to say "Fill it up!" in as many languages as you need.

Other than the drive-on-the-left rule in Britain and a few other countries, basic road rules are the same everywhere—don't cross the center line except to pass, etc. But learn peculiar local laws, and do memorize the international road signs and any common local signs. Except for rush transportation, you'll probably enjoy shunpiking, since a highway is a highway. Be prepared for narrow roads, unfenced mountain drives, and speeding drivers; in other words, be extra careful. Find the best maps you can, and avoid the tendency to read them too optimistically—it always takes longer than you think to drive over those squiggly, deceptively short lines.

Moving around in a strange city

Unless you're totally loose, just nosing around to see what will happen next, it's smart to scout out any city on your itinerary that's new to you *before* you get there. The better guidebooks have maps of major cities; handier still are foldout pocket maps usually available free from the local chamber of commerce or visitors' center (in the United States) or from the national tourism office (for foreign nations). You needn't plan a strict minute-by-minute schedule, but if there are sights you know you musn't miss, plot them on the map and see if a logical, economic order suggests itself. You'll also find that having a map on hand in a foreign city can be a great help when you accost locals to ask for directions—instead of struggling with two tongues ("Let's see, is *geradeaus* left or right?"), your Good Samaritan can simply trace the route on your map with his finger.

Driving in big cities

Don't drive in big cities in foreign countries. Except in some of the lesser-developed capitals, the world's major cities will offer you confusion, frustrating one-way streets, parking woes—all the comforts of home. This holds truest, of course, in precisely those parts of town you're most likely to visit. Public transportation, augmented by feet, allows you to see more, be more spontaneous, and "feel" the city better. Park the car and leave it.

Taxis or buses?

Taxis are, of course, usually the easiest way to get from here to there in a city. Whether you use them depends mainly on the condition of your wallet (a lot of sightseeing can run up a hefty cab bill) and your notions of travel. For many, travel isn't travel unless seeing the sights includes joining the people in buses and in subways, on streetcars and on foot. Ask your hotel clerk for advice—after all, that's how *he* travels. (Shake off his first attempt to suggest a taxi; he's only telling you what he thinks you want to hear.) Always allow time for getting lost, and learn to think of it as fun. With the right attitude, it is.

In from the airport

If you're going to splurge on taxis, getting in from the airport is probably the time for it. No one needs to get a feel for local color while his arms are loaded with baggage and he's in a stupor from hours of travel. There are usually buses and limousine services, but they're not apt to leave for your hotel when *you* want them to leave. If there is a convenient bus and you're traveling light, of course, don't pass it by. (The airports in London and Frankfurt are two with good, cheap bus services.) Otherwise, know the local rules about taxi meters, luggage charges, and the like. And beware the ploy of taxi drivers in too many cities—pooling two or three passengers and collecting full fare from each. In most places, that's not legal; you should share the cost. In practice, if it's a busy time and cabs are scarce, you may not have much choice; but at least try hard to negotiate a middle ground.

Railroad and bus stations are usually more centrally located than airports, so a simple bus or subway ride may be a good way to your bed if you've arrived by train or bus. Your travel agent can fill you in; so can an airline agent.

Finding a bed

If you travel at high season—Paris in August, Barbados in February—you must make reservations for a place to stay. Off season, it can be rewarding to go free and easy. Never arrive in a big city late in the day without reservations, however—stop at a small town on the outskirts for the night, and enter the city the following morning. For unstructured travel, carry a complete guidebook.

Making hotel reservations

· Book for the maximum stay you can imagine; it's easier to leave early than to extend a booking.
· Determine the dining plan you desire ahead of time. The most common are: European Plan (EP)—no meals included; Continental Plan (CP)—light breakfast included; American Plan (AP)—three full

meals included; and the Modified American Plan (MAP)—breakfast and one other meal per day included.

· It's not a good idea to prepay hotels in full—anything can happen, and besides, once you've paid, you have to accept whatever you get.

· Doing some business? The bigger hotels and chains offer services ranging from interpreters and secretaries to audiovisual equipment and conference rooms.

· If you want a private bath overseas, be sure to specify it—only in America is it the rule.

· If you value quiet, request a room away from the elevators, and if you stop at a hotel on a busy street or highway, try to stay in a back room.

· If you reserve a room and find yourself stuck without one, make a polite fuss. The least the hotel can do is find you a comparable room elsewhere. Stand your ground until you're offered alternative accommodations.

Something special in Europe

Western European countries—Austria, Scotland, France, and Spain, among others—abound with ancient castles that have been turned into hotels. Surroundings and furnishings are usually impressive, food is often excellent, and prices may be no higher than those of good city hotels. Check the national tourist services.

Hostels

Youth hostels are misnamed. You can buy a senior pass (over 18) and join others of all ages in dorm-style facilities the world over. (South America is the only area in which "youth hostels" are not widespread.) You need your own sheets or sleeping bag, there may be only cold water available, there's often a lights-out time, and you may be asked to sweep the hall. "Roughing it" in this manner has several advantages—the communal atmosphere makes it easier to develop interesting friendships; you often learn more about the area's shops, entertainment, and sights than you would otherwise; and you pay only a fraction of the cost of a hotel room. A few countries *do* have age restrictions and most limit your stay to three days, so check with American Youth Hostels in Delaplane, Virginia, before you go.

Camping

If you enjoy camping, you find there's no vacation spot on earth without camping areas nearby. You can find domestic directories in the travel section of a good bookstore, and local tourist offices everywhere have lists. Campgrounds abroad are very much like those in America: heavy on families and young people in couples and small groups. In some places, you don't even need to find a campground. Sweden, for instance, has an age-old rule called Allemansrätten—Every Man's Right—that allows one night's free camping anywhere but at a military base—even on private property without permission, if you

stay away from the house and gardens. A few places rent tents fully equipped so you need carry nothing—for example, at picturesque St. John, in the U.S. Virgin Islands, everything is provided for a nominal charge per day at Cinnamon Bay Campground.

Some travelers like to stay in other people's houses. Tourist homes and guest houses seem to be coming back in America; watch for signs along the road (in small towns, mostly), or ask at local tourist offices. In other countries, homeowners frequently rent rooms to travelers. In some places—sections of Eastern Europe, for example—you can find a room in a private home either officially, through the government tourist office, or unofficially (and often illegally), direct from people who hang out at the tourist office or in front of hotels, offering to undercut the going room prices. You can save money by eliminating the middleman (no share for the state), but it's at your own risk.

Renting a house For a vacation in one spot, renting a house is usually more comfortable and sometimes less expensive than a long-term hotel room. There are several agencies that can help with this. At Home Abroad in New York lists European and Caribbean rentals; Properties International in San Francisco handles Hawaiian, Mexican, and European properties. Both have rentals that range in price from modest to exorbitant. La Fédération Nationale des Gîtes in Paris offers English-language information on *gîtes ruraux*—farmhouses, rural cottages, and even castles for rent. If you'd like to swap your home for someone else's so you'll *both* have vacations, contact the Vacation Exchange Club in New York, which has been publishing directories for swappers since 1961.

A warning In Europe and elsewhere, the people who'll check you in at many hotels, hostels, and guest houses still look askance at unmarried couples trying to register together. Better to be "married," ring and all. A recent wedding explains why her passport doesn't match yours.

In Communist and some other countries, you may be asked to give the hotel clerk your passport for a while. (They are required to register you with the police.) In such countries, as well as in smaller cities in places like Mexico and Turkey, where police can be aggressive, it's smart to let the American Embassy know that you're in the country— tell the embassy where you plan to be staying, too.

When you're an alien

There are two general rules to follow when you're shopping—concentrate on handmade or unusual local goods (carved *santos* in Puerto Rico, batiks in Indonesia), and know the U.S. value of manufactured goods.

Shopping

There are good buys in pottery and silver in Mexico, copper in Chile, leather in Florence, liquor in St. Thomas. There are also terrible buys in all sorts of items everywhere. Avoid thinking that "It's not real money; it doesn't matter." It does.

Why not become a specialized collector instead of just a purchaser? For example, if you're a cook, pick up an unusual kitchen item each place you visit.

In many lands you are expected to offer half the asking price, then grudgingly bargain upward. In these places, if you pay full ticket you'll be laughed at. A good test: Grimace, say, "I like it, but it's much more than I wanted to pay," and start to walk out. If you're followed, you have a deal.

For you, $9.95

In department stores everywhere, prices are set. Still, some fine shops discount if you pay with cash instead of a credit card; ask.

Most purchases or gifts beyond a personal limit of $100 are subject to U.S. duty when you return to this country. (Notable exceptions are works of art and proven antiques over a century old.) If you can arrange to return through the Bahamas or Guam you will be allowed $200 duty free. Goods you ship home are subject to duties also, unless they're gifts valued at less than $10. (If you do ship purchases, have it done by a reliable store or do it yourself.) Some items, such as foodstuffs, plants, and items that violate U.S. patents or copyrights are never allowed in. If you plan to buy anything at all, write for "Know Before You Go," a free booklet from the Customs Bureau.

Customs

There are substantial civil and criminal penalties for failure to declare or understating the value of an item. It's smarter to carry your receipts and declare all that is necessary.

Tipping Tipping has gone on for centuries. No one likes the system. The tough part is, who's to say what's fair? What's important is that a tip be payment and encouragement for good service, not an automatic tax. If you're well cared for, tip what you believe is fair; if you're not, don't reward the perpetrator.

How much? Tipping customs vary, so it's a must to research the practices of any country you visit. Ask a travel agent or, better, an honorable native. (Don't ask the clerk what to give the bellhop.) In many foreign lands, blessedly, 10 to 15 percent "service charge" is added onto your hotel or restaurant bill and your worries are over. (Leave some spare coins if you want to be generous.) Still, if a concierge or a maître d' does particularly well by you, it's considered good etiquette to better the national rule.

In countries where Western goods are hard to come by, you'll make more friends with chewing gum, a ballpoint pen, or a pack of razor blades than with cash. Bring things small enough to get by foreign border guards, who sometimes don't let obvious gifts through.

Some think advance tipping gives an edge. But up front or later, whether it's a bellhop's quarter or a waiter's $10, never tip ostentatiously. Smile and say, "Thank you."

Photography It's a fine idea to take a camera on your trip—as long as you can keep from compulsively shooting everything in sight. Aim to capture some of your best travel experiences, not to document the places you visit with slides of everything in the guidebooks.

Equipment Even if you are—or aim to be—the world's greatest lensman, don't weigh yourself down with four cameras and a bag of lenses and filters. The zoom lens is the traveler's savior—a midrange (say, 35 to 85mm) and a telephoto (85 to 205mm) give all the coverage you need. If you buy new equipment, be sure to test a couple of rolls of film before you leave. You can buy film most places you're likely to visit, but to be sure of type and price, take some with you. Airport X-ray inspections *can* hurt film, particularly after several tests. Ask for a visual check.

What to shoot? People. You can get all the scenics and landmarks you want on postcards. Take close shots of people selling, snoozing, going about their business. Ideally, you'll use that big lens to take shots unobserved. Otherwise, ask permission—in words or through signs and smiles. (The world is not your zoo; respect people.) Try to catch your subjects doing something, avoid wooden poses. Children in most places are very agreeable to acting for the camera, although many may ask for chewing gum or another reward.

If you're far off where tourists aren't common, you may find people uncomfortable—or even frightened—about cameras. An instant camera as an extra might overcome their reticence. Take a quick shot, show the result, and then do your own shooting—but be prepared to explain that not all pictures are instant.

When you do shoot scenery, ruins, or whatever, get something in the foreground—a person, a tree—for depth and scale. Morning and night shots of the same scene can look surprisingly different. And every good photographer knows that the best pictures come from shooting a subject from every angle possible and then throwing out the bad shots—but don't be too compulsive about your picture taking; you're not the man from *National Geographic*, just a fellow on vacation.

Trouble

Whether you're cautious or reckless, things can wreck your vacation. But they're less likely to if you realize the possibilities—and have some idea of how to cope when the worst does befall you.

Swindlers

You can be cheated. A "poor college student" will gladly show you spots other tourists never see, if you pay him up front. It turns out that he knows less than you do, and, what's more, he leaves you the first chance he gets. A shopkeeper swears he's selling you a valuable antique widget, but it turns out the widget was made last month in Taiwan. In these cases there's not much you can do, and often it's not worth the effort to try. Know better next time. Also beware of tour guides who lead you to "special shops," where the only thing "special" is that the guide gets a percentage of the take. In foreign lands, make complaints about serious matters to the national tourist board, which usually really cares.

Robbers

You can be robbed. Muggings and hotel-room thefts are most depressing on vacation. See the local police, but if it's cash, forget it. Traveler's checks? Find an office of the issuing company—and you'd better have those receipts. Airline ticket? They'll make up a new one, but you have to find one of *their* offices, too. Lose all your money and want to give up and go home? The American Embassy will put you on a plane for America, holding your passport as ransom until you repay the loan.

Lose your passport? Now you have a *real* headache. First, get a written police report of the incident. Then find an American consulate. You're best off if you've recorded the number and date of your passport, and if you have a birth certificate with you. Still, it may take a day or two for a new one to be issued.

Airline woes An airline can lose your suitcase. Maximum compensation is set by the Civil Aeronautics Board. You'll need a convincing list of valuables lost. But here's a nice note—you can put in a claim for expenses due to lost luggage, such as the new tie you had to buy for that afternoon meeting. If your suitcase is wrecked, you can demand repair. Get a free copy of "Air Travelers' Fly-Rights" from the CAB in Washington.

The airline can also bump you. Planes that go bump in the night are passengers' biggest fear, and in fact people are bumped off flights every day. Airlines must now post word that overbookings may be hazardous to your reservation, but that doesn't really help very much if you find yourself in an airport and they've just told you there's no room on the plane for you.

If it happens to you, be polite but very firm. They have to get you where you were going to no more than four hours late, or hand back your one-way fare (up to $200) *and* send you at their expense. That's the minimum; you can refuse the deal and complain to the CAB if you're still dissatisfied.

Illness Most travelers who get sick can blame what they put into their stomachs. Prevention is the key. If there's no well-supervised source of drinking water, stick to bottled water, beer, or wine. And don't let the bartender use ice cubes. Never drink even crystal-clear lake or stream water—clear doesn't necessarily mean pure. Except where you're sure, don't eat raw fish or shellfish, steak tartare, uncooked vegatables or green salads, fruit that isn't protected by its own inedible skin. If you do get Montezuma's Revenge (known in medical circles as diarrhea and vomiting), plain toast and tea for a day or two usually does the trick. Or use an anti-diarrhea medicine.

In poorly developed areas, particularly in the tropics, don't sleep outdoors or swim in still waters. Go easy on liquor in mountain towns; you're high enough.

If you need a doctor, it's best to find one who speaks your language. Your hotel staff may know of one; and, of course, the American and British embassies will. Keep in mind that some travelers maintain that the British will suggest a physician who's less likely to overcharge.

You can be arrested for an auto mishap, in a case of mistaken identity, for possession of illegal drugs, for jaywalking, or just because you broke some obscure local law. Pleading ignorance rarely helps, except in the most minor skirmishes. Now hear this: The American Embassy won't do much to help; like it or not, that isn't their job. They'll try to find you a lawyer and they'll wish you good fortune.

Arrest

Don't expect that a vacation will automatically provide a great experience, make wonderful changes in your life, or even be reasonably enjoyable unless you put some effort into making it do these things. You must create your own good time.

The bottom line

Traveling with a friend may seem like a good way to try for fun—but you and the friend must be compatible. There's a difference between "Let's have drinks" and "Let's go to Europe together for six weeks." Be prepared to tolerate and compromise. What to do if you're most turned on by traipsing up mountains and through vineyards and your friend wants nothing but big-city nightlife? Joint travel is thrifty, and sharing experiences can be great, but nonstop compromise is a high price to pay for companionship. If you do pair off (or if you're already a pair and you join another), frequent splitting up helps.

Should you go with a friend?

Solo travel need not be lonely, either. Your good time may well consist of a string of encounters with the locals. If you're successful, years after your trip you'll recall best not some stained glass window but the old woman who smilingly handed you flowers from her garden, or the man who led you to the café you were hunting for and then invited himself to join you for a drink. It's people who matter.

Still, be prepared for some meals alone, some evenings with no company but your own. If you accept this—and take a good book just in case—you won't be setting yourself up for a letdown.

If you worry about lonely touring but don't want to go with a group, organize a vacation around a hobby or interest. Genealogy? Research your roots in your ancestral village. Chamber music? The Amateur Chamber Music Players Society gives members a world directory of musicians who'll meet you for a chamber session. Put your mind to it and you can think of your own variation on this theme. The idea is that having something to do besides walking and looking can provide the best time of all.

Special interests

LOVE & SEX

You can have sex without love, of course. When sex is a game, or just "between friends," you may feel fairly safe. If you're only playing, with none of the real you out on the line, being rejected or disappointed won't feel so bad. (Being rejected by someone you were not emotionally involved with can hurt your pride, of course, but it probably won't devastate your spirit.) Sex without love may be fine sometimes—to get you through a lonely period, perhaps. But over the long term, it can be lonelier than being alone. And though there are times when it seems good for your ego, sex without love doesn't do much for your soul.

Then there's sex *with* love. Sweet, fine, and gratifying. If you're a romantic, and in love for the first time, you may think this is all you need to make a go of it with another person. If you've seen a love affair come to an end, though, you know that love hurts. Hurt feels bad. In order to avoid it, you may surround yourself with plenty of defenses, going along with love just so far, but stopping before you get in too deep, keeping an armor around your tenderest, most vulnerable places. This is a shame, because the tighter your defenses and the thicker your armor, the harder it will be for anyone to love you or know you fully. You can't really be loved unless you are known. And you can't be known until you let your guard down. If you *can* let it down, get rid of your armor completely, you'll be adding emotional honesty to love—and you'll be able to expand your relationship immeasurably.

It takes courage to have emotional honesty. It means being there, as you are, with nothing added, nothing for protection. It means admitting the truth when it's flattering to her ("I need you") and when it may hurt her feelings ("I need to be alone"). It means allowing her to see who you are (a person who's been terrified of speaking up in a group ever since he got booed off the debate platform in the ninth grade) instead of trying to get her to buy a trumped-up picture of who you wish you were (smooth, cool, undaunted—*always*). Emotional honesty requires admitting things you may not even want to look at yourself (that you didn't call her for three days after you got fired because you were disgusted with yourself for needing her so much; that you chose to suffer in silence rather than let her see you down and vulnerable). Emotional honesty requires letting all the Superman (and Superwoman) games go. It means being able to cry. Needing, and letting yourself be needed. In short, letting all the less-than-wonderful things about you show.

Learning emotional honesty

You may resist the idea of emotional honesty. It may sound like emotional sloppiness. Feelings pouring out, getting out of control. Isn't that weak, womanish? Quite the opposite. Being in touch with your feelings isn't an emotional indulgence that makes you weak. Having a clearer consciousness of self and a deeper awareness of your own behavior makes you stronger.

But, you may wonder, what about *her*? Doesn't she need to believe that you're strong? Is it really all right with her for you to be open about who you are, or will some of the uglier truths about you turn her off? Is it really all right for you to show weakness, or is it just all right during the times when she feels like mothering you? And can you trust her? You may visualize her on the phone, telling her friends, "No, we're not coming to the party because he's terrified of large groups."

Being emotionally honest does involve risk—for both of you. You need to trust each other and to agree to hang on during those times when one of you simply *doesn't* understand. You need to be willing to be uncomfortable, to handle the conflicts that are inevitable when you're totally honest. And when things do move over rough ground, remember that you have a choice. You *could* opt to keep the peace. You could avoid uncomfortable topics, deny awkward feelings, appease each other with half-truths. But you pay a high price for that kind of peace: emotional isolation.

As you begin to open yourself up to what you really feel, you're bound to hit some snags. Every time you come upon something you do or feel that doesn't fit your "ideal man" picture, you'll feel yourself resist. Pushing through what you think you should be to what you really are takes work.

Some "should's" to get rid of:

- You should earn more money than your woman.
- You should be taller than she is.
- You should have more sexual experience than she's had.
- You should want to make love more often than she does.
- You should make the first move.
- You should be stronger than she is, and if you're not, you should carry the heaviest suitcase anyway.
- You should take out the garbage.
- You should be more rational than she is.
- You should be the one to get you un-lost if you ever get lost (in a strange town, in the woods, etc.).
- You should be able to hide the fact that you're frightened or upset unless you choose *not* to hide it.
- You should always have the last word, *even* if she's right and you were wrong.

The list goes on and on, in your own head—a fact that you'll undoubtedly discover once you start paying attention to yourself. All of the so-called definitions of masculinity are just so much garbage. You are *you*. Having the courage to be that "you" makes you stronger than the most rigid model of the male stereotype. Your feelings are OK. Not allowing yourself to feel them is *not* OK. Being honest about who you are takes hard work. It can be awkward. But it can be worth it. When you add being fully known to the sexuality you share in a long-term loving relationship, you have something powerful and nourishing. Even if you are not in a committed relationship, the ability to be honest about yourself can add dimension—to a fledgling affair and to *every* encounter you have.

Everybody (male and female) wants to know: How do you meet people? You want to hear that there's a secret to it, that there's a faucet someplace that you can turn on any time you want to meet a woman or pour yourself some fresh new faces. Of course there's no such secret.

Meeting people

You go to the singles' bar, and you look up your mother's sister's friend's daughter, and you do the cocktail party circuit, and *nothing*. Aunt Millie's friend's daughter may spend the entire evening talking about her dog. Cocktail parties and singles' bars may seem like places where people look at each other like so much meat on the auction block. "What do you do for a living?" "What are you 'into'?" "Where did you go to college?" "Where do you live?" All the standard introductory lines may sound cold, calculating. What type are you, who do you know, what can your image do for my image? You may feel like a "thing" meeting other "things." You may wonder why no one dares (or, it seems, even knows how) to ask the personal questions that will uncover your "you-ness" and uniqueness.

Contact without contact

When people connect with each other on this "thing" level, there's no real contact, and no satisfaction. Most of the time it's not even interesting. Even if your wit-and-charm act connects nicely with her wit-and-charm act, interest will burn off quickly unless you find a way to reach the gritty stuff of who you both are underneath. Unless you're very good at cutting through the phoniness and getting other people to do the same, going to bars and parties and on blind dates are not very good ways to meet people.

Good getting-to-know-you situations

What instead? Situations that provide something more than obvious male-female confrontations are better. Sports clubs that plan canoeing, sailing, climbing, skiing events; college courses for adults; Yoga or Karate classes; any self-awareness trip; a health spa. When you're involved in doing something you like, you're most yourself (and so are other people), and meeting people is easier. A woman you've had several conversations with over a vat of clay in a sculpture class is a likelier prospect for an interesting dinner date than someone you've yelled at over the loud music in a dimly lit bar.

Other good meeting places: elevators, bank lines, supermarkets, department stores. Sound ridiculous? If you think you can't speak to a woman in an elevator unless it catches fire or breaks down, you're wrong. You can—it just requires a certain kind of approach. If you are willing to dispense with the games and the cute one-liner openings, you can really meet people anywhere. What should you say? Just tell the truth. Which is probably something in the neighborhood of, "I'm afraid you'll get annoyed, but I'd like to meet you." Think she'll walk off, shaking her head in disbelief at what a jerk you are? She might. But so what? You haven't really got anything to lose. And chances are pretty good that she *will* talk to you. Even if she won't meet you for a drink after work, she'll probably like you a lot better if you say something point-blank honest than if you come up with something like:

The five worst opening lines

"Smile, baby, it can't be all that bad."
"Hey, I really like your outfit."
"Haven't I seen you someplace before?"
"You're not married, are you?"
"I've noticed that you often ride this elevator, and…"

These opening lines, probably the most over-used first-time greetings in the universe, will only work if the woman you say them to considers you so terrific looking that she was falling down dead hoping you'd speak to her in the first place. But before you start worrying about thinking up some really great and original opening lines, ask yourself if a simple "Hello, my name is———" wouldn't work just as well.

Starting relationships

If you're like thousands of other men and women, you may justify courting games by telling yourself that you're just playing and having fun until the "real thing" comes along. You may be a believer in the love-zap theory. This wonderfully romantic notion holds that there is a right mate for you somewhere—she's The One. And when you meet The One, you'll know it. Zap. It's love.

The love-zap theory

This idea is supported by our parents ("When I met your mother, I just *knew*..."), by 90 percent of the songs we hear on the radio, and by well-meaning friends who console us after a love failure with, "Well, you just haven't met the right girl yet." When you meet The One, you think, the games will stop, barriers will tumble down, conversation will flow. You'll mesh perfectly. There'll be an instant, natural knowing. You'll perceive and be perceived. You'll love each other totally. And you'll never be lonely again.

You're prepared for the fact that the zap may not hit you right away—it may take you a while to realize that you've found The One. Maybe after dating for a few months, you'll look at her over a pizza, and it'll hit you: she's The One.

Once you have The One firmly in tow, you expect things to *turn out*. You expect to have fights, of course, but only for spice. Fights will end up with declarations of love and further assurances that this thing is *right*. You consider yourself home safe. Fate, or whatever it is that you consider to have created this perfect match, is taking care of you. (This, by the way, is the stuff of which obsessions are made. The man who stands on the sidewalk in the rain staring up at *her* apartment window is usually a man who has found The One, but she doesn't consider that he's The One for her.) You'd think divorce would cure believers in the love-zap theory, but divorce usually leaves people undaunted. The marriage didn't end because of anything they did—it's just that she wasn't really The One after all.

This romantic slush looks pretty ridiculous on paper, but an untold number of otherwise enlightened and educated people believe in it. People who are perfectly rational in *every* other respect may be totally naïve about love. Even Plato, the greatest rationalist of all time, considered love a mystery and bought the notion that there is one right mate for every person. So if you believe that someday you'll meet The One, you're in good company. But you're wrong. And the sooner you wake up the better.

When happily-ever-after becomes what-went-wrong

What happens when you meet The One is that you turn magically into a totally giving person. And so does she. Can she borrow your Porsche? Of course. You'll even drive it over so she doesn't have to take the bus. Pick her dresses up at the cleaner's? You'd love to. Would she mind going to a hockey game instead of to the opera as you'd planned? Of course not, hockey's *nice*. You go on and on in a marathon of joyous giving, and you call it love. Eventually you get tired. Yes, you're glad to see her when she comes home, but there are times when you'd rather stay prone on the sofa with your magazine than get up and ravish her on the doorstep. But you get up anyway because she expects it (and you do too). And then one day you wonder why you feel trapped. Of course you feel trapped. You *are* trapped. Not by each other, but by the ideal images you've created and now, by God, have got to live up to. Otherwise you'll have to face the terrible accusation "You've changed," which reads, "You don't love me the way you used to."

How can you explain it? What went wrong?

What went wrong began the minute you realized that you cared. You love her, dammit, and now you have something to lose. In order to capture it and make it last forever, you begin protecting it. You eat food you hate because she cooked it and the truth—"I've always hated pork chops"—seems too brutal. Especially since she's sitting there with the candles glowing and an expectant look on her face as you plunge your fork into her own recipe. In the name of love you protect and protect—and lie and lie. They're loving lies, to be sure, but you're laying a trap that endangers the future of the relationship more than the truth ever could.

If honesty doesn't begin at the beginning, you put distinct limits on how far the relationship can go. If you want to love in a climate where you can continue to grow, can continue to discover who you are, can flop around and make mistakes, you've got to tell the truth about yourself. When the truth isn't as pretty as you'd like it to be, grit your teeth and tell it anyway. Honesty means conflict and confrontation, which most people think of as threatening to a relationship. Actually, confrontation that sheds light on the way things are can be the cement that holds a relationship together. If you want love to be a validation of your real self, then it's essential that your partner know what that self is. Maybe you're a lazy slob who'd rather sleep on Sunday morning than play doubles with the Seymours. And you knew that when you heard her on the phone making the date with them. When you pretend that the ideal you (an energetic jock who loves tennis, any time, just like she does) is the real you, you lie. And you deny who you really are (a guy who likes to kick back and watch his beard grow at least one day a week). Deny yourself and your needs too often, and resentment will start to build. Every time you lie, you poison the relationship further.

Be honest even if it hurts

Telling the truth about yourself feels risky, and at times it *is* risky. But once you're through the confrontations, you have the reward of knowing that someone can actually love you, even in all of your authentic horribleness.

The living alone option

People say that women are more ridiculed than men for not being married, but this is not necessarily true. A man who has not been married by the time he reaches his mid-thirties is considered suspect. People often think he's some kind of emotional dwarf who isn't capable of sustaining a relationship.

There *are* people who are so afraid of love that, though they need it and want it, they back away when it actually comes, out of fear that love will somehow devour them or strip them of power. Men like this always seem to be either beginning an affair or getting out of one, and they never stay around one woman for long. Perhaps once a sense of needing or being needed starts to show, it feels too threatening. At any rate, these men stop after the first stages of love, figuring that they'll quit while they're ahead. Sometimes men like this slip into marriage through a side door and hide there, cohabiting with a woman but never really relating to her.

The living alone option is something else. Actually, if the decision to get married is to be a healthy one, living alone will have been considered as a realistic option too. Many marriages that become dull and lifeless were entered into for weak reasons:

Weak reasons for marrying

"We'd been going together for two years and marriage just seemed the next logical step...."
"I knew that if I didn't marry her, someone else would...."
"I had to marry her to get rid of her."

To get rid of her? Yes. Or, more precisely, to get rid of the questions from friends and parents. To be able to stop *thinking* about it. To move on to discussing something besides *the relationship*. Marriage is visualized by many men as a peaceful valley where they imagine people will at last leave them alone—to daydream, to play with their toy trains, to build empires, or simply to relax and not have to take anyone out to dinner anymore.

Intimate relationships are the most satisfying

Intimacy is what makes a relationship satisfying—and lasting. Intimacy doesn't require marriage. Nor does marriage guarantee intimacy. In fact, the satisfying, close relationship you need and want may become *less* attainable once you marry. Psychologist George Bach says, in his book *Pairing*, "Because marriage always requires certain kinds of role playing (boss, mother, breadwinner), it often makes intimate love all the more difficult to achieve." Some men claim that they become so determined to be good husbands (mowing the lawn, putting together jungle gyms, sitting down to a proper dinner every night) that they forget who they are, and feel like characters in a play.

If getting married is something you figure you'll do to prove that

Avoid "wife-shopping"

you're a "normal" man, if you actually go shopping around for a wife, you'll try to present yourself as "good husband material" (responsible, considerate)—and a lot of the real you will be lost in the process. When you try to fit yourself into a role, you can easily ignore your own special needs. And if you're shopping for a partner and can't find the perfect one, you're apt to take the next best thing. A pretty depressing way to begin what's supposedly going to be a lifelong relationship.

The better able you are to survive happily on your own, the better the chances that you'll live happily with a mate. When you remain single *and* have an intimate relationship with someone, there are many sweet rewards. Time together, because it's not subject to the erosion of day-to-day living which involves things like washing socks and facing each other over the breakfast table, has a magic quality. Other people may call your time together, special as it is, romantic and unreal, but it is delicious nonetheless. You have more time to yourself—to watch the news at midnight instead of *having to* make love, to let the dishes pile up in the sink, or to wander around the apartment at four in the morning gnawing on a business problem without fear of waking someone or having to answer questions: "What's wrong, dear? Are you sick? Can I help?" You can have more intense friendships with other people—you have more time for them, and the friendships don't have to please "the two of you." You'll run less risk of becoming so safe with each other that the other person becomes about as noticeable and unique as the wallpaper you hung in the den five years ago. And, since you must constantly prove yourselves to each other, the reaching (though tiring at times) can make you grow. The independence of mind and of spirit you have when you know how to be alone gives you more to bring to the intimate relationship when it's time for sharing.

Knowing that you can be alone makes it more likely that if you ever do decide to live with someone or to marry, you'll be doing so not out of an unrealistic desire to get something (security, everlasting love, mothering), but out of a healthy desire to share what you've already found to be good, solid, and satisfying in your life.

Successful loners may make the best partners

Living together   You love her. She loves you. Your relationship has progressed way beyond the first flush of romance, and you want something more solid than intimate little dinners and weekends in the mountains. Marriage? Seems too drastic. It's too soon for that, for one thing, and with the statistics reading the way they do, you wonder if marriage isn't the quickest way to kill a good thing.

Why not live together? Two names on the mailbox seems far less risky than marriage. And it's so simple: she moves her stuff out of her place and into yours. If it doesn't work out, no one will be hurt, you'll both have learned something, and breaking up a roommate situation will be far easier than getting a divorce, right? Not necessarily.

Living together is very much like marriage   From what researchers have learned from interviewing some successful and not-so-successful couples, it appears that living together is not very different from marriage.

• You can get hurt. A break-up after living together can be just as painful as divorce. A living-together arrangement is easy enough to get into—you get a U-Haul van and tote in her plants, clothes, and a few pieces of furniture. But separation hurts, whether the church and state have recognized your pairing or not. And besides the emotional pain of breaking up, more than a few living-together split-ups have led to legal hassles—usually over who gets what.
• You'll fight over the same things married people fight over. Sex, money, power, children, chores, and space (both psychological space and physical space) top the list.
• You'll become possessive. If you hope a living-together arrangement will be looser and freer than marriage, forget it. Couples who live together are just as possessive of each other as married couples are—sometimes more so. When you're not bound by legal ties, your fear of losing each other can loom large.
• You may well have the same high expectations of each other that married couples have. Your easygoing "Let's try it and see" attitude may not hold up once you've settled in. She may expect you to be as tender, sensitive, and romantic as you were when you were dating, while you may expect her to start taking care of you and let you relax.
• You may need counseling to help you work through problems. Rather than just splitting when the going gets rough, you may choose to stick it out, and it may help to talk to a counselor. About 10 percent of counseled couples are unmarried, and the number is rising.

Some ways to make living together easier   Before you move in together, it would make sense to discuss your motives for living together. Put romance and love aside for a minute and ask each other why you're doing this. To test your relationship, in a kind of trial marriage? To just be together for awhile? If you see living together as the beginning of a lifetime commitment and she sees it as good for six months at most, the earlier you face those different points of view the better.

After you do move in together:

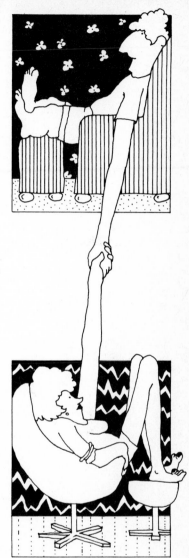

· Make changes slowly. Keep two places, at least for the first few months. If you slide into the new living arrangement slowly, you'll put less of a burden on yourselves. If one of you lets an apartment go, it puts pressure on you to make the relationship succeed.

· Divide chores. Be clear in the beginning about who will take out the garbage and who will clean the bathroom, and whether you'll alternate in the kitchen or designate one of you as cook.

· Be clear about who owns what. It may seem cold-blooded, but it saves troubles in the long run. If you buy anything together (a car, a sofa, a house), make an agreement about what percent of it each of you owns. If you ever split up, your emotional troubles will be worsened if you're fighting over who gets the car or who keeps the cat.

· Work out a budget. You're going to resent it if you suddenly find yourself paying all the bills. *She'll* resent it if you arbitrarily hand her the phone and electric bills. Decide who'll pay for what, or divide expenses proportionately, according to your incomes.

· Agree to speak up about your needs. If you want an hour of silence when you get home from work and she's all chatter, work out a compromise.

· Give some thought to what you'll tell the world. It will be easier for both of you if you can tell everyone, including Mrs. Swartz upstairs, the postman, and relatives, that you're living together. But if hearing about your arrangement will drive parents crazy, do they have to know? You're testing a relationship, not making a political statement.

· Be careful what you tell employers about your relationship. If you write "married" on pension or insurance forms and you're legally single, you're guilty of fraud. On the other hand, if you don't want your boss or your coworkers to know who your roommate is, you don't need to mention it.

It may frustrate you that the world doesn't take your relationship as seriously when you live together as when you're married. And the experimental nature of living together may actually force you both to work harder to make adjustments when problems arise than married people do. But, basically, what's wrong when you live together will be what's wrong when you're married. The living-together experience can give you the opportunity to see where your problems will be, and to decide whether you can work around those problems.

Making your relationship work

Whether you're married, living together, or considering either, if you're in love you want it to last. What's the formula for a lasting relationship? How can you keep what you have?

There is no formula. And trying to keep things the way they are is the surest way to kill what you have. People continually grow and change—there's no stopping it. For a relationship to be satisfying and nourishing for both partners, it must be a relationship that encourages growth. Growth means change. Change may take you away from one another. Knowing this and still being able to love takes courage.

Love is not enough

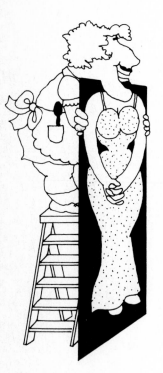

Love is a start, yes. But it's the easy part. For a relationship to work, you've got to care enough to put out effort—constantly. The problem is that loving and being loved is so soft and easy at first that it can lull you into complacency.

A viable, working relationship doesn't just happen. It must be built—and worked on daily. It takes caring. It takes recognizing what each other's needs are and helping each other fulfill those needs. It takes valuing each other as individuals, rather than valuing the relationship first and trying to squeeze each other into shapes that, however uncomfortable, make the relationship feel safer.

Why is this so hard? Because your needs will conflict. Egos will falter. Insecurity will seep in. You'll both get selfish, scared, lazy.

Even the healthiest person is a complex network of conflicting needs and fears. You need to grow, but you fear change. You need individuality, but you fear isolation and rejection. You need freedom, but you fear loss of love. You need intimacy, but you fear losing your power.

To help each other cut through the web created by these conflicting feelings takes awareness, patience, hard work, and a tough skin. It will help if you:

• Learn to admit what you really feel. You may think that you want a woman who can hold her own. That you want independence and fulfillment for her as much as you want those things for yourself. But if her exhilarating job with a film company keeps her away from home three nights a week, you may find yourself screaming, "You're my *wife*. I want you home at night where you belong." This sounds tough, powerful, and *right*. (She has a duty to you and you're insisting that she live up to it.) It is, however, a lie in the sense that it doesn't say what you're really feeling. The truth is: "I'm scared. I'm lonely here without you and I'm afraid you don't need me the way I need you." A normal enough feeling, but one you don't like to admit.

Unless you both can recognize the fear and need in your demand and be honest about what is really going on, the situation could create a gulf between you. She may not see through what you said to what you meant. And if she responds to what you *said*, her retort might be: "I'm not your possession. I love my job and I want to keep it. Don't you care about my needs at all?" Not a response that's likely to make you feel better. Telling the truth would have been more likely to get you the reassurance that you *are* loved and needed.

• Accept the fact that you need closeness. For years male conditioning has told you that it's cool to stay aloof. You may need intimacy desperately, but when she gets too close you become afraid. Maybe you'll need her too much, maybe you'll become so vulnerable that you'll lose the toughness required to survive in the world. Besides, you may argue, all that mushy stuff is feminine.

The hunger to be perceived, known totally in an intimate relationship with another human being, is not a romantic daydream spun by females, but a real human need. Intimacy doesn't mean making love. You can make love without intimacy, and you can have intimacy without making love (though when you have the two together you have the most powerful kind of lovemaking there is). To be intimate you need to drop your façade, to disclose yourself, to come out from behind the barriers that keep you protected from your own vulnerability. She in turn must care enough to listen to your disclosures without judgment, to explore with you what your self-discoveries mean, and to share her own self-discoveries with you. It's scary, and it *does* mean giving up some control—for both of you. When she knows that your macho "Get in the kitchen, woman, and cook my eggs" number means you're feeling vulnerable and unloved, it takes some of the gravel (and power) out of your delivery. It also allows her to react to your real needs instead of doing her own "I'm an independent woman and nobody tells me what to do" number on you. When you know each other intimately, it's much easier to reach out and touch each other with love. And it's much more satisfying than the hit-or-miss approach you must use when you've kept a safe distance.

Don't get stuck playing roles

• Get beyond roles and help each other find out who you are. One of the myths that has tugged on the success of relationships for years is the notion that she meets her needs by meeting yours. This isn't true—even if *she* believes it, it still isn't true. This is not to say that she doesn't get a lot of pleasure out of doing things for you. But the passive role, however much a woman may invite it, doesn't really make her happy. You can help her when she says, "Any movie you want to see is fine with me, dear," by insisting she quit being passive and speak for herself. (She returns the favor when she demands that you quit struggling to get ahead in a job you hate so that you can buy her the kind of house she "deserves.") Behind most role playing there is fear ("I'm not a man if I'm not a good provider," "I'm not a woman if I don't let him be the boss"), and you serve each other best when you insist on being yourselves, not role players.

Don't leave your socks on the living-room floor

• Share responsibility for your environment. Though a supply of clean socks and underwear in the bureau drawer and plenty of paper napkins and scouring pads in the kitchen are part of it, a loving environment requires much more than a smoothly functioning household. And even if she chooses "housewife" as her occupation doesn't mean you can peel off your socks and leave them on the living-room floor with impunity. Whatever your division of chores, it helps your relationship if you develop a sort of yin and yang approach to keeping the house running, you picking up the slack where she leaves off, and vice versa. Writer Anne Roiphe put it this way: "It used to be that men who helped women were laughed at—the Dagwood Bumsteads of the world, they were ridiculed everywhere, while men who made a lot of money or shot a lot of people dead, like John Wayne, were considered terrific. But nurturing is a very sexy thing in a man, and only the real bumblers don't know it." Slicing onions for the salad, pinching brown leaves off the ivy plant, noticing that your woman's missing a button on the blouse she'll wear tomorrow and sewing it on are the kinds of things you may shun if you feel your masculinity's a bit shaky. And that's a shame. These small acts of tenderness are a way of sharing yourself. When you reach beyond what's "normal" for you, you show a love and caring that is bound to get you double the return on your investment.

• Learn to fight. Fighting is communicating. If you never fight, never have conflicts, it means you're not confronting the truth about yourselves. Life means growth, growth means problems, problems mean upsets. If upsets don't come up, then they're simply getting buried. Being afraid to fight, to confront each other with the truth about what you feel at the moment, means you are not intimate; you're not communicating, trusting, or fully caring.

Fight, and fight fair

Fighting doesn't mean name calling. There's a difference between saying, "You selfish bitch, you knew I wanted to stay home and relax tonight," and saying, "I feel you totally ignored me when you went ahead and made plans for us without consulting me." Sticking to the facts, honestly reporting what you want and feel, is the fair, productive, and enlightening way to fight. Accusations and door slamming may feel good at the time, but in the long run they just lead to flimsier contact and murkier perceptions of each other.

• Recognize it when you're getting lazy. It's bound to happen. There will be times when it's so much more appealing to watch TV or go to a movie than to sit down and wrestle with a problem. You're tired. You need time out. That's all right, as long as you recognize and admit it

("Something's bugging me, but I'm too beat to deal with it. Let's just watch TV tonight and talk tomorrow"), and you do deal with it later. If you swallow grenades or bury problems, they'll eventually explode or sprout up bigger and more unmanageable later on.

If you ever find that you've let something slide so long that it's gotten out of hand, push through the mess it's created (everything she does bugs you, or really turns you off) and face it. The best way to deal with this is to get away from home, where there are things to hide behind (the TV, the phone, friends dropping in). Go to the mountains, the beach, a hotel in the city. Turn off the TV, toss out the newspapers, rub the sleep out of your eyes, and start talking. Remember, when you reach this stage, that the idea of making an effort will *not* appeal. And this is the hardest part of making a relationship work. If you want things to get back on the right track, *start talking.*

Talk, even when you don't want to

If your relationship is to last, it must have freedom in it. If you have to smother the real you in order to have the relationship "work," it'll only be a matter of time before you'll want out. The greatest freedom is found in being able to be yourself with another person, to be encouraged to grow and develop according to the peculiarities inside you that make you *you.* If you can give each other that kind of freedom, your chances of beating the statistics and creating a relationship that lasts are pretty good.

Sex in a relationship

Probably you've been conditioned to believe that sexual excitement requires novelty, mystery and The Chase. And one of the fears you may have when you fall in love is that once the chase is over, it won't be long before sexual boredom settles over the relationship. This is disturbing. When you've formed a relationship that has value to you, you want sex to improve, to become more and more satisfying to you both over time. Is it possible? You may hope so, but frankly doubt it. And you may push the problem to the back of your mind hoping that somehow you'll be lucky and that the feelings of excitement will last.

An exciting sex life is up to you

That passive, hoping-for-the-best attitude won't work. What you should realize is that your sex life is in your hands (and hers), and that when you approach it with the right attitude, it can become deeper and more satisfying. Rewarding sex comes of the intimacy that can only be developed over time in a deep loving relationship with another person. But it won't happen if you just let things glide along.

The best kind of lovemaking occurs between two loving adults who have developed mutual trust, the capacity for intimate self-disclosure, and a deep sexual honesty. With sexual honesty your lovemaking will validate and reinforce your identity, your sense of yourself. In a relationship that lacks sexual honesty, limits are set on where your lovemaking can go. If the lovemaking patterns you develop require that you inhibit your real self or keep it buried, sex will not be self-validating for you. You'll become sexually stunted. Excitement will dwindle. Boredom will be inevitable. It takes hard work and a good bit of psychological courage to develop an intimate relationship. However, within the context of this kind of intimacy, there can be tremendous sexual excitement.

This idea of intimacy and sexual honesty as the only way to real sexual satisfaction may not sit right with you at first. If you equate intimacy with being trapped inextricably in an emotional web, you'll consider it to be destructive, and you'll resist it. If you think developing intimacy is something like coming down with a permanent case of lovesickness, you'll fear that it will make you soft and incapable of coping in a world where a man has to be tough and in control of his emotions. But intimacy and emotional honesty can actually make you stronger. When you are aware of the emotions that are constantly operating behind your behavior, you become better able to control them—not less so. An intimate relationship helps you develop that awareness. You'll both need to stick your necks out. To admit it to each other when you feel insecure. To stop pretending that you're the confident Superman you wish you were. To confront your fears.

Few couples, it seems, know how to push through their fears, and this makes sexual honesty difficult to achieve. They can't talk about sex, can't confront their insecurities, and so they don't get rid of them.

It's often hard to talk about sex

The fear of exposing your hangups can leave you stuck. The sexual insecurities you grew up with (Is my penis big enough? Do I have enough hair on my chest? Will I be able to turn women on?) cause you to focus your attention on performance. You want to be a good lover, but there's no way to know if you are. So you close your eyes and you wing it. You know women are complex and hard to satisfy, but you want to believe it when she says, "Oh, that was good." She, just as eager to please as you are, is just as afraid. (Was it good for him? Does he love me?) So you both go along, operating blind, groping for each other in the dark, telling each other that everything is wonderful when it isn't always.

You are convinced that your sexual self-doubts make you even less attractive, so you hide them. Are you too fast for her? Are your hands clumsy? Is the way you use your tongue all wrong? And if you want her to be faster, slower, harder, or softer, you feel you can't tell her without hurting her feelings. Maybe you did try to talk to her about sex a few times, but she put you off with the plea that talking about it will kill romance. (She, of course, is over there with her own terrifying hangups that she doesn't want *you* to find out about.) So you both pretend, and maybe she goes to the bathroom afterward to cry a little and wonder why you're not interested in the fact that she's not having orgasms, and you lie there in the dark wondering if she did have one this time.

You both hide your hangups

When you deal separately with your worries and frustrations, you grow further and further apart. As long as you're ashamed to admit what's wrong, what's wrong doesn't get changed. Psychologist Albert Ellis says: "Shame, in this connection, seems utterly silly—just as silly as a husband's feeling ashamed to tell his wife that he likes eggs scrambled instead of sunny-side up and then getting angry because, somehow, she does not fathom this. Why the devil should she? And why on earth should he feel ashamed to tell her?"

Why can't you talk? Because talking doesn't feel safe. And so you hide your anxiety behind a tried and supposedly true pattern: you reach for her breasts, she reaches for your penis, you climb on top, she sighs with apparent ecstasy, and in five minutes it's over. Boring? Of course. Without honesty and openness, sex becomes a performance in which you both act without fully *interacting*. If, on a conscious level, you don't know this is happening, you do on a subconscious level, and it slowly eats away at your relationship. You both feel lonely and isolated and you don't know why. Fear of self-confrontation and of intimacy is so great that many of us pay a high price to avoid them.

Your sex life is a mirror

Sexual intimacy doesn't stand off by itself. Your sex life is like a mirror of the whole relationship. What's wrong with sex is only symptomatic of what's wrong elsewhere, and once you begin to deal with the truth, your honesty must go across the board. You can't be distant and polite and avoid conflict all day and expect to have sexual intimacy at night. Intimacy must be built into *every* area of your relationship before it can operate effectively in lovemaking.

Sexual honesty requires being willing to be uncomfortable, and being willing to make her uncomfortable as you ask questions and give answers that tell the truth about your physical and emotional feelings. It means telling the good (you love it when she runs her tongue over your ear) and the not-so-good (you don't love it when she runs her tongue over one of your nipples), and insisting that she do the same about her likes and dislikes. As the walls come down and you both see that knowing and being known isn't as terrifying a prospect as it seemed, your trust in each other will grow. You'll feel freer, and as you see that you can be fully known and fully loved at the same time, you'll feel more secure.

The rewards of sexual honesty

Sexual honesty permits you to do many wonderful things. Among them are:

• Getting out of the orgasm-as-holy-grail trap. "Did you come?" This breathless query really means, "Was it all right? Did we make it? Have we measured up?" When being known is the real prize you take away from lovemaking, you can both stop worrying so much about orgasms. They are wonderful, and important, yes. But not always necessary. In fact, when you agree to set them aside sometimes, you can enjoy a slower and even more tender kind of sensuality. You can discover the pure tactile sense of each other's skin in a way that you can miss during lovemaking-headed-for-orgasm.

• Feeling less pressure to "perform." Without sexual honesty, you often make love by guesswork. You may *think* she wants to make love tonight, and though you feel too tired, you don't want to disappoint her. So you make love, going through all the motions of passion even though you feel very little desire. She may accept your performance, but part of her will sense that you weren't really there. You may both feel empty and alone. Sexual honesty allows either of you to say, "I'm just too tired to make love tonight," and know that the other won't panic (there's always tomorrow). And chances are you'd both rather have the other say, "I love you, I'm sorry if you're frustrated," and hold you tight than to have any pretending go on. However physically frustrating the honest way may be, it's more satisfying emotionally.

• Becoming more affectionate. If she'd like to curl up against you and read, but she's afraid you'll take her cuddling to mean, "Let's make love," she's likely to put her head on a pillow rather than on your thigh. When you stop communicating via mind-reading and sign language, you'll be able to show affection for affection's sake.

• Getting rid of your inadequacy fears. When you keep things buried, they sprout roots and grow. If you go on fumbling and worrying, for example, that she doesn't really like oral sex, the fear can grow as you pile one suspicion on top of another. Talk about it in painful detail, and you may discover that it isn't that she doesn't like oral sex, it's just that she's insecure about it, and afraid she does it all wrong. Whether your suspicions are accurate or simply all in your imagination, talking about them helps you both to understand each other better and to become closer. When you both get your fears out into the open, you can begin to deal with them in a sensitive way. You can work to discover where your fears come from and to help each other get rid of them.

When you're sexually honest, you can have humor in your lovemaking. When you're open with each other, you're more secure. And when you're secure, you don't have to take lovemaking so *seriously*. You can play. You can romp in the shower, nibble on each other's toes, revel in the taste, touch, and smell of each other's skin. You can have a pillow fight, giggle and roll on the floor. You can cover each other with whipped cream and lick it off, if you want. When you're sexually open, you can have a lot more fun.

You can have novelty, too. When you're not afraid to admit your fantasies to each other, you can make love in a hammock, on top of the washing machine, in the lavatory of a 747 bound for Seattle. Maybe scooping yogurt out of her belly button with your tongue isn't your thing, but when you can be yourselves with each other, there are no rules. As long as you both enjoy what you're doing, and either one can say "Let's stop" when something becomes too scary or uncomfortable, there is no limit to what you can do. And though most of the time your lovemaking won't be of the kooky variety, it's nice to know it's there when you're in the mood.

When the walls come down and you're able to really look at each other, you'll discover a whole range of things that would otherwise remain beyond your reach. When you have honesty and trust, sexual exploring is not threatening, but lots of fun to do together. Then, sexual excitement isn't something to "hang on to," but something that has become a natural part of your continually evolving sexuality.

You can have fun

Two-career marriage Two-career marriage? It may sound like a fine idea. If you say, "No wife of mine is going to work," you'll be considered antiquated. Since there are more than 16 million working couples in the United States, it looks as if the two-career marriage is flourishing. The advantages are pretty obvious: two paychecks, more money. And when she finds her identity in her job instead of through you, it takes a lot of pressure off your relationship. You may feel very self-confident; you may feel sure you don't need to prove your masculinity by having a woman be dependent on you. And you may feel you're liberated, too, realizing that a full-time job means she's not a full-time housekeeper and that you've got to help out around the house.

But when you're both working nine to five, who'll take the packages that get delivered to your apartment at noon? What do you do when the TV breaks down or the car develops a shimmy and neither of you has time to get it fixed? What happens when you're both exhausted and neither wants to cook? Suppose you've planned a dinner party for an important client of yours and your wife's job sends her out of town for a week? When you both work, something or someone is always getting neglected. The household is often on the brink of chaos, weekends in the country must be scrapped so one of you can work overtime, the problem you were going to have a serious talk about gets ignored for another week.

Juggling the jobs Two careers mean three jobs: your job, her job, and the job of housekeeping. No matter what, there are always cereal, milk, eggs,

and toothpaste to stock up on. A weekly pile of laundry to plow through. Plants to water. Pictures to hang. Beds to make. Checkbooks to balance and bills to pay. Rugs to vacuum. Endlessly. If children enter the picture things get even more complicated—baby-sitters don't show up, children get the flu, you feel guilty about not spending more time at home. You may not want to spend Saturday morning in the supermarket or Sunday night de-clogging the sink, but if you don't your life begins to fray around the edges.

To make a two-career marriage work, you both need sensitivity, cooperation, flexibility, and a boundless sense of humor. Some of the stickiest areas:

Housework. Traditionally, housework is her problem, no matter how hard or long she works at a job. And the sense that this is how it should be is hard to shake...for men and women both. In spite of women's lib, when you run out of catsup or clean towels, there's no question, in your mind or hers, whose fault it is. And as tempting as it may be to let things remain that way, you'll make it easier on both of you if you pitch in and share the responsibility for the household, both physically and psychologically. If you don't, the guilt and frustration she'll feel every time something goes wrong will weigh heavily on her—and it will probably surface eventually in angry resentment.

Who'll take care of the house?

If you can show her that you really do consider the household a shared responsibility, you'll not only ease the burden on her, but probably make some surprising discoveries: that folding clean laundry into neat piles, turning fresh blueberries into homemade jam, slicing apples for a pie, or watching a soufflé rise magically in the oven can be pleasant, even pacifying.

Jealousy. No matter how healthy your trust in each other, the fact that you belong to separate daytime worlds can create emotional stumbling blocks. It can hurt when she likes her office friends more than you like your office friends. When she's more interested in getting the reports out than in making love to you ("You go on to bed, hon, I'm going to be working past midnight"). When you take her to the airport to send her off on a business trip and get a look at the male coworkers who are going on the same trip. And how does she feel about the velvety-voiced secretary who answers your phone, the business meetings that keep you in the office until ten P.M., the client who's an hourglass-shaped blonde? When you both work, the threat of becoming competitive with and jealous of each other is always there. If you can recognize that, agree to talk about it, and admit it when you feel raw human jealousy, you'll protect each other from unnecessary hurts.

If you get jealous, admit it

Will you insist on being the boss at home?

Power. In a two-career marriage it's necessary to be willing to share power. It can look and feel pretty ridiculous to demand that she be the child at home if she's a boss in the business world. But it can be pretty tough on you if she starts earning more money than you do. Or if her promotion comes through and yours doesn't. It takes a pretty solid ego and a strong sense of self to cheer her on when your own career seems to be stuck in one place. But if you can get beyond measuring your success against hers (or against anyone's, for that matter), you can get on with the business of working and working well, according to the capabilities that are naturally yours. In a really happy relationship, you won't be conscious of who has the most control, but more concerned with helping each other reach your fullest potential—and you'll both experience a sense of strength and a sense of love in a proper, productive balance.

What happens when you both need pampering?

Tension. There will be times when she (like you) will be overworked, and pressure will hit with a loud thwok. When pressure hits you both at the same time, the tension will be doubled. When you both come home needing a drink, sympathy, and a long consoling back rub, it can be frustrating, and probably you'll both say, "You're never there when I need you." But sometimes having to row your own separate canoes helps build a respect for each other that's as invigorating and, in another way, as satisfying as the "mothering" you give each other with back rubs. And when the tension comes to an end and you both get to flop down on a beach somewhere, the shared release can be blissful.

You can help each other chase away the bogeyman

Fear. You both fear failure, of course. And fear of success can operate too. She may fear that if she succeeds too well she'll lose both her femininity and your approval. You may fear that having too much success will cost you the ability to control your life. (The more you have to lose, the harder you have to work to hold on to it.) And there will be times when these fears operate without either of you realizing what's going on. It may be easy enough for you to give her a sympathetic ear when she's afraid she's about to be fired. But if she gets snappy and defensive after a promotion, you can feel pretty angry with her. It takes a lot of work and a lot of dialogue to be able to help each other deal with confusing feelings. But understanding what each other's fears are and how they operate will help you give each other the support you both need to make your careers thrive. That understanding can do a lot for your relationship, too.

If you have a relationship, you'll have problems. Problems are inevitable. And good. Problems help you confront things. Confronting things helps you grow. Growing makes you happy. Facing problems and finding solutions is the normal pattern of a healthy relationship. It's when problems *don't* get solved that they begin to eat away at a relationship rather than support it. If problems have begun to pile up to the point where you find yourselves in a swamp, with nowhere to turn, it's time to get some help. If you don't get help, if you just let your problems sit there, you practically assure the deterioration (and possibly the death) of the relationship.

When your relationship needs help

You should consider going for help when:

Some signs that help is needed

• You've stopped talking intimately. You avoid dealing with small and large annoyances. You use the TV set, the newspaper, friends, or children to avoid each other. You often prefer working late or going out with buddies to coming home to your woman. When she says, "There's something we need to talk about," and you recoil rather than responding with warmth and concern.

• You're often tense, and you bicker a lot. You often accuse each other of being thoughtless, and keep up an accounting of real or imagined slights. There's an unhappy current running between you much of the time.

• You have a sex problem that doesn't get resolved. Causes of sexual dysfunction are rarely physiological, and sexual problems are a symptom of other difficulties rather than a separate concern.

• One of you is having affairs. You may argue that sleeping around or having an affair is actually holding your relationship together, because you're satisfying needs that can't be met within the marriage. This "solution" may appear to work for awhile, but affairs take their toll on the primary relationship. Getting what you need outside of your marriage may make *you* feel better for a while, but to keep your marriage or any relationship healthy, the cure for its problems must come from *within* the relationship.

• You've faced a crisis that has left problems in its wake. Losing a job or having a death in the family can take its toll on the way you two relate. And you may need help in coming to terms with the way the crisis has affected you so that you can help each other deal with it.

The faster you find solutions, the better

This is not to say that an occasional spell of poor communication or spurts of irritability spell disaster. But if these kinds of problems go on in a persistent, recurring pattern, you'll need to do some hard thinking and quick acting to steer your relationship out of the shoals. Problems in a relationship are like a disease. If you put off treating them, they'll become further advanced and more difficult to cure. The sooner you get to work on finding causes and solutions, the better your chances of restoring your relationship to full health.

You may fear that your problems are so enormous that facing them will mean an end to the love between you. You may think that as long as you don't look at them they're not really "real." And getting help, or turning the light on problems, may seem threatening—you may feel that facing problems will make them loom up large and unmanageable, and that then they'll devour your relationship. The only way to assure that problems *don't* devour your relationship is to confront them, head on. If you can't do that on your own (and many people can't), you need help.

How to find the kind of help you need

There are many kinds of help available, some of them worthwhile, some of them decidedly not. There is sex therapy. There is family therapy (which involves all members of the family at some point in the treatment). There are encounter groups and enrichment weekends. There are many different kinds of private therapy. Some self-awareness programs have special seminars that concentrate on improving relationships.

The term "marriage counselor" can refer to a number of different people, from a social worker to a psychiatrist to a sex therapist. It makes sense to check out any program or counselor thoroughly before you get involved. Ask for credentials, references. Talk to other couples who've used the counselor.

Sex therapy. The most famous sex therapists, Dr. William Masters and Virginia Johnson, have their own clinic in St. Louis. Many sex therapists represent themselves as "Masters and Johnson trained," which may mean only that they've attended a workshop or read one of Masters and Johnson's books. There are actually only a handful of Masters and Johnson-trained therapists.

How can you find a reputable sex therapist in your area? Call a large hospital or medical school to find out if they run a sex clinic or sexual dysfunction program. Or you can contact The Sex Therapy

Certification Committee, American Association of Sex Educators and Counselors, 5010 Wisconsin Avenue NW, Suite 304, Washington, D.C. 20016. They will send you a list of therapists in your area. Whatever therapist you use should have an academic degree (M.A., Ph.D., M.D., M.S.W.) from a reputable school, and experience with a reputable agency.

Therapy to perk up a basically happy relationship. Many therapists offer group therapy for couples. Churches, social-service agencies, community organizations, and universities have marriage enrichment programs too. A Catholic Church-sponsored encounter group that has 30 to 40 percent non-Catholic participation is: Worldwide Marriage Encounter, 10059 Manchester Road, Suite 108, Warson Woods, Missouri 63122. It has affiliates in 40 states, including some Protestant groups. An organization that helps develop communication skills is: Association of Couples for Marriage Enrichment, 403 South Hawthrone Road, Winston-Salem, North Carolina 27013.

A counselor to help you deal with a specific problem. To get the name of a good counselor near you, you can ask friends, your doctor, or a clergy member to suggest someone who has helped other couples. You can call the department of psychology at a local university, or a clinic attached to a medical school. An organization that accredits and certifies marriage counselors is: American Association of Marriage and Family Counselors, 225 Yale Avenue, Claremont, California 91711. You can get a list of three or more accredited marriage counselors from them over the phone. Marriage counselors who belong to this association will list AAMFC after their names in the phone book, and members have at least a master's degree in one of the behavioral sciences (psychology, sociology, etc.) and two years of clinical experience in marriage counseling under an improved agency of the AAMFC.

Can counseling really help you? Isn't it painful and embarrassing? Awkward, perhaps. Painful? Not as painful as suffering with problems that never get resolved.

What can counseling accomplish?

A counselor can't save your relationship. But he or she can help you get a clearer picture of what your problems really are, how each of you contributes to their cause, and what's needed to set things right between you. Through counseling you may come to understand and appreciate each other more *and* to decide that the best way for each of you to meet your needs is to dissolve your partnership. There is value in that. In a parting of the ways that's based on understanding and respect, it's unlikely that either of you will find it necessary to paint the other as a terrible villain.

Divorcing with love   If, when you come to the end of a marriage, you feel that you've failed, you can get pretty depressed. If you feel that she's failed you, you can get pretty angry. But whatever else is behind its demise, a marriage ends because being together no longer nourishes you sufficiently to justify staying together. You have evolved and changed in different ways, to such an extent that being together doesn't work anymore. When people find the courage to move on, to realize that they require more potential for growth and happiness than can be found in clinging to the past, a kind of congratulations are in order.

You can help each other now   You loved each other once. And now, in another kind of way, you probably still love each other. So things didn't turn out the way you hoped and expected that they would. That's cause for melancholy, nostalgia, and regret, yes. But mourning? No one has died. A relationship has shifted, that's all. And once balance is restored to both of your lives, you'll realize that the shift is for the better. If you can't rejoice over that, at least relax and let go of the past. If you can let each other go with love and wishes for good things, you'll be able to support each other separately in a way that you couldn't do by staying together. To divorce with love, you'll need to:

• Dump your anger. Even if she ran off with your best friend, robbed you blind, behaved like a disgusting shrew, *let it go*. You don't have to deal with that anymore. If you sit there calling names and shaking your fist, you waste your energy and you poison yourself. If you spew out endless tales of the terrible, unjust things she did to you, you'll bore your friends. It's tempting to use your anger as a blanket to hide under. It feels good. Indignation seems so *right*. And as long as you let anger consume you, you don't have to feel the heavy weight of responsibility for your own life. You don't have to answer the question, "What am I going to do now?" What if she's in a screaming fit of anger at you.? Recognize the fear in it and don't retaliate. Retaliation will just lead to all-out war and won't do anyone except your paid-by-the-minute-lawyers any good.

• Avoid blaming yourself. No matter what kind of cruelty you can accuse yourself of now, avoid the hair-shirt routine. Instead of beating yourself, figure out why you behaved the way you did. Figure out what needs and frustrations were operating behind your behavior. If you don't use this time to come to understand yourself better, you'll be condemned to repeat the same mistakes next time around.

• Be fair. Trying to make up for what she did to you or what you did to her by demanding or giving up the TV, the hi-fi, the cat, and the entire collection of records just piles on the troubles. When you divide up your possessions and decide on who'll pay what to whom, figure out what's equitable. You don't owe her a living and she doesn't owe you blood.

· Beware of the let's-get-her-good lawyers. If the one you've got starts talking tough and nasty, get rid of him. If you possibly can, agree between you what kind of settlement you want to make *before* you call in any lawyers. If you hire a lawyer to do your hassling for you, it'll cost big money. The idea is to get things cleaned up neatly, not to start a new war.

Getting out of a marriage that has ceased to function is the first step toward making both your lives better. If you can take what you've learned and use it well, your life can begin to improve from the day the break is made. As Mel Krantzler put it in his book *Creative Divorce:* "The death of a relationship is the first stage in…self-renewal. It is a crisis that must be lived through. More than that, however, more than just a time for picking up the pieces, divorce is a new opportunity to *improve* on the past and create a fuller life—*if* you can come to terms with the past, recognize self-defeating behavior, and be willing to change it." Find out what makes you tick. Once you do, you'll be able to move on, and to look back with a minimum of regret.

Get on with your life

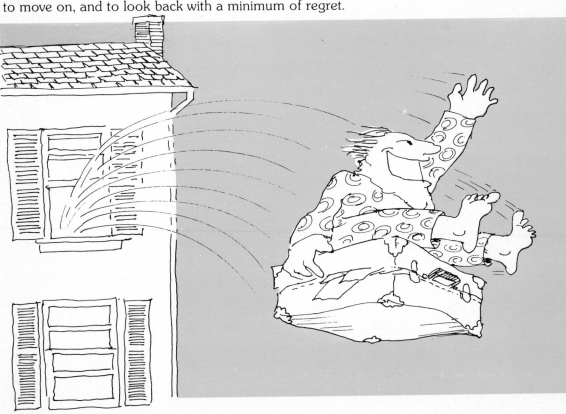

ACKNOWLEDGMENTS

Our thanks to the following people and institutions for their valuable assistance in the preparation of this book.

Marley Hodgson, Trafalgar Ltd.; William Seitz, Neighborhood Cleaners Association; Kathleen Hartz; Patrice Horn, Psychology Today; William Budinger; Roland Meledandri; Dominick Manzone, Ferrara Wines and Liquor; Dr. Arthur Davies; Dr. Stanley Goodwin; Dan King, VIP Travel; D. Robert Yarnall, Jr.; Warren V. Musser; Kim Howard; Diane Friedman; Mickey Ballantine, Ballantine Hair Styles; Manely Cuts and Colors; Alfred Dunhill of London, Inc.; The editors of Bride's Magazine; National Council on Alcoholism; National Dairy Council; Hilton International; American Airlines; Civil Aeronautics Board; Amtrack; U.S. Passport Office; Trailways; Leather Industries of America, Inc.; Levi Strauss and Co.; Blue Bell, Inc.; Men's Fashion Association of America, Inc.; Videofashion, Inc.; New York Public Library; New York Society Library.

SELECTED BIBLIOGRAPHY

THE INNER MAN

Aerobics by Kenneth H. Cooper, M.D., M.P.H. New York: M. Evans & Co., 1968.

"Doctor, Make Me Beautiful!" by James W. Smith, M.D. and Samm Sinclair Baker. New York: David McKay, 1973.

Emily Wilkens' Secrets from the Super Spas by Emily Wilkens. New York: Grosset & Dunlap, 1976.

Growing Up at 37 by Jerry Rubin. New York: M. Evans & Co., 1976.

How To Choose and Use Your Doctor by Marvin S. Belsky, M.D., and Leonard Gross. New York: Arbor House, 1975.

Man's Body: An Owner's Manual by The Diagram Group. New York: Paddington Press, 1976.

Men's Liberation by Jack Nichols. New York: Penguin Books, 1975.

Mindstyles/Lifestyles by Nathaniel Lande. Los Angeles: Price/Stern/Sloan Publishers, 1976.

Passages by Gail Sheehy. New York: E. P. Dutton & Co., 1976.

Rating the Diets by Theodore Berland and the editors of *Consumer Guide.* New York: Publications International, 1977.

The Relaxation Response by Herbert Benson, M.D., with Miriam Z. Klipper. New York: William Morrow & Co., 1975.

Shifting Gears by Nena O'Neill and George O'Neill. New York: M. Evans & Co., 1974.

Simona Morini's Encyclopedia of Health and Beauty by Simona Morini. Indianapolis: The Bobbs-Merrill Co., 1975.

Some Must Watch While Some Must Sleep by William C. Dement. San Francisco: San Francisco Book Co., 1976.

Super Skin by Jonathan Zizmor, M.D., and John Foreman. New York: Thomas Y. Crowell, 1976.

Total Fitness in 30 Minutes a Week by Laurence E. Morehouse, Ph.D., and Leonard Gross. New York: Simon & Schuster, 1975.

Up From Depression by Leonard Cammer, M.D. New York: Simon & Schuster, 1969.

A Year of Health and Beauty by Vidal and Beverly Sassoon. New York: Simon & Schuster, 1976.

THE OUTER MAN

The Butterick Fabric Handbook: A Consumer's Guide to Fabrics for Clothing and Home Furnishings, Irene Cumming Kleeberg, ed. New York: Butterick Publishing, 1975.

Cheap Chic by Caterine Milinaire and Carol Troy. New York: Harmony, 1976.

A Dictionary of Textile Terms by Dan River, Inc., New York. 12th edition, 1976.

Dress for Success by John T. Molloy. New York: Peter H. Wyden, 1975.

Esquire's Encyclopedia of 20th Century Men's Fashions by O. E. Schoeffler and William Gale. New York: McGraw-Hill, 1973.

Esquire's Wear and Care Guide, B.F. Heine, ed. New York: Esquire, Inc., 1970.

Power: How to Get It, How to Use It by Michael Korda. New York: Random House, 1975.

"Removing Stains from Fabrics," Home and Garden Bulletin No. 62, revised. Washington, D.C.: United States Department of Agriculture, Agricultural Research Service, 1976.

THE SOCIAL MAN

Stating Yourself

Egospeak by E. G. Addeo and R. E. Burger. Radnor, Pa.: Chilton Book Company, 1973.

Emotional Common Sense by Rolland S. Parker. New York: Harper & Row, 1973.

Games People Play by Eric Berne, M.D. New York: Grove Press, 1964.

Man's Search for Meaning by Viktor E. Frankl. Revised edition. New York: Simon & Schuster, 1962.

The New York Times Book of Money by Richard E. Blodgett. New York: Quadrangle/The New York Times Book Co., 1971.

The New York Times Guide to Personal Finance by Sal Nuccio. New York: Harper & Row, 1963.

Strictly Speaking by Edwin Newman. New York: Warner Books, 1975.

Up the Organization by Robert Townsend. New York: Fawcett World Library, 1971.

Your Erroneous Zones by Dr. Wayne W. Dyer. New York: Funk & Wagnalls, 1976.

Good Form
The Cosmo Girl's Guide to the New Etiquette. New York: Cosmopolitan Books, 1971.

Esquire Etiquette: A Guide to Business, Sports and Social Conduct by the editors of *Esquire* magazine. New York: J. B. Lippincott Co., 1953.

The Male Guide to Women's Liberation by Gene Marine. New York: Avon Books, 1974.

The New Emily Post's Etiquette by Elizabeth L. Post. New York: Funk & Wagnalls, 1975.

The Entertainer
The Art of Entertaining by Blanche Halle. New York: Grosset & Dunlap, 1952.

The Bloomingdale's Book of Entertaining by Ariane and Michael Batterberry. New York: Random House, 1976.

Esquire's Handbook for Hosts by Roy Andries de Groot. New York: Grosset & Dunlap, 1969.

The House Beautiful Guide to Successful Entertaining by Virginia Stanton. New York: M. Barrows and Company, 1963.

The Joys of Wine by Clifton Fadiman and Sam Aaron. New York: Harry N. Abrams, 1975.

The Single Man's Indispensable Guide and Handbook by Paul Gillette. Chicago: Playboy Press, 1973.

The Traveler
A Guide to Independent Living, Barbara Weiland, ed. New York: Butterick Publishing, 1975.

Medical Advice for the Traveler by Kevin M. Cahill, M.D. New York: Popular Library, 1970.

Pan Am's World Guide: The Encyclopedia of Travel by Pan American World Airways, Inc. New York: McGraw-Hill, 1976.

Rand McNally's Traveler's Almanac/International Guide by Bill Muster. New York: Rand McNally, 1975.

Love and Sex
Cosmopolitan's Living Together (Married or Not) Handbook by Angela Wilson and David Wilson. New York: Hearst Books, 1975.

Creative Divorce: A New Opportunity for Personal Growth by Mel Krantzler. New York: M. Evans & Co., 1973.

How to Make It with Another Person by Dr. Richard B. Austin, Jr., Ph.D. New York: Macmillan Publishing Co., 1976.

The Joy of Sex by Alex Comfort. New York: Crown Publishers, 1972.

Love and Addiction by Stanton Peele with Archie Brodsky. New York: Taplinger Publishing Co., 1975.

Male Sexual Performance by Sam Julty. New York: Grosset & Dunlap, 1975.

The Marriage Savers by Joanne and Lew Koch. New York: Coward, McCann & Geoghegan, 1976.

Pairing by Dr. George R. Bach and Ronald M. Deutsch. New York: Avon Books, 1971.

Passages by Gail Sheehy. New York: E. P. Dutton & Co., 1976.

The Pleasure Bond: A New Look at Sexuality and Commitment by William H. Masters and Virginia Johnson. Boston: Little, Brown & Co., 1975.

Sex and the Liberated Man by Albert Ellis, M.D. Secaucus, N.J.: Lyle Stuart, 1976.

Shifting Gears by Nena O'Neill and George O'Neill. New York: M. Evans & Co., 1974.

Some Men Are More Perfect Than Others by Merle Shain. New York: Charterhouse, 1973.

INDEX

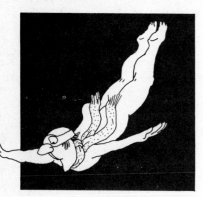

S